"YOU BELONG WITH ME, CHRESTIEN. NEVER FORGET IT."

"When you retire for the eve, 'tis hither you will come," Weston commanded. "When I bid you go to your room, 'tis hither you will come. Do you heed?"

She raised her chin defiantly. "Yea, my lord, I understand perfectly well. You've shown me that I am no more to you than so much chattel, that you can do with me as you will—including shame me. Is that not so? Surely it is, my lord. Surely I mean naught to you!"

Weston lunged at her, but found only air where her feet were supposed to be. In her attempt to avoid him, she fell to the floor. But when Weston pounced again, she was too slow.

"Oh little one, have I hurt you?" he asked, hovering scant inches from her face. "None other has the ability to anger me more than you . . . yet in the same breath I must tell you . . ." But he could not tell her. For though his heart belonged to her, he could not bring himself to say the words.

Angel of Fire

Tanya Anne Crosby

AVON BOOKS · NEW YORK

ANGEL OF FIRE is an original publication of Avon Books. This work has never before appeared in book form. This work is a novel. Any similarity to actual persons or events is purely coincidental.

AVON BOOKS
A division of
The Hearst Corporation
1350 Avenue of the Americas
New York, New York 10019

Copyright © 1992 by Tanya Crosby
Inside cover author photograph by Dawn Rakowski
Published by arrangement with the author
Library of Congress Catalog Card Number: 91-93032
ISBN: 0-380-76773-2

First Avon Books Printing: April 1992

AVON TRADEMARK REG. U.S. PAT. OFF. AND IN OTHER COUNTRIES, MARCA REGISTRADA, HECHO EN U.S.A.

Printed in the U.S.A.

RA 10 9 8 7 6 5 4 3 2 1

To my parents,
David and Isabel,
for believing in me,

To my children,
Chaise and Alaina,
for inspiring me,

And to my husband,
Keith,
for loving me—always, always for you!

Chapter 1

The odor that wafted throughout the white-washed great hall was that of Gilbert de Lontaine's favorite dish, pheasant in orange sauce. It was fast becoming a familiar scent, having graced the lord's table four of the last five eves. Great care had been taken to prepare the fare precisely to the lord's liking in hopes of his return. His twin daughters, Chrestien and Adelaine, sat upon the raised wooden dais at the far end of the old Norman hall.

Chrestien stabbed irritably at her full trencher with keen disappointment. Her father had not come home yet another night, and it made for a very fearful and queasy feeling within the pit of her belly. Worry chiseled its way through her as she deliberated the possible causes for her father's delayed return. As bid of him, Papa had hastened to the side of the Duke of Normandy, Robert Curthose, in Rouen, and from there had sent word that he would proceed to Tinchebray with the duke. Certainly, if the matter at hand could not be settled amicably between the feuding brothers, Curthose would be forced to take his men-at-arms

1

into battle, and it was this possibility that weighed heaviest on her mind.

"Oh Adelaine, 'tis now been more than three months since Duke Robert summoned Papa. He should have returned long ago. After all, 'twas merely a council he was attending! Was it not?" Adelaine didn't answer save to look askance at Chrestien, and Chrestien sighed before saying, "I'd not be so distressed had Curthose not ordered Papa to raise his levies ere making the trek."

There was still no answer from Adelaine, and Chrestien was vexed with herself. Her twin sister was sitting prettily in her chair, enjoying her pheasant and a portion of stewed vegetables with such vigor that Chrestien could not but admire her. Papa had always claimed Chrestien to be the strong one of the two. Yet, hither sat Adelaine, calm and serene, refusing to take part in the worrying, while Chrestien could barely keep down her victuals due to her brooding mind and churning stomach.

From the dais could be seen three arched doors leading from the rectangular hall; one led to the tower rooms, one to the garden, and another to the bailey. Yet another door lay behind Chrestien, beyond the wooden screen, and it led to her father's bedchamber. A large hearth was also behind the dais, nestled against the wall of her father's chamber. In that manner, the smoke tunnels could be used by both the hearth in Papa's bedchamber and the one in the hall. Chrestien stared now, unseeing, at the door that led to the bailey, and Adelaine finally spoke in an attempt to ease Chrestien's mind.

"Hearten yourself, Chrestien. It could be that Papa would come sauntering through that entry any moment."

"Pooh Adelaine! 'Twould not happen such as that, and well you know it. Ere a troop the size of Papa's could enter the perimeter of the castle, the castle guards would undoubtedly sound alarm. Moreover, only when the approaching cavalcade was duly recognized and interrogated would the guards allow entrance—especially this late in the eve, when the night's blackness conceals Papa's banner. 'Tis fruitless to hope that he would."

Knowing it was futile to argue the point, Adelaine glanced about the hall then, searching for Janelle, their ladies' maid, who indubitably was the only one able to deal with her sister. The great hall bustled with servants; some were clearing the trestle tables of food, while others began the tedious task of removing food bits from the rushes. Already the lower tables had been cleared and dismantled, as they had been devoid of occupants to begin with—Papa having taken most of the Lontaine's knights—but there was no sign of Janelle, and Adelaine resigned herself to the task of calming her sister.

Carving a generous portion of the pheasant, Adelaine placed it in her mouth to savor delicately, eyeing Chrestien as if she expected some distinct response from her. She made it a point to chew conspicuously, as if to set an example for her sister.

When she was certain she possessed Chrestien's attention, she smiled sweetly, and renewed her exaggerated chewing. But when Chrestien yet showed little interest in her meal, Adelaine began waving her eating dagger in admonishment. "Mind you, 'twould not be at all good if you died of hunger ere Papa came home," she said finally, after a fourth wave of the silver dagger.

"Oh, Adelaine, I wish so much to be like you. But 'tis not to be! Terrible thoughts war within my head—and you know how cruel my visions can be," she lamented. " 'Tis a curse, I am sure . . . as Papa once told me that Mother was oft prone to such ravings of the mind."

Adelaine smiled inwardly, knowing that indeed her sister's imagination had a way of running amok, but she maintained her reproachful expression. "A silly man lies awake at night, thinking of many things. When the morning comes, he is worn with care . . . and his trouble is yet there."

"Sweet Jesu, Adelaine, but you cannot begin that anew. If I hear aught more of those viking principles, I should go mad." Chrestien placed her hands to her ears, and only when she did not see Adelaine's lips moving did she remove them again.

Adelaine could not help but smile at Chrestien's temperamental reaction, and as she did, two almost indistinct dimples appeared upon the outline of her cheeks. But she furrowed her brow almost immediately when she saw Chrestien lay her eating dagger on the table and toss a wayward lock of honey-colored hair over drooping shoulders.

Chrestien had not touched a morsel of food, and mayhap she would have to use Chrestien's own severe tactics to get her sister to eat. "Eat, Chrestien! Lest I lose the only sister I shall ever have!" She half shouted. " 'Tis not a curse. 'Tis simply that you worry overmuch." Her tone was set to mimic Chrestien's commanding voice, but she failed to impart the desired inflections, and sounded more like she was whining.

Chrestien shook her head reprovingly, donning her most wily smile as she did. She was thoroughly amused to hear Adelaine's clumsy attempt at authority. It just did not suit to hear Adelaine raise her voice so, but she appreciated the gesture, nonetheless, and she proceeded to pick up her dagger, her smile deepening to mirror Adelaine's sweet one— so that to look upon them, you would swear to be looking at a reflection in a looking glass.

Shouts resounded from beyond the Lontaine's great twelve-foot-thick masonry walls, and the castle guards bellowed in reply. In the great hall could be heard muffled shouts coming from the bailey, and the twins' smiles brightened concurrently as they acknowledged the clamor.

"It must be Papa," Adelaine declared, her eyes gleaming with pure delight as she pictured her father and his men outside the castle gates.

Chrestien did not bother to reply. Instead, she threw down her eating dagger, bolted from her seat and wrenched Adelaine from hers. Making her way from the great hall to the crowded bailey, not even pausing long enough for Adelaine to gain her balance, she was nigh dragging her gentle sister in her wake. So delirious was she at the thought of her father's return that she barely noticed Adelaine stumbling over her skirts.

Adelaine, torn between the joy she felt at her father's homecoming and exasperation at her sister's rugged treatment of her person, snatched her hand from the pinching grip and stopped to brush the dust from her blue sendal skirt. That done, she hastened after Chrestien to the castle gate to await the emergence of their father.

The overeager villein, who had gathered into a tight band about the gates, swept to one side of the bailey to yield a clear path for their master's cherished twins. The drawbridge lowered with a thunderous crash, and a feeling of dread passed over Chrestien as a solitary rider emerged from the shadows beyond the masonry walls.

The dispirited hush that settled throughout the bailey as young Aubert, their father's squire, dismounted from his gelding swept an unmistakable foreboding through the twins, and Chrestien eyed her sister apprehensively. Fierce knots of trepidation formed within her belly as Aubert's eyes forewarned her of his words.

Aubert perused the mob of villein, then turned again to his lord's young daughters. He despised the task before him, but as squire to Gilbert de Lontaine, the misfortune was his and his alone. He was silent for a moment, while he formed the words he knew would devastate Gilbert's two beautiful daughters.

With a swoop of his hand, he wiped the gathering beads of perspiration from his brow, wincing with the pain of his own loss. With great effort, he regained his composure and spoke to them softly, his eyes revealing all the sorrow that was in his heart. " 'Tis a most dismal message I bring ye, my ladies." Inadvertently, his gaze fell upon Chrestien. Somehow, to draw upon her strength made his missive a degree easier.

All at once, Adelaine's blood rushed to her head, making her light-headed, and she swooned before Aubert could speak again. Chrestien's arms went out swiftly to catch her as if she'd anticipated her sister's response. Strength exhausted, Chrestien fell to her knees, pulling Adelaine's limp body down with her. There, she cradled Adelaine's head in her lap as she awaited Aubert's next words.

"Yer father was killed at Tinchebrai, Chrestien. . . . Duke Curthose was captured, as were many others. Were it not for the grace of our Lord God . . ." He shook his head mournfully. "I'd not have escaped, for there were many with King Henry . . . and he came with his fiercest warrior . . . the Silver Wolf."

Chrestien shuddered visibly at the mention of the much feared name, but she could not speak—too overwhelmed was she by the shocking news.

"When the Wolf's silver banner came into view, many of Curthose's men turned tail and fled the battle. Yer father did not. He stood his ground . . . fought . . . and died honorably, Chrestien. Ye've reason to be proud of him," Aubert soothed, as he surveyed her face for some sign that she would swoon as had Adelaine. But as he expected, Chrestien's face was a nigh lifeless visage.

The only features to betray her pain were her emerald-colored eyes. As she raised her gaze to meet his, he could see that there were no tears, but the sadness in their depths was heart wrenching.

In silence, Aubert reached out to lift the crumpled Adelaine into his arms, and Chrestien rose to lead the way to her tower chamber. Aubert followed, bearing Adelaine's limp body, and together they climbed the short timber stairs to the great hall.

In the hall, servants busied themselves with the clearing of the evening meal, and carefully avoided Chrestien's gaze. By now the news had swept throughout the castle and none could bear to look into their mistress's face, for no matter how much they cared for their master, they loved his daughters ever more, and they could little bear the thought of the twins' great misery.

Mindlessly, Chrestien removed a lighted pitch torch from its prop and led the way up a flight of winding stone steps to her bower. Once there, she placed the torch into a wall brace, while Aubert laid Adelaine onto the finely curtained bed.

Aubert watched as Chrestien lovingly stroked Adelaine's face. Then, feeling imbued with embarrassment for his marked staring, he averted his eyes from his sisters' bed. Gilbert and his daughters had never been aware that Aubert knew the truth of his birth—and he had never been allowed to enter their bedchamber ere this day. He felt as though, somehow, he betrayed Gilbert by being here now.

Gilbert de Lontaine had been fiercely protective of his daughters, keeping everyone from them so diligently that there were few who even knew them to be twins. Most believed Gilbert to have but one daughter, and that seemed to suit Chrestien perfectly, as she fancied to remain unwed. Gilbert, not surprisingly, had expressed a likeness in thought. He had no qualms about keeping the lively Chrestien to himself. Moreover, Gilbert had oft confessed to Aubert that he feared for Chrestien should she wed, for she was ever a most willful girl. Thus, Gilbert had taken it upon himself to become her lifelong protector, and 'twas a role he welcomed without reservation, for despite her willfulness, she brought him great joy.

A muffled cry from Chrestien broke through Aubert's thoughts and he turned to wipe a wayward tear from his eye. He couldn't recall ever hearing her cry before, and to hear it now spurred his own tears. He had grown to love Gilbert's daughters—his half sisters—and to see them in such despair did naught but to torment him.

"What of our father's friend Aleth of Montagneaux? Did he escape as well?" Chrestien managed to ask at last, suppressing the tears that threatened to flood.

"Did ye not know, Chrestien? Aleth de Montagneaux did not go to Tinchebrai . . . most likely he is at his keep."

She nodded almost imperceptibly, her breath catching pitifully in her throat. She did remember now. Papa had said Aleth would not make this fight his own. A soft sigh of relief was her response—at least Adelaine would have Aleth to turn to.

Papa had expressed a partiality to Aleth de Montagneaux, though neither she nor Adelaine knew him well enough to explain why. Chrestien could only reason that if Papa had liked him, there was just cause for it. She and Adelaine had met Aleth but twice—in times long past—but if her memory served her well, he was a kindly man. Twenty years her father's junior, Aleth was possessed of an appealing face as well as a jovial disposition.

The first time they'd met him, they'd played their secret game, where they had sworn Papa to confidence and pretended to be one and the same person—a game Papa seemed to enjoy no matter how oft it was playacted!

Adelaine had shared a trencher with Aleth for a short while, then had excused herself, pleading illness. Chrestien had returned in her place, donning a like gown, but she'd been so hungry that she'd nigh given herself away, stuffing herself with the fervor of a starved animal. Aleth had noticed naught about the fact that he was sitting next to someone new. That he thought she'd eaten enough for two merely amused him. Papa had laughed heartily over it, his chalice pitching to the side with the force of his laughter, spilling deep red wine over Aleth and sending their guest leaping from his chair in result.

The second time, Adelaine had not seen him at all, for she'd not been well and had stayed in her chamber until Aleth was long departed. But 'twas just as well that she had, for he'd not stayed overlong and his time was spent in council with Papa.

Of course, Aleth had visited Lontaine more oft than that, though not much. It was only that Papa had always kept his old friend too busy to visit with his two young daughters. Moreover, he usually banished Chrestien and Adelaine to their room until their guest had gone.

Her memory told her that Aleth was amiable

enough, and Chrestien hoped he would be a kind husband to Adelaine. "Aubert, are you certain of Papa?" She needed to be certain her father was truly gone ere setting her plan into motion.

Aubert wished he could tell her otherwise—as much for his sake as for hers—but 'twas just not so, and the ache that was so apparent in Chrestien's voice nigh throttled his heart. "I wish he were not . . . but yea, he is dead. I saw him fall to the sword with mine own eyes."

Aubert had in fact seen him fall, though 'twas a mystery to him as to how. Gilbert was a skillful warrior, and he'd had at least one other besides Aubert to guard his back—one of Aleth's hired men.

When Aubert was charged from behind, he'd turned from Gilbert to vanquish the attacker, feeling secure that naught would happen to his father, for Gilbert fought but one man. After having felled his own attacker, he had returned to Gilbert in time to see him crumple to the ground, blood spurting from a wound at the back of his neck.

Lying mortally wounded, Gilbert had forced but four words from his lips. "We are betrayed!" he'd said. "Flee!" And Aubert had complied, though reluctantly. Looking back on it now, he realized that it was Gilbert's way of protecting him from a like fate—a father's dying gesture of love to a son never acknowledged. It touched him deeply. Yet there was something about Gilbert's last words that haunted him now. Betrayed. Gilbert had said. But how?

Adelaine stirred, bringing Aubert's thoughts to the present. Through the years, it had become apparent to Aubert that Chrestien was the strong one, and Adelaine the more delicate of the two. Moreover, he had noted long ago that while their features were identical, their temperaments and constitutions were anything but, and he could not but admire Chrestien's fortitude as he watched her attend their reviving sister.

Adelaine rarely raised her voice or disobeyed Gilbert, while Chrestien was spirited and quick-witted. Adelaine was skilled with the needle and knew much of the simples. Chrestien was not. Moreover, while Adelaine was well acquainted with the books of learning, Chrestien was interested only in horses and gaming—forever begging her father to take her on the hunts.

Gilbert had even gifted Chrestien with her own stallion, Lightning, which she was never to ride in the company of guests. And she'd reluctantly agreed to take a mare for those very rare occasions when Lontaine was entertaining.

Chrestien was ever making Adelaine a part of her artful pranks. But Gilbert, instead of being angry with Chrestien, seemed ever entertained by her playful antics. He did, of course, give the pretense of being sore with her, but his scoldings lacked any substance, and 'twould not be overlong ere Chrestien was into something else.

Due to this mischievous nature, it had surprised one and all during the summer past when Chrestien had announced her wish to be pledged to the church. Had it been Adelaine to make that disclosure, 'twould not have been so appalling, for she was the one more suited to the life of a nun. But Chrestien? Lord aid the abbess of La Trinite!

The twins' mother had died in childbirth and Gilbert never remarried. The love he bore his ladywife, Elizabeth, was too great. It was a love so pure and so very rare in these times when a marital union was little more than a political game of sorts. Instead, Gilbert poured his soul into raising Elizabeth's daughters. And though Gilbert would never own the truth of it, Aubert knew his father couldn't bear the thought of being without at least one of his beautiful daughters to pamper. Thus, Gilbert had agreed not to force the issue of marriage. His only stipulation was that Chrestien go to the abbey upon his death—not before!

Though Adelaine was the most exemplary daughter a man could desire, it was fairly obvious which of his twins gave him the most pleasure. Though he loved them both dearly, Chrestien was his favorite, and Gilbert couldn't bear the thought of any man mistreating her because of her high spirits. He oft likened her to a beautiful golden wild filly, and he was loath to break her.

At any rate, Adelaine was the eldest, if only by mere minutes; therefore, she was Gilbert's true heiress and obliged to marry according to her father's wishes—only Gilbert had not lived long enough to make his choice of husband known.

The twins were a stunning pair. At eighteen, they were overage to be married, but there wasn't a man in Christendom who would not leap at the opportunity to have them yet. Too, were it to be known that there were two of them? Surely, all of Normandy would be at Lontaine's gates with the ram, ready to do battle for the privilege of wedding with them.

Adelaine stirred again under Chrestien's gentle ministrations, opening her eyes to reveal golden pupils, softly flecked with green. The eyes, Aubert mused, were the only physical way to tell them apart. Both were possessed of lovely eyes. But Chrestien's were the brightest of green, almost startling to look upon, while Adelaine's were soft and delicate. Adelaine's features seemed to work together to boast of her gentleness—not that Chrestien wasn't kind; she was, but she had never been an easy one to subdue, while Adelaine was so easily molded.

Adelaine moaned and Chrestien put her arms about her sister's neck in response. They stayed in that position, holding each other tightly, and Aubert felt as if he were intruding on the moment.

"Oh . . . Chrestien, how is it that we are to go on without Papa?" Adelaine wailed, tears streaming down her blanched cheeks.

Chrestien's voice was controlled and very soothing as she gave her response. "I know not how our hearts shall fare," she admitted, honestly. "But all would be well with us . . . as long as we go on with our plan. You must go to Aleth," she prompted when Adelaine seemed confused.

Adelaine's eyes widened with newly felt horror and the remaining color drained from her cheeks. She'd forgotten about the plan Chrestien had devised should their father not return. Why should she have remembered? She'd never thought it possible that Papa would die, so she'd quickly discarded the plan as yet another offspring of Chrestien's overactive imagination.

"Nay, 'twould never work," Adelaine declared

somberly. " 'Twould be the banter of all Christendom were I to arrange for mine own marriage. . . ." The pitch of her voice climbed higher with newly felt alarm as she realized Chrestien was unmoved by her logic. "Do you not see that?"

Chrestien's countenance remained seemingly emotionless. To show apprehension in response to Adelaine's words would do naught but undermine the only practicable solution available to them.

"Nay Chrestien! Aleth would think me unchaste and unfit as wife to be so bold!" She added with forced intensity to give validation to her refusal.

"She speaks true," Aubert acknowledged softly, unsure if Chrestien would take offense to his siding with Adelaine.

"Yea, I know," Chrestien conceded. "I'd never allow you to be so chagrined. 'Tis why I've decided to go to Aleth as your custodian."

"You cannot!" Adelaine insisted.

"I would, Adelaine! Aleth knows naught of me, and I'd tell him that I am your cousin." Adelaine's reaction was that of puzzlement, and Chrestien seized the opportunity to sway her sister. "For once Papa would be glad of our little games with Aleth, for he knows not that Papa has two daughters—and twins to boot." When neither Adelaine nor Aubert gave a sign of concession, she proceeded to give the details of how the deception would be accomplished. "I would cut my hair, and—"

"Nay, Chrestien, ye would not!" Aubert broke in, appalled that she would even suggest such a thing. He grimaced openly at the thought of

Chrestien's lost locks. Her hair had been her father's delight—such a beautiful shade of gold, with streaks of sunlight coursing through waves that fell well below her waist. 'Twas as silky and beautiful as any Aubert had ever seen—besides Adelaine's, of course.

"I would, Aubert!" she maintained. "I've no choice if I am to fool Aleth into believing I am my father's nephew. 'Twould not matter anyhow," she sighed, stroking the length of her hair, feeling an immediate loss as if it had already been shorn. "For I shall leave for the abbey as soon as I see Adelaine duly wedded to Aleth."

Aubert sighed and nodded his head in resignation, though he loathed the fact that such beauty as Chrestien possessed would be cloistered away. "Yea, Chrestien, what would ye have me do?" He succumbed, knowing he would not win a battle of wills with her.

"To begin with, how many of my father's men are left?" She was afeared that Aubert would be the only one left of her father's men-at-arms. The way to Aleth's was long—a perilous journey, with brigands lying in wait to ambush the unwary soul.

"None . . . save myself," Aubert confirmed to her dismay.

"Then, I would dress the villein in armor," she replied, resolutely, "and myself as well. . . . We would feign a small troop." She was determined not to fail. If she did, some treacherous louse would no doubt abscond with Adelaine in hopes of possessing her inheritance, and Chrestien would never forgive herself did she allow that to happen. In fact, she did not doubt there were fortune seekers on their way to Lontaine this very moment, for though Lontaine was not a large stronghold, it was only one of four sister keeps. She shuddered, repulsed by the possibility that Adelaine could be defiled by one of these vermin, thereby forced into an unwanted marriage. It did not occur to her that she would be at risk herself.

" 'Twill never work, Chrestien. Ye could never be taken for a man," Aubert assured her. He couldn't envision Chrestien's generous curves in the guise of a man and he felt compelled to tell her so.

"You'd be astounded, Aubert, at what Chrestien can do," Adelaine advised him with a sigh of defeat.

The afternoon breeze was cool, but in the confines of his armor, Weston FitzStephens was afire. The metal of his helm drew the warmth of the sun, and the extreme heat registered acutely upon his senses. He needed a break from the stifling headpiece.

He reined in his destrier, causing a stir from his troops. It was not oft their liegelord succumbed to his own discomfort, and there was no other apparent reason for the respite. Two days they'd ridden from Rouen, stopping only when exhaustion overruled them, and it confused them to see their leader halt now, when they had scant daylight hours left.

Weston loosed the nose guard and pulled the confining helm from his head, baring the mailed coif beneath. His action was not a gentle one at all, for he was on edge and could not discern why.

The task given him was a simple one—too simple in fact! And mayhap that was what irritated him . . . that Henry would have him waste his time with such a minor assignment. Any fool could carry out this mission. It presented no challenge to him—none at all.

He inspected the unfamiliar landscape, his expression brooding. The indentations the conical helm had left in his flesh were conspicuous against his sweaty, bronzed face, the moisture in the crevices reflecting the sun, making it seem that he had tiny white lines painted upon his well-defined face. The cheekbones were high, giving extra depth to his very blue eyes. And to that effect was added the grayish tint under the rims of his lower lashes, giving the impression that they were sunken blue pools. His black hair was sprinkled with early gray and disheveled as only sweat and wind could accomplish. And his thick jaw was set in a tight line, giving evidence to his displeasure.

Michel, his captain, came forward then, curious to know what was in his leader's mind. "What see ye?"

Weston shook his head, not caring to open his already parched mouth to the rising wind—though he was grateful for the cooling effect the light breeze had upon him.

"Weston?"

Weston turned to consider his captain, and when he read the concern in Michel's face he knew he would explain. Michel knew him better than any. "I felt confined is all," he admitted, raising the conical headpiece he held to convey his meaning.

Michel nodded, knowingly. What Weston really meant was that he was irritated. Ever, when Weston was angry at something, did he feel *confined*, and never did he find reason to complain otherwise. In truth, he had a penchant for driving himself and others, almost ruthlessly. A wry smile curved Michel's lips. "Ye don't much relish this duty, I take it."

"Nay," came Weston's whispered reply, his parched lips opening to the budding wind. And when he felt his tongue tingle from the dryness, he bent to retrieve a skin of water from his saddlebags. He drank from it deeply, then offered it to Michel. Michel declined.

"I'll not have ye vent yer anger on me when 'tis depleted."

Weston narrowed his eyes on his friend. "Have I ever?"

Michel raised a blond brow in challenge, making Weston chuckle. "I have mine own, thank ye, ye auld wolf," he goaded.

Weston grinned, raising his own dark brow as he lit smoky blue pupils on Michel. "Ever you mock me, Michel. . . . Wolf . . . bah! Did I know you would ride me so about my chosen device . . . mayhap I'd have taken another."

"Nay, FitzStephens . . . ye would not have. None other could have served ye as well. . . . For ye are the Silver Wolf, through and through! I cannot see yer enemies fleeing from ye—as they do so oft—if ye were the prideful lion . . . or the lofty falcon. Nay, the wolf serves ye well with all its cunning ways, leaving no doubt as to who the victor will be. I know ye to be an honorable man, but to yer enemies ye are the sly and crafty wolf, capable of things they dare not speak of." Michel chuckled as his thoughts returned to Tinchebrai. "Why, ye reduce the number of our enemies in but the time it takes to recognize that gaudy banner of yers."

Both men turned their gaze to the banner that their shared squire, Guy, held so proudly. The stark black background offset the snarling silver-threaded wolf in its middle well. The animal's dauntless, blood-red eyes glared back at them. The breeze held the banner outstretched, playing with its folds, contorting the wolf's head, and giving the impression that the animal snapped its powerful jaws in warning.

Somehow, this image, along with Michel's quip, irritated Weston, and he returned the helm to his head once more. With his knees he commanded his destrier, Thunder, and the animal carried him forward, obediently. His troop immediately fell in procession behind him—their destination . . . Lontaine.

Chapter 2

All had gone according to plan. Aubert gathered as many villein as Lontaine could spare. Then, on the day of departure, Chrestien was to disburse among them what armor could be salvaged, saving the best, her father's armor, for herself. She would have to look as fearsome as the most seasoned of warriors to make it to Aleth's unharmed. Elsewise, she reflected, they might never make it at all.

Aubert came up behind her, startling her. She'd not heard his footsteps until he was upon her. "Yer father's mail tunic is in fair condition . . . considering that it lay unused for so long, Chrestien."

"Yea, but 'twas lucky that I'd gone to the armory when I did. The armorer was preparing to melt it down—refashion it to liken it to the one Papa wore to Rouen."

"Would that it were already refashioned," Aubert lamented. "The newer design is of heavier mail, and more solidly constructed. 'Twould have kept ye safer."

"Would that it were," she agreed, readily. "But 'tis not, and I've no mind to be skewered anyway."

"Neither does the field mouse ... until he is trapped within the hawk's talons."

"Aubert, I cannot even begin to ken what you would mean by that. Compare me to a mouse will you?" she mumbled indignantly.

"My meaning ... is merely that none of us can know when danger lurks—until 'tis too late. And more oft than not, it means death for those unprepared."

Chrestien rolled her eyes. "You tell me naught I do not already know. What would you have me do? Wait the time 'twould take for the armorer to refashion this blessed hauberk? Nay, Aubert, by then 'twould be too late."

"Mayhaps," Aubert conceded. "Mayhaps it would be."

"Of course, it would—enough of your worries. You fret like an old woman. Now, tarry no longer, and gather the villein for me."

"Old woman is it? Ye can dare to call me so, when ye are the queen of upset?"

Chrestien loosened her helm and started to throw it at Aubert, but the concerned look that lit upon his face stopped her.

"Nay, Chrestien! Ye would dent the damn thing!"

"Go, Aubert ... ere I lose my temper."

"Ere ye lose it? God's teeth, Chrestien, ye never had hold of it to begin with."

Chrestien reared her arm back then and let loose of the silver helm, sending it flying to Aubert, and as she intended, it landed away from him. She'd not meant to hurt him, merely to get him moving.

Aubert picked up the conical helm and smoothed

his hand over the top of it, where it had dented from the impact of its grounding. "Look what ye've done, Chrestien. 'Tis misshapen—and 'twas the only piece of armor that was passable."

Chrestien frowned and bit her bottom lip. "Can it be mended?"

Aubert cocked his head in disbelief. "Nay! Not in the time ere we leave," he snapped. "Ye shall simply have a warped helm," he informed her. Then he smiled mischievously as he said, "Never the mind, for 'twill fit yer own head perfectly."

"Oh!" Chrestien gasped. "Get you from me, Aubert! Now!" He did so readily, but when his back was to her, he started to laugh quietly.

Chrestien sighed. Aubert's shoulders were shaking suspiciously, and she would dearly love to throw something else at him, only there was naught within her immediate reach. Oh, how she would miss him. To many, their battles would seem undignified. But she and Aubert were of like temperaments, and it seemed he thrived on their wordplay as much as she. Yea, and if she could be honest with herself, she would miss the verbal combat as much as anything else.

It did not take long for Aubert to gather the villein, and once the men were mounted, Chrestien began dispensing, selectively, what few weapons and armor she had accumulated. To some she gave battered shields but not swords. To another she held out a dented helm, but then retrieved it, rolling the silver head gear in her hands as she inspected it carefully. She wasn't sure 'twould fit over Adam's big head. Deciding it would not, she handed him the much coveted broadsword instead. The helm she gave to the smallest man. And because he was so small, she gave him a sword as well. Four others were lucky enough to receive broadswords, but to the rest she gave daggers. 'Twas a pittance, she knew. But when one had naught else, a dagger was much indeed, she reasoned. When she was finished, there were nineteen fraudulent soldiers standing before her—each of them proud to defend his mistresses.

"From close range, they would not make a body tremble," she informed Aubert in a whisper. "But from a distance they would make a cavalcade to thwart most any band of brigands—I dare to hope, anyway."

Aubert did not agree, but he would not give his true opinion either. Never had he seen such a sorry band of men, and he loathed to tell her so. When Chrestien turned away from him suddenly, he was relieved, because now he would not be forced to answer her subtly phrased question.

Saddened by her thoughts, Chrestien busied herself with the task of saddling Lightning. And though she'd forbidden herself to cry, a lone tear stole down her cheek, spurred by the memory of the day her father had charged from the gates of Lontaine to join Duke Curthose. Sweet Jesu, but he and his men had been fearsome to look upon!

Papa had worn his finest armor, and he had looked so like she imagined the legendary warrior Arthur of Britain would appear. Jongleurs yet sang of the ancient Britain's fierce bravery. And she wondered, briefly, if there would ever be ballads sung to Tinchebrai's dead.

Papa had believed, passionately, that Henry had

no right to the Duchy of Normandy and had hastened to Curthose's aid without reserve. Papa was given to the opinion that if William, the Old Conqueror, had wished his eldest son to be Duke of Normandy, then 'twas Curthose's indisputable right to hold that which was willed to him.

Henry of England had warned Papa against his support of Curthose, stating that 'twould be an act of treason on Papa's part, but Papa had not seen it as such. The dowry lands Gilbert de Lontaine held of Chrestien's mother were forfeit on her death. Had Papa not relinquished the English soil to her grandsire, then he might have felt differently. But as it was, he held land of Normandy's duke alone—had sworn fealty to Curthose even! So it was that Papa had ridden out upon his destrier, clad full in armor to meet his duty . . . and never returned.

The only comfort Chrestien could take was that the Duke of Normandy had valued Papa greatly because Papa was one of the few who were loyal to him. She could not fathom why Aleth had not defended his duke. But whatever the reason, Papa had known of it and had obviously accepted it—so then could she.

Composed now, she turned back to Aubert, again seeking his opinion of their little troop. "You are silent, Aubert. What think you of our army?" she asked, amber brows raised expectantly, emerald eyes probing.

"Oh well . . . they . . . er . . . they are a fearsome lot," Aubert said as seriously as he could muster, knowing Chrestien would not reconsider her decision to seek out Montagneaux. Once Chrestien made up her mind, she was a veritable stone wall. Too, he was afraid to pain his half sister further by telling her the god-awful truth—that her men-at-arms were naught but a farce!

Chrestien narrowed her green eyes dangerously, ready to pounce on Aubert for his quip. "Truly, Aubert, there can be no allowance for falsehoods," she scolded. "They are no more a fearsome lot," she apprised him, "than I am a man. I only wish to know if they'll pass from a distance." Her chin rose defiantly as she awaited his answer.

Aubert's face reddened at the exaggeration he'd proclaimed and he capitulated. "Yea, Chrestien, ye are correct. I only wished to ease yer mind . . . and yea, they will pass . . . from a distance," he added honestly, sighing heavily.

He stared openly at the disguised woman before him, chuckling inwardly. She did truly look like a man—or rather a boy-man, for she was whisker-less, her skin as smooth as a baby's arse!

Chrestien wore men's braies tucked into thick brown leather boots, and a hauberk that fell nigh to her shins—on her father it had been worn about the knee. If her disguise made Aubert smile, he frowned as he inspected her hair. It now fell scant inches below her shoulders—worn to a length like that of a peasant boy's. Her perfect face was black-ened with soot from the hearth to make her ivory skin seem more weathered, and she carried her fa-ther's heavy jewel-hilted broadsword in her scab-bard. Finally, Gilbert's shield, which was an elongated oval shape and bore his chosen device—a golden, winged lion, poised for flight— she carried in her hand.

Aubert marveled that she would even be able to stand upright in her father's coat of mail as heavy as it was. It had taken Aubert years to acquire the dexterity to carry the drat thing with ease. Yet, hither stood Gilbert's daughter, bearing its entire weight proudly upon her small body.

Chrestien was by no means frail, but she was every bit the woman if ever he'd seen one. Though in truth, she was more petite than any woman he'd known. She stood only to his chest in height and he could look down on the pate of her head with ease. But yea, she did look like a man at this moment. That much he would grant her. The heavy mail hauberk, worn over an ill-fitting undertunic, flattened her breast effortlessly. And her heavy boots, stuffed with cloth, hid the delicate curve of her limbs.

To give herself the appearance of one who has labored, she had soiled her hands with grime, blackening her skin with it until it was nigh a part of her flesh. Then, she applied oil to the unruly curls that fell upon her nape and face to duplicate the likeness of perspiration. The latter he had no doubt she would not need, for after a day in the saddle, clad in armor and helm, her tender skin would be drenched in sweat of her own. He was certain she did not realize how hot it could grow to be in the confines of her armor—she'd discover it soon enough!

Aubert waited patiently as Chrestien marched up the timber stairs and disappeared into the great hall. Time to fetch the reluctant Adelaine, he mused with a chuckle. And he was little surprised when Chrestien returned but moments later, dragging a struggling Adelaine by the hand.

"Sweet Jesu! But you look like a man," Adelaine exclaimed, ripping her hand from Chrestien's iron grip. "You handle me like a man as well," she mumbled under her breath. "And Lord! I would credit it not, did I not see it with mine own eyes."

Chrestien grinned, revealing a string of pearly white teeth. "Shall I do, then?" she asked, standing her tallest, smiling wickedly at Adelaine. Then, she turned to Aubert, squaring her dainty shoulders, as she awaited the verdict.

Aubert was one summer younger than Chrestien but he looked much older than his young years. His golden hair and well-chiseled features resembled those of Gilbert de Lontaine, so much that Chrestien had oft suspected him to be her father's bastard. But Papa never admitted as much, so she had long since discarded the notion. Nevertheless, he was brother to her in every sense of the word, for she could tell him aught, and he would attend her with care.

"Ye'll do," Aubert assured her with a tender smile. Then, of a sudden, his lips turned up in a jeer and he raised an amber brow, wickedly. "They'll think ye a man ... and a filthy one at that!" He teased without mercy.

Adelaine giggled at the sight of her very dirty twin sister. She was more than fascinated at the acute difference between the two of them now, and her nose scrunched prettily as she spoke to say so. "Chrestien, 'twould be most insulting to me if they thought you to be my twin now," she admonished with mock severity, but her twinkling eyes gave her amusement away.

" 'Tis good to know, *cousin*," Chrestien replied with a wily smile, emphasizing the word *cousin*. Then, on a more serious note, she reminded, "Oh, and do not make the mistake of calling me by my given name. Be faithful in calling me by the new name of Christopher, elsewise they would discover the truth," she cautioned. "And I'd not like the repercussions of that."

"Yea, Chrestien. . . . Oh, nay, I mean, Christopher. Sweet Jesu, but I shall have to practice!"

Chrestien frowned at Adelaine and shook her head in disgust. "Do practice . . . oft!" she reprimanded.

She would need to keep watch over all Adelaine said, for Adelaine was not a very convincing liar. She sighed. If ever there were an honest soul, 'twould have to be her sweet sister. And of a sudden, she felt more than a little guilty about making Adelaine play a part in this deceit. Surely, it was for her own good!

Aubert helped Adelaine settle onto her speckled chestnut mare, making certain that she would suffer no ill effects from improper positioning. That done, he turned to Chrestien. He watched, dumfounded, as she leapt onto Lightning's back, missed her target entirely and slid down the agitated horse to land in a metallic heap upon the ground, chain links grinding noisily beneath her. He could not stifle his laughter when she rose from the dust, brushed herself off and started to leap upon the poor animal yet again. 'Twas just like Chrestien to think she was capable of mounting a horse the size of her Lightning clad in nigh fifty pounds of armor. 'Twas time to go to her rescue, he knew, for never would she say die. "Allow me to assist ye, minx," Aubert chuckled, stooping to make a riser of his linked hands. But even as he proffered the aid, he had to own that he was loath to end the comedy.

Highly embarrassed now, Chrestien's face took on a somber expression. " 'Twould be wise if I were never to mount before others, Aubert, else they would know of my lack of strength ... and think to use it to their advantage." Aubert agreed, clenching his jaw almost painfully to refrain from laughing more. Then, she added as if to defend herself, " 'Tis this accursed armor that makes me seem so weak!"

Aubert acknowledged the well-given excuse with a gentle tip of his head, but to his way of thinking there was naught about Chrestien de Lontaine that was weak or timid.

Aubert knew that Gilbert would be proud to see the way Chrestien took charge of Adelaine's and her own future. She'd turned a hopeless situation into a plan that promised to resolve all: first, Chrestien had sent word to de Montagneaux, stating that Lord Gilbert de Lontaine favored a betrothal between Lord Aleth and his only daughter, Adelaine. The message also revealed that in the event of Gilbert's untimely death, any proposed marriage contract was to be negotiated through Gilbert's nephew, Christopher. Moreover, that Christopher awaited Aleth's decision on the matter at Lontaine. Did he wish to wed the lady Adelaine, or nay? As a final touch, the letter was

predated to the eighteenth of May, in the year of
Our Lord 1106—the date of Gilbert's departure
from Lontaine. The parchment was rolled then,
and sealed with wax. Finally, it had been explained by the messenger that the letter had only
recently been discovered in de Lontaine's bedchamber, thereby accounting for the lapse in time.

The reply had come speedily. Yea, Aleth did
wish to wed the lady Adelaine, and Christopher
was to bring her with all haste. It had been concluded as simply as that, only Chrestien feared
that the hardest part was yet to come. As for herself, having no wish to wed and take orders from
a husband, she planned to enter the convent post-
haste.

Chrestien shifted uneasily in her saddle. It
seemed that a thousand nervous fingers pricked
her flesh, and she could not find a comfortable position. Turning her stallion to face her faux mesne,
she began a final inspection. Seeing that the villein
were ready to ride, she gave the gatekeeper a
wave of her hand and he lowered the drawbridge
immediately. As it lowered her anxiety rose, until
her palms were moist with nervous sweat and the
silver helm she held in her hands threatened to
roll from her uncertain grasp. Unceremoniously,
she put the conical helm on her head and adjusted
the nose guard. For better or worse, she was ready
as well.

Chrestien waited as Aubert hauled himself onto
his own mount, then she led the way through the
gate and onto the great wooden plank that
spanned the dry moat encircling the masonry
wall. Hooves cantered behind her, echoing noisily

as each man crossed the age-old bridge. Once all had passed over, Chrestien motioned for the gates to be closed again, knowing that the guard would not reopen them until Aubert returned . . . alone.

The morning proceeded without incident, and after three hours the cavalcade had covered much more territory than Chrestien had deemed possible. Curious to know how far they'd come, she turned to Aubert. "Have we a great distance to go yet?"

"Nay, but as I suspected, we'll not reach Montagneaux this eve, though with luck we would achieve at least ten miles ere the sun sets. Even so, we'll not see our destination until the morrow."

"But how many miles have we to go?" she insisted.

" 'Tis hard to say, Chrestien. Castle Montagneaux is not more than twenty miles as the crow flies, but—"

"We are not crows, Aubert," Chrestien snapped.

"And if ye would have allowed me to finish, Chrestien, I'd have said so. Now, because we are not crows, we would need take the long route, which will add an additional four miles to our journey," he told her peevishly. Alone he could have well made it to Montagneaux in less than a day, but he was not alone, and the caravan of villein slowed them considerably.

Most of the men had never even ridden ere now because villein were not presented with horses. Nor had they ever donned the heavy armor that now greatly constricted their movement. As a result they were more than awkward in the saddle. Even so, they rode on without complaint, even as the sun's rays baked onto their heads.

Chrestien's own helm became an oven that nigh boiled her skin alive. Still, she would not stop, until finally her thoughts were confused—muddled by the dizzying heat—and her body was sodden with perspiration. Even then, she gave respite only long enough to rest the horses and give water to her tired men.

Time passed quickly and dusk seemed to fall ere it was due, bringing with it welcome relief from the heat. Aubert found a suitable spot to make camp, then it seemed he disappeared. Chrestien settled Adelaine into their small canvas tent, and once the guards were posted she set out to find the inconspicuous Aubert. Panicking when she didn't see him straightaway, she called his name repeatedly, and sighed audibly with relief when he came from the woods. When he told her where he'd been, her cheeks colored at once. Nevertheless, her eyes narrowed on him. "Next time," she reprimanded to hide her chagrin, "make known to others your intentions, Aubert."

"Ye wish me to tell ye when I need to relieve myself?" he mocked, with the familiar raise of his brows. When Chrestien's cheeks turned a brighter shade of red, Aubert chuckled, satisfied with the result of his teasing. "What is it ye need of me, minx?"

"Only that you are to bring your pallet to my tent. I want you to sleep so as to block the entrance—that no one would enter during the night."

"Nay, Chrestien!" He couldn't possibly abide by her wishes. " 'Twould be unseemly! Moreover, were I to sleep in yer tent," he advised her, " 'twould not go unobserved." He waved his hand in a gesture to encompass the whole camp.

If possible, Chrestien's color deepened, only this time it was spurred by her anger. "Are you daft, Aubert? Outside the tent . . . not inside, you dolt!"

Now it was Aubert's turn to bloom crimson. Chrestien turned on her heels, gifting him with a very unladylike snort. Then, shoving aside the flap, she entered her tent to join Adelaine in repast, which consisted only of bread, cheese, and verjuice—the juice of unripe grapes.

Adelaine ate silently, with such a glum expression that Chrestien yearned to comfort her, but then thought better of it. If she showed the least bit of concern, Adelaine would think there was cause for panic . . . and there might be, but she didn't dare risk Adelaine's balking again. With luck, Adelaine would sulk for a short time. But then she would realize bemoaning her fate would accomplish naught, and she would gracefully accept her destiny.

Adelaine finally breached the barrier of silence between them. "What think you of Aleth?"

"I think him most appealing," Chrestien admitted, welcoming the conversation. "Do you not?" She was certain Adelaine would find naught amiss with the man, but she desired to hear it from her own lips.

"Yea." Adelaine smiled dreamily. "He is most appealing." She removed her bliaut. Then she struggled with the undergown, deciding she would sleep more comfortably in her chainse, and her next words were muffled as she pulled the garment over her head. "Truly . . . I do . . . hope he is . . . phhmph . . . phmmph."

"What say you?"

"I hope he is pleased with me as well," Adelaine clarified, pulling the second gown over her head. She placed her apparel in a neat pile next to the only pallet in the tent. Silence.

Peeping from the corner of her eye, Chrestien noted that Adelaine was watching her with the eye of a ladyhawk, and she knew Adelaine was yet contemplating her fate. It was not but seconds later that Adelaine confirmed it.

"Think you we shall fool Aleth, Chrestien?"

"Yea, though 'twill not be an easy task," she confessed. "And were he to find out? I cannot be certain what he would do. He may think it amusing and treat it with raillery or he might be angered. In the latter case I should not know what to do . . . but flee."

Chrestien bit her bottom lip, losing herself in thought, and Adelaine settled herself onto the pallet and closed her eyes, believing Chrestien was through conversing. She recognized that faraway look in her sister's eyes—had seen it oft enough to know that Chrestien was scheming and would give her attention to naught but her deliberations.

Just as the dreamkeeper opened his magical doors, Adelaine sensed more than heard Chrestien's voice, and she opened tired eyes to look upon her sister.

"I'd not nag you on this, Adelaine, but tell not a soul of me—not even Aleth. 'Tis between us alone ... and Aubert, of course. You and I are as one, and Aubert makes two—and you do remember what Papa says?" She would use one of Papa's quotes to emphasize her point. Adelaine would understand that better than aught else. "Tell one your thoughts, but beware of two, for all know what is known to three."

"And now who is quoting viking principles?"

"It cannot be helped." Chrestien shrugged, then sighed. "I've heard them oft enough. And old habits do not die ... they simply are laid to rest and then revived."

Adelaine's brows knit in bafflement. "I cannot recall that one."

"Of course not, silly, 'tis made up."

Adelaine raised a challenging brow. "Are we becoming a scholar then?"

"Nay, we both know who is the sage in this family. Who is it that spends hours studying the classics? In fact, you've read so profusely that you'd gone to beseeching Papa to attain new collections—pleading with both Papa and Father Claude to assist you in the learning. Who can be found scribbling in her journal? Grilling Papa on our viking heritage? Hmmm? Can you tell me? 'Tis a good thing Father Claude was not of the old school, Adelaine, for the Church does not sanction such practices. Does our ancestry fascinate you so?"

" 'Twould seem so," she confessed. "Truth to tell, it helps me to understand you, Chrestien. For though you are a woman ... you are Viking in spirit, through and through! And while we are addressing it ... 'twould do you good to understand our ancestry—to know what blood courses through your veins. Papa was very proud of our bloodline, you realize—though of course, he would be the first to own that sometimes our viking forefathers took the path of violence once too oft."

"Mayhap you will enlighten me someday—now that Papa and Father Claude are gone," Chrestien suggested. Never would she admit that she had been studying already. Nor that she oft stole a peek at the journal Adelaine kept, though she did wish to tell Adelaine how moving her prose actually was. It was amazing that Adelaine could spend long hours composing such beautiful verses of love and honor, and when the words were on parchment 'twas well worth the time spent.

Adelaine nodded eagerly, glad to have finally piqued Chrestien's interest. But then her thoughts drifted again to Aleth de Montagneaux. "Do you suppose Aleth is a Viking descendant?" Before Chrestien could answer, a thought occurred to Adelaine and her eyes widened in horror. "Surely, Papa would not regard Aleth so were he a violent man? Papa was ever so gentle, Chrestien!"

"Yea, with us he was, Adelaine. But you've just spoken to me of the Norse blood that coursed through his veins. He was a different man apart from us. But you needn't worry about being beaten, Adelaine, for there's naught *you* could do to deserve a lashing," Chrestien assured as she picked at her hauberk repulsively. The chain mail was boring through her undertunic, into her delicate skin, and it irritated her that she would need wear the offensive thing at all. How could men stand it? Never would she understand men! Why not simply cease the senseless fighting? Leave others be!

She couldn't fathom sleeping in the irksome thing, but that was exactly what she was going to do—lest someone wander into camp and discover two helpless women and a troop of farmers disguised as knights. That Aubert was well trained in the skills of war was of no consequence. What could one man do against so many?

She laid upon the pallet next to Adelaine, making certain her helm and sword were well within reach, and attempted to rest. But a sobering thought came to her and she nudged Adelaine with her elbow. "You do not think me violent . . . do you?"

Adelaine opened sleepy eyes yet again, and her answer spewed forth as a sigh. "Nay."

"Well then, I cannot ken why you say I am Viking in spirit." She sounded affronted and Adelaine attempted an explanation.

" 'Twas not brutality I was referring to, Chrestien, but the pride and courage you seem to exude. 'Twas their most valued trait, you realize. Courage, that is."

"You think me courageous?" Chrestien giggled. "Why, 'tis shaking in my boots I am." She giggled again and blew out the lone candle. Content with Adelaine's answer, she settled herself into the darkness.

Morning sun filtered through the shielding canvas, and Chrestien opened her eyes, rubbing them sleepily, and sat up to dig the offensive hauberk from her aching flesh. That done, she reached over to jiggle Adelaine's arm. When Adelaine opened one eye, only to close it again, Chrestien irately yanked her coverlet away.

Adelaine reacted with a pretentious yelp, bolting to her feet, completely dressed and laughing happily. " 'Twas but a jest. You slept like the dead, Chrestien! And not for the first time . . ." Adelaine could not contain her laughter. "You snored and wheezed throughout the night." She followed this quip by snorting loudly. "And mayhap," she teased, giggling almost hysterically now, "if you do not take off that armor . . ." She raised her shoulders squarely and attempted to walk like a man to show Chrestien what she was in danger of becoming.

Chrestien gathered her boot into her fist, and in seconds hurled the brown leather swiftly across the tent. Adelaine dodged it easily, and it landed with a loud whack on the closed tent flap. Then it bounced across the tent wall to successfully smack Adelaine's leg. Suspiciously, there was the faintest outlet of breath from beyond the tent opening, but Adelaine's accusations demanded Chrestien's immediate attention. "I do not snore. . . . I do not wheeze!"

Adelaine ignored the denial. "I have been up and ready for so long, Chrestien. Oh, and I have broken my fast and seen to my toiletry." She listed these accomplishments on her fingers. "And you," she chided with a wide smile, "delay us."

Chrestien's eyes narrowed with feigned malice. But in truth, she was relieved that Adelaine was in such good spirits and was willing to overlook the barb, until she heard a muffled guffaw from behind the tent flap. Outraged that Aubert would be eavesdropping, she picked up the discarded boot and gave another firm blow to the shadow behind the tent wall. When she heard a groan of pain from the other side, she smiled wryly and victoriously tore open the flap to reveal her victim.

"How did I discern 'twould be you . . . Aubert?" she purred ever so sweetly.

Aubert said naught. He responded only by rubbing his sore cheek in an attempt to ease the sting there.

"Go, Aubert, you wretch! Saddle the horses, and let us be gone." She felt somewhat contrite as she watched a splotch of red form upon Aubert's right cheek, though not enough for an apology.

"God's strength, minx!" Aubert muttered. "Remind me to apprise the abbess of yer propensity for ungodly brutality." But he smiled drolly as he turned away from her and left to do her bidding.

When he was out of earshot, he half chuckled, half groaned, as he thought of the abbess of La Trinite. She would give Chrestien a fight to contend with. The surly old woman was none too gentle a soul herself!

Chapter 3

Castle Montagneaux loomed forbiddingly before them, the eighteen-foot-thick walls rising nigh seventy feet into the air. An aura of undeniable foreboding swept the air of what gaiety the little troop had mustered and the tiny hairs on the back of Chrestien's neck bristled in alarm at the sight of the monstrosity.

Bringing her snowy-colored stallion to a halt, Chrestien silently reconsidered the likelihood that they would dupe the lord to whom this castle belonged. Its suzerain seemed to have taken every precaution against intruders.

The castle was seated upon a solid, steep sloping hill, which was elevated at least forty feet in itself. A man-made reservoir joined a natural lake to the left, encircling the majority of the massive curtain walls. The only visible entrance was through the main gate, which was set along the narrowest expanse of water.

The curtain wall, itself, was a monumental masonry eclipse that boasted several mammoth, projective towers.

There was not a single peasant's hut below the

41

fortress, leading Chrestien to believe they would
be found within the protective arms of the massive
curtain walls. Aleth, Chrestien observed, must be
very kind to care overmuch for his people, and
with that thought came a sigh of relief. Adelaine
would indeed be safe with the lord of
Montagneaux.

Aubert brought his gelding between Chrestien's
stallion and Adelaine's speckled chestnut mare.
" 'Tis not the time for misgivings," he said more to
Chrestien than Adelaine. Nudging Chrestien's stallion with a black boot, he nodded in the direction
of the nearest tower, where the vague outline of
two men could be seen.

"They know we approach ... 'tis not like
Lontaine as it is now, wither there is but one tower
and few men to garrison the keep." He didn't
mean to remind her that her father's death had left
Lontaine in a quandry—without any real
protection—and he was saddened by the sudden
melancholy reflected in her green eyes.

Chrestien gave a curt nod. Then, without warning she started for the castle with relative speed.
Having taken a deep breath for its calming effect,
she forged ahead ere her mind could warn her
body to turn back.

The drawbridge was lowered determinedly, and
the little troop cantered across with unrepressed
reverence. Adelaine's eyes were wide with apprehension, and the villein kept their heads
lowered—half out of fear, half out of learned respect.

Aubert watched Chrestien. Her proud stance revealed none of her misgivings, nor did it betray

her irrefutable veneration as her probing eyes scanned the interior of the immense fortress. The castle was a self-contained municipality!

Directly inside the outer wall, the land sloped downward. They passed through the small barbican into the lower bailey, where row upon row of wattle-and-daub huts dotted the sloping view. A smaller curtain wall spanned the left side of the fortress, separating the huts from the middle bailey, and an open postern revealed an expansive lake beyond it. Two towers stood sentinel over the waters so that none would approach in that direction unobserved.

They were led into the middle bailey, which flourished with well-stocked gardens. Then came the last of the inner curtain walls, and beyond that lay a beautiful courtyard. At long last came the keep—an immense rectangular building, so big that it could have swallowed three of the Lontaine's tiny dongons.

From outside Montagneaux's walls, it was all but impossible to determine the vast expanse of land the fortress contained. The master of this citadel was either very extravagant . . . or he simply trusted no one. Chrestien chose to believe the former because oft a man who trusted no one could not be trusted himself. Had Papa not said so?

Aleth de Montagneaux was as striking a man as Chrestien had remembered. He was also just as amiable, albeit only to Adelaine. He seemed quite besotted with her sister, and Adelaine with him. But Chrestien could easily see why Adelaine might be so taken with her father's longtime ally.

He was possessed of such deep blue eyes, which bordered on gray. And she was certain that one look from him could weaken a woman's knees. She could not swear by it, however, for he never looked her way long enough for her to confirm it. And because she had been so young when she'd seen him last, she could not rely on her memory at all.

His hair, which was reddish brown in color, defied the standard for red hair in that it was unusually satiny looking. It made one want to feel the softness of it, Chrestien mused. He was not tall, but his chest was thick, and his elegant finery boasted of great riches. His mantle and surcoat were of a burgundy Italian velvet not oft seen in these parts, nigh covered with jewels of every sort—including a few gems that Chrestien did not recognize.

Aleth treated Chrestien with aloof respect—if it could be called that. He had allowed her to sit at the lord's table this eve—Aubert too, even though he neglected them both completely. But even if she did not take kindly to being ignored by her sister's betrothed, she was relieved that he had accepted her for whom she'd claimed to be, for it was so much easier to keep the pretense in silence.

They had arrived in time for Montagneaux's evening meal, and were pleased to find that Aleth had arranged to serve the main meal upon their arrival, instead of at midday as was the usual.

The tables groaned beneath a spread of roasted pork, beef, mutton, and herring flavored with cream and herbs. Sliced apples, pears, and peaches were arranged in the shape of a bird in flight, and an assortment of cheeses filled trays that were interspersed along the table.

The only unpalatable item was the wine. It was bitter and grainy, and a mouthful of it reminded Chrestien of the time she and Adelaine had made mud pies by the stream at home. Adelaine's mud pie had looked overmuch like a tart, and Chrestien, at five years of age, had decided to sample it.

But, acrid wine or nay, her only real complaint was that she was forced to share a trencher with an obnoxious knight by the name of Gervais, whom she'd neither met nor heard of ere now. Albeit, to hear him speak he was well sought after by all ... for he was, of course, unmatched in the skills of war. Jesu! Had he the dexterity to find his mouth when eating, he might be somewhat believable! The offensive cur! Fie on him if he thought her a fool!

Gervais's breath smelled of stale wine and poor hygiene, and Chrestien wasn't certain which was more offensive. And Sweet Jesu! Did he whack her back just once more, or recite another repulsive tale of female conquest, she was going to stab him with her eating dagger ... and accuse Sir Rolfe, Aleth's elder brother, who was scrutinizing her from across the table with the intensity of a hawk sizing its prey! Seeking out Aubert, who was seated next to the fair-haired Rolfe, she gave him a glimpse of her ire. And to her dismay, his only reaction was to laugh heartily.

Adelaine giggled at some witty remark of Aleth's, and Chrestien turned in time to see her sister's cheeks bloom with cherry color. Adelaine's eyes met Chrestien's then, and lowered in chagrin.

"What say you?" Chrestien asked innocently, smiling expectantly. She was in dire need of something humorous to brighten her spirits. But as she waited for her sister to reply, Adelaine's color only deepened to a shade somewhere this side of violet.

"I simply told her ... Christopher," Aleth provided, clearing his throat, "that I originally had arranged to wed her a sennight from today ... but that was ere I set mine eyes upon her." Aleth took Adelaine's pink-flushed hand then and started to kiss it, but stopped abruptly. Instead, he looked directly into Chrestien's eyes. "If there are no objections from ye ... I shall wed her on the morrow. Even," he assured Chrestien, "if it means I've insulted my guests by curtailing the celebration." Suddenly Aleth's very gray eyes bore into Chrestien's green ones, deliberately and with condemnation. "I simply cannot ... will not ... await," he clarified. Then, turning to Adelaine, he was at once smiling again.

It was clear to Chrestien that the guest he had not a care of insulting was herself. Sweet Jesu! But it suited her just fine not to remain in this ... this den of wolves! But that he would have such little care for Adelaine's only kin was insufferable. She kept her emotions well masked, however, and simply nodded her acquiescence, her anger deterring the telltale tears.

"Splendid ... splendid. Then I trust we understand each other when I say I wish ye a safe journey home. Wither did ye claim that to be ... yer residence, that is?"

"He has lived at Lontaine most of his life," Adelaine provided uneasily, unsure it was the right thing to say. But when Aleth accepted the answer with a curt but polite nod, she rested a little easier. Not by much, however, for she had noticed the sideways icy glares Aleth had given poor Chrestien.

It was clear enough that Aleth truly believed Chrestien to be a man, for Adelaine had noticed a distinct possessiveness in his angry looks toward Chrestien. Though, by the saints, Chrestien seemed so preoccupied that Adelaine was certain she had not noticed Aleth's disapproving looks.

The fact was that Chrestien's eyes had not left her sister all eve, though her thoughts were hard put to remain in the present. She couldn't help but remember other banquets ... at Lontaine ... with Papa. And now Adelaine, the only family Chrestien had remaining, would be gone from her life all too soon. It weighed heavily upon her, but she tried to console herself with the fact that she would be cloistered soon—that did help a trifle.

Adelaine yawned loudly, bringing Chrestien's senses into focus. "Well, my lord Aleth, 'tis been a most grueling day I fear, and I'm in sore need of rest," she explained, "lest I be far too weary for tomorrow's festivities. Shall we retire, cousin Chris?" She smiled happily for not once had she failed to use her sister's new name.

Aleth's eyes nigh burst from their sockets with anger as he focused on the direction of Adelaine's gaze. Initially, Chrestien did not comprehend the ire in Aleth's countenance. But it dawned on her all at once, and she feared 'twould be the end of

their charade. Mother Mary! She would be forced
to confess all to keep from being run through by
Aleth's blade. Jesu, but Adelaine was thick-witted!
Yea, more than daft she was!

"I am most certain your chamber is safe . . .
safe!" Chrestien repeated the word with muted anger as she stared at her sister in disbelief. She
turned to Aleth and faced his angry glare in an effort to acquit herself of his silent accusations.
"Adelaine has a fear of sleeping in unfamiliar places. If you would but assure us that her chamber
will be adequately guarded . . . there would be no
need for me to inspect it." Incredulously, she did
not even stumble over the explanation and it came
across clearly—and very believably. She turned
her emerald eyes on Adelaine, smiling tersely. "Is
that not so, Lady Adelaine?"

Aleth relaxed his menacing posture, if only
slightly, and assured Adelaine that all would be
well. "Yer chamber is indeed safe, m'lady . . . but
if ye would come with me, I would bodily see to
it." He rose from his seat, eyes still narrowed upon
Chrestien, and took a very contrite Adelaine by
the hand.

Chrestien watched as her sister and Aleth disappeared behind an ornate wooden screen. She
sighed with relief when Aleth returned but minutes later. At least Adelaine would sleep in peace.
The same could not be said for herself, however,
for she no doubt would be sleeping with all the
other men in the great hall—on the rush-strewn
floor, no less!

The tables were cleared, the servants dispersed,
and the hall was emptied, save for those men of

lesser distinction, which of course, Christopher was considered to be. She watched, numb with abject fear, as the men undressed and prepared for a night's rest on their thin, smelly, flea-ridden pallets. She cringed when she realized Sir Rolfe was yet watching her, but she was determined to make the best of this, and she busied herself with preparing her straw mat next to Aubert's—all the while cursing Aubert for disappearing yet again.

When finally Rolfe left the hall, she settled onto her pallet, fully dressed in her hauberk, and closed her eyes. She tried hard to conjure images of Lontaine . . . tried to pretend she was home in her chamber. But naught would come to her, save for thoughts of Montagneaux and her sister's coming wedding. Wither was that imagination of hers when she needed it? Solace came when Aubert's voice broke through her troubled thoughts.

"I shall not sleep this night," he whispered softly. "I'd keep watch over ye, minx."

Relief flooded through her as she opened her eyes to look into Aubert's familiar blue ones. "Thank you, Aubert. Mayhap, I'll rest easier now." And somehow, knowing Aubert watched over her, did soothe her fears.

The night air was clear and cool as Rolfe made his way to the stables. He was certain there was more to Christopher de Lontaine than met the eye. It was rumored once that Gilbert de Lontaine had twin daughters—though he'd never credited the idle talk. He'd assumed Aleth would have known of it were it true. Mayhap he should have pursued the matter.

It had wrenched his gut to know his brother was offered the beautiful Lady Adelaine for wife. But he'd masked his anger well, then had prompted Aleth to accept the young girl. Dead men had no need of women. If Rolfe carried out his intended plan, Aleth would have little need of the girl in the end. Now, for once, he would not have to settle for his brother's leavings! Having met Adelaine's cousin, Rolfe had no doubts at all that the old rumor was fact. Christopher de Lontaine looked overmuch like the lady Adelaine in appearance for it not to be so.

Mayhap Aleth was too stupid to note it, but even considering the disguise—and it was a good one at that—Rolfe could see the uncanny resemblance. The hair, though much shorter and straighter for the filth, was the same rich golden color as Adelaine's. Too, the whiskerless face, though dirty, was as smooth as porcelain—a good soaking would reveal much, no doubt.

There remained one difference between them, however: the eyes—such bright green eyes the unnamed one had—almost spellbinding. But, if the obvious were true, and Christopher was in fact a maiden . . . 'twould also be true that the unnamed one had to be the more beautiful of the two. Why else would de Lontaine keep her locked away? She was either beast or beauty, and he doubted she was beast. The look of her eyes promised otherwise, and Gilbert de Lontaine had been renowned for his selfishness. Did he not shun all men who came to his door? The man had surely turned Rolfe away oft enough! Truly Gilbert would keep his most valued treasure close to him always—it was his way.

Rolfe had stood next to the unnamed one but once this eve, and though she reeked of perspiration, there was also the unmistakable odor of rosewater that drifted from her hair. He ached to go to her now, remove her men's garb, wash her dirty face, and see what lay beneath the filth. Well, the state of her mount would tell him much. He would check her saddle and bags for evidence. Perhaps she left some telltale clue there.

But yea, she was Adelaine's twin, only why she should go through such pains to remain secret now that her father was dead was beyond him. Her efforts were all for naught, however, for Rolfe would have her.

He rubbed his chin thoughtfully as he imagined all that he would do to the girl. Aye, he would wait until she left Montagneaux and seize her then. By the time it was discovered that she was missing, who would trace her to his old castle in Poitiers? He'd gotten away with such a thing once before ... But nay! He waived away those distant memories as quickly as they emerged. This girl would make a warm and willing whore by the time he was through with her, of that he was certain. She would be nothing like Gwynith. And if Gervais was about his duty this night, the girl and her men would be far too tired to put up any resistance on the morrow. A warm flush crept to his face, even as he thought of her lying beneath him. Yea, she'd make a lovely consolation prize ... lovely indeed.

* * *

Chrestien winced with pain as the knight Gervais whacked her tender back yet again. "How can ye slumber in such a cumbersome manner?" Gervais waved a hand in reference to her hauberk, his brows furrowing with puzzlement. He didn't wait for an answer. "It matters not," he crowed. "This wench I've invited to my pallet will scorch yer ears and ye shan't sleep anyhow." He was holding a brawny red-haired woman by the waist, and he proceeded to plop her upon his pallet, his belly rumbling with laughter over his own wit.

Chrestien gritted her teeth as she sent a silent message of repressed animosity to Aubert's sympathetic eyes, her own eyes glittering with green intensity.

Aubert snickered and turned his head from Chrestien's wrathful glare. He knew she was losing hold of her temper yet again, but he also knew she would do naught to give herself away. He smiled to himself as she buried her face in her straw pallet and linked her hands behind her head in an attempt to hide from the milieu. He nigh broke into fits of laughter when she pressed her arms to her ears as well.

The torches were put out, and Chrestien lay in the darkness, unwillingly listening to the unabashed whimpers and moans coming from the shadows beside her. "Foul," she muttered, almost inaudibly.

Aubert chuckled, leaning toward his half sister to whisper softly into her tallow-redolent head. "He surely will not dally all night, Chris. 'Twould take great feats of strength to move that hefty belly about." He could hear Chrestien's muffled giggle, and he rubbed the back of her head affectionately. "He'll collapse ere ye know it, minx," Aubert teased, "and 'twill take the two of us to drag the red's body from 'neath him."

Chrestien could not contain her laughter at the image Aubert's words conjured. She felt like kissing him for it. Instead, she giggled until her sides hurt, and fell asleep content.

The troops were assembled, and after a brief adieu to Adelaine, Chrestien and Aubert led the company of villein away from Montagneaux. She was relieved to be gone from the harrowing place. All that was needed now was to get to Caen, and she would be safe. "Think you anyone suspected, Aubert?"

"Nay."

" 'Twas beautiful. Was it not?"

"What?"

"The wedding, you dolt—'twas all I had dreamed Adelaine would have. My only regret was that I was not able to help prepare her for the ceremony as I always dreamed I would."

"It did seem Aleth was possessed of eyes in the back of his head," Aubert conceded.

"He would not allow me to come within yards of Adelaine," Chrestien protested. "Much less within her bedchamber. . . . 'Twas unfair!" she declared, as droplets of rain pattered her helm.

"Yea, it was," Aubert agreed.

Chrestien sighed. "Nevertheless, I can take comfort in that Adelaine was the most beautiful bride I have ever seen. Of course, she is also the only bride I have ever seen," she lamented. "Papa never let us attend other wedding celebrations. He feared that the moment he showed the world his daughters, we would be whisked away. Of course, 'twas an embellishment, this I know. But 'twas good to hear him say so anyway." As far as Chrestien was concerned, his protectiveness was a trifling price to pay, for there was naught else she could find to complain about when it came to her father. He was good to them always, to be sure.

Aubert understood their father's obsessive ways better than anyone. Gilbert did all out of a profound love for his family. "If yer father was overly protective, minx ... 'twas because he only wished to have his daughters with him as long as he could manage it. Surely he cannot be faulted for that."

"And well I know it. Nevertheless, had he not been so sheltering, I would surely be on my way to the altar—not to take the veil but to an unwanted marriage instead. In my mind, 'tis something to be thankful for. As for Adelaine, she was made for matrimony. 'Tis in her nature to be nurturing and loving."

Chrestien's thoughts drifted back to the wedding. Adelaine had worn the most beautiful bliaut of pale blue brocade with gold thread woven intricately into its fabric and a blue velvet mantle trimmed with ermine. A chaplet of gold cord, from which fell a silken veil, had adorned her plaited gold hair. And Chrestien experienced a momentary twinge of regret that she would never don such finery, though she knew it was for the best that it would not come to pass.

The wedding feast was impressive for a last-minute affair. Food of every sort was provided, as was wine by the cask.

The only event that marred the celebration was that of the bedding. While Adelaine was being prepared by her ladies' maids, the men had hoisted Aleth aloft and carried him into his chamber. Before Chrestien had known what was to ensue, she was swept by a horde of men into the chamber with the wedded couple, where the drunken party chanted their demand.

It was then that she'd been faced with the worst moment of her life. She was to undress Aleth! Had Adelaine not realized her predicament and begged Aleth to send the mob out ... Chrestien crossed herself at her next thought. She would have been forced to—oh, Sweet Jesu, but she could not even bear to think of it!

Above them, the heavens swelled with angry blistering clouds threatening to unleash their furious torrents. As Chrestien watched the dark swirls overhead, she could only hope the blackness of them was more bluster than warning. Within minutes, however, it was sprinkling, and then the heavens burst with all the fury they contained.

Chrestien followed Aubert's quickened pace until the troop had entered the protective shelter of the forest. Then she took the lead. Aubert would tarry, she knew, in an attempt to elude the downpour. And as it was—even if they made haste—they would ride within the forest's boundaries for another hour—plenty of time ere they would be forced to decide whether to press on or make camp for the night. But even if the weather did not let up, she would prefer the rain to these sinister-looking woods any day.

"I like not the route we have taken, Aubert. The woods are filled with eerie shadows." The words tumbled from her lips. The trees had not yet lost all of their summer green, keeping what little light the sun gave from their misty domain. A shudder passed through her as she realized that though it was the shorter route, it would put them at the mercy of the hated cutthroats. "Aubert, what of bandits?"

"Who plays the auld woman now, Chrestien?"

"But Papa oft told me how they fall from trees to ambush their unwary victims," she protested, and another shudder passed through her as she looked warily about, her eyes scanning the mist, seeing all manner of imaginary beasts preparing to pounce! If only she didn't have such a traitorous mind—manifesting such horrid visions. Well, she could only hope her mesne was intimidating enough to those watching to keep them at bay. With a little luck, they would leave her and her men in peace. Yea, she decided at last, her men were deterrent enough!

Weston FitzStephens sat with his sweaty back against the thick base of an oak tree. Its aged, gnarled branches swooped toward the misty ground like huge outstretched oaken arms. His lead man, Michel Steorling, sat upon one of the lower limbs, carving a wolf's head into the limb of the old tree. He was becoming very adept at carving the likeness, and took pride in his newfound artistry.

"Shall you leave my mark upon every tree you pass?" Weston snapped, swiping at the sweat that trickled from his damp brow.

The blond-haired Michel smiled lightheartedly, and nodded that he would. "So that Normandy may look upon yer feared device and scramble home to lock their doors—say their prayers of thanks that the fierce and mighty Silver Wolf has spared them." He chuckled then, delighted with his fierce description of his liegelord.

Weston said naught, and he did not laugh. He knew only too well the truth of what Michel said. Yea, he knew Michel's words were said in jest, but his reputation was in fact worse than Michel described.

Weston had heard the tales once too oft of his ruthless ways—all greatly exaggerated. No matter that he took great pains to spare lives whenever possible . . . always it seemed the worst tales were believed. How oft had he seen gentle ladies and village folk cross themselves at the sight of him? Even in the heat of battle he would spy grown men—so-called warriors—pissing on themselves. The latter he did not mind, for their fear of him gave him an edge . . . but to see children run from him and village folk cross themselves rankled him sorely.

Yea, he did know the battlefield well . . . and he'd killed his share, but never once had he killed a man when it could be avoided. It was Henry's way as well—when a battle could be won without bloodshed, 'twas always the chosen course. But even so he had to own that there were times . . .

Michel knew that his jest had not been taken

well, and he sought to change the subject. " 'Twas wise to give the men this much needed respite, Weston. Had we pushed them forth, not only would they be tired, but ailing as well." His hand flew to a wet spot on his head where droplets of rain had fallen. "The rains would have given them the ague."

"Yea, Michel, but you needn't give me the credit. Were it not for your persistence, we'd be nigh to Lontaine by now."

"True," Michel agreed. "But we would be half dead as well."

"On the other hand, my man, the rain may have given us the advantage." Weston wiped a drop from his cheek. " 'Twould have obstructed a clear view of the perimeter of the fortress." Plucking a blade of overgrown grass to worry between his teeth, he went on to say, " 'Tis even more likely . . . that by the time they spied our approach, 'twould be too late. After all, de Lontaine left but one measly daughter to guard his keep, and she would be foolish enough not to take the needed precautions. 'Tis been my experience that women are feeble and too accustomed to having a man about to bother thinking on their own."

Michel nodded in agreement, though he did not entirely agree with Weston's logic. Woman or nay, he wasn't so certain Lontaine would surrender its mainstay to England so easily. But Weston was his liegelord—friend or nay—and he seemed so certain of it that Michel didn't dare contest him.

Weston didn't have much respect for women and Michel well knew the reason. Weston's mother was a so-called lady, his father a landless knight—not her lord husband. His mother's lawful husband had agreed to cover up the scandal—not wanting the world to know his ladywife had lain with another.

Reluctantly, Lord de Burghe had accepted Weston as his own. But the truth was not hidden long. In time, the landless knight became a lord in his own right, and had demanded acknowledgment of his firstborn son. Hence Weston de Burghe, third son of a baron, became Weston FitzStephens, bastard son of a lowly lord.

To further his distaste for the female gender, the ladies of court—especially those duly wedded—seemed to throw themselves at Weston's feet were he to give them but a fleeting glance. Weston needed but raise a dark brow to them, and they would follow him to his pallet like bitches in season. For some reason, Weston's reputation intrigued them. Every woman wanted to be the one to tame him.

Seeing the sour expression on Weston's face, Michel introduced a lighter topic. "I heard tell that the Lontaine was a gift to de Lontaine from Montagneaux."

Weston grimaced uneasily, thinking over the second half of his missive. "That should tell you how thick the blood ran between them."

"Then ye've doubts over de Montagneaux's loyalty to King Henry?"

Weston shrugged. " 'Tis not my place to doubt Henry's decrees."

"True, but 'tis not what I asked of you Weston—and well you know it."

Weston shrugged again and sighed. "Truth is, I

know very little of the man, but what I do know, I dislike."

"And what of de Lontaine? What do you know of him?"

"Not much a'tall—only what is rumored," Weston admitted honestly, "for the man was a recluse."

"Yea," Michel ventured, thinking that for once he had uncovered something more than his proficient liegelord. Weston usually made it a point to learn everything he could of his adversary before taking on a siege. "One story has it even, that de Lontaine's young ladywife died in his arms during the birth of his child . . . in the donjon tower of his keep. Some even say that her spirit still haunts the old Norman castle . . . and that the widowed de Lontaine immediately set forth to refurbishing the castle after her death to house his only daughter."

Michel shuddered visibly, remembering the tales he'd been told. "I've heard tell that she is come from the grave herself, ugly as she is—his daughter—and that is why he allows no man to enter his keep. 'Tis ashamed of her, he is."

Irritated that his men would indulge in gossip, Weston thought to put a stop to the nonsensical talk, but he had to own that it was a story that was hard to refute. Weston had learned little from those he'd questioned, save that one was rarely admitted into the well-garrisoned keep. Yet those de Lontaine welcomed within he treated like royalty—giving them every comfort and courtesy. And he'd been forwarned that nothing could be learned from the man's villein, for they were fiercely loyal to their master. None were so tight-lipped as they. It was the mark of a good man, he knew, for even the cruelest of men could not keep a disgruntled servant's tongue from wagging.

"Yea," Michel continued, reveling in the relating of this particular tale. " 'Twas said that de Lontaine would even meet messengers outside the perimeter walls, dismissing them without even the cordiality of a warm meal and a night's rest. Many have said that he would turn his own allies away did they arrive without notice. Imagine that!"

"The man was as secretive as if he concealed behind his old walls the holy sepulchre itself," Weston agreed reluctantly, "but then, he is dead now and I'd not speak of him when we know so little about him." Then, on a disapproving note, he said, "And since when have you taken to gossiping, Michel?"

Weston didn't wait for Michel's response, instead he rose from his place by the tree and brushed the grass from his braies. Then, he motioned for Michel to follow. "We should inspect the grounds," he said curtly. His words were laced with barely suppressed ire as he stalked away without bothering to look back at his lead man, feeling confident that Michel would follow. In his anger, he was completely unaware that all eyes followed his ominous frown as he made his way through the throng of men setting up camp.

They had come upon the natural shelter by accident. Michel had gone to relieve himself and had stepped into a thick canopy of trees and underbrush that much resembled a lush green cavern. A quick search of the site would make certain they were in fact hidden from view, for Weston had no wish to be bothered this eve. The place seemed to promise solitude, but Weston intended to make certain.

They were in Norman territory now and though many were pleased with the outcome of the recent battle, there were yet a few who did not welcome Henry's rule. That issue would have to be dealt with anon—but not here . . . not now! Their immediate charge was to secure de Lontaine's lands for King Henry, and that was what they would do.

Michel nudged Weston's arm and pointed in the direction of the path whence they had come. There, the distant rustling of leaves could be heard. Curious now, the two men stepped back into the sanctuary of the underbrush and waited. It was not long ere they could hear the banter of men approaching . . . and then, they saw it.

They were instantly taken aback by the spectacle with which they were confronted. Weston shook his head in disbelief and Michel nigh laughed aloud, but Weston's warning grip on his arm prevented it.

" 'Tis the most broken-down mesne I have ever spied, Weston! And consider the lead man—is he not the tiniest knight ye've ever beheld?"

"Yea, but at least in him 'tis some semblance of the standard. He at least wears the full armor."

"Standard, Weston? It is as though the helm will fall from his dwarf's head—'tis too big for the runt. Think ye he has stolen some knight's armor? Surely, it cannot belong to him!"

Weston scratched his chin, deliberating the possibility as the small troop passed clangorously by them. "Nay," he said finally. "The only other clad full in armor remains a telltale distance behind the leader, indicating his submission . . . and tell me, would you follow the likes of him unless deemed by the status of his birth?"

Michel shook his head. "God's Blood, but the rest of his men don the most pitiful armor. Look at them, some wear but the helm—no nose guard even. Others wear ill-fitting hauberks, impregnated with holes . . . and still others wear no armor at all."

"Yea, and you would take note that none bear a trace of blood upon them. . . . 'Tis obvious they are not come from battle," Weston surmised.

"Yea," Michel agreed, his voice rising with his wonder. Weston gave him a warning nudge with his elbow, and Michel nodded, acknowledging the tacit command, before continuing in a whisper. " 'Tis not possible to leave the scene of combat so beat and yet unbloodied! But the most pathetic thing about them is the horses . . . they appear in their dying days. What manner of soldier would equip himself so meagerly?"

"I know not. The only worthwhile steeds are the white stallion under the leader and the beige one his captain rides. I'd not mind possessing the white one." It was an afterthought, a desire he intended to do nothing to allay. Morning mist rose heavily from the forest floor, engulfing the legs of every horse. " 'Tis a sight, to be sure. They seem more a spectral army risen from the dead!"

Michel could not contain his mirth. He let out a sound that was part laugh, part groan at the sight before him. Without sparing a look at Michel, Weston quickly put his finger to his own lips to quiet his friend, and continued to ogle the sad cavalcade until it was well 'round the bend.

"They carry Normandy's banner, Weston. Think ye we should intercept them and discover who they are? Mayhap then ye would possess the white stallion if 'twas found they ride for Curthose."

"Nay. They could do no harm to Henry. Let them go in peace."

Michel nodded as the last of the troop disappeared around the bend and they both turned and started to camp. They had taken but a few steps when the thundering of hooves echoed behind them, and they hastened to the refuge of the underbrush yet again, in time to spy a second cavalcade.

This one flew by with obvious resolve, and within minutes the clanging of metal could be heard. Anguished screams pierced the air—the sound of dying men, Weston knew. He did not dally to hear more. His stride as agile as that of the wolf, he bolted to camp to gather his men.

Had he not seen the tired men of the first cavalcade, he'd not have interfered. But something about the pitiful troop had pulled at his heart. He knew they had not a prayer of a chance against the second, well-armed cavalcade, and he only hoped he did not arrive overlate!

Chapter 4

A t least fifteen men had fallen by the time Weston and his men came to the scene of battle. It was impossible to tell from which mesne the dead belonged as they were bloodied beyond recognition. Nevertheless, Weston had a well-founded suspicion to which they were members.

The assailants were startled by the arrival of yet a third company and their bewilderment was their undoing. Weston felled two knights before they even knew what struck them. When he spotted the tiny knight upon the white stallion, cornered, he started for his attacker but was intercepted by another. The bloodshed continued but long enough for Weston to down two more men, then the second party dispersed and disappeared into the forest, like rats at the break of light.

He started again for the little knight. With him captured, he was certain the first troop would throw down their arms and accept defeat. It was his intent to end the fighting, interrogate the little man, then let them all go. He wanted no more bloodshed. But so much for good intentions—he was thwarted again by the most formidable man in the little knight's company.

Aubert had the element of surprise on his side, and he was successful in knocking the silver knight from his mount. Unfortunately, his lance caught in a kink in the man's armor, and Aubert tumbled to the wet misty ground along with the ominous silver-mailed figure.

The silver knight was the quicker to regain his footing. When Aubert came to his knees and his eyes focused on the snarling wolf's head blazoned upon the broad mailed chest, his heart sank. He knew immediately there was no hope of defeating the Silver Wolf! Nevertheless, he would die fighting or dishonor his father! Determined to give it his best, he rose from his knees proudly, lifting his broadsword high, and was pierced in the belly ere he could regain his footing.

There was little resistance from the knight's mail shirt, and Weston cringed to hear the sickening sound of renting metal. He'd not intended to kill the man. Had he known the knight was so little protected, he would not have given his sword the strength of his arm.

Chrestien had felt relief to see reinforcements. But now? They were attacking her own troops! And the biggest one had wounded Aubert! Her knees trembled as she lifted her heavy sword. With strength she didn't know she possessed, she charged toward the silver knight standing over Aubert. She knew she took him unawares by the look of shock he wore. She saw her sword enter just below the shoulder blade, and the feel of it sickened her. Horrified by what she had done, she removed it. Blood spurted from the wound when she removed her sword, and her stomach heaved in response. But it was the last thing she saw, for an immediate darkness settled in her head and she fell to its force.

Weston grimaced as Guy, his young squire, gave his jagged wound a generous dose of wine ere applying the ivory needle to his skin. Michel stood before him, his boyish face contorted by the wry grin he sported, and Weston cursed his state that he could not give his old friend a healthy thrashing for his obvious enjoyment of his pain.

" 'Twas a joy for me to see ye so helpless," Michel confessed, as if he knew Weston's thoughts. His shoulders rocked gently with suppressed laughter and when he could control it no longer he threw his head back and bellowed. "Were it to be known ..." Michel ceased his laughter but long enough to catch his breath. "Ye were felled ... by a dwarf knight?"

Michel's merriment took the form of near-convulsive hysterics and he dropped to the ground and howled with glee. "Had I not cuffed the little elf with the hilt of my sword ..." Michel held his hand over his heart, closed his eyes, and lay still upon the ground to feign death. But he could not wipe the smirk from his lips, thereby spoiling the effect.

Weston was near the point of forgetting his injuries and belting his friend, when they were interrupted by one of his men.

"God's Wounds, Michel! Give the men a good example to follow and quit bellowing." Red-faced—half out of embarrassment, half out of anger—Weston turned to the new arrival and tipped his head knowingly. "What is it you need?"

" 'Tis the little prisoner, my lord," the boy mumbled. "We cannot revive him. I fear his head has been severely wounded, for I've shaken and shouted at him till I am hoarse yet he does not awaken." He fidgeted under Weston's scrutiny. And when Weston grimaced, he added hastily. "It has been hours, my lord!" Weston's dark look was directed at the needle piercing his skin, and the young knight, thinking the frown was for him, nigh fled from the tent. Gathering his courage, he held his ground, knowing instinctively that a coward's reaction would anger his lord further, and he struggled to keep the fear from his voice as he spoke. "And the other two have come about, only to fall away again."

"Tell the guard I will be there as soon as Guy completes the stitching of my wound." The nervous messenger turned to leave, just as Guy indicated with a wave of his hand that he was finished.

Weston rose from the stool, kicking it violently at Michel. "You, my friend . . ." He shook his head angrily. "You try me!"

Michel lifted himself from the ground, a smile yet pasted to his lips, and followed Weston from the tent, but no matter how he tried, he could not quell the laughter that was building yet again. He chuckled as quietly as he was able.

Without turning to look at his captain, Weston

warned, "Do not even think to! I would forgive you for it once . . . and none more, auld friend. Say naught more of it—I'd not have my men laughing behind my back!"

Michel knew Weston was serious and he sagely decided to put the jocularity aside. He was the only one permitted to take such liberties with the moody Wolf, but even he dared not push Weston too far.

Entering the tent he'd designated for the prisoners, Weston scrutinized the three men before him. There were but two men yet alive of the first cavalcade, and he wasn't at all sure they would not perish as well. The tallest one was badly wounded, and unfortunately it had been by Weston's own hand, but at least that one yet moved. The other one, the tiny one Weston assumed to be the leader, was lying as still as if his life were already spent.

The third prisoner was of the second cavalcade, and it was this one Weston would deal with first. After inspecting the flesh wound he'd sustained, Weston was certain that this one in particular was feigning sleep. Yanking the man's helm from his head proved Weston's case, for the man's ready scream pierced the whole of the camp, sending shivers down the spines of those who knew their liegelord little—those who did know Weston knew that he was a just man, not the monster he was portrayed to be.

A helm was worn tight enough so that when a blow was administered during battle it would not be dislodged, and the man's too-tight helm had

molded itself into his skin enough to make it painful to remove—Weston's furious hand had not
been gentle either. "Who owns your sword arm?"
The man did not answer. "Whom do you swear
to?" Weston demanded. "Tell me ere you breathe
no more."

Rolfe's man was too frightened to answer. He
knew that any response would bring the same
result—only the Wolf would kill him swiftly and
Rolfe would not. Too many times he'd witnessed
the tortures Rolfe would prefer. His response was
to hawk up a gob of spittle and spray it upon Weston's boots, which brought the black leather slamming into his face. The man's hand reached to
swipe away the blood from his cracked mouth,
smiling craftily as he did. The black boot slammed
into his taunting face again, welcoming him into
blissful darkness.

A scream from beside Chrestien sent a chill
down her spine and she quelled the urge to cross
herself, willing herself to remain calm. The ear-
piercing scream came from her right—not her left,
where Aubert was—so she would not give herself
away just yet. The crunch of heavy boots was very
near her ear, and she could hear someone spit. She
heard, as well as felt, a rush of wind in her ears as
something sped past her face. Then, again.

Turning from the insensate man, Weston knelt
beside the dwarf knight, inspecting his head gingerly. He lifted the closed eyelids briefly, then
stood and rubbed his whiskers, losing himself in
thought.

A noise caught his attention, bringing him out of his stupor, and he went to Michel, who was looking out from the lifted tent flap at some commotion spurred by the men outside. Weston peered out over Michel's head to see what the clamor was about. "What is it they quarrel over?"

Michel shrugged his husky shoulders. "I cannot be certain, but it seems ye are being defended to the newer soldiers."

"Defended?"

"Yea. From what I gather, there was a dispute about yer ... character." Weston's jaw tautened unmistakably, and Michel lifted his blond brows, a slight smile turning the corner of his lips. "I'll see to it." He knew Weston would not be amused by the discussion at hand and he moved to end it.

Chrestien had seen the tent flap stir and had closed her eyes immediately. She didn't dare face them yet because she'd not formulated a plan to escape them. They were King Henry's murderers and she hated the beasts for killing her father. Too, they had wounded poor Aubert, who in all likelihood was lying next to her perishing.

Yea, she'd noted the snarling wolf's head on the banner displayed outside the tent, and had silently cursed the murdering bastards for their carnal ways. They'd tossed her over a horse much like a sack of meal, and she had awakened en route to this ... this ... whatever this was. ... Oh Jesu, how did she get herself into these predicaments! Her head was pounding with the fury of a battering ram in time of siege. And were that not pain enough, her eyes had been plucked by one with the gentleness of a boar!

She heard his boots chew the ground as the man walked away. Then the crunching ceased. Was she alone? Or was he standing over her watching? Slowly, she lifted her heavy lids only a hair, and peered through her thick, dark lashes.

Two men were spying from the entrance of the tent, and their backs were to her. The tallest one yet had his sword in his scabbard. If she could but summon the courage . . . she could jump him and take it!

She had to at least try. But . . . if she did try and did not succeed, she would surely be killed. Then again, if she did not try . . . she might yet be killed anyway. Oh sweet Jesu! Was there no end to this nightmare? A look to her right revealed a bloody-faced, unconscious man. She could see the dirt and tiny rocks imbedded in his face from the force of the blow he was given, and her chest and throat constricted from the silent scream that threatened to burst from within her.

The unarmed one left the tent to settle some dispute raging outside, leaving the sword all alone—or nigh alone, were it not for that . . . that giant. If she could only catch him unawares? Even from the back she recognized him to be the same silver-clad knight who had felled Aubert—and herself as well, though for the life of her she could not remember how. He was now clad in the darkest black, having been divested of his armor. But sweet Jesu . . . even without his armor, he was as monstrous as she had remembered. How had she run her sword through that thing?

A chill traveled down her spine as she remembered how he had looked standing over poor Aubert. One quick thrust of his sword had brought Aubert down. Yet, he had not even fallen to her own when she'd impaled him. The smell of his blood upon her attested to the fact that she'd pierced him. But he'd only stood there, looking confounded, instead of dying as he should have—curse him!

Her heart raced as the giant squatted and put his foot forward to exit the tent. Her time was up! It was now or never—the sword was leaving. If she did not attempt this now there might not be another chance!

Chrestien bolted to her feet and pounced upon the giant's back! Locking her arm about his head with all her might, she tried furiously to unsheathe his monstrous sword. It seemed hopeless! The thing weighed more than a fat sow! Frustrated, she bit his shoulder instead.

Weston felt a thud on his back, then winced as he received a pang on his shoulder. He reached around with his left hand to pull the weight from him, but the man's hold was stronger than he'd anticipated. Weston's right hand went over his head to grasp the hair of the little demon upon his back. But when he did, he felt a tug at his own hair, and another pang on his neck. The little elf was biting him! He reared back, and with both hands tried to throw his attacker, but the grip on his neck tightened ruthlessly, until it seemed he could not catch his breath. With a final powerful grip of the bony legs entwined about his waist, he pried them apart and flung the violating form from him. The little knight landed with a thud, sprawled on his back upon the ground, but the elf flew to his feet much quicker than Weston had anticipated and charged again—this time, without success. Weston caught him in an iron grip, lifting him into the air in one fell swoop, effortlessly holding the man away from him.

"God's teeth! What goes on here?" Michel stepped into the tent to see Weston holding the little knight in midair. It seemed as though he'd left one brawl to embroil himself in another!

Weston said naught, only stared angrily into the vicious green eyes glowering down on him, making certain to hold the offending form well away from his body. The little imp squirmed and kicked like a scolded child against his firm grasp.

He watched the dauntless eyes as they glittered with malice. Then, unexpectedly they widened, filling with terror, and the squirming ceased abruptly. Weston narrowed his eyes as he studied the change in his captive. He had made the mistake of underestimating the bastard once, but he would not do so again.

Chrestien ceased struggling as the giant's hands came to rest very near her bosom. If she were to fidget any more, his hands would undoubtedly come to rest directly upon her breast. And were he to discover that she was a woman? Blessed Mary! 'Twould be the end of her virtue, and she would not only die ... but die dishonored. She was certain of it. She'd heard enough tales at Montagneaux to know that rape was intrinsic with men of this breed—warriors without soul, they were!

She stared into the giant's smoky blue eyes, afraid to move lest she be discovered. Then, when she tried to remove her gaze from him, she could not bring herself to do so. He was possessed of the most entrancing eyes—so blue, not warm . . . and yet not cold either.

His shoulder-length black hair was a disorderly mass and peppered with silver, belying his youthful countenance. Even so, it seemed to complement his lightly whiskered face. He was disconcertingly handsome—darkly so! His squared jaw had a tiny cleft in it and was taut and angry. Yet, at the same time, his lips seemed strangely soft and endearing. She wanted to reach out and feel them to satisfy her curiosity, but dared not. And suddenly, she wasn't sure why but she wished he was smiling at her and not scowling so hatefully. Oh Jesu! Now her mind would plot against her! Her breath caught in her throat as his lips parted to speak. Then he dropped her like the fruit tree releases its yield—completely and without warning. She fell to the ground with a sharp thud, her mail embedding itself into her already sensitive flesh, and watched stupidly as he spun on his heels and left the tent—none too soon, for she could not think with him glaring at her as he had!

Michel wisely stepped out of Weston's imminent path, but he eyed his friend curiously as he quickened his pace to keep up with Weston's furious gait. "What was that about?"

"The little bastard attacked me!" Weston spat, his fury begging to be released. He had intended to give the elf a sound thrashing, but when he had looked into the dirty face he had seen only the terrified boy—not a man, just the boy! The face was clean-shaven and as smooth as a baby's arse, and he had dropped the boy with such sheer disgust that such a fledgling should be made a knight! Were the boy at least capable of defending himself, Weston would not be so rankled. He himself had been knighted upon the battlefield at seventeen years.

"When I started to leave the tent," he explained in a somewhat calmer voice, "he attacked me." Weston's fingers reached to touch the spot where the elf's teeth had sunk in, and when he brought them away there was a trace of blood on them. He spat out a series of oaths and extended his hand to show Michel the red on his fingers. "He bit me. Can you conceive it? That a knight would actually bite ... me?" This last thought amused Weston somewhat, and he let out a sound that was more groan than chuckle. "Hell, none would credit it had I not the marks to prove it."

Michel bit his lip to suppress another fit of laughter. Weston's previous warning was yet ringing in his ears, and he didn't dare give insult by laughing at him yet again. He couldn't help himself. "What no one would credit, Weston, is that ye were bested *twice* by the little elf." The words were spoken as solemnly as Michel was able.

Weston furrowed his brows and glowered at his friend. "You'll not tell anyone, will you?" Weston sounded so concerned that Michel readily agreed he would not. "Good, good, 'twould be most embarrassing. I can assure you."

Michel nodded again, barely suppressing his grin. "What will ye do with him?" he asked, carefully weighing his words.

Weston shrugged. "I'm not certain. In truth, I should have left him to fight his own battle. But I did not, and until I can discern what to do with him I want three men to guard him at all times."

"So many? For such a little ..." Michel bit his lip to contain his mirth as Weston settled an icy glare on him. "Do we take him to Lontaine, then?"

"We've no choice. I'd be there on the morrow and no later."

"We could set him free," Michel suggested, pursing his lips.

It was plain that Michel was toying with him, but Weston would not give him the satisfaction of becoming angered. "Nay, Michel, he has questions to answer ... and until I am satisfied with the answers, he goes nowhere." Halting before his black tent, Weston smoothed his hand over his chin. "Give me a moment to think ... and then bring the little one to me." Michel gave an exaggerated tip of his head, then turned to leave and Weston shoved aside the canvas door flap.

Weston was furious with himself for giving his back to the prisoner, stupidly leaving himself open—not once, but twice. The first time was somewhat understandable, for he'd come to aid the fledgling. Too, he'd been preoccupied with the other one's wounds. But the second time? 'Twas unjustifiable.

Picking up the flagon of ale that sat upon his war chest, he gulped from it deeply, before stooping to right the fallen stool. He sat on it then, drinking the ale as he waited. It was not long before Michel entered, flinging the prisoner in before him, and Weston studied the boy a minute before motioning his captain to leave. His scowl deepened as he spied Michel's parting smile. Damn him!

As a balm for his anger, he fixed the boy with his most intimidating glare. "Who are you?" He growled the demand, then took another gulp from the flagon.

"Who are you?" Chrestien countered, her green eyes glistening with rancor.

" 'Tis I who would ask the questions, boy." Weston was absolutely certain now that this ... boy, was naught but that, for his voice was more child than man. He was intrigued that one so small would have courage men twice his size did not possess. "Who are you?" Weston repeated, his voice low, strained with a measure of borrowed patience.

Lifting her chin in defiance, Chrestien fixed Weston with an icy green stare. The fine line of Weston's tolerance snapped, and he grabbed the boy by the arm, twisting it harshly in warning. "You'll tell me or I will break it, boy!"

Chrestien nigh choked on her words. She didn't doubt for a moment that he would follow through with his threat. "My name is Christopher," she lied, wincing from the pain in her arm. The giant narrowed his eyes as if he didn't believe her, but released his hold on her arm. As the pain receded, her courage returned, until she could feel the heat of her anger again.

"Christopher . . . merely Christopher. From whence do you come . . . Christopher?" Weston spat out the name in disgust, and angry tears threatened to storm from Chrestien's shadowed eyes. Outwardly, she remained calm, while inside she was a binding of nerves. Sweet Mary! There was naught that was tender about this man now. His face was twisted and his blue eyes were now cold, though they blazed with the fire of contempt. "I'd tell you naught else but my name!" She offered as much disdain as she was receiving, and fought desperately to quell her tears.

The giant stood taller than any man she'd ever seen—and her father had been a big man. He was clad in black from head to toe, and he looked diabolic, with that twisted wolf's grin that curled his lip. He was of a like image to the wolf and its fanged grin blazoned upon his tunic. A quick twist of her arm served to remind her of the pain he would inflict, and instinctively she tried to remove his iron hand from her arm, digging her nails into his knuckles as she pried.

Reflexively, he tightened his hold on her wrist. "You fight like a maid," he spat. With little effort, he tossed her to the floor in front of his war chest. Chrestien hit her head on the corner of the metal chest, and her eyes misted from the pain. "If you'll not tell me," he warned, "then you'll not leave my sight. I shall get what I seek, boy . . . or you will get no relief."

It was obvious that this wolf's anger was barely tempered, and Chrestien decided 'twas best she not say more. She eyed him warily as he opened the huge chest hunkering beside her and extracted from it a thick gold cord. Realizing he intended to tie her up, she bolted. Before she could get to her feet, his hands flew out to stop her. He used the rope to bind her hands behind her back, then removed his dagger from his boot and cut the left-over cord from her wrists. The remainder he used to bind her feet. That done, he stepped from the tent and returned only seconds later with a young squire he called Guy.

Without sparing a glance at Chrestien's crumpled body, Guy immediately set to work removing the Wolf's sword belt. Then he removed the black tunic and padded leather gambeson, inspecting them mindfully as they came into his hands.

It seemed the Wolf's eyes never left Chrestien while his squire undressed him. When Guy turned his attention to the hole he'd discovered in the padded leather, the Wolf finally averted his eyes. He picked up the flagon of ale again, using it well before returning it to the chest. Arrogantly, he ran his hand through his tousled silver black hair, stopping momentarily to rub his temples.

The announcement came with a sigh. "It needs repairs, my lord Weston." As far as Chrestien was concerned, Guy spoke with an ease in his voice that defied logic. To speak so easily with one so sinister-looking as the Wolf? She just could not fathom.

The Wolf tilted his chin in acknowledgment. "Then take it to the armorer . . . but return to me straightaway. I'd have you keep an eye on Christopher this eve."

"Christopher?" Guy finally acknowledged the crumpled figure upon the floor, his brows raised quizzically as he examined the boy. Then, with a nod he turned to leave, but Weston grabbed his shoulder firmly. "And tell Michel to see to the other prisoners."

"Huh . . . oh, yea, my lord Weston." Guy lifted the flap and disappeared into the darkness.

So that was his name . . . Weston? Chrestien preferred Wolf. Yea, he was not deserved of a Christian name.

The Wolf removed his linen shirt, tossing it casually upon the war chest, then tilted his head to examine his newest injury. Chrestien was amazed at the size of his bronzed chest. As she openly admired his physique, her eyes lit on the jagged wound that held his attention. Was that all she'd done to him? He deserved to die for all he'd done to her father and her men! She mumbled a fiery sequence of oaths—though she had no idea what half the words meant—and Weston looked directly at her, his eyes darkening to a smoky shade of blue as he stared, his twisted smile appearing again.

Weston sat rigidly upon the short wooden stool and again rubbed the back of his neck and his temples. He'd noted the boy's cold indignation when the angry green eyes had lit on his newly stitched wound. The oath that erupted from the elf's foul mouth was further proof that the runt had meant to kill him—and to think that he'd gone to the bastard's aid!

He touched his fingers to his tired brow, wiping the dampness from them as he kicked off his black boots. Then he turned his attention to his cross-bands, his tired eyes unable to focus on the tangled laces.

Chrestien couldn't help but watch the muscles dance in the Wolf's arms as his fingers fumbled lazily with his laces. She'd oft watched her father's men train with the quintains—which they did bare-chested during the sweltering summer—and never had she seen such powerful movement in their limbs!

That done, the Wolf ... Weston ... gave his attention to the ties on his braies, and a chill crept down Chrestien's spine, raising the hairs on the back of her neck in alarm, as he loosed the laces. Oh Blessed Mary ... if she turned away now he might suspect. In her confusion, she could only stare, and within moments it was too late, the braies were down!

Chrestien swallowed the nervous lump in her throat as she watched his nude form rise from the stool and lean to pick up the flagon of ale from the chest. He was half turned away from her, but she yet had a perfect profile of him, and was mesmerized by the sheer strength in his powerful form, all of him muscular—though there was one part of him that didn't look so fit, she noted, satisfied with having found in him a flaw. In truth, the appendage looked rather fleshy—just there. He was not so perfect after all, she decided, feeling a little triumphant—though she could not fathom why.

She watched him take yet another gulp from his flagon, the muscles in his uplifted arm rippling as they held the object of his attention. His back was to her now and she stared, wide-eyed, at his posterior as he walked away from her toward his pallet, the muscles in his legs and backside tensing and releasing in sequence as he strode. She knew she should not be watching in such a wanton way, but he thought her to be a man so 'twould not matter to him anyway . . . and she was thoroughly amazed with his very commanding form. He ran deft fingers over unruly bangs, and with his fingertips he rubbed his scalp briskly, letting them pause there briefly, before smoothing them down to the mass of tangled curls at his nape. Every movement he made seemed to speak of untamed virility.

Guy entered the tent with a fur coverlet in hand, tossing it at Weston's feet. "Ye left it in the prisoners' tent, my lord."

Chrestien recognized it as the coverlet she'd been lying on, and she watched curiously as Weston took it, plopped himself down on his pallet and spread it over himself, leaving an enormously muscular leg ousted from the blanket. Leaning back on one elbow, he rubbed his closed lids with his free hand, then laid his head full upon the pallet. The atmosphere within the tent was suffocated with silence, save for the sound of Guy's lithe footsteps and a few muffled sounds from beyond the darkness, but Chrestien was more than relieved that he would at least give her a night's rest ere torturing her. Unfortunately, her relief was short-lived.

Guy started to extinguish the only candle lit within the tent, but Weston's roar stopped him. "Leave it be. I want you to gather Troy and John. Among the three of you ... you are to guard Christopher. He is not to sleep. I want him too tired to give me any difficulty on the morrow."

A curse was riding on Chrestien's tongue. She coaxed herself to suppress it. She was weary enough as it was, and in spite of her fear she could barely keep her eyes open. What did he think she could do against a monster such as he? Sighing softly, she rested her head on the dirty floor. She might as well rest—at least till the lackey came back with reinforcements.

Oh Aubert! She wished more then aught else that she were at his side right now. He was so dear to her, and were he to die this night ... never would she forgive herself.

Weston had planned to interrogate Christopher further, but the little fairy had stared at him so ardently that it had unnerved him. He was more than tempted to send him back to the prisoners' tent, but his threat hung heavily in the air and he intended to follow through with it, regardless of the boy's staring. He would keep this Christopher within sight ... and as long as he was watched through the night there would be no harm in the boy's staying.

Again, resting his head upon his pallet, he tried to find a comfortable position. He cringed when he thought of the burning candle and the fact that

Christopher would be awake all night to ogle him. Irately, he sat up and reached for his tunic and flung it over his head. A quick glance at Christopher revealed that the boy's eyes were wide with a curious light. With a furrow of his dark brow, he blew out the candle. That done, he lay back and tried to sleep.

Chapter 5

Chrestien's lids were heavy with sleep. She'd been poked and prodded all night by Weston's lackeys. Every time her eyes had closed she'd met with the angry butt of an elbow or foot. She knew they were taking their lack of sleep out on her. But what could she do?

Sleepily, she closed one eye to give it rest, while she struggled to keep the other open, shaking her head protestingly in an effort to wake herself—anything to deliver her poor aching body from another blow. But her efforts were of little use. Her eyes closed, her chin dropped, and she was kicked in the thigh yet again. Sweet Mary, but if she didn't have enough bruises as it was!

She heard scattered voices, but no longer cared what they said—nor whom they addressed. If she could but get some rest ... Her eyes closed again, but she was jolted awake when she was lifted, roughly, by her arms. She could not lift her lids to see who was bearing her—no matter, because she knew it was the same two who'd abused her throughout the night. She had come to recognize the pain they would give. She didn't open her eyes, and the hurt didn't last long this time. Blackness fell over her like a warm welcoming blanket in winter cold ... soothing.

The smell of wet earth mingled with human perspiration accosted Chrestien's nostrils. She envisioned herself in a deep pit next to Aubert and the other men who had died to protect her. Damp soil fell in weighty heaps to cover her body, burying her, suffocating her ... Jesu! Had she died in the night and they were burying her now? Nay, but she wasn't dead! She tried to scream ... to tell them she yet lived. Her lips moved, but there was no sound emitted from them. There was only silence and that awful feeling of being smothered to death.

She awoke in the back of a wagon, her hands still bound, her face in the soiled rushes. Only her legs were free. Her first thought was to escape, but one look about her told her that feat would be impossible. Armed knights surrounded the springless cart and she knew she would not get as far as the ground before they were upon her. Well, at least Aubert was in the cart with her, albeit deeply dazed.

As she watched her father's faithful squire, her heart swelled with pride. He had stayed with her throughout, protecting her as would a brother. And though he could have gone to offer his services to another lord, he'd not gone. Gilbert de Lontaine would have been proud of him, to be sure. That would have meant much to Aubert, for his own sire had never acknowledged him.

Chrestien's maid, Janelle, had told her once that

Aubert's father had cared for her, though he'd not loved her, his heart having been lost to another. But Janelle swore she was more than content with a son of his to love. She never spoke of Aubert's sire beyond that.

The longer she watched Aubert's still form, the more she feared, until her panic threatened to smother her accelerated breath. He lay much too still! Wriggling her sore body until she was lying next to him, she rested her dirty cheek against his nostrils. Feeling the warm air that seeped from him, she thanked God that he yet lived.

Wearily, she lay her head upon his chest, scrutinizing the rise and fall of his labored breath, and though his flesh burned with the fever, she was soothed by the rhythm of it so much that she closed her eyes and drifted into sleep again.

"They seem to be lovers," Weston muttered between clenched teeth, nodding tersely in the direction of the sleeping prisoners. "I've observed them and it sickens my stomach."

Michel had to agree. The sight was more than he could bear as well. "Mayhap . . . it would explain why the tall one called the lad's name throughout the night."

" 'Tis true then?" Weston raised a cynical brow. He'd half hoped that 'twas not so.

"Yea," Michel acknowledged. "I was awakened time and again by his calls for Chris."

"You slept in the prisoners' tent?" Michel nodded for answer. "Not alone?" Weston frowned.

"Nay, Weston, not alone, but I'd not realized ye cared overmuch." Michel winked at Weston and received another frown for his effort.

Weston's features contorted with his disgust as he digested the new information, and he resolved to keep the boy as far from himself as possible.

One wall-enclosed tower rose proudly in the distance, its quaint size belying its underlying strength. It was a small fortress by most standards. There was absolutely naught exceptional about the stronghold to look at it. The curtain wall itself seemed only of moderate height, and the rectangular keep bore tiny, well-placed arrow slits for windows.

As they neared, they could see that a profusion of well-kept wattle-and-daub huts dotted the landscape. The thatch roofs were obviously new and each hut had its own small but goodly stocked garden. Chickens scratched and children played, while the villein made busy with one chore or another.

Then it seemed time stood still. The villein ceased what they were about as the cavalcade neared. It seemed fear was struck in the heart of every one of them, and it felt to Weston as though their eyes would bore a hole through him. Several women broke the eerie stillness by crossing themselves. One woman swooned, and he knew it was because they had recognized his much feared device. It was a view he should be accustomed to by now, but it still ate at his gut to see it.

When Weston reached the gate, it remained drawn. The guard made no move to open it, so Weston removed his helm as a sign of peace. Were he compelled to, he would take Lontaine by force. But could he help it, there would be no bloodshed—even if it meant that he would place himself in danger with the gesture. "We come for Lontaine," he shouted. "In the name of King Henry of England fourth son of William the Conqueror, now ... Duke of Normandy!"

The guard upon the parapet stood silent and unflagging. The man said naught, and seemed to be studying Weston and his men as if to verify Weston's words with his careful scrutiny. Then, of a sudden, the man's dark look turned to shock and he nigh fell from his post on the wall.

Chrestien heard voices, and when she opened her eyes, her chest nigh burst from the agony of it all. She bolted to her feet, nigh falling from the wagon in the process. Sweet Mary! Nay ... not Lontaine! Did he know who she was, then? He had merely glowered at her last eve, when she'd informed him that she would tell him naught but her name. Had he known then? Nay ... he could not know. Or he would not have treated her so wickedly. Or mayhap 'twould not have mattered to Henry's Wolf.

She took a deep breath and tried to speak, but her voice was nowhere to be found. Then again, she wasn't sure she should speak anyway. The guard would not open the gate without instruction from her first. But if she did not have the guard open the gate? She looked about her solemnly. There were at least thirty fully armed knights about her. Her villein would be easy prey to them, and she'd not have them suffer for her stubbornness.

She tried again to speak, and this time, though the words were shaky, they were spoken with a resounding clarity that surprised her. "Open the gates, 'tis Aubert and I." No sooner had she voiced the words than Weston's blazing eyes lit upon her. He was seething, she realized. But had she known he was coming to Lontaine, she might have told him her identity—or at least that Lontaine was her home . . . mayhap, not the rest of it.

The portcullis was raised immediately and the drawbridge was lowered. The cavalcade made quick work of the wooden span, but Weston held back his destrier until the cart that held Chrestien was alongside him. Then he spurred his mount into a slow canter to ride alongside her.

His voice was taut with restrained fury. The muscles in his jaw twitched, and his eyes glittered as would a looking glass so dark a shade of blue were they. "Why did you not tell me you were of Lontaine?" The color of his eyes deepened until they were near as dark as the midnight sky, giving him a malevolent appearance.

Chrestien would not give him the satisfaction of seeing that her knees were shaking, so she concealed them by kneeling with the pretense of inspecting Aubert. When she regained her composure, she again turned her gaze on Weston's smoky blue eyes. "Why did you not tell me you came to Lontaine?" she retorted, her eyes glittering with defiance.

"Need I discuss with my captive . . . my intentions?" Weston spat between clenched teeth, again making the muscle in his cheek jump.

"Need I discuss with my captor—"

"Enough!" He couldn't credit that this fledgling

was countering his questions without trepidation. Many a man had cowered at the sound of his voice. Yet, this little boy-man ... or rather boy-maid ... was demanding his own answers without any real fear. He would never have figured it. Nevertheless, at the moment, it infuriated him all the more.

"What are you to Lontaine?" he insisted, his hand resting upon the jeweled hilt of his sword in a gesture that was more instinct than design. "And do not speak ... but to give me the answers I seek." His tone was low, and his eyes were angry blue flames. "What are you to Lontaine?" he repeated, enunciating his every word acidly.

Chrestien didn't dare push him further lest he decided to flog her—or worse even ... kill her. "I am Gilbert de Lontaine's son."

"Lies! He has but a daughter."

"He *had* a daughter ... and a son. My father is dead now ... as if you did not know," she spat.

"Then whither is the daughter?" Weston conceded. "She is within to confirm your tale?" He would give the boy the benefit of the doubt, but if he found the lad to be lying ... he would punish him severely. He was tired of the boy's impudence. He would give him but one more chance on the minute possibility that his tale might prove true. He would need but send word to Rouen— Henry would have access to records that could prove whether the boy spoke true, or nay.

"My sister, Adelaine, is with Aleth de Montagneaux," Chrestien admitted. 'Twas the truth and there was naught the Wolf could do to remedy it. "She was wed to him less than a sennight past."

Her green eyes glistened with unshed tears. "You'll not find her inside," she said brokenly. "You'll find no one inside but servants ..." Her chin came down to face the ground in defeat. "And shadows of my past," she said much more softly, the salt of her tears stinging her eyes.

Weston was moved by the boy's last words, enough so that he decided to have his hands unbound. He gave Guy the honor of removing the ties and watched with concealed amusement as Guy grimaced as expected, but did as was told without complaint.

Chrestien was so thankful that her hands were unbound that she nigh kissed the squire for freeing them, but Guy seemed to recoil each time he touched her hands, making her wonder if he thought her diseased. No matter, were she to kiss him, her guise would surely be discovered—were it not already. Janelle came from the great hall, flying into Chrestien's arms then. And when the sobbing maid reached to put her pudgy cheek next to hers, Chrestien nigh cried with relief ., she was home. Though Janelle was just a ladies' maid in title, she was much more than that to Chrestien. She was mother to Adelaine and herself ... home was in her arms.

Janelle aided Chrestien from the cart. Then, between the two of them they dragged Aubert from it as well. Chrestien's heart ached to see the silent tears that welled in Janelle's eyes when she looked upon her fevered son.

They started to haul Aubert to Janelle's hut, but Weston's booming voice brought them to a halt. "Nay, boy! You come with me." Chrestien's back was to the Wolf, but she knew he spoke to her. "Guy will see that he is attended."

Reluctantly, the squire took Aubert's arms from Chrestien's hold, wincing as if he were scorched by Aubert's flesh. Yea, Aubert burned from the fever, but not to such a degree as that! Angrily, she turned to follow Weston into the great hall. His footsteps echoed atop the wooden floor as he made his way to the dais. He took his seat upon her father's chair as if he were lord of Lontaine! Chrestien stopped midway, furious that he would take such liberties, but the Wolf seemed not to notice her ire, and he motioned for her to come near him.

Weston felt a strange swell of sympathy for the bedraggled-looking lad. Fairy or nay, the boy's life had been torn asunder and Weston felt partially responsible for the upheaval. "I mean you and your servants no ill," he assured the dazed boy. He would try to explain as gently as possible . . . that Lontaine was now the property of King Henry. "We shall stay hither until word arrives from your king—"

"Not my king!" Chrestien sought to enlighten him. " 'Tis your king you speak of."

"You'd best be rid of that notion, boy, as Henry would be less understanding of your impertinence. As I was saying, we will be hither until I receive word from him. Until then, I'd allow you free run of Lontaine . . . as long as you have two of my men with you at all times. Do you heed?"

Chrestien was so relieved that she could but nod her head up and down like a mute child. He would be gone ere long and she would go to the abbey as planned.

Weston debated whether to reveal any more and decided against it. Having imparted on Chrestien that message, he rose from the lord's chair and strode to the door. Two men entered at his beckoning, then he disappeared into the bailey.

Chrestien wasn't pleased about the buffoons who were sent to guard her. They were odd, to say the least. The red-haired one stood so close to her that she nigh bumped into him every time she turned around. The other kept his distance, but he seemed to have an inborn scowl painted across his much scarred face. She tried her utmost to put them out of her mind as she set out to find Aubert and Janelle.

The door to Janelle's hut was wide open. Upon entering the small but clean room, she saw that Aubert was awake, albeit in pain. He was lying upon a cot and Janelle hovered over him protectively, applying salve to his wound. Aubert groaned pitifully with each gentle touch of his mother's healing hand.

"I see we yet live . . . more's the pity," Chrestien told him with a wily smile as she kissed his cheek. A low growl sounded from behind her and she saw that one of her guards had turned his back to them. The other one was yet smiling and she turned back to Aubert, refusing to allow them to dampen her spirits. Janelle left the bedside for a moment to prepare more salve, leaving Aubert and Chrestien to speak alone.

"We are prisoners?" Aubert asked. Chrestien nodded that they were. "I remember little," he admitted, and she touched her fingers to his lips, urging him to be quiet. Inclining her head ever so softly, she indicated the guards.

Whispering, she explained, "You've been with fever since yestereve, Aubert. 'Tis why you remember so little. You do at least remember the battle?"

"Yea, though not much of it. I remember a knight clad in silver armor sweeping his way toward ye . . . I tried to intercept him. Nay, 'twas not just any knight, 'twas the Silver Wolf now that I think on it. 'Twas his device I saw ere I fell."

"Yea, it was, Aubert, though I did not know it till we were taken. 'Twas not much either of us could have done," she assured him as she took his hand and kissed it affectionately.

Another disapproving growl sounded from the door and Chrestien gave the vermin an irate glare, then turned her attention again to Aubert. "My father would have been proud of you, Aubert."

Aubert grimaced from the pain in his abdomen and started to smile at her words, but tears erupted from Chrestien's eyes suddenly. For the first time since her father's death, she let them flow, unchecked.

"I thought I'd lost you, Aubert," she wailed. "I know not what I'd have done without you." She nestled her head onto Aubert's chest. He winced against the pain, and moved her face to rest against his own, letting her salty tears stream onto his cheeks. His arms embraced her lovingly. Holding her tightly to him, he let her weep. It had been long in coming and he was only surprised that she had held her pain so long.

From the day he'd given her news of her father's death she'd played the tower of strength—at first, for Adelaine. And later? Mayhap she just didn't know how to end the charade. But Aubert had known her heart to be heavy— knew it was just a matter of time ere it burst from her grief. He'd known Chrestien all his life. She was kind and loving—even if she was extremely willful—and he loved her as the sister she was to him.

Yea, he'd known for long that he was de Lontaine's bastard. In truth, he was but five when he discovered the fact. His mother had told him, but because Gilbert de Lontaine never acknowledged him, it was a fact he was forced to keep to himself. That Gilbert de Lontaine did not call him son did not pain him overmuch, for his father had been just that to him . . . in every way but in name.

"Yer father would have been proud of ye as well, Chrestien. I noted the way ye wielded that sword." He winked at her when she looked at him, and he wiped the tears from her eyes. "Wither did ye learn to use a broadsword so?"

"You would laugh."

"Never," he denied emphatically.

"Well then, I hold you to your word." She smiled deviously, wiping a wayward tear from her cheek. "I used to watch Papa train you . . . and with sword in hand, I would mimic you. 'Twas easy," she boasted. "Though I had to practice with a much shorter sword. 'Twas not until yestereve that I ever, truly, wielded the broadsword. Jesu, but 'tis heavy," she confided in a whisper.

Aubert chuckled at her admission, and though

he'd promised not to, he did laugh at the vision that was conjured in his mind. He laughed nigh hysterically, then groaned at the pain in his chest. Then, again at the pain in his heart when he realized how close Chrestien had come to losing her life. "At least ye presented the first attacker with something to remember ye by," he told her somberly. " 'Twas a nasty gash ye put on his face, Chrestien."

Her eyes widened in confusion. "I'd not realized I'd wounded another besides Weston. Are you certain, Aubert? Did you recognize him? He did seem so very familiar to me, somehow."

" 'Tis difficult to say as he was clad in helm. I know that ye wounded him, only for the fact that I saw yer sword slip under his nose plate when he attacked ye, and there was a goodly amount of blood upon his shiny armor afterward."

Chrestien grimaced in disgust, and Aubert winced ere he spoke again. "Ye realize, Chrestien, that he had to have come from Montagneaux—his armor was newly polished, and he could not have ridden in the rain overlong without tarnishing it. Too, 'twas obvious he was after ye, and that as well tells me he came from Montagneaux, for none other would have known of ye." Aubert grunted as he repositioned himself on the cot to better study her reaction.

"It has rained a goodly amount," she admitted. "Weston's armor was soiled."

"Weston, is it?" Aubert mimicked with a frown, giving the staring guards a sideways glance.

"He made me stay in his tent through the

night," Chrestien declared as she scratched her cheek with the sleeve of her surcoat.

Aubert's eyes flared with anger, and he started to rise from his cot.

"Nay, 'tis not what you think," she assured him, shoving him back onto the bunk.

She bent low to whisper in Aubert's ear. "He believed me a boy. 'Tis only when I'd not answer his questions that he ordered his men to keep me awake . . . so that I'd not give him trouble on the morn."

"Ye . . . give him trouble? God's Mercy, Chrestien!" Aubert sneered, angry that the Wolf would treat his half sister so.

Chrestien lowered her eyes in chagrin before explaining further. "I attacked him . . . in the tent . . . when you were fevered. I bit him, and I do not think he will forgive me for it," she worried. Aubert could not help the furious laughter that escaped him now. Desperately, he held on to his wound so that it would not bleed from his efforts. "Ye bit him?" he asked incredulously. Chrestien nodded slowly, her face flushed with embarrassment.

It took him a while to subdue his laughter, but finally he willed himself to stop. " 'Twould be the banter of all Normandy to know a pretty maid such as ye has bitten the mighty Silver Wolf . . . can ye not see it, Chrestien?" Chrestien did not even crack a smile. "Have ye been wallowing in a grease pit?" he admonished, touching her cheek, when she would not see the humor of it all. But his smile returned when she wiped her face with the hem of her tunic.

He chuckled again, then groaned as Chrestien gave him a perplexed furrow of her brow. With great effort, he lifted a finger to wipe the region of her upper cheek. "Yer tunic is soiled and ye have just blackened yer eyes with it," he explained.

It was then that Chrestien realized how filthy she was, and when cued, Janelle gave a nod of agreement. Deciding it was time to bathe, she admitted, "I own that I've somewhat overdone it with the grime. Have I not?" She couldn't help but laugh to know how she must look to everyone. 'Twas no wonder she had befooled them all so well! Who would ever credit a lady lurked behind all this filth? With a tired sigh, she rose from the cot and started for the door.

"You stay abed," she demanded of Aubert, as she tried to shove her way past the guards. To her dismay, the scowling one pushed her back. The lout seemed to take great joy in bullying her, she decided, as he finally let her pass. And though she walked well ahead of them, she could yet hear the smiling one blistering the other one's ears—at least one of them sported a bone of kindness!

The walk back to the keep was a lonely one, as no one dared to come near her. But then, she had to own that the sight of the two burly guards behind her was enough to keep the devil away!

In the great hall, Weston was settled in her father's favorite chair upon the dais, and resentment welled within her to see him there again. She dared not voice what she felt lest he be angered and impose more restrictions upon her. She did cast him a ferocious glare, however, before turning to instruct Eauda, a chambermaid, to fetch her bathwater. Then she climbed the steep stairs to her bower. When she opened the door to the antechamber, sunlight streamed in from an uncovered window slit nigh blinding her, and she brought her hand up protectively to avoid the glare. She'd forgotten this room caught the afternoon sun. She'd forgotten about the guards at her heels, as well, but was quickly reminded as she stepped into her chamber and attempted to close the door. Before she could shut it, the scowling one placed his foot inside the door to prevent her from it, grinning awkwardly as he stepped in behind her.

Sweet Mary! But what was she to do now? She would not—by the love of God—bathe in a chamber full of men! There had to be a way to get them out . . . before her bathwater froze! Weston had been adamant that she have his men with her at all times, and she was certain he'd given the same instruction to her guards, so asking them to leave would be pointless.

Eauda came in just then, bringing a procession of servants behind her, each carrying two large wooden buckets. They shouldered the buckets of bathwater to the large ornate wooden tub, and one by one they emptied the contents of their pails. Finally, when the tub was filled, they left hurriedly—all of them save Eauda, who was to bathe her. Chrestien paced back and forth until anger well outweighed her distress.

Sweet Jesu! Did she wait much longer to bathe the water would be cold . . . and after all she'd endured, the least she deserved was a warm bath! She was nigh insane with anger, until at last a flicker of thought brought her out of her black mood. Jesu! But she should have thought of it earlier. The jewel-encrusted poniard, the one Papa had given her, was buried beneath her mattress.

Before she could think on the consequences, she reached for it and turned on her guards, screaming and flailing her arms with rage. "Out! Out!" The blade swished furiously and the smiling one left the room immediately. The ugly, scowling one stayed but a few seconds longer, then he too scurried off like the vermin he was.

"Sweet Jesu, it worked!" Her triumph was nigh shouted, as she motioned for Eauda to aid her in barring the door with a coffer—the wooden stake she oft used was nowhere to be found.

That done, Eauda helped Chrestien remove the heavy hauberk, the greasy undertunic, and the filthy breeches, shaking her head in disgust all the while.

Chrestien watched the repulsive garb fall to the floor with revulsion. Of a sudden, she was more than offended by the smell of them, so much so that she was nigh ill to think she'd need don them again. Poor Eauda was in agreement, for she could barely stand to put her hands on the foul garments. The maid made a hideous face, and Chrestien shrugged helplessly.

"I've no choice in the matter, Eauda." Her remorseful tone didn't seem to ease Eauda's disgust over the crumpled rags and Chrestien chuckled. "You'll have to steal a clean tunic from my father's chamber, then." Lifting a dirty leg into the tub, she sighed wistfully, and sank, exhausted, into the warm delicious water. Eauda immediately set to washing Chrestien's hair with Janelle's rose-scented soap, and Chrestien breathed deeply of the sweet scent.

The maid was more than appalled at the number of bruises on her mistress, and she frowned openly to see them. She was very curious to know about the many blue-black marks that appeared on Chrestien's fair skin when the filth melted away, but she couldn't bring herself to pry openly. If she was going to learn aught, 'twould have to be because her mistress brought it up first, so she decided to lure Chrestien into conversation. Her frown deepened when she took the shoulder-length hair into her callus-toughened hands. "M'lady, forgive me for saying so . . . but me thinks ye've made a grave mistake in cutting yer hair."

Chrestien frowned. "You'd best not remind me of it now, Eauda." Her tone reflected her fatigue. "I am not in need of another reason to wail." Remembering the lapse in self-control she'd displayed in front of Aubert, she gently fingered her puffy eyes, then closed them against the humiliation of it all.

"Think ye the giant will be angry?"

Eauda's inquiry brought her out of the stupor, and she reflected upon the question a moment before answering. "He is rather big, is he not? 'Tis most likely he shall be. But I'd not wish to think on it now. I shall need face him soon enough as it is." Stretching her tender legs out to be soothed by the warm water, she winced against the many aches that surfaced suddenly.

"Yea, m'lady. 'Tis the truth, I fear." Eauda could

see the pained expression Chrestien wore, and she decided not to pester her mistress with more questions at the moment—so much for conversation.

Chrestien was filled with sheer bliss to be submerged in the cleansing liquid. It had been overlong since she'd been able to repose in such luxury, and she closed her eyes to savor the scent of the rosewater as Eauda rinsed her hair with the fragrant mixture.

Water rushed down her face, and for a moment she pictured herself beneath a splendid waterfall, basking in the warmth of the sun's rays. Then, of a sudden, the sound of pounding reached her ears, and before she could cover herself the door flew open. Her breath caught in her throat as she watched the coffer she'd placed in front of the door topple across the floor, and she was more than acutely aware of her sheer nakedness as Weston strode toward her with a malevolent gleam in his eyes.

"You will never threaten my men again! Hear you what I say? I'd warned you that if you were to have free roam of your home, you would need have my men with you at all times—and that includes bath time, boy! And do not look so mortified, you've naught to hide that has not been seen before," he added when he saw the look of shock registered upon the young face before him.

Eauda ran from the chamber as Weston came to stand directly above the wooden tub, and Chrestien could not blame the maid, for she felt like fleeing too, but she didn't dare rise from her refuge within the sudsy water. His lips were moving, but she could hear naught Weston was saying because blood was rushing through her ears, blocking all sound save for the pounding of her heart.

Chapter 6

Weston had been furious when his men had relayed the tale of Christopher's tantrum. He'd seen women give in to such madness but never, in his nine and twenty years of life, had he ever met a man—or boy—who was so stupid—or demented. Which one of those this one was, Weston could not discern, for only an idiot would attack two armed knights with a tiny poniard.

The only reason his men had left the chamber to fetch him was that they feared to run the little imp through, thereby securing their own demise. Weston had given them explicit instruction that the boy not be harmed, but at this moment he regretted issuing such an order. His temples throbbed angrily and the muscles of his neck corded with his fury. He was so blinded by rage that he could not clearly see the person lying within the tub. . . .

He started to walk away ere he could do something foolish, but something in the back of his mind acknowledged what his eyes would not, and he stepped back over the tub to look down at the form below him.

Naught in all his years could have prepared him

for the sight he beheld. He stared in disbelief at the creamy mounds of flesh that greeted his eyes. Twin peaks rose above the pool of soapy water and he could but stare at them stupidly. Christopher was a woman, with skin as pure and smooth-looking as a baby's arse! But surely this could not be the same bedraggled lad he'd seen but hours before?

His breathing lapsed as his gaze settled on the face—features he would never have believed existed behind all that grease and grime. But what took his breath away were the eyes—the purest green pools he'd ever beheld ... as deep and enchanting as perfect emeralds. How was it he'd missed their brilliance before? His loins tautened, bringing him back to reality, but he said not another word—too stunned was he at the discovery. He backpaced until the hind of his legs touched the curtained bed, and when he realized he could retreat no further, he turned and walked away— quickly, ere his body could refuse his command.

Chrestien watched Weston back away from her in disgust. Mortification at her discovery quickly turned to self-pity—an emotion she'd never experienced ere now. The look on his face nigh brought tears to her eyes. Was she so unappealing? But cry? Nay, she would not! The echo of his footsteps ebbed and she willed herself to finish her bathing, taking as much time as she dared. Then she rose from the water, misty-eyed.

She'd not been in the company of many men, but there had been some who'd shown interest in her ... and never had anyone looked at her with such loathing as that. 'Twas as if the sight of her made the devil want to run.

"Oh, Papa," she whispered brokenly. "Could it be that you agreed to send me to the abbey because you knew that I would repulse men so? Adelaine's sweetness seems to soften our shared features. While," Chrestien lamented, "it seems that my own temperament hardens and misshapes mine."

Janelle entered the room cautiously, closing the open door to hide her mistress's nakedness. Then she took a bedrobe from a coffer. She placed the robe about Chrestien's shoulders gently, and Chrestien smiled wearily, relieved to see her faithful maid.

"Have ye gone to talkin' to yerself, child?" The reproach was given lightly, the tone gentle. "I'd come to aid ye with yer bathin', when Eauda flew past, raving about the devil in yer bedchamber. The chit was frightened beyond hope and I fairly flew up the steps to save ye from certain rape . . . but I can see yer safe enough." Just to be certain, she asked, "He's not harmed ye, has he?"

Chrestien's answer was a moan. "Nay." Without bothering to dry herself, Chrestien pulled the bedrobe closed and lay upon the bed she had once shared with her sister. She'd give aught for Adelaine to be with her now. But it was not to be, and Chrestien resolved to make the best of her predicament.

"Janelle, fetch me a gown—any one will do." Her tone bore little enthusiasm, but then she added on a higher note, "On further consideration, fetch me the gown that Papa bought especially for

Adelaine and myself—the twin gown ... that should make me feel better." She wasn't certain exactly how it would help, but somehow she knew she could draw strength from her sister by donning something that made her feel close to Adelaine. Mayhap Adelaine was wearing hers this very moment even.

The gown Janelle removed from the coffer was of bright green sendal, accompanied by a bliaut of golden silk. Papa had bought the material from a merchant in plenty, so she and Adelaine could have like gowns. It was this very one they'd worn to fool Aleth that first time, and the recollection made her giggle. Soon, she did feel better.

Placing the gown upon the bed, Janelle handed Chrestien her undergarments. With those articles on, Chrestien raised her arms for Janelle to place the remaining finery over her head. Her dress complete, Chrestien stood to smooth the folds of her bliaut. Janelle handed her a looking glass. She raised the rounded indulgence to her face—not to gaze at herself, but to see Adelaine, then sat upon the bed to watch Janelle plait her hair. "One plait, Janelle, and arrange it as you do ... did ... Adelaine's."

Janelle immediately unraveled the side plait she'd begun, scowling as she did. "I truly hope ye've enough hair, m'lady."

Chrestien shrugged. "If I do not ... then I do not. 'Tis as simple as that."

Janelle furrowed her brow at her mistress's lack of concern, straightened the lock of hair she held, and began arranging a plait across the crown of Chrestien's head. She gave up when the short hairs consistently resisted and fell to the wayside. "It simply cannot be done!"

Janelle had a way about her that was so gentle, Chrestien wasn't aware that Janelle had finished plaiting until the mirror in her hand had been yanked away and Janelle was standing in front of her.

"Did ye hear me, Chrestien? I say it cannot be done."

"What cannot be done?" Chrestien asked, stupefied.

"Yer plaits . . . and 'tis not the time to feel sorry for yerself, child," Janelle narrowed her eyes as she regarded her mistress's severed tresses.

With the oil and dirt removed, Chrestien's hair was little more than shoulder length, when just a short time ago the wavy locks would have cascaded easily to her slender waist. And to boot, with the length of it cut its innate wildness was released, and Chrestien's locks were a mass of riotous ringlets.

"Never have I known ye to feel sorry for yerself, and ye'll not begin now!" Janelle stated dryly, with the familiarity of a maid who had long been in service.

Chrestien conceded with a nod of her head, her curls bobbing her acquiescence. But even as she assented, her shoulders drooped lower.

"Ye tell me ye agree, yet ye still mope. Smile, Chrestien. Ye've too beautiful a face to be frowning so." Janelle placed her hand lovingly on Chrestien's cheek. "Why even with yer hair butchered as 'tis, one could never waive yer great beauty. 'Tis a pity ye would waste such a gift of radiance with the sour look that ye bear."

Chrestien smiled halfheartedly and stared unseeing at the maid in front of her. Janelle arched her brows, frowning at her mistress's feeble attempt at a smile. Seeing the insolent look on Janelle's face amused Chrestien, and for the first time in days she laughed, a heartfelt throaty laugh.

Chrestien had long ago resigned herself to the liberties that Janelle took. Nay, in truth, she loved Janelle's rebelliousness, for it so mirrored her own. It wasn't oft that Papa was angered by her whims, but every once in a while she and Janelle were forced to laugh in secret at her pranks gone awry. Never had Janelle scolded or moralized, and she gave a quick prayer of thanks that she at least had Janelle . . . and Aubert. "Janelle, what of Aubert? Is he improved?"

"Yea, he is healing," Janelle sighed. "And as much a male as is possible."

Chrestien's brows knit in puzzlement. She'd never thought men to be any different from women, save that they were possessed of different physiques. In truth, until the present she never gave them more than a passing thought. But after masquerading as a man, the gender was more a mystery to her than ever, so she was rightly curious at Janelle's remark. "And how so?"

"How else, Chrestien? I'd thought him to be half dead when ye arrived, but since then, my fears have been greatly appeased. He is alive and well, and the proof is in the way he orders me about. Give me this. . . . Give me that. . . . Straight my coverlet.... Bah!" Janelle deepened her voice to simulate Aubert's with little success. Instead she sounded like Janelle with a terribly inflamed throat. "In truth, 'tis why I am hither with ye," the maid confessed. "He is driving me insane with his ceaseless bantering. Worse than an auld woman, he is." Chrestien laughed again and Janelle smiled, though the gaiety did not quite reach her eyes.

Chrestien laid back on the curtained bed. The veiled silk was pulled back and tied neatly, giving Chrestien a clear view of her bower. All was just as she'd left it, though her life was none the same. She watched as Janelle pulled the coffer she and Eauda had used to bar the door back to its rightful place at the foot of the bed. A sudden attack of nerves made her rise from the bed and pace nervously upon the large woven mat alongside it.

The weary maid was sitting atop the coffer now, arms crossed, and eyeing Chrestien warily.

"Ye can do naught against this Wolf, Chrestien. He rides with the king's blessings," Janelle cautioned. " 'Tis his duty to secure this keep for his king and he's done naught but follow his directive."

"Janelle! I care not for what concerns that vile man. Aubert says it was the Silver Wolf and his troops who killed my father. And you cannot know what he has done to me. I've watched him wound your son—Aubert. You do remember Aubert?" She knew it was a hateful thing to say, but it burst from her mouth anyway. "And I bear the lump of defeat upon my sore head ... though I cannot remember when 'twas done," she appended. "I've been shouted at unmercifully, poked and kicked—not to mention the verbal abuse. Yea, 'tis true, he thought me to be a man, but 'twill not absolve him from his ignoble behavior. I care not for what concerns him, Janelle!" she repeated, her voice bleeding with sarcasm.

"As well ye should not, child." There was naught about the girl standing in front of Janelle that was childlike, but Janelle simply had never outgrown the need to mother the twins, and the endearment was merely a personal indulgence. "But to make it difficult for him 'twould be to make it difficult for yerself. Whom do ye think he will fault if ye give him trouble?"

Chrestien bit her lip and gazed at the older woman thoughtfully. During the heavy silence, Janelle studied Chrestien's features. She could read Chrestien's thoughts as surely as if they were her own, for the years had taught her Chrestien's ways well. And because she loved her mistress dearly, she would save her from herself, were she able.

Fortunately, from the look on Chrestien's face, Janelle could see that her mistress was beginning to come about, so she ventured once more onto unsteady ground to impart a few more words of wisdom to Chrestien's already brooding mind. "He'll do naught to harm ye now that he knows ye are a woman of gentle birth. He'd not risk Henry's wrath to do ye injury ... so ye are protected by the king as well. 'Tis not as though ye are a common wench such as I," Janelle added offhandedly, without derision.

Chrestien grimaced to hear Janelle refer to herself as a common wench. To Chrestien, there was naught that was common about Janelle. She was more lady-mother to Chrestien than Chrestien was ever likely to know.

Janelle had been the one to wipe her tears away, to laugh with her, and teach her. She started to say so, but a thought flashed across her mind, deterring her words. What if Henry summoned her to court? What would happen to Janelle? Would he let her bring her maid along? Surely he would? Having never been to court, she knew so little. She looked at Janelle, who was yet sitting upon the coffer with arms crossed, and quickly wiped the thought from her head. Papa had taught her to fire the crossbow one arrow at a time, and she would have to resolve this mess one problem at a time.

Weston was more than a little unnerved when he'd discovered a woman in the wooden tub, and not the boy he'd expected. Some part of himself heaved a sigh of relief to know that he'd not been ogled by a man the night before, but for the most part he was furious with himself for not realizing sooner . . . and for being bested by not a man, but a woman. But the thing that weighed heaviest on his mind was the lie itself. What could the girl have hoped to gain by such a ruse? De Lontaine had no son . . . neither was his daughter married to de Montagneaux, for she was none other than the boy, Chris.

Hours ago he'd made a hasty decision to take leave of Lontaine. He'd feared that if he remained near the little vixen he would give in to a very primitive need to throttle her little ivory neck. He'd ridden from the fortress angry, leaving full half of his men with Michel to garrison the newly taken keep, but more than aught else to guard the little lying, conniving ... beautiful, intoxicating witch. The fact that she was a woman did naught to change the way he felt about her. She was not to be trusted—nor underestimated.

The sun was setting, and Weston was loath to make camp so close to Castle Montagneaux, but he was more than certain that de Montagneaux would not receive him at such a late hour. Moreover, he'd pushed his men to near exhaustion, and a good night's rest would do them all much good—and himself as well. The morrow would prove to be a long day, having to confront de Montagneaux about his absence at Tinchebrai. Yea, he could use the rest.

Henry had given Weston two duties: the first to seize Lontaine; the second to secure Aleth de Montagneaux's fealty to the Crown ... providing that Aleth's reasons for truancy were believable.

Henry was appreciative that de Montagneaux had not taken his armies into Tinchebray and meant to reward him by allowing him to retain his well-garrisoned keep ... as well as the neighboring Lontaine.

It was no secret that de Montagneaux was possessed of armed men enough to have weighed heavily in favor of Curthose. That he'd yielded to Henry's bidding by not leading his troops into battle greatly pleased Henry. That de Montagneaux had not openly taken Henry's side rankled Weston. He did not trust straddlers, but it was not Weston's right to question Henry's decisions. He would simply carry the missive to its intended recipient as was his directive.

And the vixen? When he returned to Lontaine, he would simply inform her that she would be leaving Lontaine for the comforts of Henry's court. She was Henry's problem now. And as much as Weston loved his country and his king, he would not put up with the little termagant any longer than necessary.

Resigned to being the most quiet, obedient prisoner Weston would ever know, Chrestien had come into the great hall fully prepared to do aught he would bid of her. When she found only half of the knights at the table, and Weston gone, she'd been confused—though no more so than her uninvited guests. Only Michel's face showed little surprise when she arrived without her disguise. The rest of them gaped, jaws nigh hanging to their knees.

She felt like an oddity with all the unwavering eyes upon her, and part of her wanted to flee . . . to hide. And yet another part of her felt anger—great anger at their unconcealed censure. It seemed Michel sensed her unease and he came to her immediately.

"M'lady, ye behold one Michel Steorling, captain to Henry's Wolf." There was a moment of silence while Chrestien considered him. "I must apologize for my men's gaping . . . 'tis not oft they are gifted with such beauty as yers at table." She knew they were only kind words from a charmer's tongue. Nevertheless, his words greatly lifted her spirits, and she decided she liked him.

"Come, m'lady, join us." The tension dissipated completely as Michel took her by the hand and led her to the table. He leaned to her and whispered into her ear. "May I ask yer name?"

Chrestien couldn't help but smile. " 'Tis the lady Chrestien you would know."

Michel lifted the metal eating dagger and struck a silver chalice with it. It was a needless gesture, for all eyes were already upon them. "Fellow knights, ye behold the lady Chrestien of Lontaine." There were murmurs of approval, and with the formalities over, the hall broke into chatter, everyone speaking at once.

Jests were whispered about the Silver Wolf being bested by a woman. And finally, when it was said that Weston had fled rather than meet with his conqueror, Michel felt compelled to banish the offender from the hall. But Chrestien had noticed his soft inward chuckle ere he rose to reprimand the laughing young knight.

Michel was likable and very, very blond, Chrestien noted. His brows could barely be seen on his boyishly handsome and very bronzed face, they were so light. He was possessed of a very jovial disposition, and Chrestien took to him right away. He was so like Aubert, she mused, in that he too had a very sympathetic ear. Chrestien told him, while the other knights attended, about her father's death and her trek to Castle Montagneaux.

She told them about her sister, Adelaine, about having to cut her hair, and about the knight called Gervais. Just as she'd suspected, none knew hide nor hair of him. Michel threw back his head and laughed when she told about the bedding, and by then, all the knights had gathered about her, attending with great interest to her tales.

She told them about the wench that the knight Gervais had bedded while lying but a scant two feet from her, and that tale gained a round of laughter. But the tale to kindle the biggest roar was that of her intent to take the veil. What was so amusing about becoming a nun she could not fathom. But they did not seem to be laughing at her, so she assumed they believed she was jesting. Yea, that was it, they believed it a jest!

Michel filled her chalice for the third time, and placed more cheese and broken meats onto her trencher. She frowned when he took her hand so presumptuously. But he only pecked the back of it and declared, "Ye are delightful, Lady Chrestien." Then a smile lit upon his lips as he whispered a little more faintly. "My men are fascinated with ye, m'lady—overmuch so. I'd see yer door is well guarded this eve."

Chrestien, her head reeling with the wine, imagined that her eyes widened in slow motion. "You can't mean that they would . . ."

"Of course not, m'lady—at least not under normal circumstances—but it seems to me as though one and all are enamored of ye. 'Tis more likely that they would lie at yer feet to do yer bidding. But just as a safeguard . . ."

"I see . . ." Chrestien nodded her head in a slow exaggerated motion, though she did not see at all. The room was spinning and the air was growing warmer. Another sip of wine might clear her head, she decided.

Michel chuckled and removed the chalice from

her grasp. "I believe, m'lady, ye have indulged in this quite enough ... though of course I should take the blame. Most women I've known can consume twice the amount ye have. But then, m'lady ... ye are not most women. Are ye?"

What kind of a question was that? Chrestien wondered. Of course she was like other women! There was naught they had that she had, or rather that she did not, or that she ... Oh Jesu, but she could not think straight!

Michel's smooth voice broke into her scrambled thoughts. "Now, let us allow yer ladies' maid ..." He waved a hand, signifying Janelle. "The one waiting across the room with the dour expression ... escort ye to yer chamber."

Chrestien peered across the room to Janelle and giggled. "She's as a mother to me, you realize ..." Her chest heaved, interrupting her explication, and Chrestien found to her chagrin that she'd developed a nasty case of hiccups.

Michel laughed heartily as he pulled Chrestien's chair from beneath the table, and when she was steady on her feet, he gave her a gentle shove towards the irate ladies' maid.

Aided by Janelle, Chrestien ambled up the stone stairs to her bower. It seemed Janelle was as silent as the grave until Chrestien was nestled into her bed sheets. Then she squawked at the top of her lungs ... saying who knows what, because Chrestien was not attending.

Her thoughts were centered on the Silver Wolf. She still hated him of course, and it made her feel delightfully wicked to know that she'd been the cause of his departure—she knew that it was so, even if Michel had not admitted as much. She loathed that Weston had found her so disgusting to look upon that he would need to leave Lontaine to avoid seeing her again. And yea, she gained some measure of satisfaction in knowing she had caused him humiliation. Every one seemed to be amused that she had bested the mighty Silver Wolf, favored knight of England's king, but she would warrant that the Wolf himself was not so pleased.

The wine made her feel warm and tingly, and of a sudden, she remembered his lips. They were much too full and luscious for a man. His dark hair, with its silver flecks wild and unkempt, made him look so very dangerous—as did aught else about him. His face was unmistakably handsome . . . so masculine. There was naught about Weston that was effeminate, she mused.

Her lids closed sleepily as she pictured his well-defined face—a powerful jaw shaded with the growth of his whiskers . . . and his deep-set, blue eyes . . . mmm. Reflexively, she smiled as she recollected his smoldering gaze, then frowned when she thought of the one odious glare he'd given her ere storming from her bedchamber. Yea . . . she hated him for certain, she decided as she drifted into sleep.

Weston had been awakened in his tent well before Montagneaux's bells sounded Prime. Aleth had sent a greeting party of six fully armed knights to escort him into Montagneaux's gates. They were no match for Weston's fifteen . . . but then Weston had not come to do battle, so he'd followed Aleth's men as was requested of him.

De Montagneaux had greeted him with some measure of reserve, and only after Weston had stated the purpose for his unexpected arrival did Aleth lay every luxury at his feet—including the honor of being bathed by his ladywife, whom Weston was now awaiting.

The servants had led him to a private chamber in which a very ornate wooden tub graced the center. While he waited, he fondled the entwined nude figures which lined the rim of the tub. And as he studied them, he thought he saw the likeness of the vixen's face carved into the delicate woodwork. He shook the ludicrous thought from his mind and gave his attention to the room, which was to be his until he departed Montagneaux.

The large wooden bed wore a feather mattress and occupied the left corner, and a very large, overembellished, oaken hearth covered the wall he faced. An assortment of trunks lined the right wall, and the only door was at his back—a position he did not feel comfortable with—so he raised himself onto his haunches and turned around to face the door, just as it opened to reveal a young woman.

At first, he mistrusted his eyes. Then he cursed himself for the vision. He could not have forgotten that face so soon, and was angry with himself for allowing the vixen to implant herself in his thoughts so much that he would see her apparition in his dreams . . . in his thoughts . . . and now even!

Last night, as he lay in his tent courting sleep,

he had been haunted by a vision of her lying within her steamy bathwater. He'd wanted so much to reach out to her at Lontaine ... to assure his mind that the siren he was envisioning was in fact real. But in his state of confusion, he'd only stared stupidly, mouth agape. Then he'd left the room ... as well as Lontaine.

The apparition spoke in greeting, and in doing so, he was assured by the very real voice that he was not mad. And instead of being angry with himself, he was angry with her. How did she dare follow him to Montagneaux?

He watched as the vixen approached in her rich finery, her head covered with a couvrechef of white linen—no doubt to hide her short, ugly crop of hair.

"I see you've found your way here," he spat, but the woman still managed to smile sweetly. That did naught to temper his anger, however, for after the way she'd behaved, her docile smile did naught but make him mistrust her further. If he turned his back on her, would he find a knife in it?

Adelaine was appalled at the man's rudeness. What audacity! She'd come as soon as she was informed of her duty to bathe this guest of Aleth's. She was more than confused by his rancorous manner, but Aleth liked him, she reasoned, so she would try to overlook his surliness.

In silence, she picked up a rag along with the rancid-smelling soap at the foot of the tub, and carefully bathed the Wolf's back. But as she breathed in the stench of the lye, it occurred to her that though the offensive occupant of the tub would be clean, he would soon stink of lye, and that was an odor more foul than the man's temper was sour. Oh well, it was no more than he deserved to have the ladies running from him in terror of the smell. Smiling to herself, she resolved that as soon as Janelle arrived from Lontaine, she'd have her sweet rose-scented soap—luckily, too late to waste any on such a surly one as this.

She was glad that at long last Aleth had agreed to let her bring Janelle and Aubert to his household—her home, as he told her oft enough. She missed Janelle nigh as much as she missed Chrestien, and because Chrestien would have no need for Janelle at the abbey, she'd not feel guilty about taking them from Lontaine. Too, Aubert could offer his services to Aleth.

Aleth had sent his men to Lontaine to collect them early this morn, and 'twas then the men had come upon the camp of this . . . Silver Wolf.

Aleth had known this FitzStephens to be one of Henry's, and so was rightfully suspicious when the Wolf and fifteen well-armed knights rode into Castle Montagneaux's parklands. But when Weston had explained that Henry had given Lontaine to de Montagneaux as a gift of loyalty, Aleth had nigh laughed—partly from relief, but more than aught else because Lontaine was already his by marriage. It came to him as part of Adelaine's dowry!

Aleth was honest with Adelaine in that he was fearful of Henry. He had even confessed that he'd not gone to battle because he'd known Henry would win. Yet he'd loved her father so well that he'd sent fifty of his own men to ride under her father's banner against Henry of England even though his own heart was not in the battle. He'd also admitted that he'd do naught to rile the Conqueror's youngest son, so he'd led Weston to believe he was grateful for Henry's gift, and had left it at that.

She knew Aleth was not a craven man—had seen the proof of it herself. But she also knew him well enough to know that he took no chances where his lands were concerned. In any case, Aleth hoped to gain favor with Henry by treating his favored knight with high regard. Hence, she was sent to bathe this rude creature.

"I see the cat has caught your tongue. Can you not find your words? Or have you used every foul one of them already?" There was no verbal answer, only an angry glare from the girl. "At least tell me your name, mistress, that I may greet the devil's wife."

Adelaine had had enough. "Now you hear me well, sir knight," she snorted, waving the wet rag dangerously close to Weston's face. "I'd listen to you abuse my person, until death if need be! But never will I allow you to speak of my lord husband in such a manner! Do you attend? Need I explain further? One more remark and I shall . . ."

Weston watched the soapy rag slap at the air in front of him, and initially he backed away from it to avoid a swat in the face. Was she admitting to selling her soul to the devil, then? Could she be such a heathen?

"My Christian name is Adelaine!" she shouted boldly, gaining courage from the dumfounded look on Weston's face. So this was how Chrestien felt when she charged upon someone—so in control!

Meekness wasn't an intricate part of Weston's nature, however, and he was over his confusion rather quickly. Jumping from the tub, he grabbed the startled Adelaine, tossing her into the tub backside first.

Chapter 7

A rush of water cascaded across Adelaine's face as she raised her head from the stinking water. Tears sprung to her eyes as she watched Weston's nude form stalk from the chamber angrily and into the hall—completely unashamed to be seen in his naked state.

His voice reverberated throughout the hall, sending a chill down Adelaine's spine. He roared Aleth's name again and again. Within minutes, her husband was in the room.

Aleth gaped, incredulously, at his wife, who was sprawled in the tub with her legs skyward. Then he turned to Weston, his anger barely suppressed as the scene before him registered. "What goes on here, FitzStephens?"

Weston was too angry to notice Aleth's murderous glare. "You dare send this wench to bathe me!" It was a statement, not a question, but Aleth did not treat it as such.

"Yea, I dare. Ye dare question my wife's position in my home?"

"Your wife?" Weston's expression showed his

surprise, and Aleth, sensing there was some sort of mistake, was quick to explain.

"Yea, FitzStephens, m'ladywife. Ye've plunged my wife into yer bathwater—I told ye 'twas she I'd send to bathe ye."

Weston reentered the room and sat on the bed, still nude and deep in thought. Adelaine remained meekly in her awkward repose within the tub until Aleth lifted her into his arms, crooning softly into her wet head as he placed her upon a stool.

Never again would she dare to play at Chrestien's games ... never! Mayhap Chrestien liked such turbulence in her life, but she did not. The price of boldness was much too high!

Gently, Aleth removed the saturated couvrechef from Adelaine's head, letting her wet mane drop to her waist. He was in the process of drying her trembling body when Weston spoke again.

Seeing the length of her hair, Weston now knew this to be a different woman. "My pardon, lady, I believed you to be another ... I offer you my most sincere apologies, mistress." In spite of his dark scowl, he managed to look contrite. "I have come from Lontaine," he explained, "wither I left a most vicious female who shares the same look as you." He could only stare stupidly at the shivering, wet girl seated upon the stool before him. He still could not rationalize her likeness to the vixen of Lontaine, but 'twas now obvious they were not the same woman—the hair was much longer ... and there was something else ...

At his words, Adelaine jumped from the stool. "You've seen my sister, Chrestien? But she was to go to Caen when she departed here! Nay, tell me she is not at Lontaine!" Adelaine pleaded.

"What say ye, wife? Do ye tell me that scrawny cousin of yers was in truth yer sister?" Adelaine started to whimper, then sob in earnest at the angry glare Aleth gave her.

"How were we to know that you would be so kind, my lord? 'Twas for Chrestien's safety that we devised such a scheme. Please, Aleth, accept my apology. Did I know you would be so kind and understanding, I'd not have agreed to such a thing."

Her explanation seemed to appease Aleth, and his look softened though he said naught. Adelaine dried her eyes. Then, as she remembered guiltily that Chrestien had done aught because of her balking, she appended. " 'Tis not true, my lord. Now that I recall, 'twas for me Chrestien did aught. My father did not request that you and I marry as I have led you to believe ... and though I know he favored you, 'twas Chrestien and I who decided the fact. Only she'd not have embarrassed me by allowing you to believe me so ... so ..."

"Enough." Aleth thought to save her the embarrassment of using some ugly expression. Unintentionally, he let out a noise that was akin to a growl, and Adelaine's eyes widened with fear.

When Aleth noted her anxiety, he instinctively sought to calm her. "Never fear me, Adelaine, I'd not hurt ye, my love. 'Tis simply that Gilbert never told me he had two daughters. I thought there was trust between us. It appears not." He swallowed hard at the realization. His eyes misted as he focused upon a distant memory. "When I was a child," he explained, "your father risked himself to save me when no others were inclined to."

Adelaine gazed at her husband with sympathy in her expression. "I did not know," she said finally. "Papa never spoke of it."

Aleth nodded solemnly. "At the time, he served my father as castle guard and when my father was murdered, it was your father who protected me from harm by bringing me to the Lontaine to shelter. And he kept me there until I was of an age to govern my estates of my own."

"And what happened to the attackers?" Adelaine asked him. "Did they just up and leave Montagneaux, milord? That seems rather odd to me."

Aleth seemed deep in thought. "Huh? Oh, nay . . . my brother Rolfe was able to wrest it from them in due time. But it was to Gilbert that I owed my true gratitude." Gilbert had been close to Aleth's heart, and that had been the deciding factor to his agreement of a marriage to his young daughter.

He'd not planned to remarry ever, for he'd loved once and it had gained him naught save heartache, but he'd not counted on the fair Adelaine entering his life. The time he'd spent with her had brought him love anew, for she was possessed of both beauty and kindness. He brushed aside a damp curl from her face. "The pieces come together so well now—all the times your father refused to let me travel the distance to Lontaine. Always he would come to Montagneaux instead . . . save for those few times when I in-

sisted, of course. It hurts to know that he did not
trust enough to confide in me."

"Oh, Aleth, he did trust you," she assured him.
"But Papa was so afraid for Chrestien that he kept
it even from you. Even so, there were times I believe he wanted you to discover it." Aleth knitted
his brows in puzzlement, and Adelaine giggled at
a distant memory. "Do you recall when Papa invited you to Lontaine two years past?"

He did indeed remember, for 'twas not oft that
he was invited to Lontaine at all. "Yea, and what
of it?"

Adelaine giggled again. "Well, at dinner you
shared a trencher with both Chrestien and myself
. . . but you had not known it—being that we are
identical twins. Too, we were much too young to
gain your notice. You suspected naught when I excused myself and Chrestien returned in my place.
I watched from behind the screened partition
while Chrestien stuffed herself silly . . . and all you
could say about her overindulgence was that she'd
eaten enough for two. Oh . . . and how Papa had
laughed. Remember?"

Aleth was smiling now, for he remembered it
well. Gilbert's fitful laughter had irritated him, for
he'd not known its cause. "Yea, and if I recall
aright, he spilled his wine upon the ermine trim of
my mantle."

"He did." Adelaine smiled. "And you jumped
from the table and ran toward me, of all places!
You should have seen me bolt." She laughed.
"Poor Janelle thought I'd lost my head to see me

scurry into my father's chamber like a doe in the hunt."

Gently, Aleth plucked a honey lock of hair from Adelaine's wet face and placed a chaste kiss upon her forehead. Adelaine smiled to feel the warmth of his lips pressed to her face, and to Weston, it was a smile that was purely ethereal. Of a sudden, he longed to know if the other one possessed such a glow. In an almost musical tone, Adelaine giggled and said, "My lord, did you not wonder why I refused to let my cousin undress you?"

Aleth knitted his brow in remembrance. Then he let out a yelp of laughter as he remembered Adelaine flying from the refuge of his marriage bed to inform him, sternly, that she'd not allow anyone but him in the room. It had made no sense to him at all for her to reveal herself, only to demand that she not be displayed.

He'd been furious that she would allow his male guests to glimpse her form. Then he flushed when he remembered that he'd jealously assumed she'd uncovered herself to allow her cousin and lover a last glimpse. He'd noticed the loving looks between the two of them and had been irate. He'd even expected her to be deflowered, but had soon discovered that to be untrue.

He placed a kiss of newfound trust on his wife's cheek. He had fallen in love with her angelic face at first glance. But now? Because of her honesty, he felt a new bond with this gentle, caring woman who was his wife. Then he turned to Weston, apologetically, because he'd all but ignored the naked man upon the bed. "Please, join us in repast, Weston. M'ladywife has had prepared a most sumptuous feast for ye. . . . Would ye join us?" It was Aleth's way of mending the rift between them.

Weston nodded. He was glad that Aleth was so willing to let the insult pass, but he couldn't keep a streak of mischief from giving him the last word. He'd waited patiently while the lord and lady of Montagneaux reminisced, and now he would see the lady blush. "Yea, but I am certain you'd have me don something a little less revealing," he chuckled, and Adelaine, instantly red-faced, nigh flew from the room in her embarrassment.

Aleth and Weston shared a hearty laugh, and Aleth whacked Weston on the back. "'Tis amusing, is it not? That she would bathe yer well-endowed form without chagrin. Yet, at any other time she would nigh swoon with mortification to see ye exposed so."

"Indeed, it is." Weston grinned wolfishly. "But 'tis the way it should be. And God's Teeth, you should be thankful you didn't wed the sister. They share the same look, but they, indubitably, do not share the same disposition." Aleth laughed again before leaving Weston to dress.

The feast was sumptuous, indeed. Aleth had not spared the sparrow for the elegant spread. It had been overlong since Weston had sampled such a culinary delight—regardless that he'd spent much time at Henry's court. Usually, by the time the food was offered to the lower tables, the choicest pieces were oft gone. Even the wine, though a tad gritty, was of better quality than that of court.

Throughout the meal, Weston watched as Aleth

tossed love glances at the lady Adelaine to which she would shyly duck her head in chagrin. What difference there was between these two sisters, he comtemplated. And there was something about the identical faces that was not the same as well—though he could not quite place it.

Adelaine's hair was the same golden color, albeit much longer. But 'twas the meekness of the woman that seemed to change her entire appearance. That he did not feel drawn to this one as he had to the other confused him. There was little different about their appearances ... or was there?

Again he remembered the form lying within the tub at Lontaine, the creamy flesh of her bosom jutting above the soapy water, and it was this image that again tightened his loins and sent a surge of hot, demanding need pulsating through him.

"My lord, now that you know.... What would you do with Chrestien?"

Adelaine's sweet voice brought him away from his lusty thoughts. "Chrestien ..." The name rolled from his tongue, and he savored the sound of it. "I've not decided," he declared, somberly, as he lifted a portion of mutton to his lips.

"She would be ... we would be," Adelaine clarified, "ever so grateful did you escort her to the abbey."

"Abbey?" he asked incredulously. "The girl belongs not in an abbey!" But Weston no sooner said the words than he regretted them. Everyone within the hall was attending now, and he could see tears forming in the gentle woman's eyes.

"But, my lord," she wailed, " 'twas my father's

wish that she enter the convent upon his death . . .
and 'tis my sister's wish as well," she added.
" 'Twas her destination when she departed
Montagneaux. My dear father . . ." She crossed
herself before continuing. "He knew she would
not make a good and obedient wife, my lord, and
were she to fall into the hands of some cruel
man . . ." Adelaine ceased speaking and lowered
her head to wipe away the silent streaming tears.
She could not bear to utter the unspeakable.

Weston did not doubt that she spoke the truth.
He'd seen women as meek as the lady Adelaine
herself beaten for much less than he'd already witnessed in her hellcat of a sister.

"Which abbey?" Rolfe inquired suddenly as he
fingered the healing slash on his cheek. Now more
than ever, he wanted Chrestien—whether it was to
make her pay for the wound she'd inflicted upon
his face, or simply because his nights were filled
with the agony of coveting his brother's wife, was
not clear to him yet. He only knew that his failure
to catch Chrestien in the woods that day still
taunted him. Always, he was given Aleth's leavings. Well, by damn, not this time! He was the eldest, was he not? Yet Aleth had all, and he had
naught! All of it should have been his to begin
with, and he would have it soon enough. It was
his birthright! His!

"*La Trinite* . . . in Caen, *la place de la Reine-
Mathilde,*" Adelaine provided meekly, bringing her
tearstained face to meet the concerned gaze of
Aleth's half brother. She needed all the aid she
could to convince this . . . Silver Wolf of Henry's.

And for the love of her sister, she meant to recruit every sympathetic party.

Weston was more than aware what Adelaine was about, and he was not about to be engaged in a heated discussion concerning her sister's welfare. Especially when he'd seen firsthand how ill fitting the role of ladywife was to a such a paragon of hellfire. "I shall tell you what I'd do, my lady. I would send word to Henry of your father's request. Does he agree to honor it? Then . . . and only then . . . will I myself escort her to Caen. Agreed?"

"I would be ever so grateful to you, my lord." She looked at him then, her golden-brown eyes radiant with the light of kindness, and she smiled. Again, Weston wondered whether Chrestien was capable of such a wonder. Moreover, he wondered if he could be the tool to bring about such a sight, then quickly dismissed the thought. Chrestien's destiny did not intermingle with his own, nor did he desire it to.

He would petition Henry on Adelaine's behalf, but . . . he would be certain Henry knew that Chrestian was not cut from holy cloth—'twas only fair that Henry should know what he would bestow upon the holy Church. As it was, there was dissension enough between Church and Crown, with Henry having inherited Rufus's many quarrels. Once all the facts were presented, Henry would make the decision of his own . . . and Weston would abide by it. 'Twas as simple as that.

* * *

Colors paraded upon the horizon in an array of bold hues as if the very heart of nature were celebrating autumn's close. It seemed the heralding evidence of winter's approach left naught untouched. The forest was a backdrop of gold and russet against the amber grassland. The meadow itself was nigh devoid of wild blooms, and the birds screeched their secret alarm of winter's advance from their perches in the molting trees.

Chrestien plucked a wildflower from a lone patch of late bloomers and placed it in her hair. Then she turned her attention to Lightning, caressing his nose gently with great affection. Adelaine, Janelle, and Aubert were gone now. Lightning was a link to the past that she would never relinquish, and she spent every afternoon riding him through the changing meadow. Smiling, she took the flower from her hair, placing it to Lightning's flaring nostrils, and he reared his head in protest.

"Tickles does it?" Lightning snorted in response, and she knew instinctively that he was growing impatient with her dallying.

A lone tear came to her eye when she thought of Adelaine, and she wiped it daintily with her fingertip. 'Twas not that she was unhappy, not really. Michel and the others had proven to be aught but what she'd expect them to be—murderous, egotistical lechers. Instead, in the two weeks since her return to Lontaine, they'd been kind, attentive, chivalrous, and very entertaining. Every one of them, in his own way, had helped to make this very trying time a bit more endurable.

Michel was witty and lighthearted—much like she imagined her father would have been at his age. Too, he looked after her as if he were her mother, of all things. He made certain she was never alone in the company of his knights . . . and that she was carefully watched when she rode Lightning through Lontaine's parklands. Even now, she could see a pack of his men lurking atop a distant knoll, trying to be inconspicuous—as if she would not note them standing in the open meadow!

There was not a single place for them to conceal themselves. And they were standing sentinel in such an obvious manner that it nigh made her laugh to look upon them. But she was very grateful to Michel for taking such great care with her—it filled the void her father had left. Mounting Lightning, she kneed him in the direction of Lontaine, and the stallion galloped swiftly, knowingly toward the band of waiting knights.

It felt so wonderful to ride into the wind, and Chrestien again bemoaned the fact that she'd shorn her hair. She could nigh feel the wind rippling her long tresses in her wake as it had before . . . nigh. Because when she placed a hand behind her head, she was assured that it was but a memory. And she resolved that when finally it grew back to its full length, she would never cut it again!

The four men Michel had assigned this day stood as in a trance as Chrestien approached them. When Lightning came to stand before them, all four of them rushed to her side—like bees to a spring blossom.

"May I help you dismount, m'lady?" It was Troy speaking, and his hands flew out with unrepressed eagerness. But Derrick, who was a head taller than Troy and more muscular, successfully elbowed his way to Chrestien, pushing Troy by the wayside, and stood there smiling, the look of victory vivid upon his handsome, boyish face, his blond hair ruffling in the wind. And Chrestien giggled inwardly when she noted the bright flush that crept to his face. She knew him to be embarrassed by her lack of response to his outstretched arms, but she didn't have the heart to tell him she had no plan to dismount.

The other two, John and Ned, shyly hung behind the more boisterous Troy and Derrick, never actively involving themselves in the rivalry. Nevertheless, they yet vied in their own way for Chrestien's attention, though it seemed a smile was enough to appease them, while Troy and Derrick nigh came to blows every time Chrestien set eyes upon either of them—never would she understand men!

John was not at all what she'd expected. The dark-haired knight had once seemed ugly and ornery to her, and while he was full of unsightly battle scars, he was definitely not the ill-tempered lout she'd thought him once upon a time. His most prominent scar ran diagonally across the left side of his lip, contorting his mouth into a permanent scowl, and 'twas the effect of this scar that led her to perceive him as so.

Troy was possessed of a very handsome face, though he was short and stocky of build. And did he seem a little overzealous, he was no more so than Derrick.

Ned was tall as Derrick—not quite as tall as John—with rusty hair and freckles. He'd a nervous smile painted across his thin face, giving the impression that he smiled always. Unfortunately, it seemed this tendency caused him much trouble with the other men. He was the kindest of them all, and she'd come to deeply regret attacking him and John with her poniard.

Each of them possessed good and bad qualities, but all of them had found a place in her heart. Just as she was about to speak, Michel appeared at her side, seemingly from nowhere.

"Ye've been away long, m'lady, and I was given to worrying about ye as would an auld woman," he told her, as he eyed his pack of young dogs, silently demanding them to give the lady breathing room. Bringing his mount next to hers, he leaned into her, whispering so as not to embarrass his men. "I note ye have yer hands full with my lovesick puppies."

Chrestien smiled. " 'Tis not a burden, if that is what you mean. They are instead a boon to me," she confessed, as she watched the four men mount their geldings and start away.

"I thought, mayhap, ye would join me for a short ride," Michel imparted.

Chrestien beamed. " 'Twould be a joy, my lord." And then as an afterthought, "You spoil me overmuch, I believe."

Michel's deep brown eyes twinkled with merriment. "Nay, m'lady, 'tis no more than ye deserve."

'Twas a struggle to get the words out, he was so mesmerized by Chrestien. When she smiled, her eyes lit with an ethereal green fire, and he told her pointedly, "Ye've been told, I'm certain, that ye've a smile that could fell a mountain, m'lady." It was never his way to mince words, and this girl intrigued him. " 'Tis why ye do it overmuch, I'd venture to say . . . and mayhap," he joked, "had ye wielded that smile instead of yer broadsword on Weston, he'd not have recovered at all." He chuckled. "I suppose I should thank ye for sparing him."

"You flatter me, Sir Michel." Chrestien was embarrassed, and she lowered her face to hide the blush that was creeping to her heated cheeks.

" 'Tis for purely selfish purpose that I would do so, Chrestien. I'd have ye smiling oft, so that when I leave yer company, the light of yer eyes would be etched in my memory, and I would carry the image of ye in my thoughts always," he promised.

Chrestien's blush deepened, and she made a pretense of hugging Lightning's mane, when what she really wanted to do was hide from Michel's shower of compliments. He'd never been so full of adulation before, and though he was extremely handsome with his almost boyish looks and golden hair, she would rather think of him as she would an elder brother.

Michel noted that he was making her uncomfortable, and he moved to change the subject. "There is something I'd discuss with ye, m'lady. Will ye still request that Weston take ye to Caen?"

"Yea, I would still have it so. Think you he will

honor my request?" She was immediately anxious to hear what he would say.

"Yea, 'tis why I ask. Weston has sent word from Castle Montagneaux that he is petitioning Henry to allow ye to be cloistered." He thought he heard her sigh in relief, and was disappointed by her reaction. "Are ye certain 'tis what ye truly desire. . . . 'Tis likely ye'd be more than welcome in Henry's court." He would not tell her that he'd, in fact, already written to Henry on her behalf. With all due respect, he was certain Weston knew naught of her many worthy wifely attributes, and he did not feel it a betrayal to Weston to inform Henry of such. "Ye would be his ward, ye realize, and under his protection."

"Nay, I could not." A silent tear inched down Chrestien's cheek as she thought about her father. "My father would not have me seeking protection from his enemy."

"I ken, m'lady. 'Tis simply that I would abhor to see ye ensconced away from life, when it could be such a full one for ye. . . . Each waking breath is so priceless . . . and ye have such vigor for life that 'twould be nigh sinful to deprive the world of yer charms."

Chrestien was desperate to change the subject. "I'd not speak on it longer, my lord." And then to ease the sting of her retort, she inquired, "Michel, how came you by such an odd surname? Steorling . . . to be named for heaven's stars . . ."

Michel chuckled. " 'Twas given to me long ago, m'lady, when I was but a page in William Rufus's court." Michel chuckled again at the memory.

"Tell me of it."

"Very well, m'lady. It goes as this. One morn, Rufus was struggling with his dress. And in his frustration, he asked of his chamberlain the price of the offending boots. When the chamberlain replied that their cost was but three shillings, Rufus threw the boots at him and shouted obscenities. Then he demanded that boots be purchased which cost at least a mark of silver. The chamberlain came to me then, and bid me to find these new boots for the king. And though I searched, demoiselle, I could not find a pair for my king and was forced to purchase some for much less than the three shillings. For this I felt extremely contrite, and I decided to pay for the boots of mine own purse. But when I returned to the chamberlain with those boots of lesser quality, the explanation, and the mark of silver, the chamberlain only laughed heartily and bid me keep the coin. He assured me he would reveal naught to the king . . . and so he did not."

"Yea, but what of the name?" she insisted.

"Oh yea, well, the silver mark that was given me bore Rufus's tiny steorlings upon it. Hence was I called Michel Steorling by all who knew of the escapade. And soon I was known as thus by all . . . though but a scant few know the reason."

Of a sudden, Michel reined in his destrier and grabbed the reins to Chrestien's mount, stilling both steeds with a gentle tug.

Chrestien wanted to ask him what was amiss, but the engrossed look on his face told her that it was best she not disturb him. It was several moments later when Chrestien could finally make out a speck on the horizon. With scant seconds, an approaching cavalcade could be seen.

"Should we not hasten to Lontaine, my lord?"

"Nay, 'tis but Weston. . . . He returns from Montagneaux."

Chrestien stiffened in the saddle at the mention of the much despised name. "How can you be certain?" She prayed he was somehow mistaken.

" 'Tis his banner that gives him away."

Chrestien was amazed he could see it at such a distance, and she cupped her hands just above her brow to shield her eyes from the sun. Sweet Mary, but she could see no banner!

Noting the confusion on Chrestien's face, Michel quickly explained. " 'Tis the silver in his banner that reflects the rays. 'Tis the reason his enemies know of his approach, and would scamper like frightened rabbits ere he comes anywhere near them." There was a note of pride in his tone as he explained, but his pride in his liegelord did little to sooth Chrestien's fear.

"And that is why they call him the Silver Wolf?"

"That . . . and other reasons." He would tell her naught else. Such things were not meant for her delicate ears.

"What other reasons?"

Michel chuckled. "I'd not burn yer ears with such things, m'lady." But when her emerald eyes fastened upon him in protest, he knew he could no deny her an answer, and he sighed. "He is called so because of his device, the silver in his hair, his prowess upon the battlefield . . . and his prowess with women." Her eyes widened accusingly, and he knew he would tell her naught else! "Yea, 'tis true, the man has a silver tongue."

"Oh" was all Chrestien said. Nervously, she ran her fingers up and down Lightning's braided leather reins. It seemed to her they spent an eternity waiting for Henry's Wolf, and the strain was becoming unbearable. Impulsively, her foot burrowed into Lightning's belly, but as the stallion charged forth, Michel caught the reins and held them tight, and she had accomplished naught but to rile Lightning.

"He'll not harm ye, m'lady."

Chrestien wasn't certain that was the truth, but she nodded in acknowledgment and nervously nibbled at her bottom lip.

Weston halted his destrier directly in front of Michel, but he did not look at his old friend. He'd been wildly curious about the vixen he'd left at Lontaine, and now that he finally set eyes upon her, what he saw took his breath away.

Chrestien's beauty was beyond compare—even in contrast to her twin sister. There was something about this one that was nigh overwhelming. 'Twas the eyes, he realized. They pierced his soul as would the Welshman's arrow—with breathtaking accuracy. They were entrancing ... so deep and pure a green.

Chrestien's golden hair was shoulder length, but instead of being straight and greasy as he'd remembered it, it fell in riotous silken tendrils about her face. Streaks of white sunlight coursed through its sensual waves, making her look so like the archetypical temptress. She was as night is to day to the fair, gentle lady he'd seen at Castle

Montagneaux. They were so alike, these sisters, yet not alike at all ... and he vowed he would stay away from this angel of fire.

Chrestien's heart turned flips as she weathered Weston's obvious appraisal of her person. His azure-colored eyes locked with hers, capturing her with his controlling gaze and rendering her helpless. His handsome features were devoid of emotion—not even his eyes hinted at his thoughts. His destrier pranced impatiently beneath him and abruptly he turned his scrutiny from Chrestien to Michel.

"Why is she away from Lontaine?" he asked abruptly, the muscles in his jaw twitching in protest against his clenched teeth. His anger needed unleashing and it seemed Michel was the most viable target. His old friend was aiding and abetting his tormentor! From the moment he'd set eyes upon the bitch, she'd implanted herself within his mind—some whore's trick no doubt, for he knew she was no lady.

Michel let go of Chrestien's reins immediately and spurred his mount forward, signaling for Weston to follow. They stopped but a few yards from Chrestien, and spoke in a whisper.

Chrestien noted that whatever Michel had said, it had angered Weston enough that he waved furiously to his men-at-arms, urging them to follow. Then, without waiting to see that they obeyed, he sprinted toward Lontaine.

"What did you speak to him of?"

"Naught," Michel lied. He would have to answer to Weston later for his defiance, but he'd felt it necessary to speak his mind about Chrestien. He could not stand by and watch Weston treat her cheaply, as he knew Weston was wont to do. His intent was evident by the look in his eyes. He'd seen that devil's glare too oft—'twas his look of contempt.

Kind? Virtuous? Pious? Michel had used those words to describe Chrestien. Had she blinded him? Was he daft? The only kind thing Weston could say of her was that her beauty could confuse a man's senses. Leave her be? What gall Michel had! Leave her be. . . . 'Twas she who would not let *him* be!

Henry had not returned Weston's messenger as of yet and Weston was anxious to get the vixen off his hands. The sooner she was taken to the abbey, the better for all involved. He'd remained at Castle Montagneaux as long as was feasible to avoid a prolonged period in the vixen's presence. He was afraid he would throttle her if he were around her for any length of time—for her insolence . . . and for biting him. The marks she'd left upon his shoulders were blue-black now, proclaiming to the world his stupidity. Too, he could fault her for inhabiting his dreams. Hell! He would leave the girl to Michel, for he seemed to be having an easy enough time of it. No doubt she offered him a few of her favors for his trouble.

He did not fear losing Michel's loyalty. That was something Weston knew would be his till death— too many times Weston had come to his rescue. Not to mention the fact that he and Michel had fostered together. Nay, there was overmuch between them to suspect a turn of loyalties, so he

had no qualms about leaving her to Michel's care
... as long as Michel kept her well away from
him!

Lontaine was much as he had left it. The villein
were bustling about, minding their chores, and the
swishing and clanging of steel upon steel could be
heard throughout the bailey. The smell of sweat
accosted his nostrils and he knew that the men
had not been slack in their training. A smile
curved the right of his lips as he dismounted
Thunder and led him to the stable.

Before turning his attention from his gelding, he
patted the horse's black rump lightly, and silently
wished that women could be as loyal as his horse.
A good horse could make or break the knight.
And though a man could do without the permanent appendage of wife, sooner or later, most were
affixed with one ... and a bad one could definitely
be the ruin of him.

He usually took more time with his prize destrier, for any knight worthy of the title knew his
life depended highly upon his mount. He'd seen
many an untrained horse panic in the face of battle, leaving his rider to face certain death ... or to
be trampled amid the melee. But he'd been away
from his men overlong and was overeager to join
their training, so he hurried from the stable, leaving the care of Thunder to the stablemaster.

He strode across the bailey with purpose but
stopped dead in his course at the sight before him.
Every one of his men—save Michel, who made his
way to Weston now—had ceased his vigorous
training and was standing motionless, ogling
Chrestien. Three men rushed to her horse and held

their arms outstretched to help her dismount, and Weston shook his head in disbelief.

When Michel was standing before him, Weston finally unleashed his fury "Three men, Michel! Not one?" He could hardly believe his eyes. Moreover, the three were nigh shoving each other for the privilege. "I'd stressed chivalry to them, but this is preposterous!"

Michel did not agree, but he would not tell Weston so while he was in such a temper. In silence, they watched as Derrick managed to fight off the other contenders, then lifted Chrestien delicately from her stallion, setting her down carefully.

"She rides a damn stallion as would a man!" He'd not noticed what she rode in the meadow . . . only her face, and he cursed himself for his distraction. Nay, he cursed her for it! "What manner of woman would ride a stallion?" Michel was prepared to defend Chrestien. But as he opened his mouth to deliver the explanation, Weston cut him off. "Never the mind, for I ken the answer to that already."

Weston watched Chrestien hand the reins of her mount to John, who took them eagerly, acting as though he were just entrusted with the royal treasure! "This is overmuch!" He shot Michel a contemptuous glare, and concluded that Chrestien must be *extremely* generous with her favors for his men to be acting so. Mayhap he would have to sample them for himself.

Chrestien was surrounded by at least a dozen men, but the only presence she felt was Weston's. His darkness and air of arrogance prickled her skin until she could stand it no more and she hurried to the sanctuary of the keep.

In the hall, she felt a little less conspicuous with all the women servants bustling about. But somehow, Weston managed to invade her thoughts, and she could yet see the loathing he felt for her smoldering in his gaze. And though she didn't know why, it brought a stinging tear to her eye to know he hated her so.

Weston cursed as he watched his men follow Chrestien into the hall like lost puppies. "How can you have allowed this, Michel? In a matter of weeks my men have become witless, bumbling simpletons." Michel shrugged, knowing he would not find an answer to appease Weston. And when Weston stalked off angrily, he was more than a little relieved.

Weston shuddered to think what would happen were they to remain in her company much longer. Would he need find a nursemaid to care for them? " 'Tis ridiculous the way they fawn over the woman, waiting on her every whim." Were her favors so disparate from those of other women's?

John hurried from the stables to join the lady Chrestien. She was so kind, and her goodness made one feel so good about oneself. You could not help but flock to her warmth as does the moth to the flame, and he knew that she must at times grow weary from the lack of privacy. But though she never encouraged anyone, she also never complained of them as well, and he was glad of that, because it felt so good to be in her presence.

Remembering the night the lady had been brought to camp, a pang of guilt surged through

him. He and Troy had kicked and jabbed her
throughout the night. Every hour that passed had
brought more violence against her as they had bemoaned their lack of sleep. They had taken their
frustration out on a woman, blasted—a kind and
gentle one at that!

Chapter 8

With painstaking care, Chrestien had planned her week so as not to meet up with Weston. Up until the third day she'd busied herself within the stables, working with the stablemaster to impart some order to it. With the most worthy stallions long gone, there were very few studs to breed with the mares. In truth, she probably should not have worried herself with the dilemma at all, for she'd be off to the nunnery as soon as there was word from Henry. Too, Michel had told her that Lontaine was now a forfeit of war, though he'd not specified what was to be done with it, and she had little liking for increasing Henry's bloodstock. How absurd to enact retribution against a man now dead. Damn Henry's soul! Even so, the chore offered welcome diversion from her problems, and she embraced the challenge wholeheartedly.

All would have gone well if Weston had not ventured into the stable and eavesdropped upon her conversation with a stable boy. It seemed he was everywhere she was! Unnerved by his presence, she had started to rant mindlessly about

151

breeding, and the more Weston had listened—grinning his wicked grin—the more she had sounded like a mindless fool! Curse his rotten self!

The next day Chrestien decided to hide in her bedchamber in an attempt to avoid Weston, but about midday, she had started to wonder what he was about and had unshuttered her window to look into the bailey. And curse him if he wasn't right there, looking up at her window. Yea, he was training his men at the time, but he didn't have to catch her spying on him! She'd covered herself well, however, and had pretended an interest in Michel. Michel had waved along with the others and Weston had barked his command that they leave off with the socializing.

Later in the day, she'd busied herself with the preparations for the evening meal. Her favorite, baked capon, was to be prepared, and Eauda had set the lord's table with the finest table linen—the one Adelaine and Janelle had embroidered during the winter past. She wanted to be certain aught would be perfect tonight. Why? She couldn't discern, but somehow she needed to impress Weston. For some odd reason, she seemed to need his approval. It seemed the odious man was always frowning at her, however, and mayhap that was why she wanted it overmuch. Yea, oft in the past days she would sense his gaze upon her, and when she looked at him, he would indeed be watching her. But his face was always a mask of absolute contempt, and she wanted sorely that he should look at her otherwise. Giving the hall one last inspection, she saw that all was in order, and after looking over the washbasins to be certain the water was scented properly, she went upstairs to dress.

Tonight she would don her best gown. Surely Weston would not find her lacking then? She took from her coffers an aqua silk undertunic and a beautiful bliaut of shell-pink brocade. Tiny roses were embroidered about the sleeves and neckline of the bliaut, and each flower boasted a tiny pearl. But even without the delicate stitchery, the gown was a sight to behold, for the gossamer silk was as sheer as a silken web and it hugged her every curve with a certain passion. This gown was to have been Chrestien's wedding vestment ... were she to have wed.

Naught could be done with her too-short hair, so she had to content herself with the riotous mass of unkempt curls. 'Twas her penance for cutting her maiden's tresses! It seemed as though there was naught she could do to tame its innate wildness. She combed it oft and yet it still seemed to have a mind of its own.

"Oh curse it!" The oath stumbled from her mouth in her frustration. With a sigh, she peeped again into the looking glass and decided that all that could be done ... was done.

Time seemed to stand still as she entered the hall. It was as though ten thousand eyes were focused upon her, and all of a sudden she wished she could hide. But she squared her shoulders instead, and went directly to the dais, taking her usual seat at the lord's table.

Michel sat beside her, and Weston to his left. She could feel his eyes upon her, but she didn't dare look to see whether he was watching. She knew he was, for the hall had never been so quiet, and the hush made her skin tingle madly—nerves, she reasoned. She felt this way every time she was in his presence, and more so at this moment, because the reigning silence was overwhelming. It seemed everyone was afraid to speak. And Sweet Jesu, the stillness was near maddening!

Weston could scarcely believe his eyes. Every time he saw the woman, she seemed to grow more exquisite. She was possessed of a stunning quality about her and there was something mysteriously beguiling as well, beyond the obvious physical beauty—much like the allure of a pagan goddess.

His eyes feasted upon the gentle sway of her hips as she glided across the hall. Her waist was so tiny, he was certain that he could encircle it with his hands and his fingers would meet. Then his eyes fell on her gown and he found himself gritting his teeth. The sheer cloth clung to the curves of her slender body, accentuating her proud bosom and delicate hips. Was there no end to her wickedness? Did she intend to seduce every man in the hall this eve? No doubt she liked the way everyone watched her.

When the unnerving silence reached his ears, he knew instinctively that all eyes were upon her. But when he looked about the hall, he was shocked to find that everyone was watching him instead, with a most protective gleam in their eyes. 'Twas almost as if they would pounce on him did he say the wrong word.

The meal proceeded in the most deafening quiet, and Chrestien thought she would die from the strain. Not once did she look at Weston.

Whether it was fear or some other emotion that kept her from it was not clear. What was clear was the beating of her heart. It pounded wildly against her chest, making it difficult to breathe. When finally she could take no more of the madness, she rose from the table, squared her shoulders proudly, and left the hall for the sanctuary of the garden.

The garden was a favorite place of hers. Always, when she craved solitude, it was hither she came, as Adelaine had had her own place to go as well—the donjon tower. Tonight, the brisk night air was refreshing after the stifling atmosphere of the hall. Out here, inside the rose alcove, no eyes could prick her soul.

Ah ... Sweet Mary. But 'twas not just any eyes that pricked her, only Weston's. If the truth be known, it was a joy to receive the attention the rest of his men gave. As a child she could never receive enough notice—though her father was ever giving it—and that had led to at least a hundred childish pranks to gain more ... and at least as many scoldings.

She plucked a rose and snuggled beneath the alcove to enjoy its sweet heady fragrance—they were her mother's favorite flower. Papa had said her lady mother had brought the rose cuttings from her father's home in faraway England.

Solemn thoughts clouded Chrestien's mind when she thought about her grandsire. She'd oft wondered what he was like. Papa had never spoken of him overmuch ... save to say that he'd allowed Chrestien's mother a love match. But 'twas only so because lady Elizabeth Grey had been a fourth daughter.

Her grandsire had fathered four daughters, but to his dismay, not a single son. Even so, her mother was not in a position to inherit and was allowed her heart's desire. This one good deed did not, however, excuse her grandsire for his lack of concern toward Adelaine and Chrestien. And she would never forgive him for it. Not that 'twould matter overmuch to him, anyway, for he most assuredly did not care.

Baron Geoffrey Grey had never possessed an inkling of concern for his grandchildren—at least not for the children of his youngest daughter. 'Twould have saved Chrestien so much misery after her father's death if she could have relied upon her mother's family. But as it was, she knew naught of them, save for the name.

Weston rose from his seat at the dais and started for his chamber, but curiosity got the best of him and he went in the direction of the garden instead. The hall had nigh emptied after her departure, and if he knew what that abrupt parting meant, she would be meeting someone in the garden. What he didn't know ... was who. From her entourage of suitors, it could be anyone: Derrick, Troy, John, Ned, even Michel. God's Mercy, they were all besotted with her!

The garden was dark and shadowy, illuminated only by the light of a silvery moon, and Weston stood in the doorway a long moment so his eyes would adjust to the darkness. When the shadows cleared sufficiently, his eyes scanned the wall-enclosed garden. He could see naught—hear naught. The garden was empty but for the herbage. He walked forward a pace or two, nigh tripping over the side of a small raised compartment. A faint giggle floated sweetly to his ears, and his eyes instinctively focused in the direction of its origin. He could barely discern a glow from within a black hole in the far right wall, and he made his way toward it.

Oh, curse and rot her tongue for giving her away! She would have liked to see him fall into the herb gallery, and 'twas that wicked thought that had caused her to laugh. She held her breath as Weston came to stand directly in front of her, his huge form outlined by the moonlight. Reflexively, she put her hand to her chest to will her heart from leaping from her body. It was beating so loud, she knew he must hear it as well.

She was alone, he realized, as a cool breeze filtered past, ruffling his hair along with the sleeves of his tunic. "Are you not cold?" He wasn't certain why he was concerned, but of a sudden he was.

Chrestien was rendered speechless by his show of consideration. Her lips moved to answer him, but she could not find her voice, and what ensured was a deeper silence. She liked him better when he was angry—at least then he was predictably infuriating. To that she was never at a loss for words.

God's Breath! She had enough to say when she was with his men, he recalled. In his anger, he turned away from her and started to walk away, but her softly given reply stopped him.

"Nay, I am not." Her voice was calm, though it was not how she felt. " 'Tis the way I like it," she explained.

"What are you about . . . outside at such an hour?" He couldn't keep the accusatory tone from his inquiry, and it was not lost to Chrestien.

She bit back a sharp retort, and said instead, "I come hither when I need to think, my lord." It did not soothe her to quell the angry words, and instead of sounding agreeable as Adelaine would have, her voice flew to his ears mockingly. It just did not suit for her to be pleasant.

"When do you need to . . . think, demoiselle?" Weston drawled, as if it were a novel concept.

Chrestien noted the sarcasm in his voice and it fired her all the more. Fury shot through her limbs until it reached clear to her toes, and at once she sprang to her feet, aching to feel her palm across his too comely face. "Oh! And whither does it say that wisdom is a man's trait, my lord?" she spat out, fury swelling her chest until the inhaled breath ached to be set free. When finally she let it flow, her chest rose and fell indignantly along with her rage.

He could not see her, but he could hear her heavy breath and it unnerved him. She sounded in the throes of passion—or at least that was how he imagined her—and he forced himself to quell the sudden urge to taste her lips, remembering that he would not be the first. But then, he wasn't sure why that mattered at all. Had he ever known a chaste woman? Furthermore, had he ever refused one on that pretext? "Forgive me, demoiselle. I forget you are not the lady." It was not an answer to her question, he was merely voicing his thoughts.

His keen instincts accurately predicted her response, and when her hand flew to the shadow of his face to issue a slap, he caught her wrist and held it tightly within his fist. A sweet, heady fragrance reached his senses, making him loosen his grip. And involuntarily he moved closer to her until he could feel the softness of her breast against his ribs. The breeze shifted again and he inched closer, warming himself with the heat of her body. Catching the back of her neck in his grip, he forced her lips closer to his, until he could feel her breath upon his face.

"Unhand me, you lout!" Never had she been accused of such a thing. Her eyes misted and then she felt him against her. She was afire where her body was pressed against his warmth. And in that instant it felt as if the fires of hell had descended upon her, for it was not like anything she had ever felt ere now—nor was it a good sensation. Any moment she would disgrace herself by falling into tears.

His lips ground down into hers, bruising them, and she fought him. Then, unexpectedly, his kiss softened and her heart leapt within her breast. She moaned helplessly as his tongue slid between her lips, moist and hot, and moved deep into her mouth. With each stab of his tongue, her heart leapt higher into her throat, strangling her breath.

Weston groaned deep in his throat and his eyes closed as he savored the silky feel of her mouth. The sweet taste of her nearly drove him over the edge. His breathing labored now, and his nostrils flaring with the scent of her, he pressed himself into her trembling body, seeking out her warm curves.

Chrestien cried out as Weston's body rocked into her, nudging her most private places with his hardness. Her insides convulsed wildly and the all too brief sensation left her breathless and clinging for more.

Black rage filtered through Weston's mind as he acknowledged the fact that Chrestien was no longer fighting him, but clinging wantonly instead. Did she give so willingly to everyone? he wondered irately. His anger mounting, he whispered into her mouth, his voice both a velvet caress and a threat all at once. "Who were you meeting out here this eve, Chrestien? Michel?" he asked thickly. "Derrick?"

It took a full moment for her to realize what he'd asked. Again, she tried to slap him, too stunned to respond in any other way. And once again, he caught her wrist. She glared at him, unable to believe what he'd practically accused her of.

Weston gave her no more opportunity to respond, but took her mouth in a searing kiss, scalding her lips with his own. His hands slid firmly down her curves, releasing her wrist as his palms sought out her bottom, pressing her to him.

If Chrestien had felt something moments before, it was gone now, replaced with a mounting fear. Her senses cleared, and she cried out, shoving him away from her. His form was unmoving, like stone.

"How dare you! How dare you fondle me as if ..."

He raised a dark brow. "Me thinks thy protests come too late?"

"... as if I were no more than a common harlot!" she continued, ignoring his mocking words.

"Common?" he asked, his tone velvety smooth. "Common is the one thing you are not ... milady." With a grin he stepped away from her, releasing her. The second she was given opportunity she shoved him angrily and bolted from him, flying into the great hall and dropping the white rose in her haste to be away from him.

Weston watched as Chrestien made her way through the dark maze of raised gardens without err. When she was gone, he followed her into the hall, and as he stepped into the doorway he noticed the white rose lying amid the rushes. Stooping to pick it up, he placed the snowy bloom to his nostrils, inhaling deeply of its fragrance, recognizing it easily as the scent from the garden. She'd been holding the rose in her hand when she tried to slap him, he mused. No doubt she would have been pleased to leave a thorn or two in his face.

As he stared at the perfect bloom, Michel sauntered into the hall with Roger, the young messenger he'd sent to Henry, grinning as he led the lad to Weston. It was odd, but of a sudden Weston felt a sense of unease when he should feel elated that he would finally be rid of the vixen.

With trembling hands, young Roger handed Weston the rolled parchment bearing Henry's seal, and Weston accepted the missive, dismissing the messenger with a brisk wave of his hand. He was baffled when the youth nigh fled from the room, and he eyed the retreating form before him with censure.

Turning to Michel, he inquired casually, "And whither have you been?" But Michel only cocked a brow in response, displaying his most devious smile as he did, and Weston recognized it immediately as Michel's sated smile. "Never mind, I know what you've been about ... with half the castle wenches no doubt." The reproach was given lightly, and Weston smiled inwardly, somehow soothed by the knowledge that Michel had not been with Chrestien.

Carefully, so as not to damage the delicate parchment, Weston broke the seal. He went about the procedure leisurely, confident of the message enclosed. He knew Henry well, could predict easily what his king would do, so there was no hurry to know what news it conveyed. A flick of his wrist righted the parchment enough to read from it, and as he read the dictum, his jaw dropped, reflecting his shock.

It took a moment to regain his composure, and when he did, his jaw turned taut—a reflex which easily gave away his anger—and his eyes narrowed savagely as he waved the parchment before Michel's face. "Damn it all to hell! Have you aught to do with this, Michel?"

Weston kept his tone low, but Michel knew it to be the calm before the storm. Therefore, not knowing what the letter contained ... and recalling his own letter to Henry, he couldn't very well reply, so he stood silent, watching Weston's every action.

When it was obvious there was no answer forthcoming, Weston shoved the letter into Michel's hand and turned toward the tower steps. Damn it! Damn her! He would go to her chamber this very minute ... tell her the news ... and assure her that the deed would not come to pass. Surely, Henry had misunderstood!

Michel opened the letter then, and initially his expression mirrored that of Weston's, but that was soon replaced by a flood of other emotions: first, relief that Chrestien was not to be cloistered; second, jealousy, because she was not bestowed on him; and again relief that it was Weston who would wed her.

The mandate stated simply that Weston and Chrestien were to wed at once and send proof of the union to Henry. There was no further explanation beyond that. Briefly, Michel wondered whether his letter had influenced the king's decision, but then he quickly discarded the notion. Henry would not make a decree such as this lightly, knowing it would incur Weston's anger— not that Henry would be overly alarmed by it, for he knew he had a loyal servant in Weston. But when the Silver Wolf was unhappy, his concentration suffered, thereby making his battle skills falter, and Henry had further need of Weston's services.

Too, Michel had not asked that Chrestien be given to Weston, nor did he have that right. Nay, Henry would have another reason for this edict. And if the truth be known, if anyone could care for her, 'twas Weston, though Weston was like to pretend he was unaffected by Chrestien. Nonetheless, whether Weston realized it yet or nay, he was as moved by her as the rest. It did not escape Michel the way his friend's gaze followed the lady Chrestien wheresoever she went—nor did it go unobserved by anyone else.

Chrestien was startled by the chamber door bursting open—even more so to see Weston standing in the doorway, his massive form blocking the exit from the chamber completely. It seemed his eyes were as turbulent as a summer storm, and she had no care to discover the reason for his anger. Instinct told her that she'd best guard herself well, and her own eyes scanned the room for a weapon of defense. She blanched when she realized there was none within reach.

"What are you doing in my bedchamber ... *unbidden*." She emphasized the last word acidly, letting him know her displeasure over his intrusion. She possessed in her hand naught but a wooden comb ... and what could she do with such a thing? Pierce his flesh with it? Nay, 'twould not do. She stood squarely, in the middle of her chamber, deliberating the possible courses of action. Did she move too quickly toward the bed to get her poniard ... well, he would surely pounce on her then. But did she move toward it slowly, keeping his mind filled with her words ... mayhap then she could reach it.

She moved back a few paces, slowly inching toward the canopied bed as he stepped toward her. "My lord, I have asked why you are hither!" The loathing in his eyes was more than apparent, and oddly, it pained her. Her heart racing madly, she moved backward too quickly and fell upon the bed that had crept up behind her, her bedrobe flying open. She gasped as his gaze settled on her exposed breast, but she made no move to cover herself, so stunned was she by his dark look.

Weston could not remove his eyes from her breasts. Yea, he'd come to tell her of Henry's mandate ... to assure her 'twould never be—but of a sudden he had a change of heart. If a man must take a wife, then this one was as good as any ... and he would indeed take her to Caen—wed her this very night! After all, Henry would have good reason to issue such an edict. What his reasons were, Weston could not fathom ... and it surprised him that Henry had not explained. But Henry had reason for all that he did, and rarely issued an edict without good cause, so Weston would comply.

A few long strides brought Weston before the bed, and without a word he stooped to open one of the wooden coffers. Noting with rancor that she did naught to cover her nakedness, he took from the chest the first garment his fingers encountered, a white linen chainse, and threw it to her distastefully. When it seemed the wide-eyed Chrestien would make no move to gather it, he took it upon himself to dress her.

Chrestien did not realize his intent until his powerful hands had encircled her dainty wrists. "Nay! You will not ... you will not!" she screamed and continued fighting him the only way she knew how. Without her hands, she had use only of her body, and she squirmed and bucked against his firm embrace. Soon, Weston was exhausted with her efforts, and he put the weight of his own body over hers to cease her struggles.

It was the wrong thing to do, he realized much too late. Her body bucking against his did naught but to inflame his loins, and he closed his eyes against the feel of her beneath him. The muscles in his jaw twitched as he strained to control his rising need, as well as his anger.

"I would, and I will, demoiselle. Now hold still!" Chrestien nodded her acquiescence, but when Weston lifted himself from her stilled body, she immediately began her struggles anew, and he nigh ripped the bedgown from her in his exasperation. She was not making this easy for him. Hell, he was only a man after all!

"Nay, nay!" Her panicked screams became wails as she gave in to hysterics for the first time in her life. There was little she could do against his obvious strength, but if he was going to deflower her, by God, she would not give in to him easily. He would need fight to take what was hers alone to give, and she vowed to herself she would never willingly give her maidenhood to this . . . this blackguard.

Finally, Weston was able to pin her hands above her head, and her lower body was stilled when he sat upon her, restraining her easily between his heavy limbs. Chrestien's stomach became unsettled. Her obvious disadvantage gave her a sick, hopeless feeling as it dawned on her that alone she was no match for his great strength. Overwhelmed by the realization, she screamed again—a scream to wake the dead—realizing bro-

kenly that no one would come. Who would risk
Weston's wrath? No one, she concluded.

His intention was to stop her hysterical wails,
but hovering near inches from her, he lost track of
his thoughts. Her golden hair, though but shoulder length, fell in silky curls to frame her face. Her
lips were rosy and full ... and they seemed to
beckon to him.

The sweet, heady fragrance of roses drifted to
his nostrils. Briefly, he wondered whether it was
the white rose he'd sniffed in the garden, or
whether it had been Chrestien. 'Twas near impossible to differentiate the two. Reflexively, he leaned
closer to brush her lips with his own. The scent of
her was intoxicating, muddling his thoughts. The
softness of her lips invited him ... teased him ...
and he could feel her responding by opening to
his gentle pressure. It was more than a shock to
him when her teeth bit down upon his lip.

"Damn you, you bitch!" His right hand came up
to inspect his throbbing lip, making certain that
there was no bleeding, while his left hand kept her
yet pinned to the bed, arms secured above her
head. His fingers squeezed her wrists without
mercy, as he gathered the chainse into his free
hand, and with an effort he spread the filmy linen
over her, nigh tearing the cloth as he shoved it
over her head.

He intended to dress her! Chrestien was so relieved that he was not going to defile her that she
remained still while he smoothed the material
over her body. Her relief was short-lived, however,
because when he dragged her unceremoniously
through the chamber door, she fought panic anew.

It didn't take a wise man to know that his intent boded her no good. Freeing herself, she dropped to the floor and kicked with a vengeance.

His voice was low and his eyes narrowed as he spoke. "Get yourself up, demoiselle." Damn her! Seeing her lying on the floor with her legs exposed to him made him want to grab hold of her and take her back to her bed. Never mind that he would sustain major injuries from her thrashing legs in the venture!

"I'll not, my lord. Not until you tell me whither you would take me." She gasped with horror as he grabbed her and hoisted her over his shoulder, exposing her thighs to all who would see. Balling her fists, she beat upon his back until her hands hurt. "You . . . you baseborn . . . insufferable lout. . . . You swine . . . savage . . . unhand me." She punctuated her expletives with a slam of her fists on the middle of his back, then shut her eyes tightly to stop the flow of tears. "Whither are you taking me?" she pleaded.

"To Caen." It was no lie, though the ultimate destination was no longer *La Trinite* but *St. Etienne* instead. He would tell her no more . . . and with a little luck she would not realize his intent until they were standing before the priest. 'Twould not matter whether she gave her consent once he showed the holy man the mandate bearing Henry's seal.

Chrestien let out an audible sigh of relief and visibly relaxed. "I'd go willingly, my lord," she informed him, as if she had a choice. "You need not carry me like so much baggage." Weston acknowledged the arrogantly given request with a grunt and let her down. Keeping a firm hold on her left wrist, he carefully led her down the steep stone staircase, never allowing more than a foot-long distance between them.

Chrestien was so relieved to be on her feet again that she did not complain about his ruthless hold on her arm. Nor did she remember that she was clad in but a thin undergarment. Her back straight, shoulders squared in an attempt to salvage her dignity, she walked proudly before him, wincing to herself when he pulled her arm too roughly.

Weston on the other hand was acutely aware of her lack of dress. With the aid of the torchlight, he could see the curves of her body clearly through her thin chainse. That she did not complain about her lack of dress did naught but secure his belief that she was unpure, and he thought it fitting that she would be wed in such a telling state.

It was not until Chrestien was seated upon his black destrier with Weston's warm body burning her flesh, the chill wind biting into her nigh bare skin, that it dawned on her. Her mind had been so full of Weston that she'd unbelievably forgotten what she wore—or rather what she did not wear.

"My lord, I cannot go to the abbey so scantily dressed."

Weston was silent as he listened to her musical voice. Her head was resting just below his chin, and it was all he could do to keep from placing his lips upon the silky curls of her crown. The moonlight shone into its waves, giving her an almost ethereal glow, and of a sudden he needed to feel the silky strands against his lips—couldn't think straight until he tasted of the gold-silver threads. Reflexively, he drew a few strands onto his lips, though cautiously, lest she know what he was about. He couldn't have her thinking she possessed some control over him, could he now?

The smell of her was near intoxicating and he could feel the heat of his need surge within him yet again, quickening his breath, filling his braies. He should have taken the time to ease the pain in his groin when he'd had her in her chamber, for he didn't know how far he could ride with her rubbing her nigh bare backside against his already strained breeches. In an effort to shield her from the cold and himself from her touch, he removed his mantle and placed it about her shoulders, roughly, because 'twas her fault he burned yet again.

"My cloak is all you shall need." His statement brooked no argument, and Chrestien did not balk. 'Twas true that once she was cloistered she would have no need of her former clothing. She would be given the shapeless nun's garb to don. Still, she could not bear the thought of confronting the abbess without proper dress.

With each hour spent in his embrace, Chrestien's anger melted considerably. How could she hate him when his touch was so gentle? Moreover 'twas his disdain for her that had spurred her anger toward him to begin with—that is if she disregarded the fact that he'd wounded Aubert ... and that he'd treated her shabbily when he thought her a man. But of course, did she not disregard thus, then she would have to own some fault of her own . . . for she'd stabbed him once . . . and attacked him as well! Then, of course, she had lied to him . . . and attacked John and Ned. She was certainly in no mood to accept so much culpability.

Twice he pulled his cloak about her to shield her from the chilly night air, and each time he'd clutched the white ermine in his fist just below her breast, giving her a firm but gentle embrace. To Chrestien's way of thinking, that was not the gesture of one who was repulsed by her—of that she was certain, and she felt nigh dizzy from the unknowing affection he lavished upon her.

She knew he had no idea what he was about, for she'd not forgotten his bitter words so soon, and neither would he. His breath was very near her left ear, sending a chill down her spine. In spite of the wind, she knew it was he that caused the chill, for his body kept her overly warm. Too, it was a different kind of chill . . . one she was not familiar with. It began as a heat in the innermost part of her and radiated to her outer limbs, making her sensitive to the feel of his heated skin, and covering his own skin with gooseflesh. He nuzzled his face in her hair, and she shivered again at the gentleness of his touch.

They rode for what seemed an eternity and it was dawn when they arrived at a hostelry. Dismounting, Weston pulled the mantle about Chrestien to cover her with the rich blue velvet. "Remain thus," he warned. "I would return in but a moment." His voice was husky as he stared at her, and his eyes set a dark silky blue.

He started to leave, but noted that her chainse was visible—even with his heavy mantle draped over her—and he frowned as he returned to clasp the mantle together in front of her nigh exposed breast. Giving her his most exasperated look, he sighed and took her into his arms. "You'll say naught, Chrestien—and you'll keep yourself covered. Do you heed?"

She nodded once that she would. "Can you not speak to acknowledge what I say?"

"But you told me not to," she defended.

"Yea, but I'd meant ... ah, never mind, Chrestien."

"But did you not tell me ..."

"Yea."

"Very well, then I said I would not ... and I shall not."

"Cease, Chrestien." He didn't care to take her inside dressed as she was for everyone to ogle, and he hated to leave her so vulnerable. Damn her! He would not have needed to stop at all if he'd not left Lontaine so ill prepared. Never would he have done so had she not riled him so. But what was done was done, and no matter the kind of woman she was, he could not make her bed down upon the bare ground this eve. She was gentle born after all, and they would have need of blankets and other supplies.

Upon entering the inn, Chrestien was immediately self-conscious about her state of dress, for the room harbored a horde of men ... from every station of life. There were peasants and noble men alike spread about the fetid tavern, partaking of the spirits.

Weston singled out the innkeeper straightaway, and gently pulling Chrestien behind him, he made his way to the burly-looking man. "I'd purchase goods from you, auld man."

The innkeeper's eyes widened, and his voice gave away his fear. "Yea, sir, what would you have of me?" Letting loose of Chrestien's arm, Weston pulled the innkeeper aside, and the hefty old man scurried to do his bidding, nearly tumbling over himself in his haste.

When the innkeeper returned, his arms were loaded with goods, and Weston removed the bundle from him, handing him a few coins in return. Then, without a word, Weston grabbed Chrestien's wrist again and nigh dragged her from the tavern, angry that she would stand there so calmly while everyone ogled her.

"You need not abuse me, you know."

His eyes became hooded as she spoke, and he gifted her with his most languorous smile. "I'd give you the gentleness you seek ere long, Chrestien, and I'd warrant you'll have naught to complain of then."

Chrestien's eyes widened in response to his cryptic remark, and the color drained from her face. But at the same time, a shiver of anticipation coursed down her spine, regardless that she had no inkling of what he meant.

As they started away, she noted with a smile

the gentleness with which he commanded the midnight-colored gelding, for with but light pressure from Weston's thighs, the animal responded to his every command. It was in that same manner he commanded his men—with a silent authority.

He seemed able to relay his every want without a single word, and 'twas this knowledge that had kept her tongue tied ever since they'd departed Lontaine. Yea, few words were spoken between them, but the less he was aware of her weakness to him the better! And she was certain he was as adept at reading the mind as he was at imparting his silent commands. His face was always so carefully masked that she could not even begin to know what was in his mind. Too, she was never so certain of her own mind any longer—that it would keep its secrets. So yea, she would keep silent, and mayhap that way she could keep him in the dark for a change.

The sun rose high and fell again. When Chrestien finally slumped against Weston's arm, he knew she was asleep, but he was only slightly amazed that fatigue had taken so long to claim her. Were there one thing he would need give her credit for, 'twas that she did indeed have spirit.

Not once did she balk after he gave her his mantle—not even to complain of her weariness— and he had to admire her for her endurance. He'd not known many women who would last so long in the saddle. Had he not seen her own sister burst into tears within only minutes of knowing him? Granted, he had abused her by throwing her into his bathwater. But had not Chrestien endured over thrice as much? Yea, she did have spirit, he determined with a conclusive nod to himself.

They rode until dusk and only when exhaustion was about to claim him did Weston make camp for the night. Dismounting, he took Chrestien into his arms, laying her over his shoulder gingerly, before setting her feet to the ground. She stood, legs wobbling as she sleepily buried her face in his chest. Somehow, he managed to lay out a blanket, and when he was finished, he set her upon it carefully, so as not to wake her. Then he covered her with his heavy mantle. The second blanket he used to cover himself with, making certain to stay a goodly distance away from Chrestien.

Sleep would not come easily with her so near him, and he lay for the longest time watching the sun complete its descent. When his stomach growled, he recalled the bit of foodstuff in his saddlebag, but decided against retrieving it just yet. He would wait until Chrestien awoke ere he partook of it.

She'd eaten naught but a bit of bread and broken meat he'd purchased at the hostelry since the evening meal at Lontaine, and he would not eat himself until she could join him. Briefly, he wondered why it mattered to him, but the answer was not forthcoming, so he closed his eyes against the chill of the wind and attempted to avail himself of the much needed respite.

A burst of chill wind crept into his bones, and he repositioned his blanket. Then, looking to Chrestien, he found her shivering beneath his mantle, so he carefully slipped his arm about her waist, drawing her near to him, and then he placed his blanket over her. Without thinking, he buried his face in her hair, only to find that the heavenly fragrance of it kept him miserably awake. Irritably, he raised the mantle to lay it between them ere he slipped into a desperate slumber.

Chapter 9

She was having the most wonderful dream. Weston was holding her and caressing her with his eyes. There were no looks of contempt while she was within his arms. The heat of his gaze was upon her, beckoning, and unwittingly she moved toward the warmth of his body.

Weston was awakened by a throbbing in his loins. The night was black now and he could see naught, for it was a near-moonless night. But he had no need for the light to know that Chrestien's bottom was resting in the crook of his thighs.

Sleepily, she wiggled her rump, and though Weston knew it to be an involuntary motion, the silky massage against his already heated groin sent fire surging through his veins. She wiggled again, and he began to suspect that she did it apurpose, so he stilled her hip with his hand, hoping that she would reveal her awakened state to him.

When she made no move to continue, he concluded by her smooth even breath that she was indeed asleep. His fingers ached to wander, and he could feel the softness of her ivory skin beneath the thin material of her garment. Surely, she would not awaken were he to slide his hand very lightly across the smoothness of her thigh, he reasoned. But before he'd even concluded the thought, he found his hands skipping across her legs ... and then her buttocks, commending the satiny feel of her skin to his memory.

She wiggled again and his breath stilled as he fought the desire to take her hither and now. 'Twas not as if she were virgin. If she were, her body would not seek his so instinctively—even while she slept! It seemed the curve of her body fit too neatly into his, conforming to his manhood almost as if it were where she belonged.

Mindless with need, his hand slid across the material of her chainse, coming to rest under the swell of her breast, and he closed his eyes to regain some of the control he felt waning with every touch of her ... only his hands betrayed his will, and while his mind recounted the reasons he should leave her be, his thumb inched determinedly to the crest of her bosom. That it reacted immediately to his touch was all the more stimulating.

She awoke with a start to feel his hand upon her breasts, and she lay very still while he caressed them at his leisure. Some part of her wanted to cry out for him to cease—shout that what he did was improper—but he'd awakened a dormant desire within her and she could not bring herself to say the words. Then again, she could not consent to his boldness, so she kept silent and let him believe her asleep. It could not hurt to let him continue but a while. He would explore ... and she would discover more about this elusive feeling ... and then he would cease—none the wiser.

She closed her eyes as he gently squeezed the nipple between his fingers, and she ran her tongue over lips gone suddenly dry. She concentrated, fighting desperately to keep her breath even and shallow, but against her will her breathing quickened and her heart beat faster—and louder! She could not help the cry that escaped her lips when his hand slid under the chainse and came to rest in the valley between her thighs.

Realizing she was awake gave his hands new purpose and he gave his touch slightly more pressure as they slid knowingly across her abdomen, then back down to her mound of golden curls, expertly removing any thought of resistance she could have uttered.

It seemed as though a wave of heat washed over the lower half of her body, giving it an unbearable warmth—an ache almost. She knew if she didn't stop him now, she would reach a point of no return.

"Nay, do not." Her whispered plea was without genuine meaning, and her forged refusal was not lost to Weston. He knew she desired him to continue, and he did. "Nay." There was a little more force to her protest this time, yet not enough to convince Weston, and he turned her body, almost roughly, to face him.

He lifted her chainse to expose her, and his lips moved to her breasts as a predator would to its prey. She tried to speak again, but the warm gentle feeling of his mouth upon her breasts silenced her protest, save for the low moan that escaped her

lips—though she wasn't at all certain it was a
moan of protest. She didn't know what it was she
wanted, but the need was there and she could not
deny it.

"You will not cease, then?" She wasn't certain if
the question was meant to stop him or to assure
herself that he would finish what he'd begun.

He brought his face near inches from hers, his
mind drugged by the scent of her now. "Nay, I
will not . . . but 'tis not as though I dishonor you,
is it? 'Tis not as though 'tis your first time," he
said silkily. He was merely vocalizing his
thoughts. As the sensual haze cleared from her
mind, it dawned on her what he was saying and
it fired her with a different fire—that of anger.

Her hand found its mark in the darkness, and
he reared back at the sting of her slap, fingering
his cheek where the blow was issued. At first he
was confused by her action, then thinking she'd
planned his seduction from the start he decided to
finish what he'd begun.

Pinning her hands above her head, he held them
firmly within a single powerful fist. With sturdy
pressure, he parted her thighs. After all, she would
be his wife soon and she would learn her place!

Chrestien fought him wildly, bucking against his
great weight upon her, but Weston succeeded in
securing her legs and positioning himself between
her thighs. Bringing his free hand to her hair, he
grasped a lock of it roughly, entwining it about his
fist and pulling until the pain of it forced her to
cease her struggles. In warning, he drew it again,
holding it firmly, and she arched her head back-

ward to lessen the pain, giving him access to her breasts, which were thrust boldly at him now.

His lips came to them, warming the flesh there and making her quiver with new desire. He blazed a trail of kisses along the base of her throat, drinking of the sweetness of her, killing her will to fight him.

Having stilled her sufficiently, his fingers sought the telltale wetness, and finding it, his knees widened the gap between her thighs. Slowly, he entered the heat, closing his eyes against the exquisite feel of her, his body trembling over the control he was losing ... and then he felt it—the barrier that separated the girl from the woman ... and she was possessed of it?

Resisting the will of his traitorous body, he withdrew, feeling as though scorched by an inner fire. Pangs of remorse surged through him. She was virgin, and he would not take her maidenhood from her until he was her rightful husband.

He had withdrawn before breaking her delicate maidenhead, for though he could not quell his desire, a wall of protectiveness rose up before him like an impenetrable fortress to keep away his burning lust. The taint of his own birth hovered over him, giving him the will to suppress his overwhelming desire. It was rare enough that a virtuous woman could be found and he would not defile her—or take the chance that his child be conceived on the wrong side of the sheets, when she would be his ere long.

Of a sudden, all the anger he'd felt for her receded, replaced by a powerful urge to shield her from all who would harm her. He said naught to her. He would not insult her further by telling her that he thought her to be dishonored already, but what he did not realize was that she had already come to that very conclusion—and that more than the shame of her wantonness brought stinging tears to her eyes.

Hearing her muffled cries, he swept her into his arms, holding her close to him, and to Chrestien's consternation, she welcomed his embrace wholly. Sobbing from the depths of her heart, she allowed Weston to rock her. After a long moment he whispered into her ear, "I shall make it right." But Chrestien was no longer aware of his words, for sleep had taken her into the netherworld, where nightmares plagued her throughout the night.

Weston watched while Chrestien whimpered in her sleep, her breath catching pitifully every little while, and a whirl of emotions whisked through him all at once. He could not sleep for the confusion it brought him.

At first light, he propped himself upon an elbow to stare into Chrestien's sleeping face. With her eyes closed, her thick lashes were spread like strands of silk upon her rosy cheeks. Her mouth was so lush and ripe, and of a sudden he remembered that he had not even kissed her, and it sickened him that he would have taken her without a single show of tenderness.

He rarely kissed the women he slept with, preferring to keep the lovemaking simple and to the point. After all, 'twas naught but a means to satisfy his body, and never had he felt the urge to shower adoring kisses upon a lady friend. But this one ... she was different. He recalled having her pinned to her bed at Lontaine, and wanting desperately to taste of her—even though he had thought her defiled . . . he had wanted to kiss her even then.

Suddenly angry with himself, he rose and prepared the horse for the day's ride. When Chrestien awoke and readied herself, he placed her upon his destrier, taking great care not to look into those emerald eyes of hers for fear that he would see the loathing there.

Chrestien watched him, wanting desperately for him to say aught that would tell her he cared—if only a little—but he said naught and kept his eyes averted. Surely, he thought her a harlot.

When Weston finished securing the saddlebags, he finally glanced up at her. Tenderness had calmed the raging storm in his eyes, but Chrestien did not notice, for she turned her face as if seared by his gaze. She could not bear to look at him now and have him know what was in her heart.

His power over her was frightening, and she'd never been affected so by a man in all her life. Of course, she'd known few men, and mayhap that was why Papa had wanted her to be cloistered. Could it be she would react this way toward any man . . . in such a wanton fashion?

Papa had known she would not make a good wife, and must have also known that she would not be able to keep her virtue in the arms of a man. That thought brought a profusion of blushes to her cheeks, as she realized that her father would know of her wantonness. He'd raised her and knew her well—'twas surely why he'd kept her hidden. He didn't have faith in her.

An hour from the monastery, Weston stopped in the shelter of the woods and dismounted. Retrieving a pile of material from the burlap sack he'd placed in his saddlebags, he unfolded it to reveal a modest sendal bliaut—the muted rose color was accentuated by a border of ivory thread.

" 'Tis for me?" She was shocked. "But how—?"

His voice was low with contrition as he told her. "I bought it from a nobleman's wife at the inn. Do you favor it?"

Not able to mask the joy she felt, she nigh cried. " 'Tis beautiful . . . and 'tis for me?" she repeated, dumfounded.

Weston's remorse was eased somewhat when he noted Chrestien's radiant smile. Taking in the fullness of her lips and the gleaming whiteness of her teeth, he conceded. "Yea, I'd not have you going to your wedding in your undergarment." He'd decided it was best to tell her of the mandate. 'Twould neither be fair nor kind to let her discover it at the altar.

"My wedding, my lord? I do not understand . . . you were to take me to Caen?"

"And I shall, but not to cloister you at La Trinite, Chrestien. We go instead to St. Etienne, where I would wed you." He thought he saw a hint of a smile in her eyes, though her lips did not follow suit, and she did not protest at all, so he would leave it at that. He would not tell her it had been Henry's desire that they wed, for she was obviously not displeased, albeit a little bewildered.

Chrestien's heart skipped its normal beat. For some reason she felt strangely elated. She had expected him just to drop her at the abbey, soiled by his violation of her body. But instead he offered her marriage? At any rate she would not balk at his generous offer, because she could not dishonor the Church by entering the priory unfit. His reasons? She could not discern, for she understood naught about men. It was no little surprise that Weston had bought her the gown. And now this— who could figure it?

"You would wed with me, my lord?"

Her surprise amused him and he chuckled huskily. "Yea, I would wed you, Chrestien."

"But you know naught about me, my lord," she protested lamely.

"I know enough." His blue eyes danced with a sudden merriment, and she nodded her head in acquiescence, for 'twas true that marriages were oft arranged between complete strangers. Although Weston could surely choose another more fitting to be his bride. Why her? But then, she reasoned, he had taken her virginity, and surely he was feeling a little guilty about that?

Her curiosity moved to other matters. "And whither shall we live? Shall we live at Lontaine? May we go to Montagneaux to inform my sister? 'Tis not far from here, my lord." There was so much to know that she was all at once overwhelmed by it all.

Weston could only smile at her questions as he handed her the gown. "We'll discuss it later," he promised, smiling as he watched her take the garment from his outstretched hand. Then she disappeared into the brush, making her way into the dense tangle as regally as would a queen.

Only weeks ago Chrestien would have scoffed

at the idea of marriage—a fate worse than death! And she would have avoided it at all costs. Now? Well, after seeing Adelaine's beautiful wedding, she'd had all manner of regrets over her own future. And of a sudden it was what she wanted most: children, a home of her own, the love of a man.

Nay, she wasn't fool enough to believe Weston loved her yet, but surely he did want her. Did he not show her gentleness last eve? And guilty conscience or nay, he would not have needed to wed with her over her lost maidenhead. Love would come with time, she decided. He'd held her tenderly in his arms for long hours and comforted her? True, he was the author of her misery, but she had let him go beyond a man's physical endurance level. She never should have let him play with her body . . . and 'twas as much her fault as it was his. Then he had comforted her when it was over.

As she drew the rose-colored bliaut over her head, her mind flew back to the intimate moments spent with Weston. She had shamefully enjoyed aught he had done to her, but somehow she'd felt so unfulfilled. Was that all there was to it? Was that the way it was then? Confusion reeled her senses, until she could think on it no longer, and she waved her hand as if to swat away the pestering thoughts.

When she came from behind the trees, Weston's eyes ignited with passion. Tiny flames flickered within them, until it seemed there was a roaring blue fire behind the smoke of his eyes. Somehow, he didn't remember the gown being so lovely. It seemed to be enhanced by her beauty rather than the other way 'round. Moreover, the color of the gown had seemed indistinct before . . . now it was clearly the color of a pink rose—the same shade as her lips and her cheeks.

He marveled that her eyes never lost their power to bring a man to his knees. 'Twas like losing oneself in a maelstrom. They seemed to promise mystery and intrigue . . . and at the same time they were ethereal and pure.

Why had it taken so long for him to see the truth? That she was but a selfless maiden . . . not the selfish vixen he had believed. Then again, he had never met a selfless maiden. Even now, it was hard for him truly to trust his heart . . . and until he could be certain . . .

Chrestien sensed that he was pleased, but his face showed not a trace of emotion, save for the eyes—they were smoldering with open desire. Jesu, but they were dominating! She lowered her eyes to escape his knowing gaze, but could yet sense his scrutiny of her.

Chrestien's lashes fluttered to her cheeks, and again he was awash with desire. Reflexively, he closed the distance between them, his arms coming around to enfold her dainty waist.

Her eyes flew open to meet his and this time, though she desperately wanted to turn away to hide her confused emotions, she kept her eyes pasted to his. Green eyes fused with blue, the aqua flame climbing higher, higher, until the intensity of the moment nigh consumed them both. Without warning his lips covered hers hungrily, and in that moment Chrestien knew she was his to do with as he would.

She tasted just as he thought she would—sweet and warm, like honey-spiced cream—and his tongue flicked across the smoothness of her lips, willing them to part. Chrestien wasn't certain what he wanted her to do, and initially confusion prompted her to close her lips tightly, rousing a throaty chuckle from Weston. Her bewilderment pleased him, aroused him further, and the gentle pressure he exerted made her lips part softly. Immediately, his kiss deepened, his possession nigh frenzied as he took the part of her she'd willingly given him.

She was startled by his invasion of her person. When she came to her senses, she managed to push him away, and was thoroughly confused by the languorous smile he displayed. She turned her face from him, but could not keep her gaze from returning to him as she lifted her chin defiantly, challenging him.

Curiously, his only reaction was to grin until it seemed he would burst out laughing. But he did not break into fits of laughter, instead he lifted a challenging brow and watched the changing emotions that registered upon Chrestien's face.

Sweet Mary, but he was arrogant! she decided, as she turned her back to him and started to mount. No sooner had she lifted her foot to the stirrup than she found herself raised into the air as he lifted her by bent elbows nigh effortlessly.

For a moment, before he placed her into the saddle, she could feel the heat of his breath upon the back of her neck, and it sent a chill down her spine. Sweet Jesu! What did he do to her soul? It was as if every gaze, every touch, every movement he made sent her senses into turmoil. Never had she felt such a thing. It was as though her body betrayed her at his slightest touch—no matter how innocent the contact might be.

When they were both mounted, Weston encircled her waist with a long sinewy arm, holding her firmly against his solid chest, and his whispered words in her ear nigh made her shiver. "You have naught to fear of me, Chrestien." Having imparted that bit of news, he placed a firm but gentle kiss upon the back of her head and moved to cradle his cheek upon her crown.

God's Bones, but how did this happen? He had been prepared to hate her ... or had he? He reflected back to the first time he'd truly seen her ... in the tub. He'd left Lontaine in a rage—not because he was angry with her ... but if he could be honest with himself, 'twas because of an unexplained yearning he'd felt for her ... even then.

At Montagneaux, he could hardly keep from comparing the two sisters, and without having known Chrestien he'd yet felt a bond with her— 'twas as if he knew her ... yet did not know her. She was an enchantress and Weston wasn't certain whether she would destroy him or ... But yea, he knew ... he knew.... She was an angel sent to claim his heart. Had she done that? Yea, she had. But when? Mayhap when she'd floated into the hall last eve, dressed so prettily, coming into the room almost as if on gilded wings. Or mayhap it was in the garden when he could not see her ...

only feel her heady sweet presence ... hear her daring spirit.

He chuckled to himself as he thought of his lovesick knights at Lontaine. How many of them had asked themselves these very same questions? The obvious answer brought another chuckle, then a frown, as a powerful wave of protectiveness came over him. In that instant he knew he would kill any man who touched her. She was his! Moreover, he vowed he would keep her away from men altogether. Her effect on them was much too disconcerting. Had she not come close to turning him into a mindless, covetous fool? Yea, whether he was willing to own the truth of it or nay, she had ... nigh.

"You have not said whither we would live, my lord." They had started on the wrong foot and she would right it. True, 'twould take more than mere conversation. But she needed to show him there was another side to her. He made no move to answer and she turned to see what held his attention.

He was startled to see her emerald eyes watching him so intently, and he thought he noted expectation in them. "Did you say something, Chrestien?"

His lack of attention irritated her but she would keep her temper subdued ... at least for the duration of the journey to Caen. "I asked whither we would live, my lord."

"I have two estates; you may have your choice," he told her indifferently.

"Then you take me there soon? I cannot choose without having seen them."

"Montfort and Belvedoune are so dissimilar, 'twill not be a difficult task to choose. Montfort is near the Scottish border . . . on England's side of the Tweed." His tone suggested that no other explanation was necessary. "While Belvedoune is in the midland near Cambridge. 'Tis simply a matter of taste." 'Twas more a matter of character, he thought to himself. He loved the climate and terrain of northern England, but was certain a woman would have no part of its wildness. Chrestien would be more comfortable at Belvedoune and he was sure that would be her choice. He would have preferred Montfort but at least he would be closer to Henry at Belvedoune.

"You do not have holdings in Normandy?"

"Nay, I do not."

She would have preferred to be near Adelaine, but though she'd never stepped foot in England she'd heard much of the filth that is London and she preferred to stay clear of it. On the other hand, though she'd heard little of the north lands, what she did know was intriguing—she would love the brisk air and virgin land. Her choice would be Montfort . . . though she would not tell him quite yet. She would wait to know his preference, for never would she force him to make his home where his heart did not lie.

"Tell me about Belvedoune, my lord." Her inquiry was sweetly given, veiling the sudden repulsion she felt for the name. She would inquire of it first so he would not think her mind set on Montfort until she made her decision known.

" 'Tis not much to speak of," he told her coolly,

an almost bored tone to his voice. " 'Tis merely my brother's leftovers."

"And Montfort?" She turned to him in time to catch the wistful look in his very blue eyes.

"Montfort?" He looked away from Chrestien, attempting to mask the longing he felt for his home. " 'Tis wild terrain, uncut ... unyielding. 'Tis not the place for a wellborn lady." It was his way of making her decision a little easier.

Irritation swelled her chest until she was grinding her teeth wrathfully. "How so, my lord?" She would not tell him that she could hunt and ride with the best! Nay, not even that she craved the brisk wind in her face and the rolling countryside at her heels, nay! She would let him state his reasons, and wait for the moment when she would prove herself to him. He'd not believe it otherwise.

"I have just told you why, Chrestien." He was quickly growing annoyed by her interrogation, and the veiled sarcasm in her voice was duly noted.

"Tell me again, my lord."

His sigh was laden with exasperation. " 'Tis too cold ... too wild ... and too near the Scottish marches—forever there is strife near those borders."

Jesu! Was that the way of it, then? "Think you I have never dealt with cold, or that Normandy is free of strife? Nay, my lord. I am no stranger to aught that you mention. You would have me instead wallowing in the filth that is London?"

Weston did not answer, but a smile curved his lips. God's Truth, but the woman was a mystery. He'd given her the perfect opportunity to refuse

Montfort's wildness, and she had taken it as a challenge. He knew she would be miserable in the north, but he could not pass up the opportunity to show Chrestien her place. She would know who was her keeper! It did not occur to him that she would actually choose Montfort over Belvedoune. What woman would? The rugged north land was a man's land.

When Weston had first spied the adulterine fortress seated in the very heart of the wild, he'd thought it insane that anyone would live in such a place. With the river Tweed but a stone's throw away, and the raiding Scots beyond it, there was never a prolonged period of peace in those parts. Even Henry had debated its value. But fact was fact, and the small wooden palisade had been erected on English soil, so Henry had finally ordered it confiscated.

On second sight, Weston had fallen in love with the terrain, and Henry, knowing this—God knows how—had given the land to him. Thereafter, he'd spent the better part of a year planning the new masonry curtain walls now erected on the site. In the end, the decision to keep the fortress was a sound one, for Montfort now stood a proud, impenetrable stronghold over the troubled Scottish marches. He would give Chrestien but one more chance to refuse. "You would prefer Montfort, then?"

There were no doubts cloistered within her mind. "Yea, I would prefer Montfort," she told him haughtily, conveniently forgetting her earlier pledge to wait until she learned his preference. Jesu! Montfort would be her home whether he wished it or nay . . . and did he prefer Belvedoune, then so be it . . . he could have Belvedoune. It wasn't as if he loved her and couldn't bear to part from her side, she conceded. They would simply live apart, man and wife in name only. Of course, she would bear him heirs, but she would raise them at Montfort.

"Then Montfort it is," he asserted, trying to keep the laughter from his voice. "Montfort it is," he whispered to himself, more than pleased with the choice.

Chapter 10

The ceremony was over quickly as there was little need to celebrate with but the two of them present. The priest spoke the holy words, witnessed by the monks, then it was over and they were again in the saddle. The sobriety of the situation hung heavily in the atmosphere, mingling with the dark gray clouds overhead, their swollen bellies threatening to regurgitate their overflow. And it was not long after the couple left Caen that those clouds made good on their threat, drenching riders and animal in the tumultuous downpour.

The heavy feeling of despair had begun immediately upon entering the cathedral of St. Etienne. Its enormous rib-vaulted ceiling made Chrestien feel minuscule, unimportant . . . a prickle in Weston's side; so too did the many giant arcs—three tiers of them there were!

The rain went on for miles, sometimes slowing to a drizzle, but never ceasing, and Weston noted late in the afternoon that they were but a few miles from where he'd made camp the day he'd captured Chrestien. He made the decision to go to it, and his gelding struggled against the soft ground to do his bidding.

The forest floor was a carpet of muck, and Weston began to doubt his decision to make camp in the woods. But he pressed on and reached his destination within but a few more minutes. Reining in his destrier, he dismounted and aided Chrestien in doing the same. Then he led his wife and his horse through the thick underbrush and into the natural shelter.

A canopy of trees shielded the haven from the rain, and very little light pierced the foliage, giving the shelter an ethereal glow. Chrestien's eyes widened with wonder, and Weston thought she looked so like a little girl—a complete contrast from the vixen he'd thought her to be. Her wet hair hung in ringlets from her crown, and her cheeks were rosy against her ivory skin.

It was her wet gown that assured him she was no child. The sopping fabric hugged every curve of her body, and he noted that her nipples stood proud and erect against the now faded bliaut. His first task would be to remove her sodden clothing and warm her with dry blankets.

Taking two blankets from the saddlebag, he spread one upon the ground and dropped the other to lie on top of the first. Then he motioned for Chrestien to come to him.

Her teeth were clattering in her head and she thought any minute they would dislodge her brain, which seemed as saturated as her clothes. Taking tiny rigid steps, she made her way to Weston—her legs were near numb from the cold and she could walk no faster.

Weston frowned as he watched her amble to him. If he did not take the wet gown from her body soon, she would take ill. And at her slow pace, she would be within arm's length in another fortnight. Having made the decision to go to her, he took her into his arms and dropped her beside the blankets. When he'd removed the dripping gown, he set her gingerly upon the dry homespun coverlet he'd set out.

Her kid-leather slippers were ruined, she noted, as he removed them from her chilled feet. She was too numb to protest when he took off her chainse as well.

Weston's breath caught as he set greedy eyes upon her nude form. She was more beautiful than he'd remembered, and he reasoned that the soapy bathwater had hidden her better than he'd realized. Desire ignited within his loins, but he willed his mind to govern it while he placed a dry blanket about her shoulders.

He would not touch her this night. She was cold and miserable and he would wait until she could gift him with the fire that was between them last eve. "Are you recovered?" He prayed she was, because he couldn't bear to look upon her any longer and deny himself still.

Her teeth were yet chipping away in protest of the cold, but she nodded her head, assuring him that she was.

There was an extended silence between them as he listened to her teeth chattering, but when she started to shiver anew, he sighed and went to her, wrapping his arms about her. Instinctively, she buried her face in his chest, and he pulled her against him to cradle her within his arms, whispering softly into her wet hair. "Do you realize, Chrestien, this is the very spot whither we first met?"

She had not. Somehow it seemed so different. Raising her head from his embrace only slightly, she took a long look about her, concluding that she owed her lack of recognition to the occasion, because the shelter took on a very different air this time. Too, it had been a dark night. There had been no moon to light the night sky, and she had felt trapped in the devil's lair—for that was what Weston's tent had seemed ... the devil's lair. When she looked about her again, she realized she'd not seen a moon.

A shiver of recollection swept the length of her spine, clear to her soggy head, and then another as she realized that again tonight there would be no light, for they'd not brought candles. She thought to ask Weston to take her from the place, but when the sound of thunder violated her ears, she decided against it. She did not wish to travel during a storm.

"Somehow it seems different," she whispered finally, her teeth chattering as she spoke, and Weston frowned at the sound of her chipped speech. He let go of her then, realizing he could not warm her well enough in his wet garb, and he immediately sought to remove it. First came his boots; he kicked them off, tossing them to a corner of the blanket. "Our blanket sits on the very spot on which my tent was erected." He chuckled at her expression and rubbed his hands across the whiskers of his jaw, closing his eyes to focus upon the memory. "God's Teeth! I truly thought you a boy," he confessed with wonder.

" 'Twas the notion I'd hoped to impart. You cannot know how frightened I was you'd discover the truth," she admitted. "I thought you a fate worse than death."

" 'Twas not how you looked at me, Chrestien. In truth, I thought you a fairy you ogled me so thoroughly." He dropped his mantle, tunic, and gambeson onto a low-lying limb, and rose to his feet to undo his laces and cross-bands.

Chrestien's eyes widened, and her face immediately reddened. "I'd not meant to . . ."

Weston chuckled again as his breeches fell to the ground unhampered by the loosed cross-bands. He noted that Chrestien turned her head, cheeks suffused with blushes to see him unclothed, and she hid coyly behind the blanket she held. Without really knowing why, he took it from her, forcing her to acknowledge him, while he stood to straighten it.

Chrestien's eyes widened in response to what was revealed before her. Sweet Mary! But she did not remember that from the first time. Yea, mayhap her eyes were playing tricks on her!

A slow arrogant smile curved Weston's lips as he watched Chrestien's reaction. 'Twas the response he'd hoped to gain from her, and he was certain now that she was completely innocent of all he had silently charged her with. She was his, and his alone. Sitting again upon the blanket, he pulled the coverlet about their nude bodies, seeking the warmth their wet garb could no longer give them.

Darkness fell quickly as he lay next to her, feeling her tremble through the blanket that covered them. He reached for her then, pulling her gently into his arms, rubbing her tenderly with his warmed hands. It did not escape his notice that her skin was like cool satin to the touch. She was so soft ... so supple beneath his war-roughened fingers. God's Bones, but he would not be able to control himself! But why should he? She was his wife now. Was she not?

His lips were warmed by her flesh as he placed a trail of scalding kisses along the back of her neck, and he knew that once again he would not stop himself. She was too delicious a morsel to be put aside this eve.

Again, she was nestled within the crook of his thigh, and he vowed that he would sleep with her this way always. 'Twas meant to be. Why else would it feel so exquisite?

Chrestien could not stop shivering, but she was cold no longer. In truth, she was afire with the touch of him. Their first night together had been shameful, but even so, the memory of his gentle touch lingered nigh painfully in her thoughts, and her body yearned for some unknown thing that she knew instinctively only he could give her.

Already her breasts were anticipating the caresses he'd given her last eve, and when he brought his warm fingers to the tips of them, she shivered in response. But no sooner did his fingertips alight there than her body craved his touch elsewhere.

His lips took the place of his branding fingers, suckling and probing the hardened nubs. It seemed he spent an eternity savoring one breast and then the other, until she nigh went mad from the intense pleasure it gave her. She wanted to scream—wanted to plead that he help her find a way out of the torturous state his will evoked. She wanted him to cease ... wanted him to go on ... in truth, she didn't know what she wanted. Was it possible to die from so much pleasure?

The fire that was growing in her belly was no longer exquisite but agonizing instead. It had grown so intense that she could barely endure it— tried to tell him so, but his name rolled from her parched lips instead.

Weston reveled in the sound of his name as it came off her tongue. He knew he brought her desire to near madness, but the sweet torture was his to endure as well. He traced one nipple with his knowing tongue, then dipped to the valley between her breasts, coming finally to her lips again—his tongue following the outline of them, exerting the most gentle pressure, until she opened to his tender probing.

He traced the shapes of her teeth, enjoying the feel of the tiny ridges against his tongue. When his tongue slid into her softly parted mouth, Chrestien daringly brought her tongue to meet his, equaling his passion without temperance. He groaned his pleasure.

She was vaguely aware of his hands gliding across her skin, stopping to play in her forbidden region, and she thought to tell him to cease, but as his fingers danced their magic dance, her protests died in her throat, replaced instead by tiny pleading whimpers. She wasn't certain what she wanted from him, only knew she would have it! Whatever it was, she would have it! God's Mercy, she would have it!

The night air was cold, belying the sweat that flowed from Weston's brow. He burned as if immersed in flames, and the sensual cries Chrestien gave increased his desire tenfold. But he was desperate to retain the control he would need to make her first time less painful. Parting her thighs tenderly, his hands trembled as they fought the urge to take her with the force of his passion, and his fingers reveled in the wetness that gave evidence to her pleasure.

He continued his gentle assault, lips covering her breasts, kissing them druggedly, lavishing them with his seductive teasing, then trailed to the white of her neck. He nibbled her lobe, causing a shiver to run rampant throughout her body, and she took his hair into her hands, pulling him away from the sensitive spot . . . toward her own lips.

Covering her mouth with his own, he hungrily thrust his tongue in a rhythm that he would soon mimic in lower regions, tasting and plundering with every frenzied stroke. Holding her close, he whispered huskily, "God, I need you, Chrestien . . . I can wait no longer . . . yield to me now . . . give to me, my sweet." In answer, Chrestien took his tongue within her mouth, willing him to continue by moving her hips beneath him suggestively.

Her eagerness nearly unmanned him on the spot. Sliding his hands down to cup her buttocks, he positioned himself between her thighs, intending to enter slowly, gently. But he was overcome by the warmth of her, and he thrust into the silk instead, fully sheathing himself, breaking through her maiden's barrier in one fluid motion. Instinctively, he covered her mouth with his own to absorb the cries of pain she could not contain.

He lay very still within her, allowing the pain to subside, watching for a sign that told him she was ready. Her body went limp finally, and when he was certain the pain had dissipated completely, he rocked her slowly, building the strength of his thrust until Chrestien could bear it no longer. The blaze raged, unchecked, consuming her inhibitions, and her body arched instinctively to accept all of him, her hand tugging at his hair. She moved beneath him feverishly, arching and undulating in turn, until finally it seemed something erupted within. And when Weston felt her tremors of release, he was ignited by the feel of it so much that he was at once catapulted into his own release.

It was long ere Weston could find the strength to lift himself from Chrestien's limp form. The darkness was impenetrable now, and he cursed himself that he could not see her once more ere he would abandon himself to sleep. He could hear her shallow even breath, and knew she slumbered peacefully. Pulling the coverlet over her, he buried his face in her hair, content just to breathe of her mystical aromatic scent.

Morning broke with a shower of sunshine. The golden rays of sun fell like stars plummeting to earth, piercing the multi-colored foliage and crashing to the forest ground to burst in a flurry of dazzling brightness.

Chrestien awoke to find herself alone. Grateful

for a few minutes to see to her toiletry, she hurried to gather her displaced gown and chainse, and seeing the crumpled material sent a profusion of blushes to her cheeks as she recalled her first night with her husband.

"My lord husband," she said aloud to know the sound of it. "My lord husband," she said again with a wistful sigh as she placed her gown over her head and tied the laces. "Weston . . ." She smiled at the intimacy of it. "My lord husband . . . Weston," she concluded happily.

Weston leaned against a tree with the morning's kill in hand to attend his wife's ravings. A grin curled his lip to see her smiling so at the mention of his name, and he decided to play along. "My wife . . . the lady Chrestien." She started at the sound of his voice and turned to face him, suffused with blushes. "Or perhaps you prefer Baroness Montfort?"

"You have a baronetcy to your name?" was all she could find to say, embarrassed now by her childish ravings.

"Does it please you to know it?"

She pondered the question a moment, and decided she felt no different for the knowledge. She started to say so but decided against it, for in truth the title suited one so dominating and she would expect no less for him—in fact, would be disappointed were he not valued for the risks he took for his king.

Weston noted her indecision, as well as the emotions that were so apparent in her candid expressions, and it pleased him that she would not care overmuch for such things. He wanted no power-hungry wife to interfere in his dealings. A spark of mischief glinted within his azure eyes as he lifted a brow in challenge. "Perhaps you prefer Mistress Silver Wolf?"

The gibe was not lost to her, and she smiled haughtily. " 'Tis not as though I do not deserve the right to the name, my lord. After all, I have bested the bearer of it not once, but twice." She raised her own brow in challenge and Weston threw his head back and roared with laughter.

She was no power-hungry vixen, but she was no slip of a woman either, and the knowledge thrilled him. Forever she surprised him with her untamed spirit, and he vowed not to break her in the taming—but tame her he would!

His good humor sparkled in his eyes.

"Ah, demoiselle, 'tis true. But 'tis precisely why I have wed you. I would keep that a family secret." Chrestien smiled softly as he said the word *family*, vowing adamantly that she would give him a happy one . . . with many heirs.

Weston's breath quickened as he noted the smile that caused Chrestien's face to glow. Immediately, his eyes hooded with desire and he felt the familiar tightening of his loins. That smile was like a fire in the summer heat . . . enticing him with its magnificence . . . but the closer he ventured, the hotter it burned, until his body was naught but a torch afire, kindling in its fiery path.

His body heat rose to a fevered pitch, and he had the uncontrollable urge to kiss her soft warm lips yet again. Walking toward her, he dropped the rabbit he held, and with a singleness of purpose he made his way to her, not caring that his meal lay at the mercy of the forest's many creatures.

There was no mistaking his intent as he took her in his arms. His lips descended upon hers, branding her with his desire. Chrestien met his with equal fervor. There was no denying him, she realized, as his hands ventured beneath her chainse, touching her feverishly. He wrapped them about her waist, caressing her bare shoulders before crushing her to him. Her body quivered in reaction. Sweet Jesu, there was no denying her own need—but then, she'd not even thought to. Her arms went about his neck eagerly and her fingers clutched at the curls at his nape.

Raising his mouth from hers, he gazed into her eyes and his look was as soft as a caress. Then, he lifted her suddenly, and her legs went about him instinctively. Reclaiming her lips once more, he walked two awkward steps and set her gingerly upon a low, thick tree limb, the same aged one Michel had used as a canvas.

Impatiently, he lifted her chainse and gown over her head, tossing them to the wayside. But in removing her clothing, he had subjected her tender backside to the prickly bark, and she fidgeted, leaning toward him to ease the pinch. To Weston it seemed she offered her nakedness to him, and he was stunned by her brazenness.

Reflexively, his hands flew out to catch her, coming to rest on her hips as his eyes feasted upon the creamy mounds of her bosom. She was so beautiful. Suddenly aware of the dryness of his lips, he licked them in anticipation. His smoky blue eyes lingered upon her, devouring her, letting the fever rise between them.

His gaze alone was enough to set her afire, she acknowledged, as her lips rose involuntarily to meet his. It seemed every part of her ached to be touched by him and instinctively she tightened her limbs about his waist.

Her innocent daring fired him, and his hand slid knowingly to her silky buttocks, cupping them gently as he lifted her bodily. Slowly, savoring the moment, he lifted her until her breasts were to his lips, and he suckled each of them eagerly before dropping to his knees with her.

With Chrestien's weight upon him, his descent to the ground was awkward, and the fall hard, but the pain was all but forgotten when her legs relaxed their hold. He thought to hold her to him just a moment longer, not wanting to end the intimate contact just yet, but when she brought her legs around to support her own fall to the ground, her hips ground seductively against the hardness at his groin, and he quivered against the intensity of it.

Mad with need of her, he urged her backward upon the dewy ground, and nuzzled his face into the crook of her neck, cherishing the feel of her tender skin against his face. When he raised himself to look her full in the face he saw the redness upon her cheek caused by his whiskers, and he bent to kiss the rosiness away. Slowly, he worked his way down to her belly, and then to her thigh and a sense of urgency stole over her.

The touch of his warm silky lips upon the smooth inner side of her thigh sent shivers coursing through her. She was mindless with need of him and her hands wound themselves tightly into his hair as though she held on for dear life—and it seemed to her that she did, for the torture was unending. She was losing herself again, merging with a separate entity born of their loving, and she welcomed it fully.

Never had Weston desired to please a woman so, that he would deny his own need to such a degree as he had. She was so very delicious. Her hair was spread like a crown of golden silk upon the earthen floor, interwoven with jewel tone leaves of many colors. But her deep green eyes were the boldest gems of all. They seemed to plead silently that he continue, beckon unto him to abandon his good will and enter the emerald fire. Kneeling over her, he moved up to straddle her belly with powerful limbs, and he could not help but admire her.

She loved him. The realization left Chrestien breathless. Unwittingly, she moved her hands to the ties of Weston's breeches, unlacing them with ease. Her hands trembled, and she had to pause a moment to ease the nervous flutter in her belly.

She was such a contradiction, Weston mused—innocent, yet lustful. As if singed by her whispery touch, the muscles in his abdomen flinched. Instinctively, he knew he could not endure the wait while she fumbled with his braies. He thought to aid her in removing the tangled laces, but as he moved his hands to aid her, his laces fell away like winter snow melting in her hands.

Chrestien could not believe the beauty of her husband. His chest was so broad, corded with muscles like no other she'd ever seen. His waist was narrow, with a dark streak of hair that ended in curls of black at his groin.

Weston was stunned and at the same time touched by the open admiration in Chrestien's gaze. He grimaced as her fingers landed upon his newest scar below his shoulder blade, the one he'd received at her hands, and his hand went to her chin.

His voice was rough with emotion as he spoke. "Nay, Chrestien. Do not look on me so full of sorrow. I prefer to see you smiling."

He was startled when she looked away from him, and gently traced the healing wound with her finger. When she again raised her eyes to meet his, he thought he detected remorse amid the beautiful green pools as they glazed with unshed tears. She raised her fingertips to her lips then touched them to his body as though she bestowed the kiss of healing upon it. He shivered violently over the intimacy of that touch. It shook his breath away.

"I am so sorry, Weston . . . truly . . . I wish I had not."

Looking back on it, he wished she had not either, but he would not say so and spoil the exquisite mood. He lifted her hand from his chest and kissed each finger slowly, with great promise.

"N—Not only for the pain I've caused you," she told him breathlessly, closing her eyes against the powerful feelings that swept through her. "B—But that I was so very glad of it at the time."

He bent to cover her mouth with his own, for he

had no care to hear any more. "Hush, Chrestien. I forgive you."

Her hand flew up between their lips. "But, I—"

"Hush," he commanded softly, moving her hand away from his mouth so that he could love her lips once more. Her fingers slid softly down the length of his arms as his mouth covered hers hungrily.

The kiss was warm and caressing, sending a surge of incredible heat flowing through her body, and Chrestien abandoned herself to him then, knowing that never again would her life be her own—even so, she gave of herself willingly.

Positioning himself between her thighs, he raised her hips and plunged himself into the depths of her, groaning with intense pleasure. Another moan echoed in his ears, but this one belonged to Chrestien as her body joined the age old ritual, wildly and without restraint, heat raging as no fire ever had.

She met his powerful thrusts with eager ones of her own, and when she thought she would explode with the intensity of it, a tidal flood washed over her, cooling the blistering heat, wracking her body with tiny delicious tremors, and culminating finally with a soothing calm.

But as she lay there beneath him another flame was sparked, and she joined him once more. A primal roar sounded throughout the forest as Weston found his release, and Chrestien followed him yet again, silently, willingly into the haven of pleasure.

Sighing contentedly, she went limp in his arms,

and he crushed her to him possessively, savoring the feel of her nakedness against his chest.

Weston supplied the rabbit for their meals the first two days. But on the third morning, Chrestien awoke early and very quietly took a crossbow from Weston's possessions. She would show him how easily she could survive at Montfort, even if she had to care for herself ... alone ... in his absence, because surely he could never leave her now. And she would not bring back a mere rabbit! Nay, that would be much too easy.

The simple fact that Weston had chosen to bring back the creatures—in fact, two or three of them every meal—told Chrestien that the woods were teeming with them. Elsewise, Weston would have brought back something else, she reasoned. Nay, she would not bother with a measly hare.

At least five rabbits scurried from her path ere she came upon the boar. Had she not been stalking it ... knowing to look for its dung, she would have been caught unawares. As it was, she nigh stumbled into its path and was separated from the wild, brutal animal by a mere span of short, thick bushes.

She could see the ivory beast clearly. And the boar, sensing her presence, was ready for her, but Chrestien did not fear the outcome. Panic would get her nowhere but purgatory. Knowing this, she very calmly positioned her bow and waited for the animal to come within range.

The gnarly beast snorted and bellowed as it caught sight of her, and charged vehemently toward her. She lost sight of it as it dashed through thick underbrush, but she knew not to avert her gaze from the swaying rustling bush.

When she was certain where the boar would emerge, she aimed her bow at the spot and waited patiently. On sight, she let loose her bow. At that very moment another arrow came flying over head, and both arrows came to rest in the heart of the boar.

Chrestien held her breath and quickly but deftly placed another arrow into the bow. Nibbling her lower lip nervously, she spun about to face the owner of the second arrow. But when she turned, she found herself looking into Weston's monstrous chest. Relieved, she let go of her pent-up breath.

Weston's eyes were settled upon the bow in her hand. Noting that the arrow had not been fired made his blood boil all the more, and his voice was deceptively low as he yanked the crossbow from her hands. "What did you think to do, mistress, feed yourself to the boar?"

Chrestien's eyes narrowed furiously as she caught his implication. She'd not quibble with him, when she could show him for the fool. "Accompany me if you will, my lord." Weston, knowing his own aim was true, scoffed at her presumptuousness. The boar was lying upon its wound, and Chrestien fell to her knees, astounded at the size of the animal. She truly doubted she could move him on her own.

"Afeared to bloody your hands, mistress?" Weston taunted.

At his ridiculous remark, Chrestien narrowed

her eyes upon him, and with great effort she turned the animal to reveal two arrows deeply embedded within its chest.

Weston was puzzled to see the second arrow, and his face clearly showed his astonishment as he eyed the crossbow he'd taken from Chrestien. He was more than amazed that she had been able to prepare a second bow in the time it took her to turn about and face him—without his seeing her do it to boot! Nevertheless, his anger won over his admiration, and he angrily pulled her from the kill. Unsheathing his dirk, he stooped to cut a hefty portion of boar, eyeing Chrestien all the while. That done, he replaced the dirk in its scabbard and wiped his bloodied hand upon the grass. Then, grabbing Chrestien by the hand, he dragged her back to camp.

"Unhand me, FitzStephens!"

"Nay." The hairs on Weston's neck bristled in result of his anger.

"You have the foulest disposition, my lord. I just thought to make you aware of that flaw."

"And now you have. . . . I shall be sure to remember your words, mistress." What if she had missed? Damn her!

"I should expect so, for you are sorely lacking in the art of gentility."

"I see, mistress . . . and is that what you would have told me last eve, pray tell?"

Chrestien gasped, and within seconds her face was awash with heat. "And that is just the sort of comment to prove my point," she mumbled under her breath, but Weston was too absorbed in his fury to hear her words. He'd watched her smuggle his crossbow from behind sleepy lids, and it had amused him to know she planned to provide his breakfast ... mayhap a hare or two, he was sure. Hell! She'd passed over at least half a dozen of them before he'd even wondered what she was about—the little sneak!

He had been more than willing to allow her the honor, and had followed quietly to protect her with the intent of returning to camp well before her. But when he'd passed the boar dung she'd been studying so intently, his amusement had quickly turned sour. And damn! When he realized the boar had been her intent all the while, his fury had reached a peak. She would get herself killed just to say she bested him again? Nay, he could not believe she would be so vain. Her intent was to show him she could weather Montfort. That was the only possible explanation. She'd certainly been ruffled enough when he'd taunted her about its wildness, saying it was no place for a woman— and truly, it was not. But then, Chrestien was no ordinary woman ... that much was clear!

He couldn't help the smirk that lit upon his lips as he remembered how calmly Chrestien had taken aim at the boar. He was willing to wager that she would fit in perfectly at Montfort—unless she was intent on placing herself in such peril on a daily basis. Then he would kill her himself! Yea, he would have to watch her closely, lest he lose her to her pride—or his fury.

In utter silence they made the trek back to camp. Once there, there was no shortage of cutting looks—all from Chrestien—and Weston could not help but wonder what kind of father would allow such insolent behavior from a daughter. Her manner was like that of no other he'd ever known. She was a willful, tempestuous vixen . . . and it was not difficult in the least to imagine a man catering to her every whim. Damn her!

By her actions, it was apparent that she'd had her lord father wrapped about her little finger. Otherwise, she would have marks all over her from her many sound beatings. He would have to be careful to keep his wits about him, lest he become her lackey . . . or worse, her murderer.

Nay! He would not have it. She would learn her place and keep to it, or he would—God's Teeth, but what could he do? She was no man to beat sense into. Nor was she the fragile wench he knew her sister to be. He would need but raise his voice to the other to have her cowering at his feet like a frightened hare. But this one? She was contrary and cheeky—full of enough daring to disperse amidst a legion of men.

"You'll not touch my bow again!" he finally shouted, for lack of better words to say. "If you touch the drat thing again, I'll bind your hands together with iron cords. I swear it, mistress, I would! I'll not have you traipsing across the countryside, looking for all manner of ills . . . pretending to be what you are not. You are a woman . . . for God's sake! Can you not behave like one? Or were you never told?"

"Nay, my lord, there was never the need." She could not keep her temper schooled any longer.

"For I've never had the misfortune of meeting a man so doubtful of his own strengths that he would fear mine!" Her palm was aching to find his flesh again. Jesu, but the man was a miscreant!

"Strengths, mistress?" He gave her the most incredulous look he could muster. "Strengths?" he repeated doubtfully. "Nay! I think not." Devil take her! His mere words could set a man's knees to knocking . . . and she would dare speak to him in such an insolent tone? How, upon God's earth, could one woman be blessed with so much beauty . . . and so little brain? Did she not realize another man would have beaten her for her misplaced mettle?

"Well, Milord! You need not worry that I might disturb your crossbow, for 'twas done out of kindness. And I've no desire to please you in the future. You may rest assured of that." Her eyes were storm-tossed green pools, so deep in color that they seemed a maelstrom of emotion, threatening to pull him under their swirling depths. They were ever his undoing—forever enchanting him.

He did not doubt for a moment that she meant every word, but he would not let her see to what degree her words cut him. In one swift motion his hand flew to the back of her neck, drawing her close. And when her face was but scant inches from his, he lifted her chin with a finger so that their eyes would meet. "When I need pleasure from you, mistress, I shall take it." His voice was dangerously low, but Chrestien was not intimidated.

"You, sir, shall take naught from me, lest I desire it to be so," she spat out. Reflexively, Weston's lips crushed over her own in what promised to be a punishing kiss, but when he felt the rigid line of her teeth upon his lips, he came away.

"Never think to do that again, mistress, lest I show you just how vulnerable you really are."

A slow smile crept to Chrestien's lips, but she said naught, and somehow Weston felt she'd won this battle. Disgusted with the revelation, he shoved her away from him and turned his attention to the boar to prepare it for the spit. After cleaning the pieces, he secured them over the heat.

The fire crackled in protest to the silence, but neither Weston nor Chrestien were willing to break it. Prodding the meat with a stick, he determined when it was done, and he gave Chrestien her portion. Thereafter, Chrestien devoured her portion of the boar with a vengeance, while Weston devoured her with his eyes.

A wisp of curly golden hair fell across Chrestien's right eye as she bit into her meal, giving her a bit of the savage look, reminding him of her innate wildness, and his loins burned for the feel of her again. Even in his anger he could not quell the raging desire. The sight of her as she sat upon the low oaken branch, her ragged hem exposing her bare feet and ankles, disturbed his maleness. He watched a moment longer as she examined Michel's carving with a finger and then turned narrowed eyes upon him. He threw his head back and laughed at her censure, but if the truth be known, when her eyes met his, his body reacted immediately, and he felt like laughing no more.

Unable to stand the sight of her anymore without touching her, he busied himself with smothering the fire and packing the goods, keeping his back to her as he spoke. "Ready yourself to leave, Chrestien." There was no answer, but he could hear the rustling of leaves behind him as she rose from her seat upon the tree limb.

He was thankful she did not question him, because he planned to surprise her by taking her to Montagneaux to see her sister . . . though he wasn't certain he could tolerate the pair of them together. Nevertheless, he would take her anyway. But did she give him much ado, he would surely give her fanny something to burn about!

Chrestien inched forward until she was nigh sitting upon Thunder's neck. With each canter of his hooves she would slide unmercifully back into Weston. His touch was like a thousand fires licking at her back, and she moved forward again only to be bumped into him once more. When his hand came to rest on her waist she slapped it away irately and moved forward again. A faint chuckle and a wisp of hot breath skimmed her nape and she shook her head to dispel its effect. Another chuckle. Curse him . . . the knave!

If only she was possessed of her own horse, she'd not be forced to endure his nearness! Such a bedlam of emotions raced through her, and his touch was making her head swim with thoughts she would prefer not to acknowledge. He was making it impossible to keep her head! Were it not for his mockery of her, she would be more than willing to put her hostility aside. But even now he belittled her with his ceaseless laughing. He knew well and good of her discomfort, and was taking great pains to worsen it, to be sure!

Chapter 11

All at once the forest gave way to a familiar clearing, and it was not long ere Castle Montagneaux was within sight. "You are taking me to my sister?"

Weston had no need to see Chrestien's face to appreciate the surprise registered there. Her voice told all. Without looking, he could see her wide green eyes, slightly parted mouth, and quizzical brows. "Yea, and is that not what you wished?"

The man was a puzzle! First he treated her as though she were naught more than horse manure, then he unleashed a wealth of kindness only to rescind it. And now? What was his motive? She had asked but once to see her sister—could it be he really cared for her feelings? Even so, if the answer were yea, she would still need guard her heart well. For until the mystery of this man was solved she could not present herself wholly to him, lest he break her heart into tiny wretched pieces!

"It is. I thank you, my lord," she told him sweetly, gritting her teeth afterward. It wasn't so easy to put her anger aside, regardless of this kind deed.

Weston bristled at the formality in her voice. "My given name is Weston. Use it in future, Chrestien. You are now my wife, and I'll not have you addressing me so formally." Chrestien reflected on his request a moment, then nodded her head in acquiescence. With a sigh of defeat, she let go of her vexation ... for the moment. She was happy to be seeing her sister again, and she had to own that somehow leaving their little haven in the woods saddened her. The intimacy she and Weston had shared there was beautiful, and that spot would hold a special place in her heart always.

Thinking of the woods brought to mind the time he had captured her there, and she was of a sudden curious about that first encounter. "Weston?"

"Yea, what is it?"

"Why did you come to my aid that day in the woods?"

"Why else? You are my wife. You would have me instead leave you to the boar?" His face contorted, reflecting his puzzlement. What an idiotic question!

"Nay! I did not mean that time. I meant the first time ... when you captured me."

Weston chuckled at her curiosity, and his eyes twinkled with mirth as he recalled the day she spoke of. "I see ... well, 'tis simple. Michel and I saw you pass by our camp—you looked so pitiful—and when the second cavalcade came through, we knew you had not a chance to defend yourselves against them."

"And how did you know they came for us?" She had not forgotten Aubert's counsel, and only wished to hear Weston's interpretation.

"There was no mistaking it, Chrestien; they had that look about them ... and whether you realize it or not, 'twas you they were after."

"Me? But how—"

" 'Twas you they were after," he broke in. "Do not ask me to explain. For though I am certain of it, 'tis only a feeling, and I cannot explain. I gather 'twas from Castle Montagneaux you were come?"

"It was, but how did you know? Did Michel tell you of it?"

"Nay, Chrestien, 'twas your sister that did the telling."

Now it was Chrestien's turn to be puzzled. "Adelaine?"

"You have another, mayhaps?" Without waiting for her reply, he explained. "I overheard while she relayed the tale to Aleth."

"Sweet Mary! Then what does Aleth think of me now?"

"I cannot say, for he did not confide in me. But I'll wager he was thankful 'twas not you he married." Chrestien's back was to Weston, so she could not see the smile he sported.

"If I am such a burden, my lord, why then did you encumber yourself with me?"

"I'm certain I shall ask myself that very same question a thousand times ere I meet my maker," he jested. But in her anger, Chrestien did not hear the chuckle that escaped him.

"You uncivilized, pompous oaf! How could you say such a thing to me? I'll petition your king and have the marriage nullified! That, my lord, is what I would do! I'd not be a part of such a ludicrous marriage ... whither there is no love—nor have you given me the true reason you have wed me. And do not tell me you did it for my honor, for I know now that you did not dishonor me ere the vows were spoken." Her face turned crimson as she spoke. "My maidenhead was not taken until after . . . and you, sir, have surely taken enough innocent maidens to have known this. So prithee, why did you wed me?"

His anger was spurred by her outburst, and he gripped her shoulder hard in warning. "You'll not write for an annulment." His voice was dangerously low. "And when, mistress, has love had aught to do with marriage? Nay, I did not dishonor you ere the vows were spoken . . . but you are mine now, and there is naught you can do to remedy that—not even petitioning the king, for 'twas he who ordered me to wed with you." The words were said, and no amount of regret on Weston's part could erase them.

Great, sparkling tears inched down Chrestien's cheeks as the revelation was made, but she said not a word— nor did she break into sobs as Weston had feared. She sat erect, without moving, without speaking, and stared ahead at the nearing Castle Montagneaux.

So the truth was known. There was no love . . . nay, not even desire . . . and she could not turn to King Henry, for he himself had ordered the marriage. But why? What had he to gain by it? At least now there was no need to search for Weston's motive. He would never defy his king, and that was the cur's only motive. 'Twas plain enough to see!

The iron portcullis rose at their approach, and

Chrestien noted the way the guards greeted Weston. It was obvious they recognized him and were honored by his visit. She kept her silence until Adelaine appeared, then she nigh screamed her joy. At that moment, the devil himself could not have kept her from her gentle sister and she nigh jumped from Thunder's back in her haste to reach her. Weston, it seemed, was possessed of more strength than the devil, and held her back with but his hand. Then, with the very same hand he lifted her effortlessly from the horse and lowered her to the ground. For his efforts she gave him her most vicious scowl, then with arms outstretched she ran to Adelaine.

Weston watched as Chrestien lifted her skirts and flew to her sister. The two were locked in such a firm embrace that it was difficult to tell one from the other. Were it not for Chrestien's shorter hair and weathered gown, it would be near impossible to tell them apart! Then he remembered her other endearing quality—her blade of a tongue—and he knew he could never mistake her for the other.

"What brings you here?" Adelaine could not conceal her shock to find her sister at Montagneaux ... and with the great dark brute, no less!

"I bring you news," Chrestien said simply, her tone lacking emotion.

"What news could make you so saddened, Chrestien? Come, tell me." Adelaine was fast becoming alarmed, for she'd never seen her sister so disheartened.

"I have wed." Chrestien's eyes remained downcast, in the meekest expression Adelaine had ever seen upon her sister.

"Wed? But to whom?" Her words were uttered just as Weston came to stand beside Chrestien, and Adelaine had no need for an answer ... she knew—Chrestien had wed the giant!

"Oh Chrestien, it cannot be so awful as all that!" Adelaine rubbed her sister's back to give comfort as she wailed pitifully, and Janelle shook her head in disapproval all the while.

"What would yer father say, did he see ye now?" Janelle scolded. "Child, I've never known ye to cry so, now cease ere yer eyes get puffy and red!"

"But it *is* as awful as all that!" Chrestien sobbed. "He does not love me!"

"He has not hurt you, has he?" Adelaine interjected, more than a little concerned.

"Nay."

Exasperated, Janelle popped Chrestien on the back of the head none too softly, then lifted Chrestien's chin with an old but tender hand. "What does it matter that he does not love ye, child, if he at least wants ye?" Her question was concluded with a click of her tongue, "What nonsense you speak. Fie! When has love ever had aught to do with marriage?"

Chrestien was angered to hear those words again so soon, and she spent her fury on Janelle, shouting furiously. "But he does not even want me!"

Janelle, long having weathered Chrestien's tempers, did not cower easily. "And how do ye know this? Has he said so? Did he say so in anger, it cannot count." Janelle shook her head emphatically, emphasizing her point. "Much is said in anger that is not meant."

Chrestien annoyedly brushed Janelle's hand from her chin. "He does not need to say it, for I know it. He did not wed me of his own will, Janelle. He did so only under King Henry's behest."

"But why?" Adelaine's eyes widened immediately at the revelation. "Why would King Henry ...?"

"Oh Adelaine, if I only knew. But I can think of naught he would gain by it. . . . Lontaine is no longer mine, 'tis yours . . . and I have naught else."

"But ye do," Janelle insisted. "Ye have so much to give." Her tone was heartening as she smoothed the golden mass of wild curls that belonged to Chrestien.

Again Chrestien swatted Janelle's hand away, and she sighed. Then she proceeded to explain. "You forget that he cannot know much of me, for 'twas not known my father was possessed of another daughter."

" 'Tis ye who forgets, m'dear. He need but know of one of ye," Janelle stressed. "What have either of ye that the other does not? Tell me," she insisted. But before Chrestien could answer, she appended, "Did he know yer father had two daughters, then he also would know ye are twins. Would that not be so?"

"You put overmuch value on my appearance." Chrestien's temper was sparked, and she came to her feet to face her faithful maid and her wide-eyed sister. Her crying had ceased, and Janelle smiled to see the familiar gleam in Chrestien's eyes. " 'Twould not matter whether I were beauty or beast in the eyes of the king. If it gained him naught, he would not concern himself with me, to be sure!"

" 'Tis true, Janelle," Adelaine interposed. "But Chrestien, mayhap Weston does love you. Mayhap, 'twas he who requested your hand to his king, after all! And I have just the way to discover the truth. Do you love him? Are you willing?"

"Truth to tell, I'm not certain what I feel, Adelaine, save that it gives me great pain to think he does not care for me." Chrestien watched as Adelaine's face lit with the merry look of mischief, and she was a little amused at the turn in roles. In times past, it was Chrestien who always came up with the knavery. "What idea have you?" Her curiosity was well piqued, and she was almost eager to hear the plan.

All their lives Adelaine had been content to remain in Chrestien's shadow, never getting much attention because she never sought it, and 'twas good to know that she was getting her time in the sun. Chrestien could not help but smile to see the change in her sister. Aleth was good to her, to be sure, or Adelaine would not have gained so much confidence. "Whatever it is, I'm willing," she capitulated.

Looking about her for what seemed like the first time, Chrestien could see that Adelaine's bed-chamber was exquisite. In it were all manner of luxuries, from a curtained tub ... to twin hearths. Never had she seen the like of it before.

The windows were covered with ornate wooden shutters, intricately carved with delicate figures painted gold. The bed was a monstrous thing, needing steps to climb onto it. And the coverlet was of the finest fur, well stitched so that you could not see the seams—unlike the patchwork coverlets of Lontaine.

Chrestien's attention was drawn to the manservants who filed in one by one, carrying large buckets of steaming water. Finally the tub was filled, and in her excitement to feel the delicious warm water about her, Chrestien nigh plunged into it. After her bout in the woods without washing, she was nigh famished for the feel of clean water. "Pooh to the Church!" she whispered. How could bathing be a sin?

Stretching her legs in the huge tub, Chrestien curled her toes to contain her excitement. "Are you certain Weston will notice?"

"Of course! When you disregard him awhile, he'll be somewhat angry ... but when Aleth's men are falling all over you in earnest, he shall be livid. You will see."

Chrestien sighed wistfully as she watched Adelaine smooth the pleats of a beautiful bliaut of lavender brocade. With it came a mantle and capuchon of pure white velvet, trimmed in luxurious ermine. And when Adelaine pulled another from her coffer exactly like it, Chrestien was awed. "You have two?"

"Of course, silly. I had two made of each in the

event you came to Montagneaux. I know 'twas outrageous, for you were to go to La Trinite, but I could not enjoy any of it ... unless I somehow shared it with you," Adelaine admitted, sheepishly.

Tears sprang to Chrestien's eyes to hear Adelaine's admission. "Thank you ..." She paused to wipe a wayward tear from her cheek. "It has been so difficult to be away from you. ... You are so much a part of me."

"And you, me," Adelaine conceded. "I've missed even your tyranny, Chrestien." Chrestien giggled, and both were crying softly now—tears of joy. And then in mock horror, Adelaine added. "What would Janelle say to see the both of us like this?"

"I know not, but I've no mind to find out." Chrestien giggled again as she wiped away all traces of her telltale tears, and Adelaine followed suit. Neither wanted to be caught crying by Janelle. They'd get their ears blistered, to be sure!

The great hall bustled with activity. Aleth had invited players to remain throughout the week, and they were indeed earning their keep. A very tall juggler clad in parti-colored breeches and tunic made his way about the hall carrying a matching sack. His painted face contorted into outrageous grins as he stopped to ogle every female.

Finally, he came to stand directly in front of the lord's table. His eyes widened comically, and he dropped the sack to hide his face with parti-colored hands. Opening his fingers a crack, he peeped through them, and closed them again in feigned alarm. The hall roared with laughter as the juggler held up a flattened hand in front of his face and looked into it as if it were a mirror. Then he looked behind the faux mirror and widened his eyes as he pointed a red finger at the twins, making them both laugh at his antics.

Finally, getting back to the task of juggling, he pointed to his sack and threw out his hands as if just finding it after a long search. Tossing the sack open, he pitched a red ball carelessly into the air. Almost simultaneously came a gold, blue, and green one.

The hall sounded with clapping as the juggler settled into his practiced routine, accompanied by the heavenly sound of the lyre. Chrestien clapped loudest of all, for which she was rewarded with a comical smile from the juggler, making her laugh all the more.

Weston noted that Chrestien's smile was capturing more attention then the juggler's performance. His point was proven when the juggler himself stopped juggling abruptly and let every ball fall to the wooden floor with a loud thump, each thud exaggerated by a loud strum of the lyre as the juggler feigned being love-struck. A red ball came down upon the juggler's head, earning another round of laughter, and Chrestien clapped all the harder.

Why this petty juggler should irritate him so, he couldn't fathom. But Weston was indeed irritated, though he masked it well, drowning out Chrestien's enthusiastic clapping with his own thunderous applause.

Meekly, knowing that what he was about to do might be misinterpreted, the juggler picked up two of his painted balls, the gold and green ones, handing the gold to Adelaine. The green he gave to Chrestien after pointing out that it matched the color of her eyes. The twins rewarded him with a smile, and the juggler packed away his remaining balls and stepped away from the table as a team of dancers took his place.

"Oh Aleth, 'tis delightful!" Chrestien shouted above the din. "Papa never allowed players into Lontaine, and 'tis the first time for me."

Aleth smiled, and Adelaine whispered into his ear. "I knew 'twould cheer her."

"And I never doubted," he whispered back. To Chrestien, he said, "They'll be hither throughout the week. What say ye to that?"

"You've been so kind, Aleth!"

Weston was amazed that such a simple thing would bring Chrestien so much pleasure. The essence of rosewater drifted to him, and he longed to have his face in her hair again. The lavender gown she had donned somehow made her eyes appear so much greener, and he vowed that as soon as they were home he would have a dozen lavender gowns made for her.

Her skin seemed so like the unblemished snow of the moors, smooth and milky, without a single flaw. He'd wager that were she not already his, every man in this hall would be vying for her hand at this very moment. And of a sudden he was thankful that her first visit to Castle Montagneaux had been made in the guise of a man. Though how anyone could mistake her for one was beyond him.

A thought occurred to him, and he scanned the faces in the hall. Someone must have known who she was, for whoever led that ambush had come from Montagneaux. He studied every face in the hall to no avail. There were no telltale faces about—naught was registered upon any of them that would sound the alarm.

They were all simply enjoying themselves. Even the bold ones, who stared openly at Chrestien, were now reacting as any normal man would when caught in the act of staring at another man's wife. They would turn away in submission to his warning scowl.

The dancers moved away, and the lower tables were cleared and dismantled to make room for the guests to dance. The lyre was joined by the lute, and couples flocked to the dance floor.

There was yet to be one syllable uttered between him and Chrestien, and he was not about to be the first to break the silence between them by asking her to dance. By God 'twould be broken by her, or not at all! He had not begun the feuding between them, and he would not end it—or never would she learn her place.

Adelaine, seeing the long face Chrestien sported, urged Aleth to seek the first dance with her sister. Aleth nodded, and turned to Weston first out of respect. Weston smiled, masking his irritation as he nodded his approval. "By all means," he said chivalrously. Within, he seethed.

He watched Aleth lead his wife, gracefully,

amidst the other dancers, and he grit his teeth. Aleth had his own ladywife to attend and it was to her he should direct his concern. Surely Chrestien needed no more attention than she was receiving this eve!

He risked another glance at Chrestien, and a roar nigh burst from his chest. She and Aleth were laughing—no doubt she was amused that he sat alone. He turned away from Chrestien, oblivious of Adelaine's staring until he saw her gleaming white teeth, and he realized she was watching him, just as he watched his wife.

Was she laughing at him as well? Did she know he was angered? He looked away momentarily to wipe the scowl from his face and then returned his gaze to Adelaine. Two could play at this game, he decided, offering Adelaine his arm. "Would you care to dance, my lady?"

Adelaine smiled sweetly. Chrestien wasn't the only one who could play off a mischief! Her smile deepened as she shook her head. "Nay, but you have my gratitude. For you see . . . I've twisted my ankle somehow, and 'twould be excruciatingly painful to dance."

She denied him with such overstated intensity that Weston was certain she'd concocted the falsehood, and he gave her a frown for her efforts.

She could see the muscles in Weston's jaw ripple as he struggled to control his anger, and she knew why he was irate—he wished to make Chrestien jealous, and she'd foiled his plan. The man was besotted with her sister, and he didn't even know it. Now it was just a matter of his discovering it . . . with a little aid.

"Sir Weston, I am indebted to you for bringing my sister to Montagneaux. I've missed her terribly—we've never been apart, you know," she told him, offhandedly.

Weston's jaw twitched again, but he forced a smile.

"Chrestien is enjoying herself so. Do you not agree? She's never seen the likes of this before, because Papa never allowed players into Lontaine."

Weston's jaw twitched yet again, but this time he spoke. "So I've heard." His voice was low, and his tone was dripping with sarcasm.

Adelaine watched his gaze return helplessly to the dance floor and she smiled inwardly, biting down on her bottom lip to refrain from laughing. "She looks so beautiful in that dress ... and she dances divinely. Do you not agree, my lord?"

Weston's head turned and he gave Adelaine an incredulous glare. He made it a point to inspect her from her identical feet to the top of her head. He thought it ineffectual that she should be complimenting her exact twin so and wanted her to know it.

Adelaine realized what he was thinking when he gave her such an odd look, and she colored. He most assuredly thought her bold and vain. She would have to be careful what she said—that it would not sound as if she were complimenting herself, for she wore the very same gown as well as the very same face as Chrestien!

Finally, Aleth returned Chrestien to the table, exhausted. But Adelaine stood within seconds of their arrival, pleading faintness. Aleth stood to catch her, for it seemed she would faint upon the table, but Adelaine pushed him away.

"Nay, I am fine, my lord husband. 'Tis but that I have need of fresh air." She turned to smile sweetly at Weston. "If only Sir Weston could part with my sister for but a few more moments."

Aleth smiled, for he knew what his wife was about, and he nodded his head. The game was certainly amusing, and he decided to play along. Turning to Weston, he asked, "Would ye mind terribly if m'ladywife took yers away yet again?" If Adelaine's plan worked, he would have his wife and his chamber returned to him, for he'd given up his own chamber in light of the difficulties between his newly wedded guests.

Weston sighed irritably, but his answer was given with a smile. "Nay, I'd not . . ." Three female players had gathered onto the floor and Weston turned to them as he finished his sentence. " 'Twould give Aleth and I a chance to . . . talk." He grinned wolfishly, appraising the dancers. Aleth could but chuckle—he really was enjoying this game.

"Indeed it would." Aleth smiled as he sat in the oaken chair to enjoy the dancers. And that was the way Adelaine and Chrestien left them—staring wide-eyed at the underdressed women writhing before them.

What Chrestien didn't realize was that the moment she and Adelaine turned their backs to him, Weston's gaze reverted to her, staring until the sisters walked through the hall door.

A familiar face stood up and followed them out, and Weston nudged Aleth's arm, pointing out the man just before he disappeared behind the huge oaken doors. "And who would that be?"

" 'Tis but Aubert, their father's squire."

Weston had not recognized him, for he'd not seen Aubert since the day he'd taken him to Lontaine. But all at once he was plagued with a barrage of memories: Aubert defending Chrestien in the woods, risking his life to do so. Aubert lying next to Chrestien in the tent—Chrestien lying next to Aubert in the cart, showering him with caresses. "By God, only Aubert is it?" he muttered to himself.

"I do believe 'tis working, Chrestien! You should have seen him watching you. I thought his eyes would pop from his sockets. Oh, I do hope he will forgive me . . . for I know I sorely tried his nerves. And I did a dreadful thing—you cannot believe how mortified I was—I actually complimented you . . . not that I shouldn't. 'Tis but that we looked exactly alike this eve, dressed as we are. And you should have seen the way he gazed at me. 'Twas as if he thought me mad!"

Chrestien laughed heartily to hear Adelaine's chattering, and she caught herself trying to envision Adelaine's accounting. So intent was she on her thoughts that she didn't hear the footsteps behind her until they were nigh upon her. She swung about, expecting to find an irate Weston behind her, but what she found was a very receptive Aubert.

"Oh, Aubert! I thought never to see you again." Chrestien threw her arms around him and kissed him firmly upon the cheek. "And I've missed you so," she confessed.

"And I've missed ye, ye little minx!" He picked her up, swinging her about exuberantly.

"They tell me ye've married the dark one."

Chrestien smiled wanly. " 'Twas not my choice to do so, but yea, I've wed him."

"But are ye not happy? 'Twas my very mother who said ye loved the man." Aubert's face now reflected all the confusion he felt—never would he understand women.

"Sweet Mary! Janelle cannot know what is in my heart. She's got it in her head that I love the man, and naught that I say will sway her."

"Do ye love him, then? Are ye happy?"

"Happy ... nay! Love him ... yea," she nigh shouted. "But I've not told Janelle any of that!"

Aubert chuckled knowingly. "Ye know Mother, Chrestien. If she's got it in her mind that ye love the knave ... then whether ye agree or not, ye'd better say ye do, or ye'll not hear the end of it."

Chrestien gave him a lopsided grin and hugged him again. "How I've missed you, Aubert."

"So ye've said, minx, but I see not where ye've withered away from the pining." Aubert took Adelaine and Chrestien by the hand, bringing them both forward to lock them each in one monstrous hug. "If yer father could only see ye now." He clucked. "I've never seen either of ye look so beautiful."

"Enough about the two of us, Aubert. I wish to know of you. Has Aleth accepted you into his hire?"

"He's not asked," Adelaine interposed. "He has

this silly notion that he's not needed at Montagneaux."

" 'Tis not silly, Adelaine. Yer lord husband does not require me," he said adamantly. "And I'll not be taking charity."

"Mayhap Weston could use you," Adelaine proffered, and Chrestien nodded in agreement.

"I'll ask him as soon as we are speaking again," Chrestien promised, sighing wearily.

"Nay, if anyone will do the asking, 'twill be me . . . in any case, he does not care for me. I can tell by the way he glares at me—and what do ye mean, when ye are speaking again?" It finally dawned on him what she had conveyed.

"Exactly thus. I've not spoken to him since three days past. We argued, and he said some horrid things that I'll not be forgetting so easily. 'Tis an apology I'm after, and I'll not speak to him until I get one." Adelaine grimaced to hear Chrestien's heated words.

Aubert couldn't see the wisdom in riling the dark one's temper, but 'twas not his place to say how a wife treats her husband, so he kept his opinion to himself. He was neither a husband nor a wife. And even if he were . . . and could give sound advice . . . Chrestien would not heed it. She was of her own mind, and Aubert knew that better than any.

He remembered clearly how as a child Chrestien would come up with some wily prank, and he would try to dissuade her to no avail. Always she would do as was her wont, and no amount of pleading could stop her. "Just take care that ye do not push him too far," he advised.

"Do not fret, Aubert. I can manage." But she wasn't at all certain that she could. She was accustomed to men such as her father and Aubert, who rarely asserted their authority.

Somehow her assurances didn't help to ease Aubert's mind. For how oft had she said that only to find herself in her chamber without supper? Not oft enough, Aubert reasoned, for Gilbert had loved her too well to punish her. It pained her father more than it did her, in any case. And of usual, 'twas laughing at her monkeyshines ye'd find him.

Remembering something she'd meant to show Chrestien earlier in the day, Adelaine started to walk away, calling over her shoulder for Chrestien and Aubert to follow. "I wish to show you something," she explained.

It was not long ere they came upon a small enclosed garden, well lit with at least a dozen pitch torches. When Chrestien saw the exact duplicate of the rose arbor at Lontaine, she nigh swooned with joy. "How ever did you manage?"

"Aleth is good to me, Chrestien. I needed but tell him how much that rose arbor meant to me—to us, that is. And he had his men build it, and then he moved the roses from the herb garden. Flora, the cook, nigh had a fit from what Janelle tells me, for she uses the roses in her salves ... and as a garnish for her dishes ... but she's welcome to come hither for them."

" 'Tis beautiful, Adelaine ... and you can have the snow-white rose I favor so much."

"Yea, and there is even a very tiny replica of it.

Come, follow me." She went to a small raised garden and plucked the tiniest white rose.

"Oh ... Adelaine, 'tis like naught I've ever seen." Chrestien stared as if mesmerized by the dwarf bloom. Taking it from Adelaine, she put the tiny blossom to her nose, breathing deeply of its scent. "How did you happen upon such a thing?"

" 'Twas a gift," she said simply, pleased that Chrestien was so awed by it. "From Aleth's brother," she clarified. "I believe he acquired the rose while on crusade—brought it home to present to his mistress, but she alas was not there, having left him for another ... so Rolfe brought it here ... to give to me as a wedding gift. He's such a charmer, Rolfe."

Aubert half turned away from the pair, not able to stomach all the woman's talk, and he busied himself with shining the hilt of his proud sword, using the sleeve of his tunic to catch the smudges.

"Would that I could meet him," Chrestien lamented. "Mayhap he could find me another such rose—I would pay him, of course."

"Oh, but he does have another ... a crimson one. But there is no need to pay him, for he has already promised it to me. And when he gifts it to me, I shall simply give it to you as a wedding gift. I would just take a little cutting from it first, if you would not mind overmuch."

"Need you even ask? Of course, I would not mind." Adelaine and her kind heart would never cease to amaze Chrestien. "Whither is this Rolfe anyway?"

"Not here—he left shortly after Janelle and Aubert came, in truth. He told Aleth of a matter in

Caen he had need of attending ... but you shall meet him when he returns—and he shall soon, for he's never away for long. He's very close to Aleth, you realize," Adelaine added, offhandedly.

Chapter 12

The sun dawned bright and cheery, though it was a cool, bitter late autumn day. Turning from the window, Chrestien saw that Adelaine had removed from a coffer yet another set of twin dresses, both of a deep emerald color with an underdress of very fine ivory silk.

"Just how many sets of dresses have you, Adelaine?"

"I cannot remember this moment, but 'twas how I kept busy when first I came to Montagneaux. I missed you so."

Chrestien understood perfectly, for she'd known the same pain of loss when they were parted.

"They are yours to keep when you leave," Adelaine added indifferently.

"You are too good to me," Chrestien protested, but her smile foiled the reproach, and she hugged her newest dress happily. "Think you Weston will like this one?"

"How can he not? You will be stunning. The deep green is equal only to the color of your eyes . . . and with the white capuchon, you shall be a vision, to be sure."

Chrestien smiled halfheartedly. Only Adelaine could take their one disparate feature and make it seem Chrestien's was superior. But Chrestien felt it untrue, for Adelaine had the color of sweet honey—the color of their mother's eyes—in her eyes and Chrestien would have greatly preferred the amber color to her own stark, cold green. "Will he see us depart, then? Have you arranged it? You realize he has not spoken one word . . . nor even looked at me in nigh six days?"

"You deceive yourself if you believe he does not care for you. I have watched him, Chrestien, and when he believes you see him not, he gazes at you with such sheep's eyes. He does want you. 'Tis simply that he is overly stubborn—much more than I anticipated . . . and Chrestien, I never thought to meet anyone more stubborn than you."

"Stubborn? You think me stubborn?"

"Yea, but 'tis no more than what I would expect from you, for 'tis your nature. Though I'd have you promise me one thing . . . does he not give in today, you will go to him. You cannot sleep in my chamber another night, for I'm longing to be with my lord husband. Now, tarry no longer and dress yourself. Aubert awaits us in the bailey with our mounts."

With bated breath Weston watched as the vision before him grew in clarity. From the arched entrance of the great hall came his wife and her sister. Were it not for the vivid green of Chrestien's eyes, he would not have known one from the other because they wore matching dresses and their hair was covered by a capuchon of white velvet—but the eyes told all.

The cool emerald gaze was as captivating as ever, and he was ever stunned by its beauty. So deep ... so green were Chrestien's eyes in color that they had the capacity of absorbing his very control, making his head swim with thoughts of her.

Her gown of emerald added to the allure of her eyes, offsetting them well. And the white velvet mantle and capuchon enveloped her as would a halo, giving her an ethereal essence—almost as if she were born of the mists, and if he reached for her she would dissipate into its whispers.

Aubert was indeed waiting in the bailey, Chrestien noted ... though not alone. Weston and Aleth were with him. As Adelaine approached, Weston stepped forward and took Adelaine's hand, kissing it nobly as he told her. "You look lovely, demoiselle." Adelaine managed a smile but bowed her head to hide the laughter that threatened to erupt.

Forcing a smile, Chrestien turned away from her sister and husband to mount her own horse. His slight did not bother her in the least. He had said Adelaine looked lovely ... and in a way, 'twas as if he had given the compliment to her. That gave her something to hope for.

Just then, Aubert rushed to Chrestien's aid. A vision of her clad in armor, pouncing onto her stallion and falling to the ground, came to his mind, and he couldn't bear the thought of her playing the fool in front of her wolf of a husband.

Weston noted with sheer disgust the way Aubert ran to Chrestien's side. Had he not kept an eye on the two, knowing when they were together and when they were not, he would strongly suspect them. As it was, he did not relish them alone together. If Aubert thought he was going along with them, he would need think again!

Weston roared Aubert's name across the courtyard, though Aubert stood but a scant few feet from him, successfully gaining everyone's attention, including Aubert's. "I'll be needing you to remain hither with me this day," he explained, his tone gruff.

Aubert was puzzled, but he was not about to argue with him—Chrestien's husband or not, he was yet the Silver Wolf—and he acknowledged Weston's command with a tip of his head before lifting Chrestien into her saddle. Ahead of them, Aleth aided a giggling Adelaine onto her chestnut mare.

He watched his sisters ride from the gate, followed by five burly guards, and his knees threatened to give away his terror of the man who stood behind him. Then, gaining his courage, he turned his attention to Weston. "What will ye be needing me for, Sir Weston?" he managed to say with a calm he did not feel.

Weston noted angrily the cool arrogant way the youth kept his attention upon his wife until she was no longer within sight. Half out of fury, half out of some oddly felt respect, he clapped Aubert none too softly upon the back, and Aleth chuckled as he left the pair of them together. Weston observed with well-concealed amusement the way Aubert stood proud and erect, without so much as a grimace to ease the sting of Weston's slap, when the blow would have felled another.

He reminded Weston of himself—years back in his father's home, when he was forced to endure the backbiting his brothers conspired to give—and a sudden overwhelming compassion for the youth opened a path of kinship through the thorned weald of animosity. Mayhap the boy did not covet his wife after all.

"I ken you're wanting to find a home for your skills, lad ... and I'm needing a squire. Are you willing?"

"Sir? But I thought ye yet had a squire?"

"Guy? He's Michel's man ... and we've shared him long enough. Mine was lost to me at Tinchebrai," he explained, his voice low. A pregnant silence ensued as Weston recalled his loss, and Aubert his own. While Weston awaited the youth's answer, he thought he detected doubt etched upon the young squire's face, and he tried to smile to convince Aubert that his anger had fled, that his motives were pure. "Michel will be happy to have Guy to himself," he coaxed. "So what say you to my proposal?"

Aubert was stunned. "I should be honored, sir," he managed to utter after a long moment.

"There's but one thing I'll have you do for me first, lad. You would stay away from my wife." Weston's tone was low, as he turned to walk away, feeling confident Aubert would follow.

Aubert was doubly stunned for a moment, then he nigh tumbled after Weston's heels. "Chrestien?" he inquired, bewildered by the request.

"I have another?"

"Nay, but I cannot stay away from her," he protested strongly.

It was an arrogant denial—never mind that it took courage to proffer it—and Weston's anger was ignited again. The little bastard would risk his life just to be near another man's wife? Mayhap he'd misjudged him!

Weston stopped and turned a deadly glare upon Aubert. The muscles in his arm rippled as he fixed his grip upon his sword. "You cannot? Why can you not?" He spoke slowly, enunciating every word with a deadly calm. "You would prefer my blade instead?"

Aubert noted that Weston's hand was gripping the hilt of his sword, and he knew instinctively that his life depended upon his next words. The truth was his only recourse. "I cannot, sir, because she is my sister," he spat out, angry that he would need reveal the fact at all.

"Your sister? You lie, for she never said as much."

"She does not know," Aubert admitted. "But I have proof . . . if ye would care to confirm it." His voice was low with resignation as he started away from Weston, in search of his mother.

"I would, indeed, care to," Weston assured him. There was an air of truth about the lad's words, but he needed to verify it for himself.

Janelle's teeth clattered nervously as she disclosed all to Weston. " 'Tis the truth my son tells ye. He's Gilbert de Lontaine's offspring . . . though Gilbert never openly acknowledged it. He did to me, however, and that's what matters most. He made a warrior of a servant's son. Does that not prove the truth of what I say?"

Weston knitted his brows as he took in the maid's confession, but he said not a word, only rubbed the hilt of his sword reflexively, and his actions made Janelle all the more nervous.

"If 'tis not enough, then there's more. Gilbert told me that if aught happened to him ere he was able to make things aright, there was a letter in his chamber that would tell all. I cannot tell ye whither exactly it lies, and I know not how to read, but 'tis there. That ye can be sure of, for Gilbert would not tell me so were it not true. He was an honest man . . . Gilbert was."

A faraway look glazed her eyes when she spoke again. "Gilbert never loved another besides his Elizabeth. But after all . . . he was man, and I am woman . . . and I loved him . . . I did," she swore. "He was ever good to me—gave me free run of Lontaine as if it were my own home, and he entrusted me with the raising of his wonderful daughters. Yea, he was a good man." The maid licked her lips nervously. Her eyes glistened with unshed tears, and Weston decided he'd questioned her enough.

"Cease, woman. You've no need to tell me the rest. I believe you."

Janelle was relieved that the dark one had chosen to see the truth, but now her thoughts had drifted in another path, and she ventured onto dangerous ground by questioning the Silver Wolf at all. But she had to know what he planned to tell Gilbert's daughters. "And what of Adelaine and Chrestien? Will ye tell them, my lord?"

Weston sighed heavily as he pondered her question, but he told the weary-looking woman what he knew she wanted to hear. "I'll not tell her, but I expect either you or Aubert to do so. You may choose your time, however. I'll not be interfering."

"Oh bless ye, Sir Weston. Bless ye. We'll tell her. We'll tell her," she swore, and Aubert contorted his face, for he knew by *we* his mother meant *he*.

The sun rode high in the autumn sky. It was near Sext and they had been riding through Montagneaux's parklands nigh two hours. In past Adelaine would have grown weary of the outing by now, and Chrestien marveled that her sister showed not a trace of fatigue. Instead, she seemed nigh as invigorated as Chrestien felt. Yea, Aleth had changed her much, and Chrestien didn't hesitate to tell her. Adelaine giggled to hear her sister's praise. " 'Twould seem we are more alike than 'tis possible!" Adelaine readily agreed.

" 'Twould seem so, yet 'tis fortunate you were not gifted with my tongue, for the cursed thing has brought me more grief than not."

"Now, Chrestien . . . 'tis not so difficult a task to keep one's tongue still. After all, Papa oft said that 'tis a wise man who can conquer man—"

"Yea, I know . . . and wiser yet did he conquer his tongue. I've heard it a thousand times if once, I'll warrant!"

"To hear without listening—"

"Yea . . . yea . . . is to eat without chewing . . . anon you shall strangle upon overlooked words. Cease, Adelaine, ere you cause me to go daft! What have you done? Taken to memory all Papa's quotes, have you?"

"He was a wise man after all. Do you not miss him so? I do, terribly."

"Yea, if the truth be known, more than words can say." It was a somber mood that followed that admission, and with solemn thoughts Chrestien halted her mount and looked to the sky. It was a beautiful day for riding, though it brought back too many memories, for Papa had taken them riding oft—though only when he was certain there would be no one about. He was such a cautious man when it came to protecting those he loved.

Adelaine reined in beside Chrestien, whirling her mare about to face her sister. "There's something I've a mind to ask."

Chrestien knitted a brow in protest. "Need you always gain permission ere broaching a tender subject, Adelaine? Ask what you will. There were never secrets between us before, there cannot be now." She sighed.

"'Tis only that what I wish to know is a very, very delicate—"

"Out with it, Adelaine," Chrestien grumbled. "What is it?" She was quickly growing impatient with her sister's diplomacy. But as always, she at once suffered a pang of guilt for losing her temper with her sister.

Adelaine's face reddened. "Has Weston—? That is to say, have you . . .?"

Instinctively Chrestien understood what Adelaine was inquiring, and she thought to put her sister out of her misery. "Yea, we have." There, it was said, and now Chrestien's face was just as rosy in color as Adelaine's. "Does Aleth—? Well, do you . . . like it, Adelaine?" Chrestien bit her bottom lip, for she was quickly growing as flustered in this conversation as her sister.

Adelaine's face colored, her cheeks staining with her chagrin, but she held her breath and nodded her head, admitting honestly, "Yea, and you?"

Now it was Chrestien's turn to flush as she owned the truth of it. Satisfied that they had as of now had their first woman-to-woman chat, they were quick to leave the topic at hand for another.

"Oh Chrestien, I want you to have a wedding, just as I. And when you and Weston resolve this silly misunderstanding, I will give you a proper one . . . here at Montagneaux."

"Nay. I thank you, Adelaine, but he'll not agree to it—of that I am certain."

"You pea brain." Adelaine giggled. "The dark brute loves you, whether you wish to believe it or nay!" She shook her head reprovingly as she spoke. A glitter of sunlight erupted on the horizon, drawing Adelaine's attention momentarily, and she paused, cocking her head to examine the glare. But the flash was gone now, and she noted that her husband's men paid it little attention. In truth, it seemed that two of the five guards were making their way to the woods, and she could only reason that they might need to relieve themselves. Reluctantly, she dismissed the glint as a figment of her imagination and returned her attention to Chrestien.

Nudging Adelaine's foot with her own, Chrestien inclined her head softly, indicating an opening in the woods. "The woodland ahead is where Weston and I made camp after our nuptials, and so I shall always remember it fondly."

Chrestien sighed wistfully, recalling the blissful time she and Weston had passed there.

"So you have told me, Chrestien, but I cannot see you lying as naked as a wood nymph upon the woodland floor—in the cold rain no less! 'Tis not my idea of a fanciful tryst with the one you love. Nay, for me 'tis a warm chamber lit with scented candles . . . and soft words of love." Adelaine's amber eyes glinted gold, and her happiness was evident in the radiant smile she displayed.

Chrestien was pleased to see her sister so happy, but she scrunched her nose in response to Adelaine's fancy. "That too was my first notion of romance, Adelaine, but I'll not be finding any of that with Weston. Yet, I'd have him no other way. . . ." The truth was—though she would not tell Adelaine—that Weston's lusty masculinity was as a love charm to her.

Chrestien watched curiously as another of their guards took to the woods, and within scant seconds of his disappearing, arrows flew from the trees, felling the remaining two men. "Sweet Mary!" No sooner did she say the words than she spotted the approaching cavalcade . . . only seconds before Adelaine.

" 'Tis not Aleth that approaches, Chrestien."

"And 'tis not Weston, so we have not the time to waste contemplating the possibilities. Follow me!" Chrestien made for the forest at breakneck speed, while the clanging of armor rushed to her ears, and Adelaine followed obediently, not needing further urging. Chrestien had good instincts, while she seemed to have none at all.

Chrestien's mind raced, searching through its

store for a clue to save themselves, when of a sudden she remembered the hidden shelter she and Weston had shared. 'Twas their only chance—if only they could make it there.

The clashing of metal drew closer, and she had no doubt that boded them no good. All at once, the forest came down upon them as a ceiling of evergreens interspersed with autumn-bared oaks, severely gnarled with age. Chrestien didn't dare take the time to check that Adelaine was behind her. She knew that she was—the echo of crunching leaves indicated so.

The toppled tree was upon her before Chrestien realized it was there. Fortuitously, her mount had already noticed it, and it hesitated only momentarily before leaping over the hurdle, clearing the bulk of dead timber easily. Not even Lightning could have done it finer! But just as her mount alit upon the forest floor, its hooves grinding and pulverizing the fallen leaves, she was nigh struck with the outstretched arm of an ancient oak, her head missing it by only scant inches.

She took a deep calming breath when the obstacle was behind her, but a loud sickening thud stopped her dead in her course. Adelaine! Instinctively, Chrestien knew that her sister had not made it beyond the oaken limb, and panic found a foothold in Chrestien's heart.

Whirling her mare about, she found Adelaine crumpled amid the crushed leaves, unconscious, blood flowing from some unseen wound upon her head—so much blood that Chrestien could barely see her sister's face! Bile rose into her throat as she nearly tumbled from her saddle. Falling to the ground beside Adelaine, she whispered brokenly. "Oh, Adelaine." Then, panicked, she shook Adelaine's shoulder. Pleading now, she cried, "Nay! Oh, nay, Adelaine! Nay!" Suddenly seeing the gash from which Adelaine's life ebbed, she reached to staunch the flow. Pressing her hand against the wound, she watched in horror as the blood continued to trickle through her fingers. Suddenly sickened, she observed helplessly as the white velvet capuchon Adelaine wore stained crimson.

Her heart racing and chest aching from her pent-up breath, Chrestien lifted her sister, knowing that at any moment the soldiers would be upon them. With strength she didn't know she possessed, she placed Adelaine over her own horse, so that she lay upon her belly in front of the saddle's pommel. The rush of metal grew closer and Chrestien smacked the rump of her sister's riderless mare wildly, sending it in the opposite direction from the shelter. Then, mounting behind Adelaine, she spurred her own mare in the direction she had originally intended.

Within moments she reached the shelter and dismounted to lead the horse within, keeping a wary eye to her back to be certain she was not followed. Once inside, she ripped a strip from her gown and placed it between the wound and the capuchon. Seconds lapsed before it was soaked red, and she tore another strip, packing it tightly over the old, before kissing Adelaine's bloodied forehead tenderly. Tears clouded her vision, and she refused to acknowledge anything other than that her sister was unconscious—there was so little time to spare. She had to find a place where she could spy upon the soldiers without being seen. Only then could she escape and get Adelaine to someone who could aid her—that someone was certainly not Chrestien, for she had learned naught of the art of healing, having stupidly left that bloody task to Adelaine and Janelle.

It was not long ere the armed knights realized they had been duped, and they returned to track her. A shiver of recollection made its way down her spine as she watched a metallic figure approach her. It was the very same knight who had ambushed her the first time—there was no mistaking it. A red symbol of some sort was blazoned upon his mailed chest, though she could not see its entirety for the shield he carried. His shield also bore a symbol—mayhap the same one that he wore upon his chest, but she could not make it out for the bush. The conical helm was slit across the upper face, exposing the eyes, and an icy chill swept across her nape as she scrutinized their familiar darkness.

Whither had she seen those eyes before? She'd seen them other than the time in the woods, of that she was certain. Her heart nigh stopped when she realized that he was staring intently in her direction, and a shudder passed through her as she watched one half of his devil's brow rise in challenge. She nigh bolted from her hiding place, but fear kept her rooted to the spot. And it was a good thing too, for though it seemed he was coming straight for her, he turned abruptly, all the while mumbling to himself.

It seemed he stood before her an eternity, muttering until it sounded almost a chant. She could make out tiny bits of his ranting ... *bastard* ... *again* ... *bitch* ... Where had she heard that voice? Every part of her body came alive, nigh aching with the need to scream ... run ... something— anything! But she did none of those.

Another rider came to the first, seemingly from nowhere. And when they started off together, away from Montagneaux, Chrestien knew this would be her one and only chance to escape them. It was obvious they had not fallen for her ruse, and it was but a matter of time ere they searched the entire span of woods adjacent to Montagneaux's parklands. The time to flee was now, while his men were yet separated. Once they came together again to search 'twould be too late.

Taking the already skittish mare by the reins, she edged as quietly as was possible toward the opening in the brush. Once there, she scanned the area for a sign of her assailants, and when she could see no sign of them, with a pang of anguish, secured Adelaine's limp form to her horse, re-mounted, and made for the clearing.

The blanket of trees gave way to familiar blue skies, and behind her a trail of shouts assured her that she had been tracked. And though she did not spare the precious time to look back, she knew that she was being pursued as well.

It was all she could do to keep the exhausted, frightened mare galloping at such a strenuous pace, and she could feel the animal tense every so oft as if she were going to buck. Leaning forward, Chrestien whispered desperate words of praise near the mare's ear, hoping to reassure her, while between herself and the animal's mane Adelaine's body slipped to and fro, threatening to fall from the horse's back. But by the saints, she was able to pull Adelaine to her without unnerving the mare further. But oh, Adelaine . . . she was as pale as new parchment—and she was covered with her own blood!

The rush of steel was a roar in Chrestien's ears, and she imagined feeling the devil's heated breath at the back of her neck. She knew it was imagined, for her head was cloaked in the thick velvet mantle and hood Adelaine had given her—the mate to the one Adelaine wore now, though Adelaine's was saturated red and could no longer be recognized as such.

Unable to dispel the feeling, she turned to look behind her and was startled to see those eyes so close behind. She could see their murky gray color—angry, insane eyes. Then of a sudden there was some other emotion registered there, and if Chrestien didn't know better—know he was after her as he was once before—she would have sworn that his eyes mirrored surprise. Incredulously, he then did something she would never have expected. When she could nigh feel his arm reach out to grab her reins, the man stopped and gave chase no more.

The towers of Castle Montagneaux were well within sight, and the lead man reined in his horse, his hand clamped tightly about the shield he carried—so tightly that his knuckles nigh turned white beneath his mailed fists. His surprise had worked against him. Having seen the face of the injured one lying atop the horse's shoulders, he'd not expected to see the very same frightened face peering back at him, and it had unnerved him. He knew them to be twins, but it never occurred to him they might be identical twins. By the time he'd recovered from his shock, they were well within sights of Castle Montagneaux, and he did not dare come within range of the garrison's sight. As it was, he'd risked exposing himself by bribing the men sent to guard the damn maids!

Rolfe's voice was choked with his anger. "I think it was Adelaine . . . she saw me—damn her to hell!" Gritting his teeth until it seemed they would be ground into his gums, he threw his shield at the nearest man, nigh hitting the lad in the temple. "Damn that bitch! Damn her . . . damn, damn! I cannot credit that she has escaped me yet again, and Adelaine, she will have to die now, for I can take no chances." He let fly another string of oaths and angrily turned his steed from Castle Montagneaux, the veins in his neck pulsing until it seemed they would burst. But mayhap it had been Adelaine injured and not Chrestien? In that case, it would have been Chrestien that had turned to look at him, and she would not have recognized him.

"Gervais, ye will go to Montagneaux and discover what Adelaine knows." Gervais acknowledged with a nod of his head. "But do not go until this eve," he added, forcefully, and then he shouted, "I'd not have ye arriving mere minutes after Adelaine and that cat of a sister—that bitch has more lives than Satan's familiar."

"I thought ye wanted her alive?" Gervais inquired meekly, not sure he should even speak.

"And I do, but I shall hold the final judgment of her fate till I've known her. I've yet to know if she's as worthy as my brother's ladywife—if not I'll not have her. Do ye heed? 'Twill be Adelaine I would take." Rolfe's eyes turned skyward as he took a calming breath before continuing. "Unless of course she knows, in which case . . . 'twill be a pity, but she would have to be leaving us," he spat out.

Rolfe reined in his horse again, turning in his saddle to consider his fallen shield, and Gervais did the same.

"Should I retrieve it for ye, Rolfe?"

Rolfe's deep unexpected laughter resounded across the meadow, and it seemed to Gervais that of a sudden clouds moved in to darken the horizon, giving the land an eerie gray look, and he held his breath as Rolfe spoke again.

"Nay. With luck 'twill be found and another of our obstacles will be removed. I was not foolish enough to make use of mine own shield, you idiot. 'Twas the shield of Aleth's most trusted advisor, Roland le Blanc," he disclosed pridefully.

A smile half puckered his lips. Finally Roland would get his own. The bastard had managed to delay his execution for long enough. The eve ere the battle at Tinchebrai he'd abandoned camp and had gone to Aleth. It had weighed heavily on Rolfe's mind that Roland had gotten to his brother first. Had Roland overheard him and Gervais making plans? Had he warned Aleth? Nay, or Aleth would have confronted him with the accusations by now—his dear brother would have given him a chance to deny the allegations made against him. Nay, Aleth did not suspect! And in all probability neither did Roland for the man was too stupid to surmise aught.

Chapter 13

By the grace of God the gates were open to receive them, and Chrestien flew through them hastily, dismounting before the keep. It seemed everyone within the walls of Castle Montagneaux flocked immediately to the limp form upon the chestnut mare.

With the aid of a castle guard Chrestien took Adelaine from her mount; all the while silent tears coursed down her cheeks. And when Aleth came from the hall, she ran to him, reluctantly allowing the guard to carry her sister's lifeless body behind her.

Weston watched as Adelaine ran to Aleth, embracing him soundly. With a catch in his throat, his gaze returned helplessly to his wife, who was being carried by the faceless guard. Her body was without movement; her arms dangled lifelessly and her neck hung in the most frightening position—caught in an impossible pose. His warrior's instinct told him that her neck had been snapped, and the realization dawned with a sickening clarity.

His heart nigh burst from his chest as he ran to her, taking her limp form into his arms. He could not stop the ache that was mounting to an unbearable weight, threatening to crush his heart. A lone, silent tear trickled down his cheek as he gazed into the heavenly face before him.

Her eyes were closed, but he could remember their vivid greenness as clearly as if she were gazing at him now. And though her face was covered with blood, it was yet as beautiful as ever. Brokenly, he bent to kiss her lips, coming away with her ruby blood upon his own. He knew her to be dead—had seen the face of death too oft to deny it.

Tears streamed from Chrestien's eyes as she embraced Aleth. "Adelaine . . ." She could barely speak, for her words choked her. "She's fallen . . ."

Confusion muddled Aleth's mind as he stared at the woman in front of him. Her eyes were green, not the sweet honey-colored eyes he'd grown to love, and dread took hold of him as he stared into Chrestien's crystalline pupils. Familiar lips were moving, though he could hear naught that she said, for her eyes were not the ones he knew . . . and he knew what that signified.

Somewhere in the confusion he sensed Weston pass him by, carrying Chrestien into the hall. But 'twas not Chrestien he carried, for Chrestien was standing before him now. Shoving her aside none too lightly, he went after Weston . . . and his wife.

Weston's chest heaved, laboring to catch that elusive breath that would sustain him as he strained to hear a heartbeat. He could hear naught save for the pounding of his own heart, and though he knew it to be useless, he pressed his cheek to hers, hoping to feel her breath upon his face. It was then he sensed Aleth's presence beside him, but could not look up to acknowledge him.

His cheek was to her bloodied nose, and though he prayed fervently in his mind's heart, he could still not feel her breath. Feeling at a loss, he let her face slip from his callused hands. His heart broken, he allowed Aleth to remove her body from his embrace.

Aleth took the limp body from Weston and held it close to him, while somewhere in the distance he could hear a woman screaming—or were the screams his own? Nay, they were those of a woman. His senses were reeling and he could not make out the origin, for it seemed his soul was screaming out as well.

Weston tried to calm the distraught Adelaine, but she would not respond. Her screams of grief were wrenching, and he shook her fiercely to stop them. They were crumbling his self-control! He shook the shrieking woman until he was nigh crushing her small arms in his grip. Still, she would not stop and her voice was a dagger slicing at his soul! Curse Aleth, for it should be him comforting his wife!

The woman's head bobbed back and forth so quickly that it was difficult for Weston to see her features in his numbed state. But finally he focused on her anguished green eyes. They were green, he noted—green. Adelaine's were amber. The woman standing before him was possessed of green eyes! Then of a sudden her lids closed and the screaming ceased.

The bright blue sky belied the true feeling of the day, for it was black—as black as the darkest rain clouds ... as black as the eyes of the devil who had put her sister in this place.

The priest said his holy words and the casket was lowered unceremoniously into the black earth. Numb with grief, Chrestien took a handful of the white miniature rose blooms and sprinkled them onto the casket. As soon as she was able, she would plant the miniature roses at her sister's grave. Adelaine would have liked it thus, she was certain. And when Rolfe brought the red roses, she would place them hither as well. Yea, she would have Aleth remind his brother of his promised gift ... Adelaine would have liked it thus.

She could vaguely feel Weston's crushing grip on her shoulders, could vaguely feel him dragging her away as the soil was shoveled back into the damp ground, burying with it a part of her.

'Twas all her fault, dear God; Adelaine was an innocent! How could it be that she was lying 'neath the cold hard ground? "Nay," she whispered, brokenly. It was the first word she had uttered in two days—the longest two days of her life. A heaviness had settled in her breast that was unlike anything she had ever felt ere now.

It was as if a part of her had died ... and a part of her had, for Adelaine was more than a sister ... she was friend as well. Nay, she was more than that even; she was half her body, half her mind, half her soul!

"Nay!" she cried, falling to the ground, fingers clutching the soil as gut-wrenching sobs racked her body. When Weston tried to lift her from the ground, she threw his hands from her. His touch would bring her back to reality, and she never wanted to go there again . . . not without Adelaine.

Aubert stepped forward and placed his hands upon Chrestien's shoulder then. And when Chrestien did not push him away, he lifted her face tenderly and gently brushed the damp soil from it. "Come to me, Chrestien . . . help me to ease my burdened heart, for she was my sister as well." 'Twas the time to tell her, Aubert realized, for he knew Chrestien well. First her father, now Adelaine, and what she needed most was the closeness of two who are flesh and blood. She'd loved her sister well and truly, and without Adelaine Chrestien felt not whole. Aubert knew this as well as he knew his own grief.

To see his father fall in battle, without ever having called him son, had caused him much sorrow. But to see Adelaine buried in holy ground? The finality of it all was oh, so clear. And his duty was to be brother to Chrestien, even though she knew not that she was possessed of one.

Chrestien looked into her brother's eyes and knew what he said to be true. His golden hair and proud arrogant stance loudly proclaimed his viking heritage—his features too like those of her father. She had long suspected it, and to see the grief in Aubert's eyes confirmed it. She allowed him to lift her from the ground, falling into his arms, sobbing; for her father, for her sister, and for the brother God had mercifully given her.

Finally, when her tears were spent, she looked into Aleth's pained face. He seemed to have aged overnight. Fine lines crinkled his eyes like little bird's-feet, and on his pallid face was etched a permanent frown. He reached for Chrestien, hoping to delude his aching arms into believing she was his lost love—if only for a moment. And she went to him, embracing him with all the might she had within her, giving him her strength, her anger, and finally her tender words. "You loved her, I know, and for that I am grateful, Aleth."

"She was easy to love, Chrestien." His voice was rough with emotion as he spoke, openly declaring his sorrow.

"Yea, that she was."

"Though she came to me but a short time ago, I shall never . . ." His voice broke, and it took him a moment more to compose himself. "I shall never erase her memory from my heart, for 'twas as if she had been with me always. The only comfort I have . . . is in knowing that her murderer has paid for his act of treason."

"You know who it was?"

"Yea, his shield was found where my men said he gave up his chase."

"And so he is dead?" Chrestien wanted to hear that he had suffered—that he died without mercy.

Aleth's eyes were pits of sorrow, overflowing with emotion, and he could barely speak. "Justice has been done," was all he could say.

"Who could have done such a thing?" Chrestien cried. "Who could have despised her so much!"

Aleth's face was rigid with hatred. "Roland le Blanc, my captain," he said hoarsely.

Chrestien's heart felt near to bursting. "Why?" she asked brokenly. "Why Adelaine? My sister has never offered anyone harm."

Aleth's chest swelled with the pain he was harboring, and his eyes took on a faraway look. "For his daughter, Gwynith. He has always blamed me for her death. I simply never knew how much." His brows knit with pain, and then he looked away from her, to gaze at Adelaine's grave.

By the change in Aleth's expression, Chrestien could tell that he would speak of it no more. His jaw was set tight, and his eyes became daggers. Briefly, there was a hint of something more, a glimpse of someone else, and she shuddered at the thought of it. Then, knowing she would not hear what she sought to, she nodded in acceptance, and finally turned to Weston.

He stood apart from the others, letting them grieve without distraction. But there was a sadness about him too, she noted, and Adelaine's voice echoed in her thoughts: *The dark brute loves you, whether you wish to believe it or nay. . . . You deceive yourself if you believe he does not care for you. . . . He loves you, Chrestien. . . .*

She went to Weston, placing her hand in his, for he had turned away from her. Tenderly, she kissed his fingers, and when she looked into his eyes there was such compassion there that she wondered how she could have ever doubted his love.

Adelaine had been right. He was simply too stubborn to own the truth of it. 'Twould take time, she knew, but it would be worth the wait, for this man would give his heart only once. Papa had oft said that something worth having was never easy to attain ... and to beware of the treasure that drops into your hands, for 'tis never true, and it oft comes with the highest price.

She watched Aleth ride toward Montagneaux and then returned her gaze to the newly dug grave. By now all had gone, but for Aubert and Weston, and she motioned to them that she would leave as well. Weston mounted his destrier, and Aubert aided Chrestien into Weston's arms, then mounted his own steed.

Seated upon the black destrier, Chrestien's hand went to Weston's arm. Without realizing it, she dug her nails into his flesh, and Weston knew instinctively that she was not yet ready to go, so they sat there a long moment; Weston with his arm about her waist, Aubert with his head lowered in prayer, and Chrestien staring blankly at her sister's grave.

A sharp breeze swept her hood from her head, and Chrestien shivered but did not retrieve it. Winter was approaching. 'Twould be the first without her father and Adelaine ... and Adelaine had always loved winter, writing into her little volume of its beauty, finding wonder in all it had to give: a flock of birds heralding autumn's end, a lone crocus lifting its flowery head from the snow. Even in the dead, colorless winter landscape did Adelaine find glory ... for from the sparse limbs of winter-humbled flora came spring's flowers.

A lone tear crept down her cheek as she stared at the newly disturbed soil for a long moment, then she placed her fingers to her lips and spoke.

" 'I give to thee my song, along with that of God's, to rise unto the stars and echo in the wind.

I bid to thee good-bye with fingers to my lips, and send to thee my kiss to be carried to your soul on petals in the wind.'

"You see, Adelaine, I did take the time to read, but 'twas not the classics that moved me, but your prose instead. . . . I love you." With that having been said she kissed her fingertips and held them into the sailing breeze. In response the wind picked up and rushed through her fingers. "Good-bye, sister," she whispered after it.

There were no candles lit, but the full moon illuminated the chamber enough for Chrestien to know that she was alone. She was a shade disoriented from her long sleep, but it took only a moment to realize that she was in her chamber at Lontaine.

The ride from Montagneaux had tired her more than she'd realized, for they'd arrived at Lontaine near None and she'd only thought to take a little nap. That little nap had turned to be a dead slumber.

Weston had ridden fast and hard. And that had suited Chrestien just fine, for she had longed to be where there were pleasant memories of Adelaine. Aleth had been kind enough, offering the comfort of Montagneaux until arrangements could be made for them to go to Montfort. But Chrestien had needed Lontaine, and he and Weston had been so understanding.

She'd slept a bit in Weston's arms while on horseback, but 'twas by no means a restful sleep, for thoughts of Adelaine had haunted her. Feeling the puffiness of her eyes for the first time, she pressed her fingertips to the offending area. Then she remembered guiltily that once she'd shut herself in her chamber, every tear she'd denied had gushed forth unchecked. Janelle would need make an herbal compress to ease the swelling, she knew, and it shamed her that all would know of her lapse in character.

Glowing embers from the hearth gave her half of the room a toasty warmth, but when she went to the window across the room she was struck with the icy feel of the air there. She made quick work of unlatching the shutters and looked to the bailey below. Not a soul was stirring in the courtyard, and by the look of the sky it would yet be a few more hours ere sunrise. Reflexively her hand went to the open window, her fingers fanning the empty space there. Montagneaux's windows had boasted glass panes, and this window's lack of glass was strangely comforting. Though the pane was a luxury and helped to keep the cold from the room, it also distorted the view hideously, making the countryside seem warped, cloudy, and unnatural.

Chrestien wasn't at all sleepy, but she didn't dare leave her chamber. Janelle would be sleeping in the antechamber and Chrestien didn't wish to wake her. Janelle and Aubert had taken Adelaine's passing nigh as hard as she had. She winced when she remembered that Aubert had cried— something she'd never before seen him do. Even as a child, when he had fallen from Chrestien's horse and broken his arm, he'd not allowed himself tears. When Janelle had set his snapped bone he'd grimaced, but all the while he'd stared at

Papa. When Papa had smiled approvingly, Aubert had beamed in response. The memory was as vivid as if it had happened yesterday. The grin had spread from Aubert's mouth to his eyes, and Chrestien had to smile at the recollection. Had he grinned any wider, he'd have been smiling from the back of his head.

It was clear to Chrestien now that Aubert had always known they shared the same father. That he had never showed the least amount of jealousy was remarkable. Given the same circumstances she might not have been so caring—and Aubert was caring. 'Twas not an act either, for Chrestien would have seen through that easily enough. Aubert genuinely loved their father, and that was indisputable, because Papa had always been Aubert's first concern.

She sighed heavily. The past could not be changed, however much she wished that her father had acknowledged her half brother. But she took comfort in that Papa was always kind to Aubert—very good to him, in truth. Even so, 'twould have meant a great deal to all to have been told the truth. And poor Janelle . . . the secret she had lived with would have embittered most women, but Janelle was untouched by such an emotion.

Shoulders slumped, Chrestien made her way back to the bed, falling onto it dejectedly. She started to pull the coverlet about her when of a sudden she had a strong urge to be with Weston. It was funny how the feeling would just come over her at odd times. When she first came to her chamber, she had need of solitude. But now? It was Weston's strong arms about her and his comforting breath near her cheek, as he seemed to like to sleep, that she needed.

A quick peek told her that Janelle was indeed in the antechamber, but the maid did not awaken as Chrestien expected. Though it was dark, Chrestien could make out Janelle's sleeping form upon a pallet under the tiny raised window. 'Twas a miserable place to take one's slumber, Chrestien knew, for the night air was cold and the stone floor could put the ague into one's bones. But Chrestien knew why Janelle chose the spot. It was directly across from her chamber door and Janelle expected to keep an eye on Chrestien. That she didn't stir now proved just how tired she was, and Chrestien made every effort to exit the chamber as silently as possible.

She had no need of a candle to make her way through the small keep. She could do it blindfolded—and she made it to her father's chamber, down a flight of steps and behind the screened partition in the great hall, without waking a soul.

Crawling into the bed next to Weston, taking care not to wake him, she mindfully lifted his arm and slid into its welcoming warmth. All was well with her now, and not surprisingly her eyes suddenly felt as heavy as lead, forcing her to close them and welcome sleep.

It felt as if someone were waving a feather beneath his nose, tickling him out of his slumber. Weston opened his eyes to find it was a lock of Chrestien's hair doing the torturing. Briefly, he wondered how she'd come to be there, but he was too elated to think on it overmuch. She was here with him now, and that was all that mattered.

Smiling contentedly, he took in a breath that boasted of her fresh scent, and reluctantly removed the teasing lock of hair from his face. It was such a womanly fragrance she wore—a sweet delicate scent so unlike that of the ladies of court. Unable to help himself, he buried his nose in her hair to catch the elusive fragrance once more. She stirred when he turned her face to place a tender kiss upon her cheek, and their lips met instead. She opened her eyes to his.

"Good morning, my sweeting," he whispered hoarsely.

Her answering smile shone even in her eyes. "Morning," she whispered back, stretching lazily.

"You slept well, I take it?"

"Aye, and you?"

He chuckled softly. "I would have . . . if some little vixen had not tortured me overlong with her curly mane of hair." His languorous smile spoiled the effect of his scolding, and Chrestien could not help but laugh softly in return.

He was so handsome . . . and when he smiled at her so, it made her heart skip a beat. She decided to play along. "Then you would prefer I slept in my own chamber?" she asked and started to rise from the bed.

Weston's arm snaked about her waist, and he drew her firmly against him, facing him. "If you were to do that," he whispered huskily. "I might would not sleep at all, little one." His lips brushed hers again, so softly that her heart fluttered at the caress.

She couldn't tear her gaze away. The glitter of silver in his almost black hair, once so sinister looking, was merely another of his endearing qualities—part of his undeniable allure, proclaiming his mastery by experience. Driven by impulse, Chrestien reached to smooth her hands through the curls at his nape, and Weston drew her closer yet. His eyes burned a smoky blue as he watched her.

Chrestien bit her lip nervously. Suddenly curious over his age, she allowed one hand to weave its way through the brilliant silver-black strands as she told him, "You don't seem so very old, Weston."

His brow rose. "I don't seem so old?" he repeated soberly.

"Aye, that is what I said, milord. How many years have you?" she asked seriously.

He chuckled softly. "Nine and twenty."

Chrestien's brow furrowed. "Well," she said and let the word hang in the air as she gathered her thoughts. "That is older than I first thought . . . but the silver of your hair proclaims you should be at least two score or more and I knew that it could not have been so."

Some choked sound escaped him. "That old?" he asked and his eyes widened with mock alarm. "You would have me aged before my time, sweet Chrestien?"

Chrestien smiled sheepishly, then chuckled when he dropped his jaw in indignation. Unable to help herself, she told him, "You've such beautiful hair for a man." Her hand flowed with the waves in his hair down to his nape, where her fingers stroked him softly, but the effect was much too intense and Weston caught her wrist in his hand, stilling her. Their eyes locked and neither of them spoke for a long moment. The air was charged between them.

" 'Tis why they call me the Silver Wolf," he said hoarsely, never taking his eyes from her. "My hair," he clarified.

Chrestien blinked, as if to clear her mind. And then, when it dawned on her what he had said, she looked at him as though she didn't believe him. "That, milord, is not what I was told," she returned saucily.

"Yea?" he asked gruffly, the sound a caress. "And what is it that you've been told?" he challenged softly, certain that she was bluffing.

Chrestien tried to recall Michel's words exactly. "Well, for one," she said, " 'tis been said that you are a great prowess on the battlefield."

Weston tried not to laugh. "That I have great prowess, Chrestien. You cannot be a prowess ... prowess is something you have," he corrected. "It means more or less that I've exceptional skill in battle."

Chrestien's eyes widened with sudden understanding, and her eyes narrowed accusingly as she again recapitulated Michel's words. "I've also been told you've a prowess with women."

Weston's smile remained, but the humor faded from his eyes. "I've not heard that. Tell me, Chrestien, these are Michel's words, are they not?"

Chrestien nodded. "Christ!—Never listen to a thing that cur tells you," he muttered irately.

Chrestien nodded again. Then, as her thoughts traveled another vein, she told him. "I must thank you for giving me time to grieve for my sister, milord, you've been so very good to me."

He shrugged his shoulders. "You are my wife," he said simply, and loosened his hold upon her. Her simple words of gratitude did much to cool his ardor.

Chrestien wanted to hear that he loved her too, but Weston said nothing more, and she knew that it was too soon for him to own as much. "Adelaine was very dear to me," she admitted. "In truth, when my father died ... I was devastated, for we were very close. But when Adelaine left me ... 'twas more than that even. We were rarely apart, and it was as though I'd lost a part of myself—'twas not at all like the first time we parted, for though I thought I would die from the loneliness, I knew she would be in good hands with Aleth." A flicker of a smile lit upon Chrestien's lips, but disappeared as quickly as it surfaced.

"What thoughts bring such a wan smile?" Weston asked softly.

"I was but remembering the day we set out for Montagneaux—Adelaine and I," she told him wistfully, and the admission brought back her smile and a tear. She brushed it away. "Would that I could relive those days again. I'd not have made her go so readily."

Weston looked away from her, to the window, not able to bear her sadness. "You never told me how you came to the decision to present Adelaine to Aleth. Did your father request it?"

Chrestien shook her head. "Nay, 'twas my idea," she admitted easily. "Papa had long since had a bond with Aleth, though he never really told us what it was that linked them. He was very private, you see."

"So I've gathered. That Aleth did not know your father was possessed of twin daughters, is hard to credit. Did he never come to Lontaine, then?" Weston asked, incredulously.

"Not oft, though he did come. But because he and Papa would closet themselves away in the solar, we were never in his company together. It seemed Papa went out of his way to avoid it. I simply happened to overhear a discussion of theirs once." She blushed as she assured him, "Really, I never intended to eavesdrop, but I did overhear Papa proposing a betrothal between Adelaine and Aleth, and 'twas a snatch of that dispute that led me to my decision."

"I see." Weston grinned, noting Chrestien's rosy cheeks. "And what was said in that ... discussion?"

" 'Twas simply that Papa desired Aleth to wed with Adelaine."

"And why the quarrel?"

"Aleth had only one. He was to have wed another, is all."

Weston frowned. Chrestien's explication was beginning to drive him daft. "Aye, Chrestien, but Aleth did wed your sister. Now tell me, why is that so if he was already betrothed? Did he not ever wed his love?"

Chrestien shrugged. "The lady Gwynith disappeared mysteriously and they did not wed, after all. Papa assisted in the search all those years ago, but nothing was ever found of her. 'Twas said she set out to ride alone one day and never returned—nor was she ever found." Chrestien looked suddenly as if she would cry. The tip of her nose turned pink and her eyes glistened. "You know, I believe Aleth did wed Adelaine for my father . . . yet it seems to me that he came to love her in the end. He was so sad when we left Montagneaux. Was he not?"

"And who was the family of this Gwynith?" Weston persisted.

"So many questions, Weston. What is it you are thinking?" He seemed preoccupied and his eyes narrowed further with each tidbit of information she'd relayed to him.

It was Weston's instinct to smell danger much like his namesake, the wolf, and there was no mistaking the stench of it now. "Naught," he lied. "I simply am curious to know who her family was, for 'tis an interesting story you tell." He didn't wish to alarm her by voicing his fears. She thought her assailant dead, and until he had proof he would say nothing to infer otherwise. Something was amiss at Montagneaux, though he could not quite place it. He knew only that there were too many deaths and too many coincidences.

"Gwynith's father was Aleth's captain . . . Roland le Blanc," she declared. "His daughter was said to have had great beauty, though I must admit I never saw her myself. But Papa said Aleth was smitten by her . . . so much that he'd not cared that she came to him without a dowry."

The pieces were coming together. Weston's dark brows knit as he came aware that it was this same captain that Aleth had slain. Anger had directed Aleth's actions that black day, and nothing Weston could have said would have dissuaded Aleth from what he was wont to do.

He recalled that when Aleth's men had shown him the fallen shield he'd paled noticeably. And it was unfortunate that Roland had come into the hall when he had, for Aleth's blade had severed the captain's head without mercy. So blinded by rage had Aleth been at the time, that he'd not even allowed the man to utter his defenses.

Afterward, Aleth had seemed strangely removed from it all, but had proffered no explanation for his rashness, save to say that he'd always known there were doubts. That statement in itself had offered nothing in the way of enlightenment, and there was but the moistness of Aleth's eyes to reveal his regret. He'd gone completely silent after that remark. 'Twas only with Chrestien's accounting that light was shed on the matter, however minimal it was.

It seemed to Weston that the captain must have blamed Aleth for his daughter's death. But to Weston's way of thinking, the blaming alone was no crime, and there would be more to the tale, or Aleth would not have given him *le coup de grace* so easily.

Even more puzzling, was that Aleth did not seem the type to judge so unfairly. And to not allow a man his defense was indeed unjust. What

more had passed between them to seal the man's
fate so? That was a question to ponder further,
and in its resolution lay the solution. Somehow, he
knew that whoever was responsible for the maid's
disappearance, was also responsible for
Chrestien's ambush. It was only a gut feeling but
a strong one nevertheless.

Cold air coalesced about him, and he looked up
to see that Chrestien had risen from the bed. She'd
unlatched the shutters and stood watching the
sunrise from the open window. The morning still
held the night's cold bite in its mists and he was
surprised to find the shutters wide open to the
cold, but he said nothing, only watched her.

As he lay in the bed, his arms linked behind his
head, he thought he'd never seen a more fetching
sight as his wife. Her hair was set afire by the
sun's soft glow, her face tinted a soft pink. And
she was a vision to behold, with her white linen
chainse blowing so gently in the morning breeze.
Surely, he'd fallen into a dream, for no woman had
a right to be so lovely.

The ache in his groin assured him that he was
not dreaming, and he rose from the bed to retrieve
his temptress of a wife. Lifting her in one sweeping motion, he carried her hastily to the bed.
Chrestien started to protest that she was about to
begin her morning toiletry, but Weston silenced
her with a long hard kiss. His lips nearly crushed
hers with the fervor of his need. When her arms
came about his neck of their own accord, he
groaned his approval. And when she gave him her
tongue, he nigh went mad with hunger for her.

A light kiss upon the hollow of Chrestien's neck

sent her senses reeling with desire. His touch was magic, she decided. Why else would her body respond thus, with but the briefest touch by him? A wave of heat flushed over her as he turned her around and placed a hot kiss upon the back of her neck as well.

A trail of kisses from her nape to the small of her back left her quivering with longing. His fingers, scalding and magical, traced the curve of her spine. When he placed her upon her back again and rained more kisses upon her belly, her hands tugged eagerly at his hair, bringing his face to her own lips, where she kissed his closed eyelids tenderly. All the while, she silently urged him to kiss her mouth again in that slow rhythmic manner that foretold of other pleasures to come.

Rising to his knees, he drank in the sight of her beneath him, until he was drunk with passion. Lifting her hips to his mouth, he kissed her belly again. Then, he wrapped his arms about her and pulled her to him as he lay back onto the bed, taking her with him until she was lying full atop him.

Catching the back of her neck in his grasp, he gently guided her mouth to his own. His lips brushed hers tenderly and he paused to revel in her reaction to him. Her eyes were closed, her expression erotic, and he smiled because he knew she waited for more.

Effortlessly, he raised her above him, until her breasts were level with his lips, and he suckled them lovingly. Then, taking her into his arms, he rolled atop her to continue his exploration.

His lips were the weapon to bring about her surrender as he trailed his knowing tongue across her tender breast, causing her to erupt with goose-flesh. At the same time, his hands started a war of their own in lower regions. Heat unfurled within her and a sweet burning need filled her.

Somehow, Weston's husky voice penetrated her thoughts. "Touch me, Chrestien ... I need you to touch me." His plea broke into her sensual haze, and she reached out to him, stroking him in much the same way, he had stroked her. She recalled and mimicked every touch he'd given her, and when her hands swept over his chest, she felt his muscles ripple beneath her fingers. She marveled that she could make him react so. Emboldened by the discovery, she replaced her fingers with her tongue, wetting the path her fingers had followed, tasting the salt of his skin. A low carnal growl from him was her reward.

Weston's need for her was so great that he could barely think. But from the moment of their arrival he'd heard nothing but praises of Chrestien from Michel and his men, and some of the old suspicions had crept into his mind. That, more than anything else, was why he'd allowed her to sleep alone in her chamber. But now that she was in his bed—had come willingly to it—there were no more doubts. He was certain that her heart belonged to him. Only he needed to hear it from Chrestien's own lips. "Tell me you love me, Chrestien." His tongue swept into her mouth, stabbing deeply. "That you want only me," he demanded hoarsely.

Aye, she did. She loved him, and she didn't care that he knew it, but she wanted him to admit it as well. "I love you ... want only you ... love me . . ." The last two words were a question, not a request, but Weston did not recognize it as such, or he would have told her that she alone held his heart. To him, it was a plea that he make love to her, and she did not need to ask again, for he shifted above her and lifted her hips to join with his own.

Chrestien's passion was finally unleashed, and she unabashedly let her instinct take over. It was a wildcat he was loving, Weston realized as her nails bit into his shoulders. To look into her face when she was so unashamedly loving him back was his undoing, and his body quivered violently with the force of his release. She cried out, and his answering growl was fearsome. He crushed her to him suddenly, and though he'd come to his climax, and she hers, he continued to move into her, not quite able to cease the lovemaking. Dear God, how he loved her.

Chapter 14

hrestien had fallen asleep, spent. And when she awoke again, it was to find Weston gone. A quick peek from the chamber door told her that not a soul was about the hall. And grabbing her bedrobe, she ran as quickly as her bare feet could carry her up the flight of cold stone steps that led to her bower.

Opening the door to her bedchamber, she found Janelle holding a pale green brocade bliaut over a steaming tub of water, trying to smooth the wrinkles from the fabric. Five new trunks had been brought up, and one of them lay open, revealing some of the gowns Adelaine had given her.

Chrestien colored crimson when she realized that Janelle would know whither she'd spent the night, and she skirted into the room, keeping her eyes averted from those of her faithful maid.

"You've no need to hide from me, child! There is no shame in going to yer lord husband's bed." There was no answer from Chrestien, who was standing behind her now, and the perceptive Janelle knew that Chrestien had in fact been to Weston's bed. She chuckled then, delighted with the confirmation. "Come now, Chrestien, I've prepared yer bath," she clucked. "'Tis time ye went to him, ye realize."

Chrestien considered that as she undressed and stepped into the tub. There was a length of silence, until Chrestien sighed, and Janelle patted her shoulder reassuringly.

"What ails you, Chrestien? Tell me, child."

Chrestien shook her head, unsure of how to begin. "I cannot help but wonder how Papa would have felt about Weston. Have I betrayed him, Janelle?"

"Bah!" Janelle protested. "How could you think of such a thing? Chrestien, what choice had you in the matter? The only choice you truly have is whether to make the best of what the Lord has given you, or to make everyone, including yerself miserable over your fate."

Chrestien's expression remained troubled. "But what if Weston did kill Papa, Janelle? How can I live with that?"

"No man shall ever know who killed yer father, child, but know this . . . If 'twas Weston, then he did so only because it was his duty. Your father would not have thought twice about running your husband through, I assure you!"

Chrestien nodded thoughtfully, but still her expression remained troubled.

"There is something else I should tell ye, Chrestien . . . something Aubert told me. 'Tis possible that your father was betrayed. By whom, we know not. But Aubert swears yer father spoke of betrayal before closing his eyes."

"Betrayed?" Chrestien gasped, straightening abruptly in the tub.

Janelle shook her head and then shrugged her shoulders for good measure. "I know not, child, I know not."

"Betrayed," Chrestien whispered, and then settled back down into her bath to consider the possibility.

"Ye love the man, Chrestien, so do not be regrettin' it!" Janelle scolded.

"I do not regret it!" Chrestien defended. "He is my lord husband after all!"

Janelle's eyes twinkled over the confession Chrestien had inadvertently given her. It made her heart glad to know Chrestien had found love—and she had, for Janelle had not missed the looks her husband passed her way when he thought himself unobserved. Now, it was time for the two of them to work things through of their own. She chuckled suddenly, unable to resist one last barb. "Besides, look at ye. 'Tis the most color I've seen in yer cheeks since ye locked yer poor father in the guarderobe and he threatened to take a switch to ye. Going to yer husband's bed has put life back into that body of yers!"

"I never locked Papa in the guarderobe!" Chrestien protested. "That was Adelaine and she did it by accident. I only took the blame because I thought she'd cry away every tear her body owned!"

Janelle laughed at the memory, satisfied with the result of her teasing. The last thing Chrestien needed was to be brooding over her father. It was time to remember the happy moments. "There now," she crooned. "That's the Chrestien we know and love!"

" 'Tis just like Papa you are, Janelle ... teasing me so!" Chrestien gave Janelle the devil's eyes as she concluded, but Janelle remained unaffected, and proceeded to lave Chrestien's hair and scrub her body.

It did not help that Janelle's expression remained so smug, and it played on Chrestien's nerves—ever did Janelle bait her! When it seemed her body was scoured until it felt raw, Chrestien took the coarse rag from Janelle and after giving it a malicious glare, she tossed it into the water. "Jesu, it feels as though you wash me with sand. Whither is the finer linen, that you would need to scrub me with this coarse rag?" She knew she sounded the overindulged child, but it was the only thing she could find to protest about—and she needed to ease her frustration.

"They are to be cleansed." Janelle's smile disappeared and she prayed Chrestien would not inquire further, for it was not Janelle's wish to inform her mistress of King Henry's imminent arrival. Janelle knew full well the anger Chrestien felt over Normandy's new duke. Fortunately for Janelle, Chrestien accepted the explanation without further ado. Rising from the tub, Chrestien took the drying rags Janelle held in plump arms. When she was dry, she dressed, finishing her gown with a circlet of silver about her waist.

"Whither is my lord husband now, Janelle? Have you any idea?" Chrestien finally asked to Janelle's consternation.

Janelle bit her lip and prayed again. "Gone with

Michel to inspect the battlements." She tried to sound as complacent as was possible. "I hear tell that Weston has gained Aleth's permission to remain at Lontaine until after Michaelmas, and he's wanting to be certain all is in order." With a little luck, she could dance around the subject, not really telling Chrestien anything. And when Weston returned, he would tell her—as was his duty. "He's much like yer Papa, you realize, needing to be certain that we are well protected ... but he'll find naught amiss, for yer Papa was too thorough a man."

Sighing, Chrestien went to the window and unlatched the shutters. From the bailey could be heard the sound of metal clashing with metal, and she closed her eyes to fight the tears that threatened—such an odious ring it was. She would hear that sound the rest of her life, for it was the way of things. But how many times would she hear it ere she did not connect it with Adelaine's death? "One too many," she whispered. Forever, the roar of clanging armor and weapons would bring pain to her heart and tears to her eyes.

"What say you, child?"

"Hmmm, oh ... 'tis naught, Janelle. And Aubert, whither is he?"

"Gone with your lord husband. After all, who knows Lontaine better than Aubert and yerself? And Weston would not worry ye with such things."

"Lontaine is safe enough," Chrestien acknowledged. "We've never been breached before," she said plainly, wiping the wetness from her cheeks with the sleeve of her bliaut.

" 'Tis not reason enough to leave it unprotected now, Chrestien. Lord Weston must do what he must."

"I suppose 'tis true, but the only menace we've ever faced is long dead. . . . Aleth killed him."

"Yea, child, and ye mustn't dwell upon that any longer. 'Tis done with and naught can e'er be done to change it. Adelaine and yer father would have wanted ye to go on—not spend the rest of yer days crying over something that cannot be altered."

"I know . . . and at least I have you and Aubert. Why did you not tell me of him sooner?"

" 'Twas yer father's wish that ye not know. He was afeared that ye'd think he'd dishonored yer mother's memory."

"Nay, Janelle, how could we assume such a thing? He loved my lady mother and there was no mistaking it. How many times had he said so? Did he not stay hither at Lontaine to be near her grave when he could have gone to another of his keeps? And he spent his every moment with Mother in the beginning. Did he not go to her grave nigh every morn for a time? Nay, we would never have thought her memory dishonored, Janelle."

Chrestien went to the dressing table and picked up a silver comb, raking it carefully through her tangled damp hair. "My hair has grown. Do you not think so?" Janelle's back was to Chrestien, and when the maid nodded in agreement but did not turn around, Chrestien went to her and found tears in her eyes.

"What thoughts bring such tears?"

" 'Tis naught to concern yerself with, child."

"But Janelle, I'd know if something has upset you," Chrestien insisted, wiping a wayward tear from Janelle's cheek.

" 'Tis only that I'd forgotten how very much yer father loved his Elizabeth." There was silence for a long moment as each of them became lost in her own memories.

"You loved Papa . . . did you not?"

"Yea." There was no use denying it. Janelle's eyes were glassy with unshed tears. "But there could be naught between us, for he loved yer lady mother, and I was but a lowly ladies' maid. Still, I'd have lived my life no other way. Ye see, yer Papa gave me the means, and told me I could leave Lontaine if 'twas my wish. But he also bid me to stay if I would . . . and I chose to stay, for though I knew I could never have his love, he gave me all else he had to offer. Even when the years had left me plump and unattractive, he was good to me still—naught more could have been expected. Please do not judge me for it, Chrestien. I did love him so."

"I'd not judge you for what is in your heart, Janelle. You were as mother to me. My only regret is that Adelaine did not know of our brother, and 'twould have been so wonderful to have shared this with her."

Janelle mopped soft brown eyes with pudgy fingertips, and took Chrestien's hand in her own. "She knows, Chrestien." She gave Chrestien's fingers a gentle squeeze, and when Chrestien's eyes widened accusingly, she added hastily, "Nay! I've not told her, but somehow she knows. I can feel it—just as I know she'll be with us always. Overmuch a part of us she is to be lost to us ... even now ... even now."

Now that Chrestien understood Janelle's meaning, she smiled and gave a nod of agreement. " 'Tis true, her memory will remain with me always, though I shall miss her gentleness in my life. She was my other half, Janelle. She was what I could never be. What I lacked, she possessed, and the opposite was true as well."

"That may be so, child. But all is not lost to ye, for Our Lord has given ye another to share yerself with. And though it may not be quite the same, ye'll need put yer love and trust in Weston, for without trust ... love is meaningless."

Chrestien was silent, taking in all Janelle told her. She knew Janelle spoke true and that 'twould serve her well to heed the words of wisdom. And besides, 'twould not be a difficult task at all, for she'd already given Weston both. Warmed by the thought, she hurriedly finished her toiletry and went in search of her husband.

The hall was empty save for Ned. His back was to her as he stooped to retrieve something from the floor. None other had that shade of red hair, so there was no doubt as to his identity. A quick tap on his shoulder brought him whirling about to face her, eyes wide and a paleness in his face. It seemed, even, that his freckles had faded, and that thought made Chrestien giggle.

"M'lady, 'tis put the fear in me is what you've done. I'd not heard you approach."

"What is it you are about?"

"Settin' the place to rights. Sir Weston despises a disorderly hall." With his face a deep shade of red, he admitted, "And I know he would not relish seeing my belongings lying amid the rushes while King Henry is in residence."

"King Henry! But why? And when?"

Ned shook his head and shrugged his shoulders. "I've not an inkling, m'lady. I know only that he is to arrive this eve . . . or on the morrow at the least." Chrestien's brows were frozen in an obvious scowl, and Ned didn't quite know what to make of her apparent aversion to his king, so he promptly made his excuses and scurried away ere she could question him further. He liked Chrestien, but he was loyal to Sir Weston and his king . . . and he wouldn't like to have words with her over them.

"Whither is my lord Weston now?" she called after him, but Ned only shrugged his shoulders again before disappearing from the hall.

Jesu! Whyever would King Henry bother with Lontaine? But as she asked herself the question, she suddenly recalled who her husband was—the king's favored Silver Wolf. Somehow, she could see him as the much feared, ruthless warrior no longer. But there had been a time when she saw naught but the devil in him. Now, however, he was simply her gentle Weston.

She could clearly recall the day she'd first seen him. Yea, he was handsome, darkly so. There had been a harshness about him as well, his eyes violent blue flames—dark, smoldering blue, she recalled. She'd likened him to Satan with his dark looks. A shudder passed through her as she thought of him in that manner, and she decided vehemently that she would prefer not to think of him as Henry's Silver Wolf—yet another thing to dislike King Henry for.

In but a short time, she would be obliged to make the odious man welcome in her father's home. How ironic it was that the very one who caused her father's death was to be entertained and wooed in her father's beloved hall. Even more odious yet was the fact that Weston would give his suzerain the best chamber for his use—her father's very own, for that was the way of things. "Oh Papa, I'm so very sorry," she whispered to herself, suddenly feeling more than a little defeated.

What she needed was to feel the wind in her hair—smell the crisp scent of winter-fresh air. 'Twould do much to soothe her, she decided, and after fetching her riding habit, she would ready Lightning . . . and do just that.

The familiar odors of the stable filled Chrestien with a sense of peace, and a smile came to her face, lighting her eyes, when she spotted her snow-white Lightning. "My pretty boy," she cooed pridefully as she caressed the stallion's fine frosty mane. " 'Tis been overlong, yea it has," she wooed, and Lightning snorted in reply. Chrestien continued her cooing as she saddled him and led him from the stall. "But I've not forgotten you," she promised. "Nay, I have not, my pretty boy."

Naught could make her feel so alive as speeding with Lightning across the countryside, and she was filled with the thrill of anticipation as she mounted the expectant stallion. As a consideration to Weston she sat as if she were using a side-saddle—as any well-bred lady would. But once she'd passed through the castle gates and was certain there were no eyes upon her, she hiked up her skirts excitedly, hugging her thighs knowingly against her prize steed. Lightning recognized his cue and immediately abandoned the conscientiously dignified canter. By the time she'd reached the open meadow she was galloping at full pace, with the cool wind whipping at her face.

It had been overlong since she'd ridden so! At Montagneaux, she'd felt compelled to refrain from doing aught that would embarrass Adelaine. Too, she'd not wished to disenchant Weston. He was fickle in his affection as it was. But because he was otherwise occupied at the moment, she was unconcerned that he would discover her in such an unladylike state.

Involuntarily, she giggled softly at the look she imagined Weston would sport were he to see her riding in such a manner. Jesu, would he be appalled! He would frown, of course, she knew. Then he would masterfully empty his lungs of all the outrage he felt. She giggled again, not really knowing why that thought would fill her with such mirth. Surely there was naught humorous about his bellowing. Oh Adelaine. . . Papa . . . how many times have you instructed me on my contrary nature, only to find me as bold as ever? Why did you humor me so? " 'Tis as much your sin as 'tis mine!" She shouted her accusation into the wind, and laughed contentedly, uninhibitedly, when a cool hefty breeze swatted her in the face.

Tugging at the reins, she brought Lightning to a

halt when she reached her favorite glen. A small pond graced the center of it, hidden well by gnarled oaks and elms. She and Adelaine had oft come hither to wade in the spring and summer ... and fall—inconceivably, winter as well. True, 'twas frigid in winter, but something about wading in naught but a chainse sent a warm thrill through her—enough to where it warmed her bones as well as would a cozy fire.

Who would know it if she took a quick plunge into the waist-deep water—for old times' sake. Surely there was none to see her, for this immediate spot was well hidden. True, the bushes and trees were well on their way to being winter bared, but still the twining branches were thick enough to conceal her sufficiently. None would see her, she concluded, as she dismounted and tethered Lightning's reins to a low, gnarly branch.

"The old masonry walls are unbelievably well kept," Weston capitulated.

"Yea." Aubert was proud to accept the praise for his father, and continued to crow over Gilbert's resourcefulness. "He was particular, as I've said. 'Twas never his way to leave aught to chance. 'Twas the only reason he would leave his daughters at all. He knew they would not be in danger with the keep so well maintained. If you will note, there are no trees within a furlong of the curtain wall ... and the keep rises to a height so as to make it facile to utilize the tower arrow slits safely—'twill not endanger our own men. Nor will we lose countless arrows to trees that shield the enemy," Aubert explained.

Weston had already fathomed as much; he'd utilized the same concept at Montfort. Only Montfort was much larger, and sported a double curtain wall. The outer one came to a mere eight feet, sitting well below the inner, which rose to a goodly thirty feet or more, thereby giving him double protection against intruders. But he could see that Aubert was proud of his father, so he masked his amusement and allowed the lad to continue his explication.

"The moat is dry now, but only because 'twas emptied for cleaning just before ... well, before Tinchebrai," Aubert stammered. "Gilbert left it thus, for lack of time and rain to refill it."

"Did he not worry that it would make for an easier target by those who would take advantage of his absence?"

"Immensely," Aubert admitted honestly. "But there was no help for it. Curthose demanded that Gilbert raise and make use of all available levies, and it took some time to round up those who would defend the duke. Nevertheless, Gilbert was not taken lightly as adversary, and there would be none in these parts to oppose him." Aubert chuckled then, " 'Twas rumored that he was an eccentric, my father. None would anger him, lest he loose the dark spirits that live in the donjon tower." Aubert laughed openly at this fallacy.

Weston's lips turned into a sneer, and he waved a hand, dismissing the tale. "And there are those who would believe a tale such as that. Surely Gilbert did not encourage it?"

"Nay." Aubert chuckled again. "He did not." Then, on a more sober note, he added, " 'Twas only rumored so, because his young wife died in that tower." The men looked to the brooding turret above them. "The topmost chamber has never been occupied since," Aubert continued, "because the memories were too painful for Gilbert. 'Tis as simple as that. There are no spirits ensnared behind that oaken door." Aubert's eyes reflected his pride as he mused. " 'Tis not a large stronghold, but 'tis sufficient."

"Yea, it is," Weston agreed somberly as he mounted Thunder and started for the southern wall of the fortress. Aubert immediately mounted his own steed and rode beside him. Michel lingered behind, silently contemplating the prior conversation. De Lontaine had indeed been a thorough man, for from what Aubert had imparted and Weston had verified, there were very few repairs necessary, and the few were minimal. If Lontaine's remaining two keeps were in as fine a state, Henry would put them to good use—mayhaps giving them to one of his many liegemen. In Weston's hands the strongholds would prosper, Michel knew.

A lone rider in the distance caught Weston's eye, and when he noted that the rider sped from Lontaine, instead of toward it, an alarm sounded within him. King Henry was not due until nightfall, and the messenger the king had sent had gone an hour past to inform Henry that Weston was indeed in residence. None of his men would defy his orders and leave the castle when they were expected to prepare for their suzerain's arrival. Who, then, was this lone rider stealing away in such a charge?

He spurred Thunder, and the animal lunged forth immediately, knowing instinctively that his master was in pursuit. Weston was possessed of a gentle way about him when he was not in combat, and his gelding knew by the swift blow of Weston's boot that it was not a pleasure ride his master was about. By now, Michel and Aubert had spied the rider as well and were no more than a few paces behind Weston.

When Weston neared the rider sufficiently to discover his identity, he realized that it was none other than Chrestien hugging the immense white stallion, and he was stunned enough to rein in his horse and simply gape stupidly, entranced by the vision before him. Irately, he noted that Michel was watching her as well. His captain was nigh salivating at the sight of his wife. Moreover, the disheartened look upon Aubert's face told Weston that this was not Chrestien's first such ride, and the knowledge gave him a pang of jealousy—that someone else might have spied her thus.

He was torn between admiration for her skill and a nagging desire to take a switch to her pearly white fanny. Mayhap it was the fact that her skirts had flown nigh to her waist, exposing her long silky legs, that unnerved him so—or mayhap it was the way she laid so low over the animal, nigh lying upon its back in such a provocative pose. Her every motion was fluid with that of her stallion, merging both horse and rider in a pagan dance of sorts. When animal and rider disappeared behind a thicket, he regained his wits and kneed Thunder to follow.

He kept his gait slow while he tried to discern

what he would say to her—that he was pleasantly surprised she could ride so, but that she was never to employ such a revealing pose e'er again? Somehow he did not think she would take kindly to such a command. Nevertheless, she was his wife and she would do as was bid of her.

Never again would she wander alone ... or in that wanton manner! Then again, he did enjoy seeing her ride, and 'twas not her fault she could conjure such wicked thoughts in men. Mayhaps he would allow her to enjoy her sport ... while in his company alone—and never in the presence of others! Yea, that was what he would tell her. That decision made, he quickened his pace, anxious to be in the company of his wife.

What he saw when he reached the hidden glen took his breath away, filled his breeches, and at the same time spurred his anger anew. A trail of clothing dotted the bank of a tiny pool he had not known existed. Chrestien was splashing in the waist-deep water with naught on but her filmy chainse—singing nonetheless! She had the nerve to be singing, damn her!

He looked behind him to be certain Michel and Aubert were not attending, and when he saw them ride for Lontaine he sighed his relief. No doubt the two of them foresaw what she was about, and that realization did more to ignite his anger than aught else. Aubert's knowing was not so irritating to him, but to think that Michel might have spied her at her mischief brought his blood to a boil.

* * *

The icy water was so invigorating, and Chrestien could feel it tingling her skin wheresoever it touched her. Another would describe the water as frigid—swear that frostbite had set in—but not Chrestien. To her 'twas like a purifying of the soul.

"What do you think you are about, mistress?" There was no mistaking Weston's roar and Chrestien started at hearing it. But her timid reaction lasted little longer than it took to bat an eyelash, and she countered with a question of her own.

"What does it seem I do? I bathe, of course, my lord." Her tone was acid as she answered her own question. She could tell Weston was in a mood again . . . and did he think to make a meal of her with his words again, then he had a thing or two to discover. There was naught to be gained with a biting tongue, and she would make that fact known to him!

It did not occur to her that he would be angry over her state of dress, for she had forgotten that simple fact in her anger. And when she recalled that it was he she could thank for his king's unendurable visit, she was filled with a deeper anger. How dare he be upset with her when 'twas his fault she had ridden from Lontaine in the first place! If he was about to rail at her for leaving, then by the saints, he would also accept his part in it!

"Remove yourself from that pool, Chrestien." His tone was strained with anger, but Chrestien only implanted herself more stubbornly in the frigid water, curling her toes in the bottom silt.

And though of a sudden her bones were feeling the bitter chill, she refused to move toward him.

"Out, mistress!" Weston shouted, finally losing what control he'd managed to attain. His breath was heavy with fury, and his voice reverberated through her.

Chrestien winced at the tone, knowing she had never seen him so angry, and was suddenly afraid that she'd pushed him too far. It was this new fear that kept her firmly rooted to the spot, and she was totally unprepared for what he did next. Belatedly, she started to wade to the opposite shore, in an attempt to escape his rage.

He was beside her within mere minutes, still seated atop his black war-horse, towering above her in all his warrior's glory. His horse had not even hesitated upon entering the frigid waters. A quick glance at her husband's face told her that his mouth was set tight, and she could see the flesh on either side of his jaw twitch with the potency of his anger. Before she knew what was to ensue, he had her by the waist and hoisted her over his powerful shoulder like a pitiful sack of meal.

When they reached the bank again, he dropped her to her feet. "Dress yourself." His teeth were clenched as he spoke, his voice too smooth for her liking, and she knew she would not balk. She would do as he bid in order to allay his temper. Gathering her personal items hastily, she dressed promptly, and it seemed that ere she could even smooth the wrinkles from her crumpled bliaut Weston had her over his shoulder again. With Lightning's reins in hand, he headed back to the keep.

All eyes were upon the Wolf and his quarry when they rode through the gate of Lontaine. Janelle, who was looking from Chrestien's chamber window, crossed herself when she saw her mistress hauled up like so much baggage.

Not a word was said between Weston and Chrestien, and the longer the silence, the more Chrestien feared she had made an enemy of her husband. But nay! He would not forget what had passed between them. He could not! She'd sworn her love for him. Had she not?

When Weston handed Lightning's reins to Michel, who was waiting in the inner bailey, and carelessly tossed Chrestien into Aubert's arms, she knew without a doubt that his fury had reached its peak.

Tenderly, Aubert aided Chrestien to her feet, and when she'd gained her balance and recovered her pride, she made her way into the hall. Within seconds, however, she was overtaken by Weston. "I do not recall bidding you to take your leave, my sweet."

She refused to let him goad her into a quarrel this time. "I beg your pardon, my lord," she said sweetly, lifting her skirt delicately. "May I then?"

Weston didn't quite know what to think of her sudden complacence, but he nodded his approval with controlled effort, then followed behind her as she made her way up the winding stone steps. Halfway up the stairs he realized she was going to her old chamber and his arms went about her waist again. Roughly, he carried her to his own chamber, kicking open the door and tossing her backside first upon the bed. It was then she decided she'd had enough of his ill treatment.

"You belong with me, Chrestien. Never forget it. When you retire for the eve, 'tis hither you will come. When I bid you go to your room ... 'tis hither you will come. Do you heed?"

Her chin lifted slightly in defiance, but ere she would refuse his command, she was going to show him that he could not just lift her and throw her as if she were a pile of manure on a spade!

"Yea, my lord, I ken perfectly well. And shall you bid me to go to my room when your king is in residence? Surely you will, for you've shown me that I am no more to you than so much chattel, that you can do with me as you will—including shame me to your suzerain. Is that not so? Surely it is, my lord. Surely, I mean naught to you!" She spat the words with all the contempt she felt, narrowing her eyes upon him to reveal her fury.

Chrestien was standing upon the bed when Weston lunged at her, but he found only air where her feet were supposed to be. In her attempt to avoid him, Chrestien fell to the floor, taking most of the impact on her padded backside. But when Weston pounced again she was too slow in recovering to avoid him, and her chest took the substantial impact of his weight, knocking the sense from her. When she regained consciousness, Weston was hovering scant inches from her face.

"Oh, little one ... have I hurt you?" He was so relieved when she opened her eyes. "None other has the ability to anger me more than you ... yet in the same breath I must tell you that ..." God's Teeth! What was he saying? He could not tell her.

For though his heart belonged to her, he could not bring himself to say the words. To do so would be to open up a vein from which she might draw his lifeblood! Experience told him that was the way of it. Nay, he would not tell her until he was certain she would not use it against him—only then ... only then.

"Tell me what, my lord?" She so desperately wanted to hear the words he was about to say, and when his answer was not forthcoming, and she only received the scrutiny of his powerful gaze instead, she pounded her fist into his chest. "You cannot allow your king to sleep in my father's chamber!" It was the only thing that would come to mind to shout at him about—and she needed to shout!

" 'Twould be an insult not to allow it, Chrestien," he informed her, thankful of the change in topics. "He'll sleep in this chamber and I'll not hear another word of it."

"You cannot, FitzStephens. I shall not allow it!"

"You shall not ... allow it?" A dark challenging brow lifted to frame incredulous blue eyes.

"You are despicable, you realize. But he is *your* king—not mine ... and I'll not cater to his every wish. His men—your men killed my father! And I can never forgive you for that."

The truth of what Chrestien said filled Weston's chest with an unbearable weight and brought him to his knees. For if he could be honest with himself this once, he would need own to himself that he wanted her—needed her, even. And to hear her say that she would never forgive him nigh crushed his heart.

He rose from his position over her, expression blank, and left the room. Yea, she had professed to love him, but words said in the heat of passion could not be credited. Somehow, he would make her really love him, and when she said those words again 'twould be because she truly felt them.

Tears brimmed over green pools, and Chrestien ran from the chamber, up the stone steps. But she didn't stop at her bower. Instead, she continued on up to the tower chamber and threw open the door. Whereas Chrestien had her sacred thinking spot, so too had Adelaine. Adelaine's was this very chamber, lain unused but for her private moments.

The chamber was dark and Chrestien unlatched the shutters to allow light to enter within, revealing the utter emptiness of the room. It had been so long since even Adelaine had used it that dust had gathered upon the floor, and webs covered the high nooks and crannies. Wiping a place at her feet with her skirts, she sat and contemplated her state.

She knew Weston had come very close to vowing his love—knew she should have been more patient, not blurting out something so hurtful. Yea, she blamed Henry of England for her father's death. Likely, she always would, but there were too many men at Tinchebrai for her to think Weston had been the one to thrust the sword. And even with the possibility that Weston had been the one, he was merely defending himself and his king as was his duty. She could not fault him for that.

Her eyes blurred, and she swiped at the wetness

puddling onto her cheek. Once Henry took his leave, she would make it up to Weston—would show him how false her words were, that she did truly love him . . . and yea, she did love him. She wasn't quite certain when she had realized that fact, only that she did. "Adelaine, oh that I were you," she whispered brokenly. "Never would you have opened your mouth as I have. Such patience you were gifted with."

The light from the window illuminated the majority of the room, but where the shutters caught the rays of sun a shadow was cast upon the wooden floor. Reflexively, her fingers fondled the dust where a glimmer caught her eye, and to her surprise she uncovered a silver chain. Pulling it from the filth, she found that a crimson amulet adorned with a rose was attached, and a smile lit upon her lips.

Of a sudden she remembered a time when she and Adelaine were young . . . not more than six summers, mayhap. Both Adelaine and herself were crying impatiently for Papa to take them riding, and she could swear that she remembered Adelaine crying the loudest. Adelaine was not gifted with patience, it dawned on her. Nay, Adelaine had learned it, having to compete so oft with Chrestien for attention. So if Adelaine could learn patience, so then could she!

Dropping the amulet, she rose from the floor, brushed the dust from her skirts, and went to find Janelle and Eauda. Between the three of them they would set the place to rights, and Weston's king would want for naught.

As she started down the steps, the cold of the

stone bit into the soles of her feet, and she realized for the first time that she was barefoot. Now how was it that she had not noted such a thing before? Shrugging her shoulders she decided that it was surely because she had burned with the heat of her anger. But her shoulders slumped when she realized where her footwear had been discarded. Her leather boots, the ones Papa had given her, had been abandoned at the pond. And ere she could do aught else, she would need retrieve those boots. Briefly, she considered asking Weston to accompany her, but she knew he would be too busy preparing for his king's arrival to spare the time. She would go alone rather than take anyone from his set tasks.

Chapter 15

I the distance could be seen the king's banner soaring from silver-tipped lances, their metallic points twinkling in the afternoon sun. Helms and shields trimmed in gold joined the dance of sun-fires, and when the cavalcade had neared enough, the sound of clinking chain mail could be heard as a song to a warrior's ear.

Though his army was stunning in all its grandeur, no plainer man in dress could be known than William's youngest son. For all the riches he had available to him, Henry preferred the plain garb. And though the material of his garments could certainly be described as rich or fine, he chose not to adorn them in a gaudy way. So when a man of large build, with black hair cut straight across his forehead in the Norman fashion, dismounted and came to Weston's side, onlookers never guessed that it was the king himself. But as he spoke in greeting, his regal bearing was evident in his words, carefully weighed, and articulated with grace. Half out of fear, half out of respect, the villein quit the bailey and went about their chores.

It was clear by the smile on Henry's face, and

that on Weston's, that there was great affection between the two men. When Henry swatted Weston's back forcefully, it was more out of care and respect for his loyal knight than aught else.

"It has been long, my friend."

"That is has," Weston assured him with a gentle nod, acknowledging the fact. "That it has." Henry was ever the diplomat, and instinctively Weston knew that his king was anxious to know something of him—and he had a suspicion as to what it was. He knew Henry would be concerned as to how he'd taken the mandate that he wed Chrestien, and smiling his wolfish grin, he let Henry know that he was aware of the reason for the sojourn.

Henry laughed to see that his friend knew him so well, and conceded, "I received the writ stating you were wed and have come to meet your bride."

"But my lord, you need only have asked and I would have brought her to you."

"True, but I had need of this time away, and have brought with me a guest besides." It was then Weston noticed the heavyset man, well into his older years, standing behind his king. Hair that was golden blond had receded until there was but a patch of hair on either side of his head and a fringe of gold covering his chubby neck behind. "This is Baron Geoffrey Grey of Edinburgh ... grandsire to your ladywife," Henry explained as the man turned about to face them.

"Grandsire, my lord? I was unaware that she had family other than a sister, who I am aggrieved to say has died less than a sennight ago ... oh, and there is a half brother as well."

There was a heavy silence out of courtesy for the baron, and it was Grey who broke it finally, eyes downcast. There was a tightness in the baron's voice as he croaked, "The girl you speak of who has died ... she was the eldest?"

"She was," Weston assured him.

"And you have wed the youngest?"

"Yea." Weston was unsure of where the questions were leading.

Baron Grey cleared his throat, and his voice wavered.

"Then the one dead is de Lontaine's only legal offspring." It was not a question, but Weston answered anyway.

"Nay, they were twins. Henry has not told you?" Grey looked to Henry and cocked his head in question.

"You speak of me as if I were not present, my friends. Nay, I did not tell him, Weston. Your letter was too vague—Michel's as well—speaking mainly of Chrestien. And you, my old friend, mentioned Adelaine only once and left it very unclear as to her exact relationship to your ladywife. So nay, I did not tell him ... though I must own, I did suspect."

A smile turned the corners of Grey's lips as he turned to Weston and spoke again. "You said there was a half brother as well. Then he was acknowledged by Gilbert?"

"Not directly," Weston conceded. "But when you consider the fact that he was son of a peasant, taught the skills of knighthood by Lontaine himself, you are led to believe Gilbert at least knew of it. And when you see the boy you would know immediately that he bears resemblance to Chrestien, with hair the color of gold . . . much like that which you bear."

That remark brought a peal of laughter to Henry's lips. And though the hysterics were at the balding Geoffrey's expense, the baron shouted his laughter all the same. Weston knew immediately that he liked the man. Anyone who could laugh at himself so easily was none too bad a soul, indeed. He would venture that Chrestien would be delighted to know her grandsire had come along with Henry. Mayhap it would ease the rift between them.

Chrestien's boots were just as she had left them, lying just under the bush she had tethered Lightning to. Having brushed the winter-dead grass from them, she pulled them onto her bare feet, anxious to return to Lontaine.

As she started to remount Lightning, she was distracted by an approaching rider, and thinking it was Weston, she turned her back to him momentarily, bracing herself to receive the brunt of his anger. Again she started to mount, but the voice that called to her was not Weston's, and in her curiosity she turned to see that it was a strange man clad in a rich blue tunic and mantle, carrying, of all things, a potted rose. Had he not been carrying the item, she'd have known enough to be frightened. But the miniature rose gave his identity away, and a smile came to her instantly. This could be none other than Aleth's brother, she knew. Rolfe.

"Ye are Chrestien?" Of course, Rolfe knew she

was, and by her smile he could tell she did not recognize him. Good . . . good.

"I am. And you, I presume are Rolfe, sir. Am I correct?"

"Ye are, Lady Chrestien. How astute of ye."

"Nay, sir, 'twas your pot of roses that gave you away. Aleth said you would bring them. But I thought, surely, you would put them on Adelaine's grave yourself rather than bring them here?"

"I thought to, my gentle lady, but that honor belongs to ye."

"How kind of you, Sir Rolfe. I thank you for your consideration." Chrestien smiled, grateful for his gesture of kindness. She curtsied daintily, and watched as he neared. But as the raven-haired man dismounted from his stallion, she saw no kindness in his gaze and her smile fled. Moreover, he seemed to move with a purpose, she noted. But when he just stood there and looked at her for a long moment ere handing her the pot of roses, she decided that her imagination was running away with her again.

She thanked him again, setting the pot down to mount her stallion. "I shall have to impose on you to hand them to me, sir, for I cannot mount with such a thing in my grasp." He smiled and nodded, but in turning to Lightning she caught a glimpse of the scar upon his right cheek. It lay just below the high cheekbone, and was pink and newly healed. Aubert's words came to her then, ringing a warning in her ears: *'Twas a nasty gash ye gave him, Chrestien.* And belatedly, she noticed the color of his eyes—murky gray. In that instant of realization, her hesitation gave her away and Rolfe stepped into her, his chest pressing her backward until she backed into a prickly bush. When she could move no more, she finally lifted her eyes to meet his, and said simply, " 'Twas you." Her chin rose proudly while she awaited the answer she already knew was to come.

A truly wicked smile turned the corners of Rolfe's cruel mouth. In seconds, his hands went about her neck, squeezing until she could not control her fear any longer. She parted with the beginning of a scream, but his lips came down over hers, and his tongue filled her mouth to silence the rest of it.

His kiss was cruel, crushing her already bruised lips against her teeth. In another instant he was pulling her toward his horse. Reflexively, she kneed him in the groin, not really knowing why she did so. But when he let go of her to shield himself, she started to run, tripping over the forgotten pot of roses in her haste. Rolfe grimaced, his face contorting against the pain, and he doubled over immediately, though it seemed he recovered too quickly and was upon her within mere seconds. He held her fast, grunting against another wave of pain. Then the hilt of his sword came down upon her skull and blackness engulfed her once again.

Unceremoniously, Rolfe lifted Chrestien, tossing her onto his horse clumsily. As he did, his foot nudged the overturned pot just enough that it rolled down the bank, splashing into the pond and sinking to the bottom with a profusion of little

bubbles popping in its wake, leaving only a handful of blood-red petals to mark the spot.

The great hall was filled to the brim with the
king's entourage. There were more men about
than it seemed possible for the moderate-sized hall
to accommodate. In total, there were near thirty
large trestle tables squeezed in together until it
seemed they were all one enormous table.

Weston eyed the circular staircase, hoping to see
Chrestien emerge from the arched entrance. He
knew she was no longer in her father's chamber,
because when he took Henry to it to show him
where his quarters would be, there was not a sign
of her. He'd thought to go up to her chamber and
announce her grandsire's arrival himself, but then
decided against it. She would yet be angry, if he
knew Chrestien—and he fancied he did. He did
not wish to subject her grandsire to an unseemly
quarrel, which might escalate to dangerous levels
as others had in the past. But an hour had gone by
without an appearance from her and Weston knew
she must hear the clamor. It was this curiosity that
furrowed his brow.

"Weston . . . Weston, my boy, I was inquiring of
you whether my granddaughter would be down
anon. I'm anxious to see her, you know. I didn't
come all this way to see your pretty face, you realize." He laughed.

Michel laughed heartily, and Weston chuckled
as he nodded his acknowledgment. Then he motioned for Aubert to come to him from the lower
tables. "I was just thinking the same, Baron. I'll
have her brother go and fetch her straightaway."

"Excellent, I'd meet him as well," Grey said, his eyes widening at Aubert's approach. He had little need to ask, but he did nonetheless. "This is he, then?"

"Yes, Baron, it is." Weston smiled knowingly, and turned his attention to Aubert. "Aubert, this man to my left is Chrestien's grandsire, Baron of Edinburgh." Aubert acknowledged the older man with a smile and a proud tip of his younger head. Long, thick, golden strands fell to Aubert's eyes as he did, and all at once Henry burst out laughing. Grey's booming voice followed, and Weston could only chuckle softly to see Aubert's consternation. Weston knew Aubert would think he'd said something cockeyed, and sought to reassure him. " 'Tis not you, Aubert. They jest with me for an odd remark I made earlier . . . er . . . about the baron and yourself having the same head of hair." Aubert looked from the balding man to Weston. Then to Michel, eyes wide and incredulous. At once, his hand flew to his thick head of hair, and then he caught the smirk Weston wore, and he smiled meaningfully, nodding as he acknowledged the blunder.

Aubert reminded Weston of himself more each day, and he had to own that he liked the lad. "I'd have you go and fetch your sister," Weston told him, smiling approvingly. Then he pulled Aubert closer and whispered for his ears only. "If you must, tell Chrestien about her grandsire—that he is here. And if that fails, then tell Chrestien I owe her her heart's desire."

"Bribe her?" Michel teased, having overhead.

"We'll not use that word." Weston frowned. "But yea, do it, Aubert."

Aubert nodded, and made his way through the tangle of tables. And as Weston watched him retreat, he dared to hope that Chrestien would submit to this one request. His thoughts drifted to Chrestien as he'd left her in the morn, sleeping so peacefully. She was possessed of the face of an angel when she slept, and he had not dared wake her. He'd sat himself upon the stool next to the bed, watching her slumber for the longest time. He didn't know how long he'd remained there, but at some point the need to touch her had grown so strong that he knew he would have to leave the room ere he spent the entire day abed.

Henry's voice broke into his thoughts. "I can see you are happy, my friend. Do you thank me now for ordering the marriage, or shall you be stubborn as always and deny that you are pleased?" He crowed.

"He shall be stubborn, of course, my lord," Michel goaded, nudging Weston's arm with an elbow.

A smile crept to Weston's face to hear his friend's teasing, and he took a swig of wine before answering, letting the curiosity fester. "I'll not be stubborn," he imparted finally. "And yea, 'tis pleased that I am. But tell me, my lord, what prompted you to give such an edict?" Finally, he would have some answers!

" 'Twas simple enough." Henry waved a regal hand in the direction of Baron Grey and started to explain. " 'Twas his notion originally, for he has none to leave his estates to—at least none he approves of. There are no sons, and his eldest daughter died years ago in childbirth—her lord husband is a lily-livered coward. The baron's second daughter has been pledged to the Church years now." Henry sighed, weary with the accounting. "His third just will not suit. Elizabeth, Chrestien's mother, was his fourth child, and until now . . ." He trailed off, and shrugged, ending his explication.

"I never acknowledged them," Grey admitted with marked regret. "I never forgave Gilbert for Elizabeth's death. She was my favorite, you know. I let her marry de Lontaine because . . . well, because whatever Elizabeth would ask of me, I could not deny her. And once she was gone from this life, I could not bear to be reminded of her." He spoke softly, brokenly, as he paused to wipe the gathering moistness about his eyes. Composed then, he continued. "She was possessed of the greenest eyes, my little girl . . . so deep a green. 'Twas as though they were emerald pools . . . and her hair so rich a flaxen color that it seemed 'twas made of spun gold."

The baron's eyes clouded again with unshed tears, spurred by painful memories, and Weston smiled soothingly, knowing full well the image the baron described. He could vividly imagine the pain he would feel were Chrestien to leave him now.

"She was beautiful," Henry broke in, spent on the woeful subject. "And I can't wait to see her daughter." 'Twas past time to change the subject, and Henry didn't wish to see the old baron weep yet again—once was more than enough to watch a grown man sob—and he'd already done so twice!

"But you have not said why you decided to give her to me for wife, my lord?" Weston asserted.

" 'Tis simple, that," Henry stated, knowing that Weston would not cease until he had the answers he sought. "Baron Grey needed a strong hand to protect his lands ... and you were yet unwed. 'Twas destiny at hand," he avowed. "For your letter arrived just as the good baron and I were determining the girl's future."

"I've many regrets, FitzStephens. For one, would that I had come sooner," Grey lamented. "For I'd have known Adelaine as well. But what is done, is done, and I'd make it up to Chrestien ... for all that I have done—and not," he corrected.

"Adelaine was as good and kind as ye say her mother was," Weston assured the older man.

"And what of Chrestien?" the baron demanded. "What sort is she?"

Weston cleared his throat, raising both dark brows, and parted his lips to begin. But it was Michel whose voice sounded, while Weston only smiled, his eyes flashing a devilish light.

"She is kind as well, though Weston seems to have a little difficulty with her." But Henry couldn't help but note that a light in Weston's eyes twinkled at the revelation.

Aubert appeared at Weston's side then, without Chrestien, and Weston immediately assumed she'd denied his request. But Aubert's grim expression told him there was more to it than that. "She's gone," Aubert told him, with a worried catch to his tone.

"Gone! What do you mean, gone?" Weston repeated incredulously.

"Not there, my lord Weston?... We should go after her. I was told she was seen leaving Lontaine more than two hours past. She would not be gone so long ... after today's—"

"I'll have someone's arse for not telling me sooner!" Weston exploded, shouting the threat. "Come with me, Aubert. I know whither she's gone." Springing from his chair, he shoved the table angrily from him and started for the door.

"Wait, Weston, you may need some aid." Henry stood to follow, feeling a sense of urgency, as did Michel and the baron, but Weston was well out of hearing distance before the last words were uttered. But even if he were not, his rage made him deaf to their offer.

Anger surged through Weston—fury as he'd never known. He'd brought her home mere hours ago, only to have her turn about and leave again! Had he not told her explicitly not to leave without permission? Nay, it dawned upon him suddenly. He had not gotten around to it. She had angered him so with her accusations about Henry that it had turned his thoughts from what he would tell her. Well, by God! He would be certain to let his laws be known in future, and she would not do this again did he have to bind her to his bed for the duration of her life!

Weston rode as if possessed, taking the lead and leaving all in his furious wake. Only Aubert kept the pace, and Henry noted that he, too, seemed to ride as if the devil were at his heels.

It was pure outrage that flooded through Weston when he saw that Lightning was left untethered by the bank. But when he did not see Chrestien, his anger was replaced by a gnawing dread. He noted immediately that there were signs of struggle in the winter-dead grass—long broken marks, signifying that something or someone had been dragged unwillingly.

His heart nigh stopped when he saw the red puddle closer to the bank. But upon closer inspection he found it to be only a handful of red flower petals, and he said a silent prayer of thanks that it was not Chrestien's blood. Nevertheless, he could not shake the nagging sense of danger growing within him—for whither was Chrestien?

"My lord." Aubert's voice broke into Weston's thoughts. "Chrestien would never leave her Lightning untethered as he is, and she loved him too well to leave him at all." The toe of Aubert's right boot was drawn to the red that caught his eye, and as he raked the tiny rose petals across the ground, a vague memory plagued him, but he could not place it. There was something about these petals, he knew. But because there was more to be concerned with than a handful of paltry flowers, he turned his attention back to Weston. "She's in danger, my lord, I can sense it."

" 'Tis my fear as well," Weston admitted, his head pounding madly from so much blood rushing to it.

Henry, Michel, and Baron Grey brought their mounts to a halt just as the breeze picked up and caused the tiny petals to fly into a swirl. As Weston stood there watching their bright color stir from the colorless ground, he knew fear for the first time. His trembling hand rubbed his throbbing temple as he tried to compose his shattered thoughts, for he knew without a doubt that Chrestien was in trouble.

The room was dark, lit only by a sliver of moonlight penetrating the one tiny window. The silvery light fell well away from her, leaving her in the shadows and illuminating naught but a bare section of wall. There was little Chrestien could see to help her determine her whereabouts. 'Twas night, she knew, but that was all she could discern. Only how long had she been here?

Instinctively, she tried to move her hand to soothe her aching head, and it was then she realized that her hands were bound with heavy rope. The coarseness of it bit into her numbed flesh when she pulled at it, and she resigned herself to the wait as she attempted to calm the melee of her mind.

It wasn't long before her captor made his appearance. When the door creaked its warning, she closed her eyes and prayed fervently. His footsteps were heavy, their sound echoing cruelly in her ears. When they stopped so near, she knew he was looking down upon her. A rush of wind fled past her cheek as something soft fluttered onto the bed. Oh, Sweet Jesu, she prayed. Give me strength! Through her fear, she managed to peek through her lids just enough to see him hazily, but the slight flitter of her lashes gave her away.

"We've come back to the living, have we now?" Rolfe's voice was a sneer, and when she opened her eyes fully, she could see him clearly by the light of the pitch torch he held in his hand. The bright light brought swirls of color before her newly opened eyes, and she closed her lids to settle her tumultuous belly. "I thought I'd killed ye," he said simply, without a trace of emotion, sounding as if he thought her more trouble than she was worth. "I've brought ye a change of clothing . . . on the bed," he indicated. A flash of silver swept before Chrestien's eyes, and she dodged it, blinking her eyes instinctively to avoid it.

"Why have you brought me here?" She moaned, closing her eyes against the pain in her head and the nausea that threatened to rise with her fear.

" 'Tis where ye belong, my lady," he drawled, laughing abruptly at his own quip.

With the poniard he proceeded to sever the braided cord binding her wrist, and she winced to hear the way he said the last words—so much emphasis upon the word *my*. "Why do you say it . . . it . . . so," she stammered. "As if I were your . . . ladywife." The flesh of her arms was tingling oddly, and she tried to rub them, but somehow could not. She had little control over her deadened hands.

"Because it should have been so," he told her simply. "Ye should have come to me, Chrestien . . . and were I lord of Montagneaux, ye would have been offered to me first."

"Nay, 'twould not have been so," she denied, "for my father had pledged me to the Church."

Rolfe's reverberating laughter was wild, without reason, Chrestien decided, and she knew she'd not argue with him further.

His laughter stopped abruptly then, and he

shrugged his shoulders indifferently. "Then 'twould have been Adelaine. There is naught different between the two of ye ... save that she is dead and ye are not."

"Why must you want what you cannot have? Why Adelaine? Why me?" she screamed.

Rolfe's look was cold. "Because the Lontaine should have been mine. Because I went through much trouble to reclaim my birthright and your whoreson father fouled my plans!"

"How dare you?" Chrestien hissed. "How dare you speak of my father so?"

"I think it only fitting that his daughter should pay for his meddling!" Rolfe continued, ignoring her words. "Don't you?" he taunted.

"No! No! No!" she cried out, as tears pooled in her eyes.

He smiled meaningfully, and for a fleeting moment his eyes took on a gentle look, almost kind in appearance.

"I'll not harm ye, Chrestien," he promised, his fingers coming to rest upon her cheek. It was all she could do to keep from recoiling at his touch as he fondled the softness of her skin with his thumb. "I cannot wed with ye, my pretty, because the Holy Church would not grant me another man's wife, but ye'll be all to me that a ladywife should."

"Nay, I'll not!" she said adamantly, and would have screamed but knew the futility of it.

"Ahh, but ye will. Time will make ye mine, Chrestien ... for ye'll not leave from within these tower walls again."

"Will you keep me locked away?" she spat out, not able to mask the contempt she felt. As the prickling sensation ebbed from her arms, Chrestien felt a sudden rush of pain shoot into them, and she hugged them to her chest, wincing against the pain. She would not cry though—would not give him the satisfaction of breaking her.

Seeing the pain registered upon Chrestien's face, Rolfe merely stood there and watched, some unnamed emotion etched within the frown lines of his face. And when Chrestien's face relaxed from its contortion, he smiled warmly with sudden respect, his gray eyes hooding with a fierce desire. Involuntarily, his hand went to the curly mane of golden hair that was once Chrestien's glory, twirling the silky strands between his fingers. He stooped to bring his lips to them.

Chrestien turned her face from him. His loathsome hand wound itself tighter in the lock of her hair, bringing her closer.

"Do not turn from me, woman." His voice was ragged, a pleading whisper, as he brought his lips to hers, slowly, as if to savor the moment.

Tears flooded Chrestien's eyes as Rolfe tried to pry her lips open with his tongue, forcefully bringing its disgusting wetness into her mouth. When she would not yield sufficiently, he bit down upon her lip with blade-sharp teeth, cutting until he could taste the salt of her blood. She opened to him then, and strangely his kiss was gentle, belying the roughness of his handling—though it did naught to ignite the fire she once knew in her belly. She cringed when he moved to her neck, exploring there until he had the need for more of her. Then he moved to her breasts, ripping the fabric from her chest ere settling his lips there.

"Please ... please ... do not," she pleaded, and when it seemed he would not cease, she began to cry uncontrollably. His kisses ceased abruptly then, and he buried his face in her hair, straining to control his desire, trembling with the potency of it. When he composed himself again there was no tenderness in his gaze. His teeth were clenched and his twitching lip betrayed his barely contained fury.

"There will be a time, Chrestien, when ye'll welcome my touch—plead for it, even. There will be a time," he warned. "That I can promise ... because ye will never leave here," he reiterated. As he rose, his gaze rested on Chrestien's trembling legs, which were exposed to him. He smoothed his fingers along her calves, sliding up the length of her legs roughly, and stopping just above her knees. He nudged her torn skirts higher as he settled upward. Derisive laughter escaped from deep within his throat as he caressed the smooth skin there. "I cannot fathom how anyone could think ye a man ... Christopher." His sudden peal of laughter chilled her to the bone and she trembled involuntarily before him.

"You knew?"

Rolfe nodded, grinning. "There is little I do not know," he crowed.

"You are vile, Rolfe. Aubert was right—and Weston will come for me. This I know," she shouted hysterically, losing hold of her control all at once. "Set me free," she pleaded. "He shall kill you when he comes for me—if you but let me go,

I will not tell him of you. Please!" Rolfe's face was devoid of expression, and she could not determine whether he considered her proposal or nay, but it was her only chance. "I would tell him that I had need of time away—to think—that I made my way to Caen alone."

Rolfe's brow crumpled together in amusement. "And ye think he would believe ye? Think ye England would have an idiot for champion?" He turned to go, leaving his mocking laughter behind. "I thought ye more clever than that, Chrestien. Nay, I'll not let ye go," he assured her as he closed the door, bolting it after him. But even through the thick oak doors she could hear his next words, and they sent tiny chills down her spine. "He'll not come for ye after that quarrel ye had. He'll think ye've left him. But if he comes ... I would kill him."

He knew of her quarrel with Weston! But how? Silent tears flowed as she rested her head upon the rancid-smelling bedding. Her bottom lip, which had been numb with pain from his biting her, now felt warm and wet and a cold trickle ran down her chin. Suddenly aware of the pile of rags Rolfe had tossed upon the bed, she seized it and wiped the blood from her chin. It was then she realized that the faded blue cloth was in fact a ragged gown, and her eyes glazed yet again. He would have her wear servants' rags? "Oh, Papa, if you could see me now ... how ashamed you would be. After all is said and done, I have no courage when 'tis needed most. . . . I am the weepingest fool!"

How long would she be in the hands of this madman ere Weston came for her? A feeling of despair settled over her. She had to consider what Rolfe said. Mayhap Weston would not come. Closing her eyes to stop the flood of tears, she lay back on the bed. And when she could deny the hot liquid drops no longer, she cried until she was weary enough to drift uneasily into sleep.

Chapter 16

S eated atop his stallion, Henry turned from Weston, scratching his chin as he deliberated. Weeks had passed, and not a sign of the lady Chrestien. For Weston the search grew more intense by the day. His man could not sleep, eat, or rest until his wife was found, Henry knew. Again he turned to Weston. " 'Tis not my wish to leave you thus, Weston." Weston looked ready for the grave, weary as he was, Henry noted, and not for the first time.

Weston's voice was rough with emotion as he spoke. " 'Tis my dilemma to solve, but I thank you for your concern. You've lingered long enough as it is."

Henry nodded his acknowledgment. "Allow me to leave you fifty of my men, then. 'Tis the least I could do."

"Nay, I cannot accept them, my lord. 'Twould leave you with but three to guard your—"

"I'd hear no more of that drivel. In past, I've traveled with as few as two . . . as you well know, for you were oft one of the duo, Weston."

"Yea, but were you at the time England's king?

Were you newly called Duke of Normandy? Nay! And I'd not have you so little protected. 'Tis not England's roads you travel, my lord, and Normandy has yet to settle 'neath your rule."

"Still, I'd leave these fifty men with you. If it please you, then we will say it suits me to aid you ... if 'twill ease your guilt. After all, what good are you to me in the state you are presently in."

Accepting Henry's words for true, Weston nodded his acceptance. "I thank you, then. In truth, I shall need all the aid that can be attained." In Weston's heart, he could not believe that Chrestien would leave him. She needed him, and naught the old baron could say would make him think otherwise. Grey had suggested, time and again, that mayhap his wife had fled from him in fear. The old man in his anguish was worse than a woman with his absurd accusations. Weston would never mistreat Chrestien, and he resented the implication that he would.

Henry had tried to console the old man. But ultimately Weston could endure no more of his bantering, and he'd sent the baron away from Lontaine, promising to send news promptly. Reluctantly, and with a little persuasion from Henry, the old baron had finally gone.

His thoughts drifting back to the discussion at hand, he turned to catch the concerned gaze Henry sported. "I would accept your offer if only you'll allow me to accompany you partway ... wait ... do not deny me, my lord. It would ease my guilt, having taken from you your guard." He knew Henry's offer was significant. For how oft had Henry confessed his nagging fear of assassination? It was something Weston knew that his king admitted to few, but plagued him much, and he was greatly affected by Henry's beneficence.

Appreciative of Weston's fierce loyalty, even in this time of his distress, Henry favored Weston with a magnanimous smile and conceded, "Very well, then. Mount and come along, my friend."

Weston wasn't much good to his king, with his mind returning to the search as it was wont to do. But he kept his word and rode with Henry to Caen, then returned straightaway to search for Chrestien. Aubert and Michel kept the grueling pace without complaint; Aubert because he was nigh as worried about his sister as Weston. And Michel . . . well, Weston could not discern whether it was his liegeman's concern for Chrestien or his loyalty for Weston that drove him. Whatever the motivation, Weston could only be grateful for their aid.

The search continued night and day, none of them sleeping more than an hour or two hither and there, returning to Lontaine only to confer briefly, for Michel had taken full half the men to search other regions. He knew Henry's knights, as well as his own, grew weary. But somewhere out there, Chrestien needed him, and he would not fail her. Nay, he would not!

Rolfe came at least twice a day, every day. Mercifully, he would only watch her, and on occasion he would ask her questions. Then, when he was bored enough with her clipped answers and forced silence, he would leave. Sweet Jesu, but she would not know what to do if there were a repeat of the night she had awakened.

While he sat, staring at her, she would recite any number of prayers—unspoken of course, lest she offend him. It had become apparent to her that as long as she faced him squarely and did not display her unholy fear of him, he would not harm her. 'Twas only when she showed her weakness that he would leap for her throat—much like the snarling red lion he wore upon his mailed shirt. She was beginning to believe Rolfe's words of warning—that Weston would not come for her. But somewhere in the depth of her heart she yet clung to hope of rescue from the demon that was Rolfe.

But the days she'd counted now numbered ten . . . and if her calculations were correct, the twelve days of Christ's mass would be upon them in but a short time.

From the high, narrow tower window Chrestien could tell naught about where she was. There was naught familiar about the landscape, and Rolfe had yet to tell her whither he'd brought her. For all she knew she could be in France . . . or even faraway England. But she doubted it was England, for there was little difference in the lay of the land, and she'd heard England was full of rolling hills and dells.

Not a soul passed by the old decrepit castellan, and she could not fathom why Rolfe would not at least give her a candle to give light against the night's blackness. But then again, why would she have need of a candle? There was naught for her to do in this tower prison! Yea, he'd given her the wares to stitch with, but she knew naught about sewing and managed only to prick her finger with the needle near a dozen times already. There were at least a score of red blotches on the cloth where she'd bled onto the canvas.

At night, the tiny window allowed little light into the room, and the wind whistled into open crevices somewhere about the chamber. She'd not found where the draft came from as of yet, and mayhap 'twas naught but a figment of her mind. Nevertheless, the cold was as tangible as the dismal gray stone of the cobbled walls.

Worse yet was that as of late she had to fight the growing nausea she felt in the mornings and eves. At first she'd been afeared that she'd grown sick from the foul meals he brought her. But of late the food had improved greatly, and she guessed Rolfe had grown tired of having the chamber pot emptied of bile. The nausea persisted, however, and she could not imagine what illness had taken hold of her. She was never ill ere now. This very moment she was well enough, but 'twould come upon her so suddenly that it was all she could do to make it to the chamber pot ere spewing out her guts.

A distant click, click of spurred boots could be heard upon the stone steps, and Chrestien closed her eyes against the fear of seeing him again. She knew it was Rolfe, for he never allowed anyone else to attend her. It seemed he didn't want anyone to know she was being held. When the door creaked open to reveal him standing in the light of his guttering torch, she quickly let go of her pent-up breath and sat upright upon her bed, forcing a stoic expression.

Rolfe came into the room and kicked the huge oaken door shut behind him, then placed his torch in the iron brace upon the wall. In his other hand he held a wad of bedding and clothing which he tossed upon the bed. His eyes lit immediately upon the plate of half-eaten food and his murky eyes narrowed upon Chrestien. He frowned his displeasure. "Ye'll not make yerself well that a'way, Chrestien."

Chrestien's throat constricted painfully. She could not answer him, as much as she wanted to shout her hatred of him—wanted to leap at him and scratch his evil eyes from his face, and she only shrugged her response.

"Would ye rather that I fed ye myself?" he threatened. There was yet no answer from Chrestien, and Rolfe felt a twinge of some emotion he could not place. Was it pity for the weakening girl? Or mayhap regret? Nay, he did not regret taking her, even as sickly as she'd become—and he could not abide the stench of her retching.

Impulsively, he left, bolting the door behind him, and returned only minutes later with a bucket of warm water and a rag. She was so beautiful . . . this girl who haunted his dreams. Her hair had grown much since Montagneaux, and even in its dirty state it never lost its lovely luster. Her face, with its delicate high cheekbones, was of regal bearing, and her lush little pink lips were a tempting sight indeed. He cringed with remorse when he noted the bruising that was yet so apparent on her bottom lip. He'd bitten her severely, he

knew. But it could not be helped at the time—
she'd angered him.

When Rolfe came to sit next to Chrestien on the
bed, she recoiled from him instantly, and regretted
the subliminal response almost immediately. When
it was obvious he only wanted to wipe her face
with the cloth he'd brought, she slackened her
posture and decided to let him wash her without
contest. She had little fight left in her anyway . . .
and she did feel horribly dirty, after all.

Rolfe's hands were gentle as they brushed
Chrestien's face with the damp cloth and she
could sense a tenderness about him this eve. A
chill ran the length of her as he gently smoothed
her hair from her face. She nigh flew into his arms
to sob away her fears, so great was her anguish.
She did not, however. All that was needed to keep
her from it was to remember that 'twas he who
had brought her here . . . to this hell.

Rolfe started to lave her body as well, but something stopped him, and he handed her the cloth
instead. He would let her complete the task.
Standing, he turned from her briefly, to allow her
privacy, and in doing so he noted that her chamber pot had been abused yet again. A scowl dark-
ened his face as he turned to observe her. He
stared at her for a time, coming to the obvious
conclusion.

"Ye are breeding?" Chrestien turned to him,
startled by his words. Then his skeptical gray eyes
focused upon Chrestien's confused expression,
and he pondered her reaction. " 'Twas not clear to
me at first, but I know now that ye are. Ye carry
FitzStephens' child." It was all he could do to ac-

knowledge the fact without venting the anger he'd
learned to conceal so well from her. He knew she
was afraid unto death of him—in spite of the
brave face she put forward.

Oddly enough, it was that dauntless nature of
hers that made him respect her so. Even though he
oft felt the urge to beat her into submission, he
could not allow himself to do it. He had been prepared to hate her, for he'd not known it was possible for him to love her. But surely he did—how
else could he explain the need to woo her?
Though his desire for her was great, he could not
bring himself to force her. The biggest part of him
needed her acceptance of him ... her consent.
Moreover, if he could be honest with himself ...
he needed her love, even—and he would gain it
... if it took his entire life to accomplish it!

Chrestien swallowed hard against the weight of
Rolfe's words. Why had she not realized it sooner?
But then it dawned on her that she could not have
known when there was no one about to reveal
such things to her. She knew absolutely naught
about breeding, for no one had ever enlightened
her. There was never a need; she was to go to the
Church. Sweet Jesu, how could she have known?

Rolfe sighed deeply and turned to look out the
unshuttered window. He didn't know what he
would do about the child.... Damn, yea he did.
How oft had he cursed his own father for his lack
of care? He would not make such a mistake with
this tender babe. With a conclusive nod, he decided that he would raise it as his own. And he
would be a better father than his own had been.
Though his father had acknowledged him as his il-

legitimate son, he'd not ever treated him with any affection. Aleth had been his only concern . . . his only heir. Rolfe had wanted so much to have something, anything of him that would say, "You too, Rolfe, are my son." But there was never anything. Rolfe couldn't bring himself to regret having the old man murdered, and he would have had Aleth killed as well, but for Gilbert's damned interference.

'Twas good that de Lontaine was dead. Rolfe could not bring himself to regret that either. But he had to give the man his due. He'd raised a daughter worthy to be the wife of a warrior. She was her father's daughter through and through. Turning from the window to assess the girl once more, his lip curled into a sneer. Even unto the end, Gilbert had fought like the golden winged lion he wore upon his shield. Yea, and he did think to escape his death on those fiery wings as well, Rolfe mused.

How fitting that Gilbert's device would be the golden winged lion, and his own should be the snarling red. Together, he and Chrestien would make many fine sons. Looking back on it now, it was no small wonder that Gilbert had kept Chrestien to himself, for it would take an extraordinary man to be worthy of her. "I take it you did not realize ye are breeding," he said finally.

Tears brimmed from Chrestien's eyes, and after a long moment she managed to whisper, "I did not."

"Well ye are . . . ye are. No matter," he started to say, but then thought better of revealing his feelings over the situation. It was best the girl not know of the hold she had over him. Noting her tears, he closed the distance between them and took her head to cradle within his arms.

Chrestien stiffened immediately against Rolfe's hold, but when the first frantic sobs broke through, she let go of her will and gave in to her anguish. And yea ... she could not help but allow Rolfe to comfort her, for there was no one else to ease her heartache. Why did Weston not come for her?

Weston sat, eyes closed, upon the lord's chair in the great hall of Lontaine, his fingers entwined about the near-empty flagon he held in his grasp. He'd searched every inch of the woods ... and whither he had not searched, Michel had. He'd checked every abbey and hostelry ... Montagneaux even. None had seen her!

Aleth had even sought out his brother's aid as far away as Poitiers, though he doubted Chrestien could have gotten so far alone—having to cross the river Loire, and all. Two months, she'd been gone ... two miserable months, and yet there was naught to be found of her.

A deep gulp from his flagon emptied the remaining stock, and he lay his head back to ease the tautness in his neck. He'd hoped to give her a memorable Christ's mass ... one to take the grief from her existence ... to make a new beginning for their wedded life. And when the celebration was over ... he'd planned to take her to Montfort. In time, he'd hoped she would learn to love him. That he wanted more than aught else, for he now knew that he loved her more than life. God's

Mercy! She had to yet live! Hell, what would he do if she did not?

The muscles in the back of his neck ached from too many hours of high tension, and he rubbed them, closing his eyes and laying his head back upon the wooden chair to focus on a vision of her. She oft came to him in his thoughts now—an angel bathed in iridescent light . . . with fiery emerald eyes that she wielded like the longsword to penetrate the very depths of his soul.

Who could have guessed he would come to love her so much . . . only to lose her. Nay, he could not lose her! If it took the rest of his days, he would find her and bring her home to him . . . home to Montfort. That he would swear upon his honor!

Leaning forward in the chair, he rested his elbows in his lap and buried his face in trembling hands. Silent scalding tears flowed from his eyes, and he had to will himself to remain composed. Never had he been driven to tears ere now— never! And though he only allowed himself that brief private display, he stayed in that crouched position for what seemed an eternity. With fingers tightly pressed against his weary eyes, he sent shooting pains into his pupils to keep them from betraying his schooled emotions.

A gutteral moan escaped from his lips as he raised his head and irately tossed the tankard onto the wooden floor. His head was reeling, and he was now angry with himself for giving in to the wine when Chrestien had need of him. He should be out there now, searching—damn it all to hell!

Agitated, he ran tired hands over his thick growth of whiskers and his voice was a hoarse whisper. "Oh, Chrestien ... Chrestien ... whither have you gone?"

The answering whisper was faint, swirling amid the melee of his thoughts. *"You are despicable, you realize ... your men killed my father ... and I can never forgive you for that!"* What could he have said to that? There was no way to determine in battle who had slain whom. It could have been one of her father's own men, for that matter, and no one would have ever been the wiser. Yet in her eyes, Chrestien saw him as her father's murderer. And the worst part of it all was that he could never be certain. It could have even been him, for all he knew. From his constricted throat came a tormented growl, and he lifted his head from his hands. What he saw at that moment, framed by the arched entrance of the stone staircase that led to the tower rooms ... was Chrestien! She made her way up the winding steps, just as she had the day of their argument. He closed his eyes again, shaking his head to determine whether what he saw was real or nay. And when he again opened his eyes, she was gone. All that remained was a dark blur where the door should have been. And though he knew it was merely a vision conjured of his drunken stupor, he yet hoped. Calling to her, he bolted from the seat, nearly tripping over the edge of the dais in his haste to reach her. She was not on the stairwell when he started his ascent, and he roared her name, letting the anguished cry echo before him.

Chrestien! Chrestien! The name reverberated throughout the keep, returning to him unanswered, and he flew through the antechamber, throwing open the door to her bedchamber. Aubert raced in behind him, having heard his sister's name, but the chamber was empty save for the two of them.

Blindly shoving past Aubert, Weston bolted for the narrow stairway again and made the climb to the donjon tower, taking the steps two at a time in his recklessness.

The door to the tower chamber was wide open, but the room proved to be empty—wholly! There was naught in it—never had been, from the looks of it. Thick cobwebs graced nigh every nook of the room. So unlike the rest of the keep, it was filthy from the years left unattended, though oddly enough the shutters were unlatched and lay open to the budding wind.

Again Aubert came in behind him, his expression full of confusion. "What is it? Have ye gone mad, Weston?" There was no insult intended. Aubert's words were given with the ease and familiarity of two friends fused by a common love.

"Yea, mayhap I have," Weston admitted, raking his scalp roughly, and his jaw tightened against the admission. His throat lumped and his Adam's apple wavered from the pain of holding back his anguished growl. "I thought I'd seen Chrestien," he confessed.

Aubert's eyes fell to the stone floor to hide his own pain . . . as well as his growing sympathy for this man who loved his sister so much. And it was not right that everyone he'd ever cared for—save his mother—had been taken from him. Brushing away the telltale wetness that gathered about his eyes, Aubert swallowed hard. It would not suit to allow Weston to see him in such a state—crying like a babe! A spot of red caught Aubert's attention as he glanced about the room, and he went to it, lifting the tiny crimson token in trembling hands. As he turned the amulet in his fingers, inspecting the painted rose in its middle, a memory was sparked.

"God's Teeth! Why have I not seen it sooner? Weston . . . the petals!"

Weston's face was the image of confusion and inner turmoil. "Petals?" he repeated stupidly, rubbing strong hands across his heavily whiskered jaw in a gesture that was purely instinctive.

Aubert could not contain his growing exhilaration. "Yea, the petals . . . they were scattered upon the bank the day Chrestien disappeared." With quivering hands Aubert held the silver amulet to Weston, offering it into his hands. " 'Twas Adelaine's . . . she oft came here to read—and the rose in this pendant . . . seeing it now brings to mind something I've been a dolt to overlook. At Montagneaux, Adelaine made mention of a tiny red rose . . . saying that 'twas brought home from the crusade by none other than Rolfe de Montagneaux—Aleth's brother. He has her, Weston, this I know, for 'twas also said that these tiny roses were not of a common variety. In truth, as far as I know—and my mother knows—there has never been another found such as this."

"You are certain?"

"More certain than ye can know—and do ye not recall that ere she would leave Montagneaux, Chrestien made certain that Aleth would send word to his brother . . . that he should bring the plant so that she could grace Adelaine's grave with their rare beauty. 'Twas her very words if ye will only recall—he was to bring the blood-red rose to lay beside the pure white one she'd already planted thereon. That was her wish!"

It seemed a blast of wind rushed by, slamming the wooden shutters in its wake and leaving the room in darkness, lit only by the distant torchlight upon the staircase wall. Aubert was jolted to hear the unexpected clatter, but Weston was little affected by it, his mind filled with a sobering fury.

Illuminated only by that dim orange glow, Weston's features were transformed. His eyes were hard, narrowed with the anger that flowed through him, and Aubert shuddered to see the acute change in him.

"If you are certain . . ." His voice was even, controlled, from his years of authority and battle experience, for that was what he had suddenly become—the fierce knight Aubert had first encountered. "Gather my men, Aubert. We ride for Rolfe's stronghold . . . now!" he shouted, when Aubert seemed to move too slowly.

Aubert nigh jumped from his breeches to hear the last command, so angrily given, and he did not wait to be told again. He was halfway down the steps when he heard the deafening war cry given behind him, and ere he'd reached the bottom step, Weston had flown past him.

Wrapping her arms about herself to ward away the chill, Chrestien tiptoed to look from the high window. It was times such as this that she wished she were a bit taller. There were many voices below—an odd thing for this nearly deserted keep. Curious now, she clasped the stone sill and raised herself to peer below. Straining, she was able to catch a glimpse of the people below before losing the strength to keep herself aloft. It looked to be the very same man she had seen in Weston's tent so long ago. So that was how Rolfe knew so much. Jesu! What she wouldn't give for a stool or something else of that kind that she could place below the windowsill in order to see better the happenings below.

Dropping to the stone floor, she picked up the discarded stitchery beneath the table and removed the needle. Then, glancing over her hands, she grimaced at the many tiny puncture marks. Sighing, she dropped the needlepoint. Lying back onto the cool floor, she began to sing mournfully ... a verse Janelle had taught her. It was an old piece often sung by the bards in Normandy; the tale was said to have come from Norway, and it told of a beautiful and gentle woman, with hair the color of midnight, eyes the color of the sea. She was the fair Genevieve of noble birth, cruelly cast aside from her family ... merely for the fact that she at birth was bestowed with the gift of prophecy.

Opening the door slightly, Rolfe found Chrestien lying upon the cold floor and he made a mental note to bring her a mat to cover the cold stone next time he came. He had no wish that she should take the ague. As it was, she was growing thinner by the day. But at least this moment she was singing. Did he dare hope that he was winning her over? "Ye sing beautifully, Chrestien. But why don't you move to the bed, where you'll be warmer."

Startled, Chrestien bolted to her feet. "I am fine." Knowing Rolfe would keep his distance, she was not overly alarmed. He'd not attempted to touch her again since that first night, and strangely, it seemed he was wooing her, for he'd resorted to bringing her gifts.

Entering the chamber, Rolfe proffered a tightly closed hand, keeping the other behind his back. Confused, Chrestien only stared at his closed fist. "What is it?" she asked more sharply than she'd intended.

"Look and see for yerself," he urged, ignoring her suspicious tone.

Warily she obeyed, and placed her hand beneath his, whereupon he dropped an amulet into her palm. "It was my mother's," he said. When Chrestien looked puzzled, he explained. "I wish ye to have it."

"I cannot accept it, Milord!" She thrust it back at him, but he refused it.

Bringing his other hand from its hiding place behind his back, he revealed a small basket filled to the brim with food. As much as she would have liked to decline it, the odors of fine white bread and cheese accosted her nostrils and she knew she would not.

Rolfe could not help but note the eagerness betrayed by Chrestien's lovely eyes. "Ye are pleased . . . good!"

It would do little good to deny it, Chrestien knew. And it would do naught but anger him—in that case he might take the basket of food away, and she was famished. The bouts of nausea had subsided, but Rolfe had not realized this and he'd not brought much food in the last days. "Aye," she answered warily, taking the basket and sitting herself upon the bed.

"It does my heart good to see ye happy, Chrestien." He watched contentedly as Chrestien delved into the basket of treats. Happy? Chrestien thought miserably. Nay, but she would not shout her denial this moment, not when he held her life in his hands!

Chrestien dropped the silver amulet at her side. Eying the amulet, Rolfe reached for it, fingering it gently. "It was my mother's—a gift from my ... father," he murmured. His words were a measure of pain, and Rolfe's face contorted like that of a young boy fighting his tears. Chrestien took pity on him, and tried to seem interested in his words. Encouraged by her attention, he continued. "She prized this one gift he gave her above everything else—she was mad, ye know."

"Mad?"

"She was demented. . . . She died when I was but a youth of fourteen," he revealed.

"How awful for you and Aleth," she sympathized. But she regretted her words almost immediately when a scowl appeared on Rolfe's face and his black brows collided violently.

"She was not Aleth's mother!" he barked.

Regretting his harsh tone, he amended, "Ye could not have known." Seeing that she had retreated behind her protective silence once more, he sought to bring her back to him. This was the very first real discussion they'd ever had. Taking the amulet and chain, he placed them about Chrestien's neck, where the pendant rested against the swell of her bosom, bringing his attention to her very faded blue gown. He'd only brought her two coarse wool gowns as of yet. "I shall have to purchase cloth for ye anon. I have one girl who is skilled with the needle, though she's never attempted anything so fine as to be worthy of a lady such as ye." Noting that Chrestien seemed little interested, he attempted to engage her in conversation. "I see ye are better. Are ye not?"

She didn't respond.

"There is a bit of sweet cake at the bottom . . . and honey, too." Chrestien nodded that she had seen it, and reached for the treat, eyeing him warily through her lashes.

"Is there anything ye need, Chrestien?"

She shrugged her shoulders, the gesture belying the anger that was building yet again. She needed to go home, a voice within her screamed. She needed Weston, the father of her child. She needed Janelle and Aubert! "Nothing," she lied, her heart pounding madly.

"Nothing," he repeated. "Nothing at all?"

Shrugging her shoulders, Chrestien let her mind wander aimlessly, and her eyes focused upon the window. "Mayhap a chair . . . if you would," she dared. "So I can sew by the window," she added hastily, when she saw that his gaze had strayed to the open window.

Knowing she could not very well escape from such a great height, Rolfe agreed. "Very well then, consider it done." Intending to get the chair and mat right away, Rolfe rose then, clasping

Chrestien's hand as he did. Raising it slowly to his lips, he kissed it tenderly, frowning when she removed it from his grasp. "I shall return before long," he promised, and Chrestien nodded her acknowledgment, not really caring one way or the other.

Somewhere outside her thoughts, a door closed softly and she was only vaguely aware that she was alone once more. Falling back upon the bed, she was suddenly very tired, and her eyes closed of their own will. Why didn't Weston come for her? Wearily, she drifted into sleep, where sweet dreams of Weston awaited her.

The fifth day of December brought a flurry of activity to the courtyard below as a number of Rolfe's castle guards departed to make their way home for the Christmas celebration. Chrestien thought it odd that so many would be leaving, but when she'd confronted Rolfe he merely shrugged and said simply that the men's contracts had terminated. They were off to Montagneaux to keep the Christ's vigil with their families. She dared to hope that one of them might have learned of her plight—that he would tell Aleth. But then another thought came to her and she despaired. What if Aleth already knew and did not care? The days passed more quickly now, but the nights were long and she passed them in utter misery. At first her dreams of Weston had been pleasant and left her longing sorely for his gentle touch. But of late, they did naught but leave her confused and frightened.

Most of the dreams she could not recall in de-tail, but one in particular haunted her days as well as her nights. Deep in slumber her body would respond to her lover's touch. Weston's arms were so strong and safe. Then she would look into his face and would find Rolfe holding her instead. Screaming, she would run until she could run no longer, and in her panic she would trip into a pit. Only it was no pit—instead, she found herself within a common grave along with Adelaine, her father, and her unborn child. Anguished screams echoed within her ears, and she tried to shut them out. Covering her ears, she cried uncontrollably, and would see again Adelaine's bloodied face as it was when Chrestien had found her amid the crumpled autumn leaves.

A hoarse whisper from across the room broke into Chrestien's troubled dreams, and she awoke to see Rolfe sitting upon his chair, staring yet again. She'd grown accustomed to it by now— waking to find him watching her—but never would she feel at ease with it. Rolfe never touched her, but his gaze made her feel ravaged nonetheless. Yea, he'd not been cruel to her through the passing weeks, but as of yet he'd still not allowed her to leave her chamber at all.

The room was still sparsely furnished, but there were now two thronelike chairs set below the window. Several coffers filled with new clothing were strewn about—most of which she'd not even seen, for she lacked the interest to inspect them. The main difference was that the walls were covered with beautiful ornate tapestries: one depicting the betrayal of Christ by Judas; another, the halo-enshrined Virgin Mary holding her blessed son. A third tapestry, depicting a scene of battle, was strewn upon the floor to prevent the cold from taking the room. It seemed every day Rolfe brought something nèw in an attempt to please her.

"Ye are awake?"

"Yea," came her soft whisper. "I've had yet another dream."

Rolfe didn't need an explanation, for he knew which dream she meant—that of the FitzStephens. He knew now that it was overmuch to hope for that she would love him someday. She could not, for her heart belonged to another.

Though it was not yet physically apparent, with each passing week her babe grew . . . and with it her love for its father. Lord, would that it were his own child . . . and Chrestien his ladywife! 'Twould make up for all that he had suffered throughout his life. He would do aught to gain her love, but knew it to be a futile dream. This beauty, who should have been his, would give her heart but once . . . and the deed was all but done. Her love belonged to FitzStephens, and him alone. "I've brought ye another blanket—ye did say that the chamber was still a mite chilly, did ye not?"

Chrestien nodded, smiling wanly, and Rolfe knew that what he was about to do would be the hardest thing in the world for him . . . but it had to be done. She had to be given a choice in the matter, for she grew more pallid and melancholy each day. Yea, her heart had softened toward him, but he thought he detected a measure of pity in her eyes as well, and he could not bear to acknowledge it.

Vague memories came back to torment him, memories that he'd hidden in the darkest recesses of his heart and mind—a dark haired beauty from his youth ... Gwynith was his first infatuation, and she too had spurned him for his younger brother. Be damned if Aleth didn't get all ... and Rolfe?—not a bloody damned thing!

Gwynith had killed herself rather than remain with Rolfe. She'd grown to hate him that much after her babe had been taken from her. But there had been no help for it ... he'd never have made a good father to the girl child when every time he looked at the tiny young thing, he saw only his brother. And why wouldn't she have looked like his accursed brother, when she'd been planted in Gwynith's belly by Aleth's own seed.

In that moment of remembrance, as if the dam of his emotions had burst with the surfacing of those old memories, a flood of Gwynith's hateful words bowled him over. *I love Aleth, Rolfe ... never you ... never you. How can any woman love you when you are less than a man should be? You are naught but spittle to be wiped from the face of the earth ... you are spittle ...spittle ... spittle ... to be wiped from the face of the earth! Even your father despised you ... your father despised you!*

Gwynith's words echoed painfully in his mind, until he could take no more and he rose from the chair, shaking his head to dispel the memory. He went to Chrestien's bed and sat there watching her lovely face for a time. Even though he'd taken Chrestien in much the same way that he'd seized Gwynith, Chrestien had yet to treat him with the same contempt.

Rolfe's voice broke with the burden of his over-wrought emotions. "Ye are so beautiful, Chrestien. FitzStephens is a fortunate man."

As if seared by his words, Chrestien turned her face from Rolfe to hide her tears. She could not allow him to read the pain in her eyes.

"Ye will love him always, will ye not?" He watched her nod again, though almost impercepti-bly. Nevertheless . . . she had given her acknowl-edgment. "I'd only ask . . . that in time . . . ye would come to think of me kindly." Taking her hand, he whispered, "Can I hope for so much?"

Chrestien's green eyes met his gray ones squarely. "Yea, milord, I can think of you kindly . . . though my heart can never belong to you," she told him honestly. She'd given up hope that he would someday let her go, and it was obvious Weston cared little enough about her. He would not come for her as she had once hoped, and it was best she not anger Rolfe, but she could neither deny what was in her heart.

The look in Rolfe's eyes resembled too much that of an injured animal, and she felt a swell of sympathy for him. Impulsively, she removed her hand from his grasp and reached to touch Rolfe's roughly whiskered face. His body trembled at the sweetness of her gesture, and he willed himself to remember her words—that she could never love him. But as her hand brushed his bangs from his eyes, as a mother would a child, he nigh rescinded his vow that he would give her the means to es-cape him . . . hoping against hope that she would choose to stay. "There was a time when I feared you, Rolfe," she admitted somberly. "But I fear you no longer."

Those simple words meant more to Rolfe than aught else in his life, and he knew for certain that he would grant her the means to leave him ... if it was her wish. Taking her delicate hand again, he brought it to his lips to bestow his kiss upon it ever so gently. Then, holding it tightly against his chest, he began again. "Chrestien, I am so sorry about yer sister. I'd not meant to cause her death. I meant merely to have ye ... and did not concern myself with the cost. If only I were to have the chance to relive it ... she would be alive today."

Tears sprung to Chrestien's eyes almost immediately as she pleaded with him. "Please ... cease! I cannot hear this again. I cannot bear to hear it!" She would never truly forgive him, but neither could she listen to his accounting.

"But ye must! I'd have ye know it all ere I leave this room. Adelaine did not deserve to die ... and I hold myself accountable for her death—for your grief."

"Please! No more!" Anger filled her heart. Because of his need for revenge Adelaine would never again take another breath!

"I was so blinded by my hatred of my brother. I've told ye all about my father's loathing of me ... and ye know what scars it placed upon my heart to harden it so. I do not excuse what I've done, nor can I change what I am.... I'd just have ye understand me a little better. Ye are the only one I've ever loved in this life.... I never even bore a care for my demented mother. And when she died of her madness, my only thought was that I was well rid of her. Yea, and do not look so shocked at my words, Chrestien. I never bore her any love," he reiterated to emphasize his meaning. "I only ask that ye think kindly of me . . . when ye think of me . . . if ye think of me."

You know nothing of love, her mind screamed! But his words confused her. Why would he tell her these things unless he was going to let her go free? Her heart nigh burst with that new thought. *Mayhap he will set you free!* a voice inside of her screamed, but she remained composed and silent, masking her thoughts.

Rolfe rose from the bed and stood there gazing upon Chrestien for a long moment. He would leave the pitch torch in the wall brace so that she would not fall and break her neck upon the slippery stone steps. Opening the door, he walked through and turned, just standing there gazing into the room, not really wanting to close the door behind him. In his heart he knew that when he returned, she would not be there.

When finally he closed the door, he climbed the tower stairs instead of descending to the hall. He would go to the roof to watch her unobserved for the last time. He'd instructed Gervais to saddle the white horse that was so similar to Chrestien's, and to fill her saddlebags with supplies. Moreover, the castle gates were left wide open, and once she rode through them Gervais would see to it that she made it safely to Lontaine. He would follow at a distance, cluing her in the right path.

Chrestien's breath was heavy and her heart beat wildly when she did not hear that familiar click of the bolt as Rolfe closed the door. He'd not locked it! Nay? Could she hope for so much? She bolted from the bed, dressed quickly, and went to stand by the hated door ... afraid to try it—afraid the latch would not give way to her fingers. Finally, taking a deep breath, she lifted it to find it unbarred.

Her breathing quickened nervously as she snatched the torch into her trembling hands and made her way down the narrow steps. Silent tears stung her eyes as she hurriedly descended the long stairwell, scanning the shadows apprehensively like a frightened rabbit afraid to be caught by the hunter's snare. She was certain Rolfe had left the door unlocked apurpose and terrified that he would change his mind.

'Twas no more than mere minutes that Rolfe waited upon the battlements when he saw her stealing across the courtyard, her torchlight flickering lightly against the breaking dawn. Could she hate him so much? His face was numb from clenching his jaw overlong and was soaked with tears he'd not realized he'd shed. Shutting his lids tightly to stop the tears, he groaned haplessly.

When the unwanted tears finally ceased, Rolfe opened his eyes and immediately spotted the approaching riders—an army of them! Anger, his old companion, took its place at his side as he watched them ride through his open gates. There was no mistaking the leader ... 'twas FitzStephens!

From his perch atop the tower roof he saw that Weston had already spotted Chrestien scampering into the stables. And at that moment he knew he could not live the rest of his life knowing she would be in his arms. He knew he gave himself a death warrant by facing Weston alone as he was, but he could ne'er live this way—knowing he'd had her and let her go!

Chrestien was little surprised to see the white horse so similar to her Lightning fully harnessed for travel. The bulging saddlebags confirmed to her that it was by Rolfe's design that she was escaping. Setting the torch into a brace, she led the immense horse to a railing and climbed atop it, lifting herself over and onto its back, but ere she could get completely into the saddle she heard his words echo unto her heart.

"And what do you think you are about, mistress?" His voice was a caress as he sent his months of worry to her ears.

Slipping back to the railing, Chrestien nigh fell off in her haste to reach him—that voice could belong to none other than Weston, she knew. He had come for her, after all! Turning to him too swiftly, she took two steps and swooned, falling into the straw at his feet.

"Chrestien!" Dropping to his knees, Weston drew her carefully into his arms, wholly terrified that she was injured somehow.

Carrying her into the morning light of the courtyard, he saw that her eyes were open and observing him, and her smile was deep, reaching clearly to her beautiful emerald eyes. He was loath to speak or move her the wrong way lest she disappear again—loath to break the spell that brought her to him.

Chrestien's eyes were filled with tears. It seemed to her that she was ever crying these days, and too, they obstructed her view of Weston. Swiping at them hastily to see him more clearly, her heart fluttered and she could not help the smile that came to her lips. But when suddenly he stiffened and dropped her to the ground at Aubert's side, she knew instinctively the reason . . . Rolfe.

She turned to see Weston making his way toward her captor, and of a sudden she was afeared to see them battle. One of them would die, she knew—and she could not bear it if it were Weston. "Nay, you cannot fight for me. Let it be!" she cried rashly.

Weston could not stop himself. Anger and revenge had been his shadows ever since he'd known who her captor was—and he could not let it be!

Rolfe sauntered toward Weston, grinning wickedly, cursing and laughing hideously. "Ye'll not attend that harlot, will ye, FitzStephens? Ye'll duel with me." Rolfe could see the blinding anger in Weston's eyes, and he knew FitzStephens would play his part. "Yea, ye will match me . . . because I'll not let ye go untried," he baited.

Fighting the tremendous urge to leap at Rolfe's throat and silence him, Weston stood his ground and smoothly unsheathed his sword. Rolfe had openly called Chrestien a harlot, but to lose sight of one's anger was a deadly sin in the heat of battle, and Weston would not allow himself to give Rolfe that advantage.

"Yea, I've tried her many favors by now . . . as ye well know," Rolfe taunted. "And I'd have a taste of ye now . . . FitzStephens!"

Rolfe's blade sliced the air twice in front of Weston, coming well away from its mark, and Weston was dumfounded as he observed Rolfe's tactics. They were not those of one who would win, rather they were clumsy and amateurish.

When Rolfe laughed again, Chrestien covered her ears to block the sound. She could not believe Rolfe would malign her to Weston so. It was apparent that he was trying to anger Weston, but still . . . she could not attend any more of his lies!

"The king's champion knight . . . hah! So ye would have all believe 'twas so. . . . But ye are naught but a common bastard . . . as I am. Let me try yer . . . *favors* . . . Weston!" He mocked.

The hair on Weston's nape bristled in response to his growing ire. He could tolerate being called a bastard, but to know that Rolfe had used Chrestien for his base needs was his undoing. Rolfe would have died a thousand deaths if Weston could have arranged it so, but since the manner of combat was set, each of them wielding the broadsword, Weston would settle for wresting the last breath from Rolfe's vile body—carving his heart from his ignoble breast.

Neither Weston nor Rolfe wore shields, Aubert realized suddenly. He knew this would be a short battle, for the first to take a substantial blow would more than likely fall to the other. At least Weston had the added advantage that he was clad full in armor. Rolfe, unbelievably, was not.

If Rolfe fell, then justice would be done, Aubert knew. But if Weston fell. . .? Then he would champion Chrestien's honor himself. Did he fail? Then after him, so would each and every man in Weston's company. Either way, his sister would go free, but he prayed that Weston would be victor so that Chrestien would know of Weston's love firsthand, not through his secondhand tales. Aubert wasn't much good at flowery speeches as it was.

They circled each other, assessing each other's weaknesses. Rolfe feinted to the left and sliced the air before Weston's face. The clang of metal rang in Chrestien's ears as Weston parried, bringing his sword up to deflect Rolfe's. Weston released the pressure upon his blade, and Rolfe toppled forward as he lost his balance. Upon the ground, Rolfe rolled free as Weston lunged after him. Rolfe swung his blade angrily, indiscriminately, but unbelievably he was able to pierce Weston's cheek with the gilted edge. Encouraged by the blood he'd drawn on Weston's face, Rolfe swung high. Weston parried. Seeing an opening, Weston dipped his point to Rolfe's belly and slashed his tunic, drawing blood. Rolfe lost control, feeling suddenly as though he'd already lost the battle, and he swung madly.

Weston could only gape as Rolfe swung his weapon about him. The man was crazed! He'd had at least a dozen opportunities to run the man through, but was beginning to wonder if that were not Rolfe's intent all along!

A lump rose in Rolfe's throat as he glanced at Chrestien, and he dropped his sword. God, he loved her . . . he did . . . love her. Could he bear to be without her? "Nay!" he groaned aloud, dropping to his knees. A tightness engulfed his chest, bringing with it unbearable pain, and he knew he was going to die this day without a shadow of a doubt. It felt as though his heart would fail! Driven by the pain, he rose from his knees, clutching his chest—his decision made. . . . Better to die like a man!

Weston's sword was yet extended, though at this point he considered sheathing it. It went against the code of chivalry to kill a man so at a disadvantage—and Rolfe was indeed at a disadvantage. He was not given the time to make a decision, however. Of a sudden, Rolfe gave a blood-chilling war cry and lunged at Weston's extended sword, impaling himself on it fully. Confused by Rolfe's actions, Weston just stood there, bewildered by what he'd just witnessed. When he again gathered his muddled thoughts, he eased Rolfe to the ground and slid the blood-smeared sword from his body. As Rolfe's body released it, a pool of blood immediately covered the ground beneath him, his life spilling onto the hard turf.

In her haste, Chrestien nigh tumbled to the ground as she ran to Weston and embraced him. She never wanted to release him! Behind her, Rolfe's voice sounded weak.

"FitzStephens."

Chrestien turned to look at Rolfe as he coughed. When he did, blood found a new outlet through his mouth.

"FitzStephens," he croaked, and his words were barely audible. Weston turned away in his disgust of the man at his feet. With great effort, Rolfe lifted himself from the blood-soaked ground, and his hand darted out to ensnare Weston's leg. "Heed my words . . . Chrestien is far too noble a woman to be used like a harlot. I released her from my keeping ... because ... because, I knew she would never give her heart to me ... Her love belongs to ye," Rolfe relented grudgingly.

There was a moment of silence as Rolfe allowed Weston to digest the information. Then feeling his strength ebbing, he continued, again spewing blood before speaking. "And the babe she carries is yers ... " Rolfe's eyes closed against the pain, but his hand still firmly held Weston's leg. When he opened his eyes again, there was the shadow of death nestled within the dark grey of his irises. His next words were said to Chrestien. Her eyes closed, afraid to meet his gaze.

"I would have you carry a message ..." Rolfe gagged suddenly, sprewing forth a river of blood from his mouth. ". . . to my brother for me ... tell him that Gwynith is not lost to him ... tell him that she bore him a daughter ... Terese ... before her death. He will find the girl at La Trinité. You would have come upon her had you gone there, for she has been in the Abbess' care since the year following her birth. It should delight him to know that his Gwynith never loved me ei..ther."

A sharp pain forced him to stop speaking, and he closed his eyes then. He did not reopen them, but still he held on to Weston's leg as he finished. "Gwynith ... killed her ... herself rather than give her love to me ..." He bucked suddenly, and his body shook as if wracked by spasms.

Chrestien cried out and turned to bury her tear-stricken face into Weston's chest, unable to bear any more. Rolfe coughed again, then grunted hideously. And with a parting sigh, his breathing stilled at last.

Weston's hand curled about Chrestien's neck, holding her face more firmly against him, while his other hand offered her solace, caressing her back softly. He could not bring himself to regret Rolfe's death, but at the moment, he was more than grateful for the admitted words. And he knew they had not come easily to a man such as he. Rolfe had said that Chrestien loved him! She loved him! And Rolfe had not touched her . . . she carried his babe! Nothing else mattered now. His voice was hoarse with emotion as he said, "It's over . . . he is dead Chrestien." Chrestien nodded and her arm went about his neck. She raised herself to nuzzle her face into his neck, seeking the safety of his embrace.

His breath fell near her ear, his lips rested upon her wet cheek, and his arms were warm and comforting. His words were spoken with a silkiness that made her shiver. "You love me?" It was an arrogantly phrased question, one that left little room for denial. But there was no need to deny it any longer—not when she had spent months praying for the occasion to tell him . . . not when she carried his child in her womb . . . not when her every thought was centered on him and her body pleaded for his touch. Nay, she would not deny it.

"I do love you, FitzStephens." As Weston lifted her into his arms, he kissed her lips delicately before setting her upon his destrier. Hoisting himself up to sit behind Chrestien, he slid his arms about her waist, patting it gently as if to acknowledge his babe, before placing a tender kiss on the back of her head. Then, very gently, he molded her shape to him, basking in the warmth of her love, and a smile broke, rivaling the brilliance of the morning sun as he issued his command. "We ride for Montfort! To my lady's home, one and all!"

Epilogue

Elizabeth Adelaine FitzStephens lay in Janelle's arms more quietly than a four-month-old babe should, and Janelle sighed deeply. Ah well, mayhap this tender babe would be the image of Adelaine. Reflexively, the old maid's eyes misted at the memory of the gentle maid. Janelle sorely missed Adelaine's tenderness to offset Chrestien's mischievous nature. What a blessed demon that Chrestien was!

Never mind ye . . . she'd warned Chrestien more than enough . . . and if Chrestien wasn't willing to heed Janelle's words then so be it. Weston would have her hide—traipsing about the woods as she was. Fie! Weston did have his hands full! Poor man, he'd gone to retrieve Chrestien's grandsire as a surprise for her.

Chrestien had been angry at first to know her grandsire had deigned to visit Lontaine after so many years of not showing a speck of care. But after she'd received a letter from him, telling her of his great love for his daughter, Elizabeth, and owning to his many mistakes, Chrestien's kind heart could deny him no longer. She was only sorry she'd missed meeting him at Lontaine. And she was especially touched to learn how distraught the old man had been at her disappearance.

Baron Grey had turned out to be a very honorable man. Without question, he'd acknowledged Aubert, even though he well knew that Aubert was not his daughter's true issue. The baron had taken Aubert into his home. Mind ye, named him as his male heir, even!

Oh, and Chrestien would be so thrilled to see Aubert again . . . and to meet the baron. The smile that played about Janelle's eyes was soon replaced by a face-crinkling frown. If the girl did not kill herself first! Whyever did that chit think she had to go off looking for boar with that puny bow she'd fashioned? Weston would have her fanny lashed, for sure! Drat the girl!

Weston reined in his destrier. Seeing the white streak ahead of him, he immediately knew it to be Chrestien, and he scowled. What was she up to now? Hell, he would need follow her yet again, but she would have her way. He knew intuitively what she was after. She'd pretended complacency—one virtue she was not possessed of—and it was so out of character that he had known she was up to no good when she practically booted him from the door without so much as a single question put to him, save to ask when he would return. Yea, he knew she wanted desperately to prove her skills to him once and for all, and he would allow it this once. Even so, it could not hurt to follow behind her . . . to keep her from harm.

Turning to Aubert, Michel, and Baron Grey, he grinned. "Proceed without me, I will join you anon." Aubert and Michel smiled knowingly, but the baron seemed confused at Weston's abrupt dismissal. Fortunately, Aubert pulled him away to explain, saving Weston the trouble. The rider in the distance disappeared behind an opening in a curtain of trees, and Weston made his way toward the aperture.

Chrestien marveled at the beauty that was Montfort. She had been justified in insisting that it be her child's home. In any case, Weston seemed to be relatively happy with the decision, and all was well—more than well, for she'd never been so happy in all her life—such freedom she was permitted! How grand to be lady over Weston's house, for she'd never known life to be so full. Yea, she did miss Adelaine . . . and she was certain she always would. But as Janelle had once said, Adelaine was never far from heart or mind, so in a way Adelaine was truly home.

There was one area of her life she intended to alter . . . Weston's restrictions over gaming. Soon enough he would know that she was more than capable. For at least a month she had worked on this bow in her hands, using the best of all she could put into it. No finer one could be bought, she decided with a measure of pride. Weston would arrive tomorrow eve, in time for the evening meal, and she could vividly imagine his shock to find boar on the table. Amused by the vision her mind's eye had conjured, she could not help but giggle.

She'd spotted the fresh boar dung less than a furlong back, and the animal should be hither somewhere ... she could sense it. A rustle amidst the bushes to her right caught her ears, and she turned to it, studying it carefully, her bow ready. There was a quick snort—but a snort nonetheless—and the bush rustled once more. Standing motionless, her senses keen, she dared not move at all. More rustling came to her knowing ears, but the animal did not make its appearance—nor did it make another sound—and she reasoned that this one was cunning enough to know when it was being stalked.

Weston had to stifle the laughter that was building. He'd taken the boar unawares, and the animal had not had a chance against his exceptional crossbow. The wooden mechanical instrument sent the arrow slicing through the air to land with the accuracy born of a warrior's mastery. But there remained one problem ... how to fool Chrestien into believing that 'twas her that killed the animal? Stooping, he shoved the boar to its side, and he attempted to remove his telltale arrow. That done, he propped the boar as best he could, frowning at the obviousness of his ruse. He could hear her approach and he ruffled the bushes a little, snorted as best he could, then started away from the spot.

Hearing no more telltale sounds from the bush, Chrestien instinctively backed up a few paces, suddenly aware of the naïveté of her actions. Ridiculously, she found her skirts caught in a tangle of limbs, and she hurriedly bent to free herself from the briers. In stooping she caught a glimmer of white in the bushes before her. A white boar, she was certain, for in her crouched position she could see the outline of its rear, barely, but nevertheless discernable. Popping her gown from the thorns that held it, she positioned her faithful bow.

Another snort and rustle from the bush told her that it was time. The beast was growing impatient. But she had the advantage—a clear shot through a small opening in the bush. Deftly, she released her arrow, accurately ringing the leafy void.

The roar that followed more than startled her. It was surely not the cry of an animal! Nay, 'twas human! Running through the thick tangle of bushes, she wondered what poor man she had wounded. Sweet Mary, let him not be fatally injured! How could she have made such a mistake? Jesu, 'twas her punishment for disobeying Weston. And what a horrible punishment it was, knowing she'd killed a man. Her soul would be damned for all eternity!

The sight before her widened her emerald eyes with astonishment. There was indeed a white boar upon the ground . . . but Weston was also there, lying upon the earth before her, knees ground into the soft muck of the forest floor. His leatherskinned breeches were soiled beyond belief, and his pallid face was half buried in the boar's snowy-white side. But the thing that held her frightened gaze . . . and threatened to send her screaming for aid . . . was the small arrow imbedded in Weston's arse. Jesu, he just lay there, gritting his teeth to ward away the pain . . . and it seemed to Chrestien that he was growling!

"Weston! What are you doing here?" It was not

what she meant to say, but somehow it rolled from her tongue anyway.

"Damn it, woman! I have a blasted arrow in my arse and that is all you can say to me? Get the thing out of my flesh, now!"

His angry words brought her out of her stupor, and she fell to her knees. "Oh, Weston, yes ... of course I shall." Inspecting his wound mindfully, she noted that it had not penetrated very deeply— had only grazed his flesh, in fact. The thick leather breeches had taken the brunt of the damage, and she rested a little easier. Haphazardly, the words tumbled from her tongue. "Weston, I love you, I'm so sorry ... so sorry ... really I am ... so sorry!"

"Damn you! I love you as well ... but get the drat thing out of my arse! Now, Chrestien. Stop your quibbling. The time for reckoning will come later," he warned.

Immediately, Chrestien began to remove the arrow, and then it dawned on her what he'd said. Never had he said those words to her before—as much as she'd hoped he would after the baby was born. She needed desperately to know whether he meant them. "You what?"

"What do you mean, what?" Reaching impatiently to the arrow still imbedded in his backside, he decided Chrestien was not going to remove it and he would have to. Chrestien slapped his hand away, none too lightly.

"I shall do it. You would only cause more damage with your rough handling." Securing a hold on the small arrow, she tugged softly, removing it in its entirety. Then she deliberately rent a larger hole in his breeches to better inspect the wound. It really wasn't deep, the breeches having lessened the force of the arrow's impact. " 'Twas just the itsy bitsy tip," she assured him, "and it does not even bleed much. Now, did you say you loved me?"

Angrily, Weston came to his feet, looking down upon the crown of her lowered head unbelievingly as she knelt before him. After a moment, he pulled her up with his right hand—his left hand went instinctively to shield his wound. "God knows why! But yea, I do . . . damn it!" Grabbing both of her hands now, he backed her into the nearest tree and trapped her there with his arms. "If you ever touch another bow, Chrestien . . ." His voice took on that low, dangerous tone Chrestien had come to recognize so well, and his fingers bit into her arms in warning. "If you ever touch another bow . . ."

Weston noted that Chrestien's mouth was quivering, and he couldn't tell if she was about to laugh or cry. Hell, did it really matter? He did love her, and he didn't know what he would do did she disobey him again. What could he do? "If you ever . . ." His words were lost as his lips came down hard on hers, branding them with the force of his kiss, then softening immediately ere he stopped to gaze into her lovely jewel-green eyes. "You need not prove yourself to me, Chrestien. . . . I love you as you are. God knows why," he laughed, "but yea, 'tis true."

"Then tell me, Weston, why has it taken so long for you to say so?" Waving the small arrow she held in her hand, she informed him haughtily, "This is all your fault, you realize." A faint smile played upon her lips as she finished. "Making me wound you, that is ... because I felt so ..."

"My fault, love? Yea, I see. ... And shall I need declare my love for you every day to keep you out of trouble?" Chrestien nodded her head in agreement, glad that he finally understood. "Very well, then, I shall." He smiled wolfishly. "But not because you will it...." He kissed her again softly. "Only because it felt so good to finally say the words. But," he warned, "if you ever dare tell anyone of this ..." Taking the arrow from her hands, he flung it aside, and Chrestien smiled mischievously in return. Leaning to kiss her, he glimpsed her impish smile. "Chrestien! You'll not tell a soul. I'd not have my men leering at me—jesting that you've bested me again.... I'll not abide it!"

"Very well, my lord." She ducked beneath his arms and started away from him. "But you shall pay a hefty price herein, I assure you. For I would hear those words at least every day." Her wicked smile deepened as he came after her, limping slightly against the pain in his arse. "Nay, I think at least ten times a day," she ventured. "Does your wound hurt overmuch?" she added when he flinched.

"Your point is made, sweeting. And yea, it does hurt. Did you expect it not to?"

"Nay, but what are you doing out here, at any rate? You were not due back until tomorrow," she protested, her tone defensive.

"I had a surprise for you," he told her simply as he rubbed his sore arse. "But I've a mind not to give it to you now." He sighed as he ceded, "I knew you were about some mischief and I followed you."

"And it was you that killed the boar?"

"Hell, Chrestien, it wasn't you."

"But I could have ..."

Raising a brow, he stooped to pick up the small arrow resting upon the ground. " 'Tis fortunate for me that this puny thing could not have killed an insect."

"Unfair, my lord, and 'tis not true. Anyone skilled with a crossbow could land a fatal blow with an arrow such as this!" She yanked it from his grasp then, fuming within.

Turning his wounded backside to Chrestien, he goaded. "You call this a fatal blow, Chrestien?" When she turned away, he grabbed her by the arm and started to haul her away. "Let's get back to Montfort, lest they come looking for us and find me thus."

"Without my boar?" She struggled against his firm but gentle hold.

"Yea, without your boar. I'll have someone fetch it later."

"Very well," she pouted. "You shall need say those words at least twenty times a day then ... and you'd best start now."

"You cannot force my tongue, Chrestien."

She sighed sweetly. "I know." Her acquiescence was overmuch like music to his ears, and so out of character that he thought to encourage her obeisance. "I love you, Chrestien," he told her softly, and she smiled mischievously.

"That would be one."

"Nay, you do not understand, Chrestien. . . . I said that I love you."

"Two." She was ready for him when he lunged at her, and she was unhampered as he was by the pain in his arse. The end result was that she was quicker. Running, she reached Lightning and hauled herself into the saddle as Weston came to a halt beside her.

"Chrestien! I cannot ride until my wound is stitched," he lied. "Dismount and walk with me."

"Now, my lord husband . . . you've a body filled with the scars of many battles. You cannot tell me that this one tiny wound would keep you from the saddle—or is it your pride that is bruised?" she goaded, and Weston frowned at her, twisting his lips wryly.

"I love you," he coaxed, with a wolf's gleam in his eye.

Chrestien sighed, smiling inwardly to hear those words. "Very well, then, I shall walk with you," she ceded, and dismounted Lightning. But no sooner had her feet touched the ground than Weston had her over his knee. Within seconds more, his hand sounded on the cheek of her padded rump, not once or twice but three times—once for each time she'd forced his words. The first sting brought a pout to her lips, but the second and third had her laughing, nigh hysterically, for he'd not even really spanked her. It felt more like a gentle love pat than a spanking.

Weston turned her about slowly, smiling as he did. "I love you, Chrestien."

"And I love you, FitzStephens." His lips covered hers in that moment as they dropped to the grass.

He kissed her mouth tenderly on their slow descent to the ground, whispering love words into her ear. Then, suddenly curious, "How did you think to get that hefty animal home?" he asked her without separating his lips from hers. Chrestien merely shrugged. "Damn you, Chrestien." But his admonition was whispered into her mouth, tempered by the awful thought that the boar might have killed her. He kissed her closed eyes with all the gentleness he possessed, burning the soft closed lids with the heat of his lips. "Did your father beat you much?" Chrestien giggled, shaking her head nay. In mere seconds he'd undone the slim, laced belt at Chrestien's waist, and with a knowing hand he raised the gown to expose her breasts to his eyes.

"Ahh, you are so lovely, Chrestien—did your father banish you to your room oft?"

"Nay, husband, but you needn't worry about little Lizzy. Janelle says she bears Adelaine's temperament."

"Thank God!" Weston chuckled, and Chrestien slapped his jaw. "Damn you are brutal, woman!"

"If you wanted someone gentler, you should have married elsewhere," she chided.

"Nay," he whispered huskily. "I'd not have one such as that for wife ... with all due respect to your sweet sister." Chrestien smiled, and Weston secured her arms to the ground, kissing her breasts druggedly. He managed to tear himself away from his desire long enough to tell her, "But I'd not have one such as you for a daughter!" His admission brought a boyish laughter to his lips. Ignoring the fact that she struggled vehemently against his hold now, he brought his lips to her breasts again, stilling her easily with his loving touch. Knowing he'd roused her passion sufficiently, he set her arms free and she brought them about his neck faithfully.

Her breath was light upon his lobe. "I'd not either," she confessed. "I'd not either . . . ever I have been a most willful child."

"Cease your prattling and kiss me, Chrestien." She bit back a sharp retort and obeyed. There was something to be said for compliance, and she gave herself up to Weston's touch completely; her heart was his, her body his, and her will . . . though not his, would surely never be her own.

Avon Romances—
the best in exceptional authors and unforgettable novels!

THE EAGLE AND THE DOVE   Jane Feather
76168-8/$4.50 US/$5.50 Can

STORM DANCERS   Allison Hayes
76215-3/$4.50 US/$5.50 Can

LORD OF DESIRE   Nicole Jordan
76621-3/$4.50 US/$5.50 Can

PIRATE IN MY ARMS   Danelle Harmon
76675-2/$4.50 US/$5.50 Can

DEFIANT IMPOSTOR   Miriam Minger
76312-5/$4.50 US/$5.50 Can

MIDNIGHT RAIDER   Shelly Thacker
76293-5/$4.50 US/$5.50 Can

MOON DANCER   Judith E. French
76105-X/$4.50 US/$5.50 Can

PROMISE ME FOREVER   Cara Miles
76451-2/$4.50 US/$5.50 Can

Coming Soon

THE HAWK AND THE HEATHER   Robin Leigh
76319-2/$4.50 US/$5.50 Can

ANGEL OF FIRE   Tanya Anne Crosby
76773-2/$4.50 US/$5.50 Can

America Loves Lindsey!

The Timeless Romances
of #1 Bestselling Author

Johanna Lindsey

PRISONER OF MY DESIRE 75627-7/$5.99 US/$6.99 Can
Spirited Rowena Belleme *must* produce an heir, and the magnificent Warrick deChaville is the perfect choice to sire her child—though it means imprisoning the handsome knight.

ONCE A PRINCESS 75625-0/$5.95 US/$6.95 Can
From a far off land, a bold and brazen prince came to America to claim his promised bride. But the spirited vixen spurned his affections while inflaming his royal blood with passion's fire.

GENTLE ROGUE 75302-2/$4.95 US/$5.95 Can
On the high seas, the irrepressible rake Captain James Malory is bested by a high-spirited beauty whose love of freedom and adventure rivaled his own.

WARRIOR'S WOMAN 75301-4/$4.95 US/$5.95 Can
In the year 2139, Tedra De Arr, a fearless beautiful Amazon unwittingly flies into the arms of the one man she can never hope to vanquish: the bronzed barbarian Challen Ly-San-Ter.

SAVAGE THUNDER 75300-6/$4.95 US/$5.95 Can
Feisty, flame-haired aristocrat Jocelyn Fleming's world collides with that of Colt Thunder, an impossibly handsome rebel of the American West. Together they ignite an unstoppable firestorm of frontier passion.